THE IMMIGRANT

PART TWO

THE IMMIGRANT
PART TWO

SANDY SIMON

The Cedars Group
Delray Beach, Florida
2013

Published by
The Cedars Group
220 MacFarlane Drive, Suite PH-6
Delray Beach, Florida 33483

www.sandysimon.com

This book is dedicated…

to my father, Alexander Eassa Simon Chalhoub and my mother, Linda Helen Zaine Thomé Simon whose lives inspired this book.

to all those tenacious, resilient, and dedicated immigrants from Lebanon and Syria who, since 1850, have sought freedom and opportunity in America, and have contributed their heritage, culture, and wealth to the fabric of their adopted country.

and, finally, to St. Jude Children's Research Hospital in Memphis, Tennessee, which will receive a portion of the proceeds from sales of this book.

ACKNOWLEDGEMENTS

I am most grateful...

To my mother and father whose life stories inspired this book.

To my family in Douma, Lebanon for their hospitality and insights.

To Papatya Bucak, Professor of Creative Writing at Florida Atlantic University, for her guidance and support.

To Consul General du Liban, Abdel Sattar Issa in Marseille, who graciously enlightened me to the historical presence of the Lebanese-Syrian community of Marseille, the *Panier*, and Marseille's role over the centuries.

To the late Richard Shadyac, my brother and mentor, for his incisive counsel.

To Sally Benson for her advice.

To my cousins, Hanna, Nicola, Ibrahim Chalhoub, Douma, Lebanon.

To my brilliant cousin, Cezar Thome, Sao Paulo, Brazil.

To my graduate school roommate, W. H. "Bill" Stuart of Bartow, Florida, and to the Kissimmee Historical Society.

To my dear friend, Bill Finley, WWII B-17 pilot, Eighth Air Force, U.S. Army Air Corps for his detailed, first hand recollections, counsel and encouragement.

And to Sheryl Ameen Feigel, Washington, DC for her insight into the historical and cultural mores of Lebanon.

Especially, I wish to acknowledge that this book could not have been written without the support, patience, and nurturing of Christiane Collins and to Mary Strobel, for her professional, expert and patient editing of my manuscript.

TABLE OF CONTENTS

Your Friend Is Your Needs Answered
Kahlil Gibran

CHAPTER 1

"I know they are up to something that will change Europe forever," Philippe Moreau told his superiors in secretive French Intelligence meetings in Paris. "There are hundreds of German undercover agents operating all over Belgium, Austria, and Denmark. This man Adolph Hitler is crazy! He's taken over the German Workers' Party and renamed it the National Socialist German Workers' Party... the Nazi party. He hates France and blames Germany's economic depression and the plight of the German workers on France's Versailles Treaty demands. The Nazis have co-opted many Frenchmen as well. These are difficult times, and I am convinced they are going to get much worse, and very soon." But Philippe's was a lonely voice seeking to alert the indecisive politicians who were too consumed with disputes to respond. His was a lonely, futile effort. If they would just listen. But they didn't. The French government drifted during most of the 1920s, still believing they had defeated Germany forever.

Later, on a visit to his offices in Marseille in the summer of 1924, Philippe called on his good friend, Hanna Chalhoub, in the Lebanese section. The Lebanese were skilled at operating under occupation and during political turmoil with ubiquitous spies and compromises. They would know, especially Hanna, of subversive activities in Marseille as they related to the local media and to shipments in and out of the busy port and the rail station. Because the *Panier* district, with its large Lebanese immigrant community, was strategically positioned between the docks and the rail yards, he knew Hanna was his key man in Marseille.

It was during one of these visits that Philippe met Daniella and Madeleine at a dinner engagement with Hanna. Philippe was immediately struck by Madeleine's vibrancy and beauty.

Later he inquired, "Tell me, dear friend, what is the story about Daniella's daughter, Madeleine. She is the most beautiful creature I've ever met."

"Aah, Madeleine," Hanna replied, she is a magnificent woman. You are correct, *mon ami*. Madeleine is the finest. She is just twenty years old, and yet, she is an exciting, insouciant woman, Philippe. She also has a beautiful son, François, who is nearly four years old."

Hanna felt a strange sense of conflict of loyalty and betrayal while introducing his good friend to the lover of his nephew. While Daniella and Madeleine had finally informed Hanna, they had obtained his promise not to tell Iskandar of his love child. Madeleine was insistent that the child not be the reason for Iskandar to return. She was absolutely convinced he would return to find her when he could, that he loved her as completely as she did him, and that he had had to go to America or he might always regret it and ultimately blame her. Certainly, if this was true, she felt, she did not want him ever to blame her or his own child for ruining his life. "This way is better," she told Hanna. "He will come. I know it. But it must be for the right reasons. Telling him he has a son in France is not the right reason for his return. Trust me, *Maman*. Trust me, Hanna," she pleaded that day before they left for Paris "for family reasons."

"Well, I would like to see Madeleine, my friend. Can you help me? I realize that I am much older than Madeleine, but I am entranced by her, and cannot get her out of my mind. Perhaps in time I can become important to her as well."

Hanna put his arm on his friend's shoulder and spoke candidly to his friend, "Philippe, these are difficult times, and Madeleine is doing her best. She is raising her son by herself as the boy's father left France to go to America in 1920. I'm certain he does not know he has a son. She has worked hard with her mother, and yes, she needs a good man. But I think her heart belongs to, and will always belong to, the father of François. You must know this from the outset, *mon ami*."

Philippe looked directly at his friend and replied, "You say she has not seen him since 1920? If that is the case, perhaps there is a possibility for me then, Hanna."

"Perhaps, Philippe, perhaps."

Madeleine found herself frequently being visited by Hanna's friend, Philippe. He was always kind and charming, and took her to dinners at the finest dining establishments and to cultural events in the city. Over time, she became more willing to accept Philippe in her life.

"I love the bouillabaisse of Marseille, especially at Henri's by the *Vieux Port*," smiled Philippe as they taxied to his favorite seafood restaurant. "His fish are freshly caught each day. Remarkable! Paris doesn't have bouillabaisse like this."

While he spent much of his time in Paris, he returned every available weekend to Marseille. His excuse was to see his family and to meet with his colleagues, including Hanna, in the Marseille offices. His real but unspoken desire for being in Marseille was to see this enchanting twenty-year-old beauty named Madeleine. Within weeks, he knew he was falling in love although he was twenty-five years older than she. But she was a mature, delightful, feminine young woman with a child, making her way with her mother, an excellent and popular couturière, graceful, cultured, and fully aware of the fashions of the day. Madeleine, like her mother, made her own dresses that reflected the *au courant*, creating a stir wherever they went together. They emulated the latest designs of Paris so to inspire the ladies of Marseille to visit them and order their wardrobe from these two esteemed fashion models and designers. Strikingly attractive, tall, slender, and finely attired, Daniella and Madeleine personally maintained their shop's reputation.

Philippe felt very proud to have this stunning beauty on his arm even though he knew some looked askance at the "May-December couple." Some were perhaps envious, some judgmental,respectfully holding back, with a stifled smile, the query, "Oh, Philippe, is this your niece?"

He could only smile without comment. But he didn't care. He was quite self-assured. His hope and concern was to somehow gain her affection, and in time, her love, by overcoming with his physical presence and charm what her son's father couldn't provide in his absence. This, indeed, was becoming the principal emotional focus of his life. *I will win her over*, he kept telling himself.

Times were difficult for Daniella and Madeleine as with so many others in Europe during the mid-1920s as social and economic conditions seemed to worsen each year.

"Philippe is a handsome man, and yes, he is much older than you, Madeleine, my child. But you must understand the realities of life. Europe is in great difficulty. Our income is not so good anymore. Philippe is wealthy and from a fine family. He has a good job with the government, and will provide for you. All things considered, for your welfare and that of your son, I think you should accept his proposal. François is growing up. He is four years old. He needs a man in his life, Madeleine."

"But, *Maman*, Iskandar is his father, and I still yearn for him. I always will. How can I do this? I do not love Philippe. I have told him so. I know what love is, and I have that with Iskandar."

"You can grow to love him in time, Madeleine, even though he is much older. This has been quite acceptable, and not only in France, although we understand these things better than most," she added with a flourish of French liberal pride.

There were many such discussions between Madeleine and her mother during the growing number of months that Philippe called on Madeleine. From time to time, Daniella would inform Hanna of the situation. Hanna would listen intently, and wisely not offer advice unless requested. Philippe was a close friend to Hanna who felt uncomfortable in this conflicting situation. Still, it had been nearly five years since Iskandar sailed off to America.

"I have to refrain from my own opinion on this, Daniella. Iskandar is my family, Philippe is my friend."

"I'm sure he has created a new life in America. And although his letters came every week for a long time, they stopped coming when Madeleine didn't reply during the two years we were in Paris and there have been none since then. Thank you for your understanding in never mentioning Madeleine's pregnancy to Iskandar, dear Hanna. You know we had to leave Marseille for Madeleine's sake. I am so grateful you came to see us so often."

"But of course, my dear, of course."

"And what do you hear from your family in America these days, Hanna?"

"I only know what my cousin Mike tells me from Boston. Iskandar and his father somehow survived the heat and the bad weather storms and have done well in Florida. They tell me Iskandar has a small store of his own in their village." Hanna didn't feel a need to expand on his cattle business and other growing ventures. "And, just last week, I received a letter saying that Iskandar and his father are travelling to Boston for a month. Iskandar will stay with his Uncle Sam, and Abraham will stay with Mike. I think Sam wants Iskandar to meet Helene, the sister of his wife Julia."

Daniella continued to counsel her daughter during these visits from Philippe while Madeleine kept resisting. "Be realistic, Madeleine. We are alone, Iskandar is in America. Even though you still love the memories of Iskandar, Philippe is here...now. He cares for you and is a man of position and wealth. And we are struggling. I have heard you speak with kindness and love to François each time he has asked about his father. I hear your prayers and cries at night. I feel your sadness, *chérie*. And I see you constantly fondle the gold cross he gave you. You're in a difficult position, to be sure, having to overcome your conflict of love against reality. It is the eternal struggle, my child. And yours has gone on for more than four years. That is a long time, my child, a very long time. It is time for you to change your thinking...for the boy."

"But how can I accept Philippe's proposal to marry him when I still love Iskandar and will wait forever if I must. How can I betray both of them?"

"Madeleine, listen to me, *chérie*. You are being unrealistic. Don't be foolish. The world is changing very fast. Iskandar is in America and you have not heard from him in years. Be with Philippe. You will come to love him."

Madeleine had never responded to Iskandar's letters because she didn't want to describe François, his son, and make him feel guilty or obligated to return for her. And now it was too late. François's future was solely dependent on her, and she must decide how to respond to Philippe's urgings of love.

Ultimately, Madeleine came to realize that she had to be practical. Philippe Moreau was a well-established man of wealth with an excellent social reputation. He had a high position in the government, though she did not know what it was. His family was prominent, and he had many times expressed his love for her. She also knew he would eagerly provide for her and François. And she realized, too, that more and more she was enjoying her times with Philippe. "He makes me laugh, *Maman*, and he's very kind."

In late 1924, Madeleine decided to solve her emotional dilemma by accepting Philippe's entreaties.

"Philippe, you know I find you very attractive, and I truly enjoy your company. I know you understand my love for my son François, and that Iskandar, my first love, remains in my heart. I expect I will always love him even though it has been four years since I last saw him. Yet, I am growing to love you and believe we can be happy together. So, dear Philippe, with that understanding, and, my assurance to you that I will be a good and devoted wife to you, I agree to accept your marriage proposal."

Philippe was ecstatic. "I will make you a good husband, Madeleine, and in spite of these difficult days, I am sure we will be happy together."

They were married in late 1924. They spent two weeks on their honeymoon at Philippe's family estate near the spa in Vichy.

It was the same year that Alexander wed Helene in Boston.

And let your best be for your friend.
If he must know the ebb of your tide,
let him know its flood also.
And in the sweetness of friendship
let their be laughter, and sharing of pleasures.
Kahlil Gibran

CHAPTER 2

Madeleine and Philippe

During their extended honeymoon, and for several months after, Madeleine and Philippe often traveled the one hundred seventy-five miles by train from Vichy, Philippe's family's home, to Paris to enjoy the city. Daniella cared for her grandson, François, during these absences, and all seemed well for everyone.

Within weeks following their marriage, Philippe and Madeleine skied at Chamonix-Mont-Blanc. It was a happy time for both. Madeleine was now enjoying wonderful experiences and visiting different places for the first time in her life. Her youthful responses delighted Philippe beyond his dreams. He adored Madeleine, and she was a good and loving wife. But both knew there was a place in her heart where Philippe could not enter. Still, for several months, both enjoyed each other's company, and Madeleine grew closer to Philippe. Eventually they returned to Marseille where Madeleine could be closer to her young son and mother. Philippe began spending more and more time at government meetings in Paris.

By August 1926, Philippe Moreau was back in Paris alone, more often than not. Political tensions in Europe were growing. Germany was creating major difficulties for the weak and divided French government. Angry, unemployed French were frustrated with government corruption, disarray, internecine political battles, and the depressing economic conditions during the long decade. Philippe's intelligence-seeking teams were becoming stretched thin trying to keep up with the growing subversive activities of the German infiltrators. They had already placed themselves in the press and local political organizations as functionaries in charge of overseeing the utilities infrastructures, including railroads, bridges, tunnels, and the like where they could and would eventually create havoc all over France in coming years.

Each winter, Philippe took Madeleine and François to his chalet in Chamonix-Mont-Blanc for skiing holidays, and then for weekends to Cannes in the late winter and spring. But that was all the time he could afford to leave his job, which was growing in national importance by the month.

As the years passed inexorably into the early 1930s, Germany was becoming chaotic. Adolph Hitler was defeating his domestic enemies one by one and challenging the Communists. He was able to obtain the nation's bankers as supporters who were forced to choose between the lesser of two evils: Hitler and his Socialist Party or their anathema, Communists. With their reluctant financial backing committed at a gathering in Munich, Hitler began building his nation into a fascist state with unstoppable determination. By 1935, he became chancellor. German workers became fervent in their renewed sense of destiny only he could inculcate. His mesmerizing speeches enthralled the nation. The demand for more land and resources grew and grew. German outrage over the draconian post-World War I Versailles Treaty, for which they blamed France, created the fiery determination in the German people to make Germany become the most powerful country in Europe once again. More German spies were sent into all its neighboring countries. England, Belgium, Denmark, Poland, the Baltics and, especially, France, which were politically weak victims just waiting to be conquered, and he intended to exacerbate their political problems.

"I will dance in the streets of Paris!" Hitler boasted. "They wait for us, as weak poultry waiting to be plucked," he declared, laughing, to his legions of followers. "They want us. They need us."

From 1930 through 1934, France had twelve presidents. No one seemed able to deal with the seemingly unsolvable depressed economic conditions, fomenting even more instability and outrage among the populace. The United States, even with so many Roosevelt social programs, could do little to help even if it was concerned with Europe, which it wasn't. Many Americans were also leaning toward Socialism, Communism and neutrality. "Stay out of Europe's business," advocates would declare. Even Charles Lindbergh visited Germany and promoted neutrality. It would take the Pearl Harbor attack on December 7, 1941 to change the world and bring America out of isolation.

Very late in the mid-1930s, the French government woke up to Germany's growing threat and finally prioritized it by totally re-organizing its counter-intelligence agency in Paris to track the German "businessmen" who had infiltrated completely and were actually developing intelligence and significant influence within the country's industry, its media, armed forces, and government.

Philippe did not tell Madeleine that, as early as 1933, Germany was going through enormous political and economic upheaval and becoming a major, impending threat to its neighbors. The depressing economic conditions in Europe were causing dangerous unrest among unemployed union members. Germany especially was under great stress as it was still paying France what they considered exorbitant reparations for World War I. Millions were unemployed, demanding revenge. The Bolshevik Revolution in Russia in 1917, and the creation of the Soviet Union in 1933 placed enormous pressure on virtually all the governments of Europe, especially of those confrontation states abutting the new Soviet Union now led by the fierce Joseph Stalin. Communist parties were growing everywhere across Europe, feeding on the massive unemployment caused by the Great Depression and little opportunity for labor.

"The rich get richer while the masses starve," declared the Communists. "We must take over society and make it equal for everyone."

Philippe's work in Paris made him acutely aware of the political risks and actions by France's neighbors, partially the result of the huge German reparations bill of one hundred thirty-two billion marks that was still not paid, pursuant to the Versailles Treaty of 1918.

At a presumably secure, crucial meeting in Paris in 1934, Philippe was among many high government officials when President Daladier spoke to them in confidence. "Gentlemen, I believe we should clearly understand that we must now deal with this man, Adolph Hitler. We cannot wait. He intends to take over all of Europe in my opinion, and bodes no good for the French people. His National Socialist German Workers' Party, euphemistically called the Nazis, is ruthless. We must prepare. And we must prepare now."

"Philippe Moreau," the President said in a somber tone, turning toward Philippe and extending his open hand to him, "I call on you to immediately lead a new government agency of counter intelligence services to investigate, monitor, and undermine all German subversives in France. We are under enormous political pressure, as are the other governments of Europe. Because of internal conflicts, we are weak and cannot command the people to take up arms. You must pick your best men and begin surveillance at once. We may already be too late. All areas of France are vulnerable. Our major ports, from Le Havre to Marseille, even Paris itself, and our transportation infrastructure are potential targets, especially the railroad system."

"Of course, sir, I will begin today," responded Philippe, with a respectful nod of his head, in the presence of the group. Others in the meeting showed a variety of concerns. Already, however, there were German sympathizers in the room, perhaps even a few German spies fluent in French, some of whom Philippe knew had now, at this moment, become his adversaries and he theirs. He showed no emotional response, remaining stoic, yet determined to protect his beloved country. He knew he had to completely devote himself to his new organization, the French National Intelligence Agency (FNIA), precursor to the M.U.R., and enlist as quickly as possible former *Resistance* members who served during the first war. Most were now in their 40s and 50s, and many had served with him. He trusted them and knew of their devotion to France. Around them, he would build his new agency. Yet, he knew he had to gather younger, dedicated French citizens, both men and women, to achieve his important mission.

By 1937, Philippe was spending most of his time either in Paris or traveling about the country establishing teams in every city, building his organization, and bringing in disparate groups who also believed in his mission. He ventured to other countries to coordinate his efforts with his counterparts in London, Oslo, Vienna, Tallin, Warsaw, Zurich, Amsterdam, and Copenhagen. He had very little time to return to Marseille and Madeleine.

"Philippe, I do not want to complain, but must you continue to travel so much? I do understand you have important government work, and yet, you are away from us a great deal," Madeleine finally spoke her feelings.

"Madeleine," he replied, placing both hands on her shoulders, and looking directly into her eyes, "I want to be with you and François all the time, but conditions in Europe are strained and getting worse almost daily with the emerging political turmoil. The communists in Germany, Poland, Italy, Austria, and even here in France appear to be gaining power. The French government is splintered and weak. There is so much happening in Germany. Hitler's influence is growing very fast. I am quite concerned, my dear...quite concerned."

As often as he could, Philippe took François, now a handsome and precocious teenager, with him on his trips. Francois sought the opportunities to accompany Philippe to Paris, where they dined in the finest restaurants, and stayed over in the Maurice, Philippe's favorite hotel in Paris. As a result, François was being groomed with global sophistication.

War was in the air, and Philippe was France's intelligence advisor to the President. The climax of Philippe's efforts came in late August 1938.

"Mr. President, I have just come from Poland. Its army is marshalling along the German border at Lidzbark, near Warsaw. They are quietly preparing against an impending attack by Germany." Philippe was making an urgent report to the nation's leader, the president, keeping him abreast of events.

"My concerns have been growing for some time. It is getting very serious now. I believe the fuse has been lit, and an enormous explosion will soon result. The Germans are poised to invade France to their west, and are building up their forces on their east at the Polish border. Now, just this week on the twenty-third, they signed the German-Soviet Union Non-Aggression Pact with Josef Stalin who, as we know, can't be trusted. That makes me believe Poland is first and France is next."

Even sooner than Philippe had speculated, on September 1, 1939, Germany brutally invaded Poland by sea, by air, and by land. Their blitzkrieg had begun. Philippe immediately went to Marseille to meet with his agents at Marseille's port and rail yards, and to be with and comfort Madeleine.

On Sunday, September 3, 1939, just two days later, England's Prime Minister Neville Chamberlain declared, "England is at war with Germany." So, too, France declared war against Germany.

"What is this madman doing, Philippe?" pleaded Madeleine, asking what most French citizens wanted to ask.

"Hitler has made his move into Poland, my dear Madeleine. You won't believe this. He actually concocted a ruse by posing a dozen German criminals as part of the Polish army. He dressed them in Polish uniforms and, after injecting them with lethal doses, had them shot inside Germany. He then declared Poland was invading Germany! He actually declared war with a trick he called 'Operation Canned Goods.' Can you believe this crazy man? And now, the Soviet Union has invaded Poland also. I believe our beloved France is in their gun sights."

"Philippe, you have been telling me for months that this Adolph Hitler is crazy. But France is in no position to defeat him. What are we to do? Are we safe here in Marseille? What about François? Must I lose him to the army like my father? I am very frightened."

He wrapped both arms around his wife. "*Mon chérie*, I am convinced, although I cannot convince my naïve superiors, that Hitler intends to rule all of Western Europe, if not this month, then soon. Therefore, I must ask you to prepare yourself and François to be ready to leave Marseille with little notice." He paused, thinking. "I have to speak to Hanna to do the same. I don't know what his plans are, but he and your mother should be ready to leave too."

"But where, Philippe?" she pleaded. "Where can we go?"

He had no answer yet. Africa was out. So was Sardinia, even Spain. Italy was about to join Germany. Where can I send them?

During the following days, life for Madeleine was tenuous at best. While war was declared by France and England, no battles had yet taken place. But times were frightening. News from neighboring Poland was terrible…thousands of lives lost…too many German successes. One day at a time was all they could look forward to. Impending disaster was in the air. The waiting was very difficult for everyone. Hour by hour, day by day, tense and fearful citizens crouched by their radios, frustrated by the waves of static. Or they assembled in the public squares seeking the latest bulletin, frightened and frozen with no ability to resist. The entire nation was tense.

While France's political negotiations were widely described in the press, little was clear about what was happening. Fear began to build into paranoia. Neighbors became frightened of old friends. Many became convinced that no one could be trusted. The French economy was in chaos; the government was torn apart and weak. The communists were hard at work as were the German subversives.

Even so, as always, the spring of 1940 was a time of rebirth, of hope. Madeleine revisited the spot on *Les Calanques* overlooking the sea where she and Iskandar had shared so much. She would sit, think, remember, and pray. "Protect my son,

Philippe, and my love, Iskandar, dear Lord, and bring us together. I believe it is Your will. I hope it is soon. Then pausing, she whispered, "Please save us, Lord. Amen." And she would cross herself, believing in this with absolute faith.

Though she had no way of knowing, that beautiful, deceptively peaceful Sunday afternoon in June was the last Madeleine would ever enjoy in Marseille.

For how can a tyrant rule the free and the proud,
but for a tyranny in their own freedom and the shame
in their own pride?

Kahlil Gibran

CHAPTER 3

Escape from Marseille

By May 1940, the situation in Europe was critical. Poland was nearly completely defeated and occupied by the German army. Between April and June 1940, the German army overran the nations of Belgium, Holland, Norway, Luxembourg, Denmark, and the Baltics. Northern France was completely and quickly occupied. Soon too was central France. In time, even southern France would become occupied and under the military control of Germany even though the citizens under the new French Vichy government, subservient to the Germans, were allowed to come and go. And yet, while knowing much of their freedom was gone, and with it, southern France, the people somehow maintained a sense of *joie de vivre*. Thousands of the wealthy fled Paris, escaping to southern France with their treasures. Chaos began overtaking French society.

On June first, Philippe said goodbye to Madeleine as he boarded the train at the station near the *Panier* and went to Paris where he would likely remain. The situation was now critical. He urged Madeleine to prepare to leave France immediately. He would make arrangements for her and François.

"But, Philippe, where shall we go?" She sobbed at the thought of leaving France. "What shall I prepare for?"

By the summer of 1940, with Poland and northeastern France invaded, Free French Army Forces were being destroyed in northern France. The British began evacuating from France and disembarking at Dunkirk. It was a terrible disaster. Thousands of lives were lost at Dunkirk at the hands of the German forces. It was a horrendous humiliation. More than 300,000 troops escaped to England to return and fight Germany another day.

The President declared in a meeting, "It appears all is lost. You were right, Philippe. God help us for our ignorance. We were wrong. We delayed too long. We must rush to organize and unify the scattered *Resistance* teams with you as the leader."

"Of course. I will do what I can for France. I must go to Marseille and prepare. I promise to return in two days."

"No longer than that, Philippe. There is little time. It appears the German army will conquer our armies at any moment. This information is only for you. We are keeping secret what we know to avoid panic in the streets. Go now, and come back quickly. Already many Parisians are seeking safety on the southern coast."

Philippe returned to Marseille and Madeleine. He described to her that what he believed would happen was now actually occurring. "The Germans have defeated the Belgians, the English, and the French in the north. They are moving at this very moment toward Paris. I am to lead a new *Resistance* and cannot return to Marseille for some time. While I do believe you are as safe here as anywhere in France, I think all of France may soon be conquered and occupied by Germany. It is possible the full German army may not come this far south. However, millions of Frenchmen and their families will escape the north, people of Paris and the major cities will come here to the south. It will be very difficult if not impossible for you here. Thousands will descend on Marseille. The S.S., spies, and even German units will come here in droves. They will need lodging, food…everything. They will take what they want. People will be abused. I cannot let that happen to you and to François. Those bastard Nazis! You must leave immediately, my love."

"Philippe," Madeleine replied looking into his eyes as hers filled with tears, "there is no place to go. North Africa is under siege, especially French Algeria. Italy is not possible, nor Sardinia. Spain is dangerous, Egypt is weak and, anyway, the Germans are there already."

Philippe, in his fashion when he became very serious, gripped her shoulders, looked straight into her eyes and declared resolutely, "Palestine is out. Lebanon appears to be the only nearby place that is safe at the moment, while it is protected by the French. But Beirut itself will not be safe for you. I am a marked man, and there are many German spies in Beirut. You share my name, which means you may need protection. Go into the mountains in the north. There is a deep valley there that has been a safe haven for centuries. It is near Bsharre, in the Batroun province."

"Northern Lebanon?" asked Madeleine with a sense of irony. "There is one place I have heard of that could be perfect for us. I will take François to his father's village in the mountains. It is very near a place they call 'the Valley of Passion.' I know of it. We will be safe there, Philippe. The village is named Douma."

Philippe nodded and smiled, relieved and confident in her proposal. Suddenly he remembered, "Hanna is from that village. His cousin, Elias, is in Beirut. I will alert him and get you there through him as much as I am able. Please do not hesitate. There is no time. You and François must go now, Madeleine. Tonight."

"Then it is settled, Philippe," she answered, now committed, still very nervous, yet finally knowing where they were going, and struck by the fact that she could possibly be in Iskandar's village, perhaps with his family if not with him.

"I will take François to Douma until France is free once again. And, Philippe," she whispered as she embraced him, "I must say to you, you have been a wonderful husband to me, and father to François. I pray you have been as happy with me. You knew from the beginning my heart was full with love of Iskandar. Forgive me, Philippe…I was a young girl…he was my first love. You understood, I pray. Yet, these years with you have been wonderful and I do love you so much, Philippe. Now go, be safe, and as Hanna would say, '*Allah ma'ak*.' Be with God. I will pray for your safety each day."

Philippe listened to Madeleine's words, feeling the painful sting of truth, but not surprised at what she was telling him. He sadly understood, and yet was grateful to have been with this magnificent and beautiful woman for fifteen wonderful years. He deeply loved her. Knowing full well he was now a marked man and might not survive the German onslaught, he nevertheless sought to convey his strength, his noblesse oblige, and his inherent sense of loyalty to his country. He could not leave France. And there were places he could not accompany Madeleine. Yet he knew too, she was who she was. He had swallowed that bitter pill early on and had, as much as he could, come to accept his destiny with his lovely, nurturing wife.

He had to reply to her honesty with his own honesty, though it was difficult. He sighed deeply and paused before he spoke, holding her hands in his as they faced each other, "Madeleine, while I have loved you so much these years, I must say, it tested me throughout our marriage far more than I have ever confessed. It has been hard for me, Madeleine, very hard. But I also know your special love for me. And you know how much I love you. I will have you with me each day, Madeleine." Philippe whispered in her ear, "Your face will be with me forever …goodbye, my love…" As he caressed her and savored this special moment, he could not help but believe it would be the last time he would see her…hold her … feel her close…

Before they parted at the train station, hands outstretched, fingers touching, she blew him a kiss and, with moistened eyes, whispered, "*Au revoir* and *Allah ma'ak*, Philippe."

When the train was out of sight, she went to Hanna to tell him of the news, and to obtain his assistance in obtaining passage as soon as possible to Beirut.

"You will be safe, very safe, with my family in Douma, Madeleine. But they must never find out that Iskandar is François' father. It would be a disgrace for the family. It would be a terrible mistake. Be *en garde*. Now, my child, you must get ready this minute to leave France. Your mother and I will be safe here in Marseille. We will bury ourselves in the *Panier*. No one can find us here. We'll let you know when it is safe to return. But you must get François out of France or he surely will be taken by someone's army."

After meeting with Hanna and her mother, she went back home, located François in his room, sat with him on the bed to quickly explain and prepare him for their escape. "We must leave France immediately, my son. We will go to Lebanon this very night and find your father's village. Hanna has arranged passage for us. He believes your *mémé* and he can be safe here deep in the *Panier* in Marseille, but we all agreed he cannot protect us. You are at an age that surely you will be taken into someone's army, perhaps even into a German prison. We cannot know, François. I lived through the horror of my father dying during the first war, and I am not going to let that happen to you. We must leave France tonight."

"Tonight, *Maman?*" Suddenly aware of the urgency in her tone of voice, he composed himself and responded, "Alright, *Maman*, then let's get on with it." He wanted to be strong for her too.

And so, at 4 a.m. on June first, Madeleine and François boarded a small nondescript Lebanese steamer at the port near the *Panier*. Customs officers were becoming more prevalent and more enforcing, especially trying to keep young French males in France. Hanna had believed Philippe's predictions months ago and prepared for this event. François, by his father's birth, could have had dual citizenship, however, Hanna obtained a counterfeit Lebanese passport for him. To ensure a smooth escape without a paper trail, he also had gotten a Lebanese passport for Madeleine.

Madeleine and François left France just five days before the German armies were on the outskirts of Paris. With all of France threatened and panic driving millions to the south, France officially surrendered on June seventeenth, only four days after Madeleine and François safely reached Beirut.

Earlier, General Charles de Gaulle had left Algeria for London to set about organizing the Free French Army of the Interior (FFI). Most of those who joined did so in England and Algeria. Gen. De Gaulle organized the *Dauxieme*, the intelligence section of his staff. They were to coordinate with Philippe Moreau. Philippe was the French intelligence director of all domestic *Resistance* forces. His biggest challenge was in uniting the various underground splinter factions, principally three power groups which included the communists, also staunchly anti-Nazi. It was difficult at best trying to coordinate their efforts, reduce territorial protectionism, increase their effectiveness, and remind them of their common enemy. It seemed that Philippe had to be everywhere at once, all the time.

*And if it is a fear you would dispel,
the seat of that fear is in your heart and
not in the hands of the feared.*
Kahlil Gibran

CHAPTER 4

Escape to Beirut, June 1940

Even before their small Lebanese steamer reached the point where the city could be seen, Madeleine felt tremors within her soul. She had known it would happen. She had known the moment she and François stepped onto the ship that she would emotionally reconnect with her lover and François' father, Iskandar.

"All these years, *chéri*, and now I must come to Lebanon. To your very village," she whispered aloud, as she stood at the bow's railing, eagerly looking for the Pigeon Rocks Iskandar had described to her as they lay on the grass on top of *Les Calanques* where they had loved.

"You will know Beirut by its off shore rocks hollowed out by the sea, and by the Corniche, the promenade high above the shoreline," Iskandar had said.

And now, she thought, here I am approaching this Middle Eastern city known across the Mediterranean Sea. Beirut, capitol of Lebanon, long aligned with her country, France, where most Lebanese Christians speak fluent French. Lebanon was a country where she prayed they would be safe.

At the onset of the war in Europe, during the late 1930s, Beirut was occupied with French forces. It was a safe haven for many who were willing to leave France and escape the onslaught of the German war machine. Others fled to Algeria and embattled Sardinia. Beirut was also a rich haven for thousands who had different, more sinister agendas. Many walked the streets who were ostensibly businessmen from Germany, France, Switzerland, Italy, and the Soviet Union. Most of these, it turned out, were actually spies gathering information much like their counterparts in other fertile cities such as Geneva, Zurich, Basel, and Vienna seeking secret information, following couriers, and stalking runaways. Now, as a result, Beirut was becoming a dangerous and overcrowded city. Most *émigrés* of late were from France since Lebanon was still a protectorate of France as a result of the terms at the end of World War I in 1918. There were transients in Beirut from America,

Germany, Italy, Greece, Austria, Palestine, Iraq, and the Persian Gulf. It had become the epitome of a truly "international city," casually bridging east and west. Beirut easily became labeled the "Paris of the Middle East," and Lebanon, "Switzerland of the Near East."

When Madeleine and François arrived, it was a very active city, with locals inundated by European informants, Iraqis, Arabs, and escaping Jews.

∾

The last sixty minutes on the steamer passed by agonizingly slow for Madeleine. Anxious to land, she paced the decks. Abruptly, she stopped at the bow, gripping the steel top rail, her pulse racing.

"Oh, François, I hope all is well in Lebanon. I worry so."

"*Maman*, it'll be alright. It's all very exciting, isn't it? I'm going to be stepping on the very soil of my father's homeland. I thought I'd never go to his village. I'm feeling great emotions, *Maman*. As you told me, he was my age when he left Beirut to sail to America. I think his spirit is still here."

"Yes, my son, and I too am sensing his presence...Oh! ... Look!" Her heart leaped as she spotted the rocks offshore that Iskandar had described in detail. Unique to Beirut, as *Les Calanques* to Marseille, they stood as proud sentinels. "François, can you see the high rocks there? They call them Pigeon Rocks."

"They're beautiful. You can see right through the large one!"

It was almost noon when the boat finally maneuvered to tie up at the docks on the north side of the city. Madeleine and François prepared to disembark, gathering their valises, hardly all their worldly goods, but all they could carry with them as they rushed, shrouded, in the night to leave Marseille.

"We'll have to do the best we can, François," she spoke anxiously. "We have so little. We'll both have to purchase new clothes here. We'll just have to take each day as it comes. But first, we must find Hanna's cousin, Elias," she said to François as they both quickly stepped onto the dock, waving goodbye over their shoulders to the friendly captain.

Looking all around her at the city's buildings, people, and mountains, she realized that here she was in Iskandar's country, no longer in France, her home. It was a strange, emotional moment for her as she felt Iskandar next to her. She knew she had to go to his village in the mountains. But first she had to find her single contact in Beirut...Iskandar's Uncle Elias, Hanna's cousin. He would help them.

After twelve agonizing, boring and unpleasant days at sea, stopping, it seemed, at every port between Marseille and Beirut, it was good to finally arrive in Lebanon. Both had gotten seasick more than once on the miserable voyage from a mix of the rough seas, poor food, the smell, and their anxiousness to leave Marseille before the Germans arrived.

As they walked down the pier and looked around, they were agape at the bustling activity of all the disparate people in this Middle Eastern trading center and surprised by the abundance of Europeans at the port area. Businessmen carrying leather briefcases seemed to be everywhere seeking deals that would provide them substantial profits as a result of the skyrocketing rents and values of all kinds of commodities. Jews from Germany, Hungary, Poland, the Soviet Union, and even Romania were flooding into Beirut seeking Lebanese passports so they might reach Palestine and safety. Likewise, evacuating Palestinians were seeking shelter in Lebanon and Syria. Products from America and France, including tires, Chrysler trucks, engine parts, even automobiles, were available in Beirut in exchange for goods from other countries, like Syria, Transjordan, Iraq, and Saudi Arabia. International traders were everywhere. Older men, ignoring the turmoil, sat at café tables along the streets, much as in Marseille, playing *towleh* and dominoes, and puffing on their *aguilas*. The pungent fragrance of blended tobacco and fruit wafted through the streets as though the war in Europe was of no concern. Perhaps they were in denial. Perhaps they felt they could do nothing anyway, as conquerors always came and went.

"This city is exciting…like Marseille in many ways. Hanna would be at home here." François smiled as he spoke to his mother, his eyes dancing across the scenes absorbing everything. While he could not know, he was feeling many of the same exciting emotions his father had felt that day in 1920 when, with his friend Butrus, Iskandar first stepped on the Joliet docks in Marseille.

By luck, after several fruitless inquiries, Madeleine found Elias at his office on the second floor above a ladies dress shop in the chic Hamra District. Elias was seated in a leather chair behind his desk, opposite Madeleine and François who nervously sat down on his matching dark red leather couch. They noticed that his office looked much like Hanna's, but with sketches of the mountains and snow covered cedars unique to Lebanon adorning the otherwise vacant beige painted stucco walls. Fresh air entered through the two open windows.

After sharing customary polite greetings and hot tea, Elias, speaking in polished French, described the unsettled and unsafe conditions for her and François in the city, urging her to get out of the city at once and go to Douma. He cautioned, "Go today to Douma, find Milhelm, and I will contact you later through him. You must leave the city immediately for your own safety and that of your son, my dear, before the Germans here in the city find out who you are. They would like nothing better than to kidnap the wife and son of their dreaded enemy, Philippe Moreau. Let me have your passports. We'll have to get you new ones with different names. It is very dangerous here in Beirut for anyone connected with the French government. Just yesterday a Free French agent was shot and killed on this very street."

He stood abruptly, and with a sense of urgency, keenly aware of the imminent danger she faced in Beirut during these chaotic times as Philippe Moreau's wife, extended his right hand to Madeleine and then to François.

"Go quickly now. Get to Tripoli as fast as you can. *Allah ma'ak*."

He reached for her and with a friendly embrace, kissed each of her cheeks, did the same to François, and then motioned them to the door hurriedly in concern for their safety. To Madeleine, it was a good sign that Elias embraced François also, perhaps welcoming them into the family. "My young cousin, Nabil will accompany you to Tripoli and stay with you until you are safely out of the cities and on your way up the mountain where you will be more than safe."

"*Merci*, Elias. *Allah ma'ak*," she waved as they left his small, efficient office.

"François, we must now leave the city and find our way to the only place that is safe for us. Philippe has told me that there is a crush of immigrants in Beirut and few if any places for us to safely stay. And, now with the Germans in Africa, Cairo, and Italy, we must stay in a remote place. We can only hope Iskandar's village will accept us."

Nabil quickly found a French officer doing his best to maneuver traffic at a busy intersection filled with wagons, pushcarts, trucks and pedestrians. He approached him as he stepped to the curb for a break and inquired in his native Arabic, "Can you tell us how to find Douma? I know it is in the mountains in the north near Tripoli."

"*Oui*, Monsieur and Madame," he gestured with a kind salute, tipping his cap, watching the trucks and cars pass by. "I know of Douma. It is in the North, in the Shimal," the officer told them in deference, also speaking in French, although with a slight Middle Eastern accent. "You must go to the rail station over there," he pointed, "and take the train along the coast past Jounieh to Tripoli, only one hour north. From there, you will need a ride up into the mountains. Though small, it is well-known in the province of Batroun. If you cannot find a driver, perhaps a horse and wagon will be available in Tripoli. Ask there. Everyone wants a job and money. They will accept your French francs, and they all know where Douma is."

He continued, pleased at the respite she had given him, "These are strange times, Madame. People are fleeing from all over Europe

It took Madeleine and François all day to reach the tiny village of Douma. In Tripoli, she was able to enlist a man from Farhilde, near Douma, who had delivered his harvest to the markets in Tripoli. He gladly accepted one hundred francs to allow her and François to ride on his horse drawn wagon and eagerly stuffed the money into his pocket.

The winding dirt road up the mountain to the village was steep, curving and dangerous. But the farmer knew the road, as did his heavily burdened horse. They traveled very slowly, stopping at a mountain ridge to rest as the sun began to hover above the horizon.

"We are not far. It is down there. You can see the village, can't you?" gestured the farmer.

"Look at the rocks everywhere. There are hardly any cedar trees," François exclaimed to his mother, pointing in every direction.

"Yes, François," she replied, looking around. "Look. There are so few trees up here. Iskandar told me every conqueror took their giant cedars."

Throughout the ride up the mountain road, Madeleine found herself enthralled with the vistas, the rugged sand-colored, stone-filled mountains, and the cool, dry air. It was as though she had been here before. *You told me all about these mountains, Iskandar. It is a feeling of déjà vu. It is amazing that I know each of these hills and vistas, just as you described them.* Her emotions were ascending in concert with their climb from sea level to the view above the village at a point more than three thousand feet above the sea. Each step of the horse pulling the wagon closer to her destination was felt by Madeleine's soul. She could see her hands begin to tremble slightly.

"This is a very different and ancient place, my son, but it is where your father was born and lived as a child."

"It's much higher too than Marseilles and southern France!" exclaimed François.

Late in the day, they stopped at the lookout point, the curve of the road above the village. Stepping onto the road from the cart, they could not know this was the precise spot where Iskandar paused for his last view of his beloved village and picked up a small stone to take to America. This was the place where his journey to find his destiny began nearly twenty years earlier.

They looked down the mountain to the village far below. "It looks like a scorpion, *Maman*," François said as his finger traced its shape in the air.

Madeleine shivered as a cool breeze brushed across her face. "Your father said the village was beautiful from the curve in the road above the village. He said the rooftop tiles are red...to remember those who died in the wars, so the legend says. Perhaps this very spot is where he told me he looked back for the last time when he left his home for America. Isn't it remarkable for us, François? He may have stood right here and looked down as a young man just as you are doing now." *Maman?"*

"He stood here in this very place, *Maman*."

She embraced her son as she drew him close, almost as though Francois was his father, better understanding the stories Iskandar had told her so long ago. She found she actually wanted to cry from her heightened feelings of joy and nostalgia. "God brought your father into our lives many years ago to provide for us a safe haven from the dangers in Europe. Can you imagine? If I had not met your father when he was exactly your age, we might still be in danger for our very lives in France.

"God works in strange and wonderful ways, doesn't he, *Maman*?"

"Time to go, Madame," the farmer interrupted. "Hold fast to the wagon as we begin our descent to the village. It can be tricky going down this steep mountain. The village is more than one thousand meters higher than where we met in Tripoli, and three hundred meters beneath us at the moment."

It was late in the day when the wagon pulled into the village *souk*. The golden sun was lingering, almost hesitating, over the western mountain tops above the town. There were a few villagers still in the street, shopping and visiting at the last minute. Most shops were closing for the night.

"*Bonne nuit*, Madame et Monsieur, *et bon courage*. It's been a pleasure. Do you have a place to stay?" asked the farmer as he helped her off the wagon.

"No, we don't, Monsieur," replied Madeleine with a furrow in her brow. "Can you help us?"

"Well," he thought as he stroked his chin, "I have a few cousins here in Douma although I live in Tannourine down in the valley, near Farhilde. Perhaps they know of someone who will take you in for the night."

It didn't take long for the remaining villagers in the small *souk* to note the two strangers arriving in the village, for indeed, it was very small with only a few hundred residents. Most shoppers had gone home for the night.

"*Ahlen wa sahlen*," said a friendly young girl, smiling as she walked up to the wagon. "Are you visiting Douma? Do you have family here?" the young girl asked in fluent, though accented French.

"We are from Marseille," replied François in French also to the pretty, dark-eyed teenager. "We are hoping to find a place to stay. Can you help us?"

"Perhaps," she replied. "We do not have a hotel, but there are families here who have spare rooms they let out. Everyone is hoping for francs and dollars. You must be hungry after your long journey up from Beirut."

François thought, If she only knew we've been on a boat for days!

Madeleine ventured cautiously, "Do you know the Thomé-Chalhoub family?"

"Oh," the girl replied quickly with a smile, "the Chalhoub family makes up much of the village. She continued, "I am a Thomé. And what may I ask are your names?

"My name is Madame Madeleine Moreau, and this is my son François."

"Are you Christian?" asked a smiling, hopeful François of the girl, wanting to break the tension.

"Yes, I am Orthodox. We have several churches here. This is a Christian village. And you? Are you Catholic? We have a Catholic Church, a Melkite church, Orthodox, and a Maronite church." She laughed, "It is said we have more than one seat in our churches for each citizen. Thus, we must be a holy and safe village. Everyone attends church at least every Sunday. For us, life is our family, our church, and our education."

She tossed her head with a sense of pride.

"I apologize, but now I must go. I am going to have supper at my *Sitty's* house tonight. If you have no place to go, please come with me. You must meet my father, Milhelm. I am sure he and *Sitty* would be happy to help you."

"Milhelm?" Madeleine asked, almost stunned. "Is *Sitty* your grandmother?"

"No. She is really my great-aunt, but I call her *Sitty* out of respect."

"*Ahlen wa sahlen*, please come in," spoke the silver-haired woman standing in the doorway of the small stone house, wiping her hands on her apron, wearing a welcoming, sincere smile. Sara, sister-in-law of Iskandar's mother Katrina, was elderly now. As a widow, she was taken in by Milhelm and his daughter, Katrina. They all lived in *beit* Thomé Chalhoub on the main road in Douma. It was the family home Abraham had built with his own hands more than fifty years earlier.

As they entered the small, stone house, Madeleine noticed the brightly painted white walls were mostly bare, save for a crucifix over the couch, a painting of a church with mountains in the background, and photographs of family members. The floors were gray cement with Oriental rugs scattered around. They could not help but notice the enticing garlic-laden smells of cooking emanating from the kitchen.

The young girl introduced them, gesturing toward her guests, "*Sitty*, these people are from Marseille. I met them in the *souk*. They need a place to stay so I told them you had space for rent. Is it alright?"

"Please come in," nodded Sara with a slight wave of her hand. "Of course we will be happy for you to stay with us, but you will have to share a room. Ours is a small house." Then, looking over at the woman and young man, she paused and motioned for them to drop their bags on the floor. "All we have is a warm home, food, and beds. We have no money but we have our hospitality." She smiled proudly. As she walked into the center of the immaculately clean main room that was sparsely furnished with a small table and a few chairs, she said, "Please sit and tell us the news. Would you like tea?"

"*Merci*, Madame, *merci beaucoup*," replied Madeleine with a nervous smile. "We have come to Douma for safe haven. My husband, Philippe urged me to leave France soon after Germany invaded Poland. He did not believe it would be very long before Hitler occupied France, so he hurried us out of Marseille...we brought only what we could carry."

Wiping her brow with her handkerchief, apprehensive about being in the home, in the midst of Iskandar's world, she tried to explain her dilemma without upsetting the woman. "Philippe said Hitler hates France because of the penalizing Treaty of Versailles, and will not stop with Poland. He also told me that while Lebanon is the safest place for us, Beirut is filled with immigrants, transients, spies, German sympathizers, and Jews from all over Europe seeking refuge, so he urged us to go north into the mountains of Lebanon. Hanna Chalhoub, my mother's dear friend in Marseille, also urged us to come here. He thought this village would be the best place to stay. Elias, his cousin in Beirut, told me the same thing."

Madeleine, nervously twisting her kerchief in her hands, glanced around the room then brought her eyes back to Sara, hoping for a positive response, asked, "Can you help us?"

She recalled Hanna's admonition that she did not want the family of Iskandar or anyone in the village to even know of his out-of-wedlock son, François. It would mean certain embarrassment and shame. Madeleine knew that in some countries, the child would be killed to protect the family's reputation. She and François had to keep their secret to themselves.

"We won't be a problem for you, Madame, I assure you. At the moment we are refugees." She almost broke down hearing her own words. It was horrible for her to admit aloud that she and her son were homeless...without a country...because of Hitler's invasion.

Gathering her composure she continued, carefully choosing her words. "My husband is with the French government as the Director of Counter-Intelligence, the *Resistance*, based in Paris," she said with pride.

"He sounds very important to me," responded Sara as she leaned forward in her chair, and noticing Madeleine's cup was nearly empty, asked, "Would you like more tea? Katrina, bring a plate of my pastries, please...the ones with the sweet pistachio centers."

Madeleine froze and stared at the young girl. "Did you call her Katrina?" she asked with a look of astonishment, then recoiled at her reaction. She squeezed her hands together anxiously.

"Yes, she was named after my wonderful sister-in-law, mother of Milhelm, Lena and Iskandar. The moment she was born we noted her fair skin and light brown hair. She looked just like my sister-in-law, Katrina...so beautiful. Unfortunately, she died during the famine in 1916. *Allahyurhamek*, may she rest in peace. Her eldest son, Milhelm, still lives here in Douma, but Iskandar is in America with his father and sister. We miss them so much."

"They are in America? Do you know where?" Madeleine asked cautiously, not wanting to pursue the subject too much at this time.

She shrugged her shoulders. "I don't know. I believe they live in Florida somewhere. We have many cousins in Boston, Rhode Island, and then, Miklos... Mike...in Palm Beach. But I think...I...I'm not sure." Sara bowed her head modestly, not truly understanding the location of the places she had just mentioned. "There are Lebanese people all over America," she laughed.

As Madeleine and François listened intently, nodding at each new bit of family news, they grew more relaxed, feeling the welcoming warmth of this gracious family.

After a simple dinner of *tabouleh*, rice and lamb, Katrina insisted François play a game of cards with her on the table while Madeleine visited with Sara as she resumed knitting a wool comforter lying across her lap.

As they visited, they could hear footsteps outside the door. Then the door opened. Standing in the doorway was a tall, broad-shouldered man. His arms were muscular and his face ruddy in complexion.

"*Ahlen wa sahlen*. Come in," Sara announced as she looked up from her knitting. "We have visitors, Milhelm. Come meet Madame Moreau and her son, François."

Madeleine found herself standing up and staring at the man in the doorway, stunned at his appearance. *Mon Dieu, he looks so much like Iskandar!*

François, picking up on his mother's surprise, and recognizing Milhelm's name from the stories she had told him, almost knocked over the table, disrupting the cards as he stood up abruptly at the sound of the name of his father's brother. This was the man who had saved his father's life on the mountain. He couldn't help but stare at the formidable figure. Milhelm immediately looked twice at François, stunned at his similarity to his brother. But he said nothing.

Madeleine, realizing her astonished behavior could seem strange to the others, signaled to François to remain silent. She turned away slightly, so as not to draw too much attention. She was amazed at how much Milhelm, while older now, still resembled her beloved Iskandar. She almost stammered as she finally spoke, "I...hope...you don't mind that my son and I seek refuge in your home. We're from Marseille, running from the Germans. It appears the mountains of northern Lebanon are the only safe place outside America these days. Perhaps it would be better if we stayed in another family's home?"

"Well," Milhelm replied in French, opening both arms in a welcoming gesture, clearly surprised at the presence of this lovely, cultured lady, "you have arrived here just in time. In Tripoli, everyone is talking about the German invasion of northern France only a few days ago."

Then, nodding to Sara and Katrina, he added, "You are welcome here, Madame. Though we are simple people, what we have we will share with you."

Madeleine was now a bit more relaxed in his presence, yet still caught off-guard by the sensations that raced through her as she actually felt Milhelm's large, strong hand grip hers. "You look so much like Is...uh" she caught herself, "uh...like what I imagined a strong man of the Lebanese mountains would look." Embarrassed, she lowered her eyelids in modesty and resumed her seat, placing her hands on her knees and remaining silent.

"These times are not as terrible here as they were before," Sara said, looking into space, remembering. "It has been worse, much worse, but there are many people coming to Lebanon now. They bring all their money and spend it in Beirut. And because the mountains are so beautiful, they come here, but only in the summer. It's too cold and there's too much snow in the winter. The world is in a strange way these days," she added, waxing philosophically, "but we don't feel the political problems here in Douma. Nor do our cousins in the other mountain villages north of here, especially Ehden and Bsharre, where the cedars grow in abundance. They are very popular summer resorts. But in the winter the snow gets very, very deep. Only the French escaping go there."

Madeleine, remembering all that Iskandar had told her about his village, the mountains, his mother, his brother Milhelm, and his Aunt Sara, wrapped her arms around her breasts feeling a shivering sense of relief somehow, feeling very safe and very comfortable. She looked over at François, sensing in the dim light of the kerosene lamp glow, how much he resembled his father. And there he was playing cards with his cousin, 16-year-old Katrina. *My, my, how the Lord works in strange ways*, she thought to herself. François and Katrina reminded her of Iskandar and herself. Madeleine carefully reached into her bodice to verify that the gold cross Iskandar had given her was still well concealed. *I must be very careful that no one sees it in Douma*, she reminded herself. *This is no time for a family secret to cause us to have to leave the only safe haven available to us.*

Thinking that they would stay in this house for only a few days before finding another, perhaps larger home, Madeleine could not have known that this would become their home for much longer.

For a divided house is not a den of thieves;
it is only a divided house.
Kahlil Gibran

CHAPTER 5

Germany Occupies Paris, 1940

"PARIS OCCUPIED BY GERMANY" blurted the headlines in the Beirut newspapers on June 15th of 1940.

Then, even worse, on June 23rd, the headlines announced "FRANCE SURRENDERS."

"Oh, my God, what are we to do now?" Beirutis asked each other. After all, the French Army had occupied all of Lebanon and Syria as their "Protectorate" since World War I, more than twenty years. Many Syrians and Lebanese believed, and said to one another, that perhaps it was time to consider ending the French occupation of Lebanon. Members declared at Parliament, "We must be free. Perhaps it is time for Lebanon to take control of its own destiny."

It took the Germans little time to exploit the politically weak, divided French people, at least half of whom did not even support their own government. By June 22, 1940, the new government of France was surprisingly and quickly formed at the spa of Vichy, south of Paris. Henri Philippe Omer Pétain, an 84-year-old former general and father figure, was appointed by the new President Albert LeBrun to be the new premier to lead the new French government in Vichy. He immediately sought a "friendly alliance" with Germany. Soon, his new government became a puppet regime, adopting most of Germany's harsh fascist positions.

The politics of the time caused this new government to reach a painful one-sided armistice, agreeing to four basic terms: (1) the terrible unconscionable turnover of all Jews in France to the Germans, (2) the surrender of the entire French Army except for 100,000 to maintain order, and as a result, 1.5 million regular French soldiers were captured by the Germans and immediately imprisoned, (3) no member of the armed forces was to leave France, and (4) France had to pay for all costs of occupation.

Consequently, Germany occupied the northern 60% of France while the Vichy French, overseen by the German army, monitored the southern 40%. The Vichy government was much too accommodating to the Nazis, adopting many of the Third Reich policies. France quickly became unsafe for nearly everyone. Millions of citizens fled the country, tens of thousands fled to Marseille, Toulon, and other parts of southern France. And tens of thousands of Jews sought refuge in Palestine and Lebanon.

For four years, Pétain led the new right-wing government, completely allied with Germany. In 1943 a secret police agency loyal to the Nazis called *Milice* was created under the direction of Philippe Moreau's longtime adversary, Joseph Darnand. It boasted 35,000 members by 1944.

"Cowards," Moreau labeled them.

In Douma, Madeleine fretted about Philippe's safety.

"I do hope Monsieur Moreau is in a safe place," Sara commented to Madeleine when she heard about the German occupation, trying to comfort her new friend, touching her hand as they sat at the breakfast table.

"As do I," whispered Madeleine with sadness in her eyes. "France is filled with Germans once again." She began wringing her hands at the table, twisting her handkerchief, then wiping the tears from her eyes. "I lost my father during the first war when I was just a child. And now I fear for my husband's life. This is awful." She bowed her face into her hands.

"But perhaps," Sara consoled, "he knows exactly what to do and where to stay. His business requires that he maintain his safety. Is it not so? Perhaps all we can do is be optimistic and wait."

Madeleine appreciated Sara's empathy, using "we" instead of "you."

Within weeks, the new French government in Vichy had converted its protectorate government in Syria, including its province of Lebanon, to conform to the Vichy alliance with Germany, making conditions much more difficult in Beirut and the major ports of Jounieh and Sidon.

There was little news in Douma although Milhelm heard that quiet preparations were being made by the English in Syria, Iraq and Palestine, together with the Free French forces to rid the region of the Vichy French army.

"I heard from my cousin that the *Resistance* is greatly disrupting the Germans in southern France. A *Resistance* group in Beirut is trying to find out the conditions in Marseille because there are so many Lebanese there."

It wasn't long before Milhelm obtained more information through his channels in Tripoli. He learned that, in fact, Philippe Moreau was safe and in hiding in the *Panier* near the port in Marseille.

"Thank God," Madeleine told Milhelm as he told her the good news. "Thank God he is safe. I believe he is with Hanna and my mother. Can you find out about their welfare too?"

Milhelm's cousin was happy to relate any other information to him. "Of course.

We have contacts who can find out about their well-being. The people of Beirut and Marseille have been very close for a very long time and much information is possible through the captains and crews of the boats that go back and forth even during wars. It never seems to stop them. They are clever men, those fishermen. And very independent."

The Vichy government kept troops in Lebanon and Syria, utilizing their strategic location on the eastern shores of the Mediterranean. The English and Free French, fearing German Luftwaffe bases being established there, decided to bombard and invade Lebanon and Syria from Palestine and Iraq. By June 17, 1941, the English captured Damascus and signed an armistice with the Syrian Vichy government on July 12th. As a result, pro-British forces controlled Lebanon and Syria until the end of the war. The Druze, a Muslem group and fighters for centuries, especially in the mountains above Beirut, bitterly fought the corrupted Vichy army in Lebanon. Consequently, after mid-year, better information was getting through, although generally weeks late, and for the remainder of the war, Madeleine was kept informed from time to time of Philippe's whereabouts and of Hanna and her mother's safety in Marseille.

"As long as you stay within the *Panier* district, we can protect you," admonished Philippe or his agents to Hanna.

By 1942, Philippe Moreau had achieved remarkable results, having brought together the disorganized underground forces. As a matter of history, in 1941, the *Resistance* was officially formed to unify a civilian rebellion force against the German occupiers. The *Resistance* movement emerged as the only possible counterforce opposed to the Nazis. It rapidly became stronger under Philippe's leadership by filling the vacuum and became an instant rallying point for those French loyal to their country and not drawn to Germany-allied Vichy. Thereafter, instead of mere sporadic and isolated annoyances to the German army, the *Resistance* took on more and more productive means of tying up the German army so it would be less effective against the Allies. Stealthily, and almost at will initially, armed *Resistance* teams dynamited key bridges and tunnels, German army convoys of trucks, rail yards, and almost any target the French loyalists could daringly attack with hit-and-run tactics. By late 1942, Moreau's strategies and communications systems were becoming highly effective. His teams caused the German army to divert enormous amounts of manpower and materiel from the front to the interior due to *Resistance* actions.

"Daniella," Hanna said with a proud smile, my friend and your son-in-law Philippe is doing a remarkable job leading the new *Resistance*. Just this morning I heard his colleagues tell me they have quickly changed from spilling wine on German officers as they dined, mere annoyances, to now immobilizing their cars and trucks and misdirecting trainloads of tanks and arms so they do not reach their planned destinations. They are really now making a difference to the effort and causing Hitler many new headaches." Just this week alone, they even rescued several British pilots who had to parachute from their damaged planes, got them to the northern coast and put them on fishing boats that took them back to Dover, England."

The formerly disparate groups were rapidly becoming a coordinated paramilitary unit working across the country, more in concert with one another. As their impact grew, so too did Moreau's image and reputation. Awareness of the growing unexplained costs of the Germans' efforts was also reaching upper levels of German officials. "Get Moreau" was the order of the day. As the *Resistance* became more and more effective across France, Philippe Moreau became a marked man. Rarely did he sleep in the same bed two nights in a row. His drivers were double checked daily. His food was tested at every meal. His schedule was never known. After the autumn of 1942, Philippe Moreau's life was a dichotomy; on the one hand, he was planning multiple and coordinated attacks on the hated Nazis throughout the country, and on the other hand, he was constantly detailing his own safety. An escape route, an "exit strategy," was always preplanned no matter where he was located. He met, dined, and slept only at "safe" houses.

When in Marseille, he stayed in one or another of Hanna Chalhoub's apartments in the Lebanese-friendly section of the *Panier* district near the docks and rail station. He ate only in one of Hanna's restaurants, guarded by loyalists at all times.

Because the Vichy French government, a puppet regime under the Germans now governed and occupied Lebanon and Syria, in 1941, Beirut and the port cities of Jounieh and Tripoli came under a blanket bombardment from the sea, by Allied Naval forces.

"We are prisoners in Douma," declared Milhelm angrily. "We cannot even go down to Tripoli for fish! It is not safe once again for the Lebanese people."

"Will we always be subject to the world's wars?" begged Sara, almost in tears as they listened to the Naval barrages pound the region nearby. "I'm very frightened, Milhelm, and the children are so scared, huddling in their basements day after day."

Meanwhile, the English launched attacks from Palestine into south Lebanon, seeking to remove the Vichy forces stationed there. Beirut was in chaos. Those who could, fled into the northern mountains as far north as possible, and as far from the coast as the roads would take them. Those in Douma and other villages in the remote northern Lebanese mountains were safe, despite the nearby bombardment. But once again, the villagers had to deal with the shortages of nearly everything, including food and coal. It would be a very cold and bitter winter for the villagers and their new guests, Madeleine and François DuBois.

Madeleine and François found themselves more and more involved with the hospitable and friendly villagers after their confining first winter months, and were asked to help out during the summer months into the autumn season's harvest. There were olives to bring in from the groves along the Farhilde River below the village. Sacks of *zeytoon* were piled on the donkey-drawn wagons, or in bags simply slung over the donkeys' backs. The young men were called on to see that these heavy loads made it to the presses on the eastern most edge of the village. Olives and the coveted Douma virgin olive oil were then delivered to markets in Tripoli. Grapes in the vineyards and fruit in the orchards had to be harvested and delivered.

François was anxious to help, especially when Katrina, not knowing she was his first cousin, cajoled him. "*Yallah*, François, come and join my cousin Marina and me. It's more fun when we do it together." Then, pointing up the mountain, with a devilish smile, added, "Next week we will walk up the trail to the fruit groves above the village to pick the apples and pears in Figarie."

Little did François realize, Figarie was high atop the mountain reached by a severely curving, steep dirt path at least 3,000 feet higher than the village. Although Katrina and Marina were accustomed to the climb, it would test his physical endurance beyond anything he had experienced before.

"But I lived in a seaport city all my life!" he complained good-naturedly.

That next week, Katrina led François to the torturous path behind the village that led to the fruit orchards. Half way up, François was getting testy and weary.

"How long will it take to get to the top, Katrina? My legs are killing me already!"

She couldn't help but laugh. "Come on, my city-boy Frenchman. We'll make a man of you yet!" As she spoke, she teasingly grabbed his hand and pulled him up the path.

And so the autumn passed, day after day of neighbor helping neighbor bring in the bounty of the groves. After the pressing of the *zeytoon*, Sara would boast each time, "Douma is known for its pure olive oil. It is considered the finest in all Lebanon."

"And our apples!" added Katrina, "Dear, *Allah*! They are the largest, most delicious in the entire Mediterranean."

"And what about our grapes?" added Marina.

Indeed, the apples, about which Iskandar had boasted to Madeline, were larger than most Europeans had seen, and they were so juicy and sweet. After biting into one of the samples Madeleine received from Sara, she exclaimed, "Oh, Sara, these apples are so wonderful! They are just as sweet as Isk...ah..." She stopped herself after almost blurting out what Iskandar had told her with pride. She finished, "...as sweet as can be!"

Katrina and François grew closer and closer.

The autumn season turned into winter in November with the first snowfall and more time was spent inside as the temperature dropped. Madeleine fondly remembered Iskandar's story of being a child at the age of ten, caught in an early snowstorm that nearly cost him his feet. Looking up to the mountains he had climbed, she would often think of him.

Each event in the village reconnected her with Iskandar and bonded them in her heart and mind spiritually and emotionally. And each evening, while alone with François, she would tell him of these emotional bonds. Her heart would swell with pride for Iskandar. She felt great joy at actually being among his family and in his village. Her senses absorbed all that she saw and felt as she realized she was, indeed, growing closer and closer to the Lebanese culture and the people.

François too, felt like he was with his own family, but knew better than to refer to Milhelm as "uncle," although he was in fact his nephew. And he knew that Katrina and Marina were his cousins, but he absolutely could not divulge anything of their connection. This continued to create certain tensions and nervous behavior in François and Madeleine, ever on guard not to err even slightly. They had discussed many times the risks of exposure at length. She had admonished him over and again to be very careful with what he might say or how he might react to a situation.

"We must be quiet about this or we may be told to leave the village. We must not embarrass anyone, especially your father, Milhelm or Philippe. It would be too terrible, I fear, so it is our secret to keep, François."

Your hearts know in silence
the secrets of the days and nights...
you would know in words
that which you have always known in thought...
Kahlil Gibran

CHAPTER 6

Beirut, 1941

In June of 1941, just a few months before the United States entered the war in December of that same year, the Vichy government and its forces were ousted from Lebanon. Lebanon was no longer in the crosshairs of the Allies' war machine, and Beirut was safely under the control of pro-British forces. Beirut's port activity became slightly improved throughout the war, and the mountains of northern Lebanon became even more attractive to those fleeing the European and African fighting zones. Mountain villagers watched nervously as more and more strangers passed through Douma.

Two years later in November 1943, after the siege and complete removal of the occupying Vichy government, Lebanon was actually able to declare its independence. The country was finally free after so many centuries of occupation that had begun with the Turkish invasion in the 1500s and ended now with the French. Lebanon immediately formed a democratic government with a representative Parliament, the first in the Near East However, the new Lebanese covernment, particularly driven by the powerful Maronite community, maintained its strong cultural, social, and economic ties with France. Under the new constitution, Lebanon's president would be a Maronite Catholic Christian even though Christians at the time were only a slight majority. "It feels so good, Sara", Milhelm sighed one evening over dinner, we now, finally, have our own government".

"Now with the French gone, Milhelm, how well do you think we will do on our own?"

"We are free, Sara, yet, as it is written, 'With freedom comes responsibilities, and choices we never had before. I pray we will have our own government make those correct choices. We have lived five hundred years under the Ottomans, then thirty years under the French. Let us pray we can now live in peace in Lebanon."

"*Inshallah*, my brother, *Inshallah*."

But that would change soon as Palestinians, both Christian and Muslim, escaped the Zionist onslaught in Palestine and entered southern Lebanon by the thousands. Actually, seeds of internecine rivalries germinated at this time of independence would emerge and re-emerge even decades later. Yet, during the war years, those positioned in trade prospered. The best traders, of course, were the coastal Lebanese. The businessmen and the bankers were near enough to Europe, but far enough away to safely provide excellent and often surreptitious international fund transfers.

Wealthy Europeans, including escaping Jews found difficulty in Switzerland whose politicians in many ways, cooperated with the Germans. As a result, many sought refuge in Lebanon, Syria, Iraq, and Palestine, countries that were still protected by the British and Free French forces. Some European Jewish entrepreneurs even forged strong and trusted business partnerships with prominent Lebanese businessmen.

"Cousin Elias tells me his business in Beirut is doing very well, Sara. He has joint ventured with one of the Kabani trading companies and hopes his sons and maybe my sons can join him as he expands."

"Milhelm, have you noticed how many new people are coming through Douma? Are they tourists leaving some money with us, or are they not good for our little village?" she asked with a worried look on her face.

"We must always be alert, Sara. There are all kinds looking all over Lebanon for opportunities, enemies and places to hide."

Europe was experiencing painful difficulties of rebuilding their shattered cities as a result of the war. But, while in America where Alexander and the other cattlemen of Central Florida were flourishing, Lebanese bankers and traders also prospered from the massive, growing regional demands for industrial goods, and commodities required by the burgeoning economies of the oil-producing Arab states. Although their country had no major natural resources, yet enjoyed open ports, a convenient location, and tradition of free trade, the Lebanese survived those war years with their business acumen.

Thousands of immigrants flowed steadily into the eastern Mediterranean ports of Beirut, Jaffa, and Jounieh, often by way of Cyprus and even Sardinia. Those cities burst at their seams with so many new people...some coming to safety, and others to fulfill their own agendas...and still others who would be threatening to the indigenous population, contrary to the terms of the Balfour Declaration, in which England announced its support for a Jewish state in Palestine with the restriction that the rights of the indigenous population would not be abrogated. Fortunately for the family, staying in the rugged mountains enabled Milhelm and the family to remain separate from the impact of all the influx of new immigrants.

One day in late 1943, Milhelm, returning from Beirut in a borrowed truck, anxiously drove in less than one hour to Douma. He quickly went to his home and found Madeleine. He was very worried and gave her the urgent news.

"Madeleine, there are people searching for you in Beirut. You must hide. They are French *Milice* members and German Gestapo who are paying anyone who can be bought to bring you to them. They are saying they intend to kidnap you and your son for ransom. Your husband is wanted by the German government as leader of the *Resistance* because his organization is causing them so much disruption. They want to make him stop his activities. I am sorry, but you must go farther north from Douma for a while. I think they will trace you here."

"But where will I go, Milhelm?"

"The Valley of Passion is not far away, but we have cousins north of here in Bsharre. The snows there will get very deep soon, so it will be too difficult to go there until the spring thaw. There are a few Europeans there, and many caves for hiding. You must take your son and go now. My cousins will help you. If these men come to Douma, I will see to it that they do not follow you. You must go now...this very minute," he urged. "I will take you."

Nervously, Madeleine and François immediately grabbed their meager possessions, climbed into the borrowed truck, and were driven thirty miles across the winding road along the crest of the mountain range to the north. They were to stay there until Milhelm sent word that it was safe to return to Douma.

Milhelm returned to Douma and alerted the villagers to be on the watch for suspicious strangers. "They may be two or three or four men. They may be Germans who speak fluent French or French members of the *Milice*, the Vichy secret police. Alert me," he admonished, "if you see such people. They are not friends, and they are looking to take Madame Moreau and her son." When the villagers saw a worried look on Milhelm's face, they knew to respond as he asked.

Only one week later, a hired truck drove into the village *souk* bearing two such men who, speaking fluent French, began immediately inquiring if "a Madame Moreau and her son, François Moreau, had been in the village lately. We wish to help them."

When told of their arrival, Milhelm went to work with his plan.

Milhelm met with the two strangers, and, nodding his head stupidly in mock understanding, directed them with great detail to the road out of town toward the east.

"The Moreaus went that way several days ago, there, through the safe passage," he said, pointing to the narrow winding road that traveled along the eastern edge of the 7,000-foot mountain range, the same crest where Milhelm's young brother, Iskandar, was trapped in a freak snowstorm some twenty years earlier.

One day later word was sent to the Gibran family in Bsharre that Madame Moreau and her son would soon be able to return safely to Douma. "Regrettably," it stated, "the two blonde-haired German secret police who had come to Douma searching for the Moreaus had left to the east on an old abandoned road and had carelessly driven off the curving mountain roads and had gone over the edge near Douma. Their truck crashed more than 300 feet below and burst into flames. There were no survivors."

Two weeks later, a second group of Germans came to Douma. This time there were four men. Milhelm actually rode with them until they reached the crest where he got out and began walking back to Douma. Then, very soon, he saw their truck careen off the ridge into a deep valley and explode, killing all its passengers. Thereafter, there were no further visits to Douma by the Germans or sympathetic French.

Milhelm then sent word that it would be safe for Madeleine to return to Douma. When she returned to Douma, she never asked Milhelm how the clever kidnappers had become so careless. It forever remained his secret.

"Madeleine," Milhelm later said to her, his sensitive eyes reminiscent of Iskandar's looking softly into hers as he held her shoulders firmly, "I have watched over my brother, Iskandar, protected him, and revered his life since he was a little boy. For some reasons I cannot fully explain, I find I am compelled to guard over you and your son in the same way. He reminds me so much of my younger brother, Iskandar."

That is all that was ever said. Madeleine began to believe that in his heart, Milhelm felt a connection between her and her son and his brother, but neither he nor she ever explored the very sensitive issue, perhaps fearing what they might not want to hear. He never brought the subject up again, although he couldn't help being puzzled.

Apparently, as the war progressed, the German SS determined kidnapping Madeleine and François was not the best solution to their "*Resistance* problem." And as a result, they instituted more direct plots in several cities of Europe to stop their nemesis, her husband. He was quite elusive. He avoided their snares for many months, causing the Wehrmacht great frustration, culminating in the summer of 1944 with his critical coordination of the Allied invasions at Normandy, then Toulon and Marseille.

But Philippe's luck finally ran out. In late August 1944, he was shot and killed in Copenhagen while having dinner in a "safe" restaurant as he met with local agents. As it turned out, members of the French *Milice*, the Vichy secret police, machine-gunned the group at their table. An agent of Moreau's adversary, Hitler-aligned Joseph Darnand, had finally found his enemy and would be generously rewarded for his efforts. With a promissory note significantly signed by General Joseph Paul Goebbels of 100,000 Deutsche marks in his pocket, he was cut down by Philippe's guards, but too late. "We got him!" Goebbels shouted when he heard the report. The Nazis considered Philippe the most wanted man in France. Now he was eliminated.

"Daniella," Hanna whispered at dinner two days after. "I have terrible news."

"What is it, *mon ami?*"

"Our dear friend, your brave son-in-law, Philippe Moreau has been killed."

"What?" *Mon Dieu!*" This terrible, Hanna! By whom? When?"

"He was gunned down with his colleagues in a restaurant by the *Milice*. In Denmark, I believe."

While in Beirut during his frequent visits, Elias informed him that word on the streets was that Philippe Moreau, Director of the *Resistance* had been killed.

"Oh my God," Milhelm exclaimed to his cousin. "Are you certain?"

"That is the word, Milhelm. We can rarely be certain about anything these days. It's always in someone's interests to spread rumors like this. But I feel it must be the truth, for the details were quite accurate."

"How was he killed, Elias? I must know before in inform Madame Dubois."

"It was a fellow Frenchman, a member of the counter-*Resistance*, the Vichy secret police. He was in Denmark, I believe." When Milhelm spoke with Madeleine and reluctantly and sadly informed her of Elias' report, she was simultaneously deeply shocked and very angry. *His own countrymen? Philippe was protecting France every minute of everyday day. He loved his country so much. France meant everything to him.*

"But that is the problem," Milhelm calmly and thoughtfully responded as they received the news. "Which France? Those brutal idiots of the *Milice* think France's future is to be an ally of the scum Adolph Hitler. This is terribly depressing news." He frowned as he lowered his head. "Madeleine, I'm so very sorry this has happened. But, your husband is revered by all loyal French people. He is our hero also and will be remembered for generations, I assure you."

"Thank you, Milhelm," she nodded sadly. "This is just so awful. The first war took my father, now my dear husband, Philippe. Damn those Germans! Damn Adolph Hitler! Damn!" she shouted in anger.

Too many of all those she loved were being taken away from her, including Iskandar. But that loss had to remain a secret in her heart. She began worrying even more about the safety of her mother and Hanna. "Dear God," she prayed every night, "please keep them safe, out of harm's way."

Philippe Moreau had done his work well. Indeed, his accomplishments would long be remembered. His organization of the planning and direction of the *Resistance* was especially effective in coordination with the Allied invasion of Normandy in June, 1944, and preparing Toulon and Marseille for Operation Anvil, soon after. These efforts were invaluable in significantly reducing German resistance. Through his adept organization skills and exquisite planning, French railroad engineers delayed deliveries by cleverly crisscrossing the country as they carried hundreds of German tanks away from the French northern coast where they were supposed to fight the Normandy-invading Allied landing forces. In addition, by disrupting German communication lines, their efforts saved tens of thousands of lives of young American, British and Free French soldiers during the Normandy invasion. Even General Dwight Eisenhower properly recognized the brilliant planning and coordination of the French *Resistance* under the leadership of Philippe Moreau, and noted that the Normandy invasion especially could not have been successful without him.

His death occurred precisely during the second Allied invasion in the south, the Allied bombardment of Toulon and Marseille in August of 1944 during "Operation Anvil."

It was during that bombardment that Hanna and Daniella were killed.

Somehow, with all the European fighting, thousands of deaths in France, European starvation, prison camps, and brutalities, Madeleine and François were able to safely endure the war years in remote, quiet Douma, the village of Iskandar, ironically for them, the safest place in Europe and the Near East.

Ironically, it was soon after the Normandy invasion that 19-year-old Michael Chalhoub Thomas of Kissimmee, Florida, François DuBois' half-brother, began his tour of duty as a lieutenant in the United States Army Air Corps, piloting a B-17 bomber over strategic sites in Germany.

After the European war ended, the Lebanese breathed a collective sigh of relief. Many who had fled during the Vichy presence and the devastating Allied bombardment slowly began to return to Lebanon. Beirut began rebuilding into a very prosperous period of post-war exuberance while it was still under control of pro-British forces, and safe. Fears of rampant inflation were unfounded. Commerce and employment flourished. Madeleine marveled at the incredible resilience of the Lebanese people.

Among the leaders of commerce in Beirut with connections throughout the Arab world, was The Kabani Group headed by Marcel Kabani, a most influential industrialist and entrepreneur. Respected for his integrity, loyalty, business acumen, and generosity, he was able to operate easily throughout the region.

Marcel Kabani had remained at his offices in Beirut from where he had so successfully operated during the war years. He also managed to travel to America, Iraq, Brazil, and other lands where trade was possible.

"I go where I must the best way I can," he would explain later. "Thankfully I have extended families all over South America."

But by war's end, his devoted and sophisticated wife, Marina, had become ill and unable to take care of herself. She stayed in residence in their fabulous villa in the hills overlooking the city of Beirut near the Casino du Liban in Jounieh, one of Marcel's varied and most profitable partnerships.

You work that you may keep pace with the earth and the soul of the earth.
Kahlil Gibran

CHAPTER 7

One sunny Saturday afternoon in the autumn of 1944, Katrina invited François to join her and her grandmother in the family vineyards on the slopes above the village. She smiled and waved her hand, "Come, François. Let's go harvest the grapes. They are full and ripe," she giggled as she ran ahead. "Come with me!" He was eager to join her, as they had grown close during the war years. She had not yet learned that they were actually cousins. "I packed some olives, hummus, bread, and wine. We'll eat under the trees after we collect the grapes this morning."

François now a handsome 24-year-old, and pretty, coquettish Katrina, 20 years old, rushed down to the village road past the *souk* carrying their baskets and pulling their wagon together. As soon as they could, they turned left at the vineyard path, parked the wagon, and entered the family vineyards of terraced rows of rich, full bunches of ripe grapes, swollen and ready for harvest. The family's land, worked by the Thomé family for many generations, was tended carefully, and defined by loose stone walls three feet thick and four feet high. Some of the stone walls traced their origin to the Greek occupation nearly 2,500 years earlier.

"You see that old stone box-like building above the village by that large stone outcropping, François?" Milhelm had asked him the day before, as he pointed across the slopes. "Well, that is now a small monastery, but legend tells us it was built by the Greeks three hundred years before Christ as a hospital for their army. Imagine if you can, wounded Greek invaders here in these mountains being treated for everything from arrows to sword wounds. At the same time, my ancestors built the first of those stone walls that separate our land, our vineyards, and our groves of apples, pears, and persimmon. My family has been here a long time, y'eini. I am part of this land, and this land is a part of me. That is why I could not leave Douma, even when my brother, whom I loved more than myself, left for America when he was younger than you."

François, visibly impressed with all he heard and saw, had replied, "This place is so incredibly imprinted with history," "How do you remember all these things, Milhelm?"

"It is my heritage, my life. This is where my soul lives, François."

Interrupting his thoughts, Katrina teased, "I'll cut the grapes, François, and you carry the basket. This will be fun, you'll see." As Katrina bounded from vine to vine cutting the lush, deep burgundy bunches and, placing them in the basket, she declared, "Now that the fighting is over in Beirut and the French are gone, there is a good market for our harvest."

After more than three hours of cutting and harvesting the grapes, Katrina pointed to the cluster of trees. "The sun is growing warmer, and I need a drink of water. Let's go down to the olive trees, sit, and rest for awhile. Would you like that?"

He didn't want to let her think he was tired, so he shrugged at her welcomed suggestion of relief. "Sure, if you are tired," he emphasized, "we can rest."

Katrina smiled at François' response knowing that although he clearly was tired and was getting too burdened, he would never let her think he needed a rest. Men! she laughed to herself. They always want us to think they are made of iron.

Finally they found just the right spot of grass under an ancient, gnarled olive tree. She gestured to him as she bent over to spread the tablecloth. "It's cooler here in the shade. The air is dry but it's very warm today, especially when we're working so hard." She wiped her brow and cheeks. "The sun is especially bright up here high in the mountains."

"Katrina, this is a great day. I love Douma. It has become my home. You must know these past years have been very happy for me. I feel a part of the family, and I'm glad we are close friends."

He liked being with her and looked forward to sharing time with her. "You are my best friend, Katrina."

He smiled, realizing he may have been saying that to his grandmother, Katrina.

Above them, Sara was approaching the two, carefully picking her way down the slope.

"Oh, *Sitty*," Katrina called to her grandmother, "over here," she waved, "under the tree. We are resting for a few minutes. Look how much we harvested. Isn't it wonderful?"

"Oh, yes, Katrina, "Sara nodded as she reached them. "You and François have done very well today. But of course," she admonished, "more must be harvested before we can send our load to market tomorrow morning."

François, now really tired and wanting to cool off, drank heartily from the jug of water as he tipped it over his shoulder, wiped his forehead, and pulled his tunic over his head. Suddenly aware of what he had done, he abruptly glanced to his chest. *Oh, my God, I forgot to take the cross off after church.* He had found it in a drawer and, without telling his mother, had worn the cross to church that morning to feel closer to his father. Hoping Sara and Katrina would not notice, he reached to quickly hide his father's gold cross he was wearing around his bare neck by covering it with his hand. But he was too late.

"Shoo? What? Let me see your pendant, François. Where did you get it?"

Astonished, Sara gingerly stepped over to where François was sitting in the shade leaning against the tree trunk, reached to his chest and gripped the gold cross.

"Where did you get this, François?" she repeated, staring into his eyes as she pulled the cross against the chain. "It looks very familiar to me," Sara exclaimed with furrows growing on her forehead.

"It is my mother's," he replied nervously. "She let me wear it to church."

Sara stood straight, her face now glowering at this young man, who, at her invitation, had lived in her house for all these years. Now, it seemed, he was a stranger. She wondered, *Who is he?*

"Let me see it better," Sara demanded, looking closely at the pendant. "It looks...it looks so very familiar to me. I believe it is very much like a cross I had made many years ago in Beirut. How did your mother get this cross?"

"How can that be, *Sitty*?" interrupted Katrina. "How is that possible?"

"I don't know, Katrina. I don't know but I want to look at the cross more carefully with my glasses." She brushed Katrina aside, very concerned and suddenly suspicious.

François put his tunic back on, covering the treasured gold cross. He was so worried and frightened now that he couldn't talk.

After Katrina and François had completed their harvest, the three silently walked back down the slope carrying their harvest to the family wagon that they had left at the road. Avoiding each other's eyes, they loaded the wagon and walked along side it to *beit* Thomé, their home. Tension filled the air, and suddenly the group became estranged, no longer bonded. Doubt and fear had breached their relationship.

François pulled the loaded wagon down the road alone. Katrina silently helped him park it by the house.

"I'll tell my mother we are back, Katrina," said François hurriedly, as he ran directly to the house.

He quickly entered the house and located his mother in the bedroom where she sat on the small bed sewing a new dress.

"*Maman*, I am very worried," he whispered hastily, staring out the window. "I think I let you down. *Sitty* saw your cross on my chest and believes she recognizes it. I made a mistake...no two mistakes." His eyes turned to his mother. "I wore the cross to church without asking you, and I forgot to remove it before going with Katrina to cut grapes. I was hot in the vineyards and took off my tunic, exposing the cross. Sara now wants to look at it more closely with her eyeglasses. What shall I say to her, *Maman*?"

Madeleine was stunned, yet resigned. She covered her mouth with her hand, her eyes opened wide. She put her hand on her son's shoulder as she replied softly, "Ohhh…one day, my son, I knew this had to happen. There is only one thing we must do." She quietly let out a deep breath, looked down, and shook her head. "I must immediately be honest with our hosts and tell them the whole truth." She opened her arms and apprehensively shrugged her shoulders. "I don't know how they will react. They are wonderful, caring people, and they have been good to us for nearly four years. But we have kept our secret from them. So, my love, we must finally tell them who we are and pray they understand."

Her soft comforting voice was so familiar to him whenever times were serious.

Madeleine beckoned to him to sit beside her on the bed, placing an arm over his slumped shoulders. "Your father was given this special gold cross by his mother when he was twelve years old. I told you this story when you were a little boy. Do you remember as we sat overlooking the sea in Marseille?"

He shook his head, not remembering.

Madeleine held François' hands in hers as she carefully chose her words, looking lovingly into his eyes.

She continued, very concerned as she held the cross on his chest, "This cross was the most valuable possession your father owned. He gave it to me when we pledged our love to each other. I have treasured it all these years. And now, as we walk the paths of Douma and tend to the vineyards, I feel as though I am walking in his footsteps. And you are beside me also walking where he walked as a boy. And when we walk up the hills and the mountains to the east, I feel the pain he felt as he suffered in that snowstorm. I almost feel I am now Lebanese. I love this cross and one day it will be yours."

François, thinking of his beloved father as a boy, embraced his mother. "I feel the same emotions you feel, *Maman*. I think everyday about how difficult his life must have been. I don't know if I have the courage my father had, to survive the terrible famine, the locusts, loss of his mother, and the Turkish occupation. The story you told me of when he nearly lost his feet in that snowstorm really makes me respect him so much. Can you imagine? The pain, the love of my grandmother to rub his feet every day for two years to save him. If she had not been so devoted to him, you might not have met him and I might never have been born. And to think he left all that he knew to go to America when we was younger than I am now. I can't believe it. One day I must see him. Even today, he doesn't even know I am alive." He whispered to her, "It's difficult for me, *Maman*. I want to be with my father, to know him, to embrace him. Someday, I promise, I will join my father and his family."

"Yes," Madeleine whispered, "yes, *chéri*, one day you will know your father. I know he loves me very deeply and I believe deep down he will come to find us. You will know your father. I promise."

"*Insha Allah*," he responded in the Arabic manner.

"Now, François, we must go speak with *Sitty* and Milhelm and discuss what we should do." She gripped his hand and stepped to the door.

With a sense of impending disaster, they left their small room.

...And For That Wrong committed must you knock and
wait a while unheeded at the gate of the Blessed...
Kahlil Gibran

CHAPTER 8

Douma - The Discovery, 1944

Sitting side by side, Madeleine gripped François's hand tightly and as she looked into Sara's squinting, wise eyes. Milhelm, with a quizzical look on his face, sat opposite Madeleine and François near Sara in a chair in the small stone house where Iskandar was born and had lived until he went away to America. The family still lived in the same house built by Iskandar's and Milhelm's father nearly seventy years earlier. Two rooms and a cement floor had been added by Milhelm following his father's death in 1935, but the ceiling still consisted of olive tree limbs tied tightly together holding up the eighteen inches of stone-filled, hard-packed earth that was the rudimentary roof, rolled with the same marble column remnant.

Haltingly, Madeleine spoke. "Milhelm...Sara...I have something to tell you."

Nervously, Madeleine twisted a handkerchief in her hands. She could feel her forehead moisten as her hands began to perspire. She hoped she conveyed sincerity, yet she felt deep concern, almost fear, as her eyes moved from Sara's and then to Milhelm's. She hoped and prayed she would be able to hold onto their love as she carefully and slowly described what she knew would shock them.

"Please, I think you should know the truth about François and me...who we are."

"Yes," Sara interjected brusquely, with a frown. "It is past time, I think." She was quite upset.

Madeleine hesitated, trying to accept Sara's comment. Looking straight into their eyes clearly embarrassed that she had not been forthright from the start, she began.

"I want to tell you a story of my life that begins in Marseille when I was sixteen years old. It has everything to do with your family."

Turning anxiously to her son, and then facing them again, she said, "You deserve to know the complete truth."

Sara nodded silently.

Madeleine slowly and deliberately began her story, recalling the evening she and her mother met Hanna and Iskandar for dinner. Although she knew she was doing the right thing, it was a terribly painful experience, knowing she had betrayed the trust these kind people had granted her.

Choosing her words carefully, pausing often, touching her eyes with her fingers, wiping away her first tears with her handkerchief, she slowly described in detail the exciting events of the incredible six weeks she and Iskandar shared together in Marseille. She paused before coming to the most important part of her story, that portion that forever changed her life so completely, the events that she had carried alone in her heart for more than twenty-four years. She was clear and honest in every detail.

"Iskandar and I loved each other so much. We believed it was God's will that we should consummate our love that day."

Feeling the need to relax for a moment to release tension, Madeleine stood up and stepped away, touching François' shoulder as she passed him. She walked just a few steps before she returned to her place, hoping Sara and Milhelm were prepared for her story, praying they could understand her young love with Iskandar despite the cultural constraints in their village.

"That afternoon on the grassy lawn overlooking the sea, after we gave our love to each other, and promised our eternal love, I gave Iskandar my treasured gold ring given me by my father who died in the first war to symbolize my total love and life-long commitment to him."

"And this treasure," she said as she reached into her bodice retrieving the gold cross made for Iskandar in Beirut so long ago, "this cross, he gave to me for the same reasons. We loved each other so deeply, so completely that nothing would ever still that love. It was magical, I must tell you." She stopped to take a deep breath before continuing. "He was, and remains even today, each day, this day, my first and total love, and I was his first. I was a very young girl and he was also an innocent. We shared in our souls a love that only Almighty God can bring to two people who welcomed God into their love. Our love of each other, dear Sara and Milhelm, is truly our life's path."

Then, pausing, hoping to get more than a silent nod, she continued, "Too soon," she murmured, "much too soon he had to go away to America to fulfill his destiny as his mother, Katrina, wished for him, to be with his father. And, as much as my heart ached, I understood. I was in great pain losing him, not being with him." She felt her eyes fill with tears, remembering. "I cried every day for months and months. It was a terrible time for me. I was just a young girl, and I didn't know what to do. It was an impossible situation. We both understood that."

Sara could only nod, wondering where this was going. Milhelm's heart went out to Madeleine, but he was content to simply let her complete her story.

Stopping to muster her strength, Madeleine nervously smoothed her dress on her lap, shifted in her chair, brushed new tears from her cheek and took a deep breath. She knew she had come to the most serious statement, the confirmation of François' heritage. There was no turning back now. She looked to François now, as she knew François, too, was hearing these details for the first time. But he was old enough now to know the complete story.

"It was only after he left that I learned I would give birth to Iskandar's child. I was just sixteen years old. I was scared. But he would be Iskandar's child, our love child, and that strengthened me. Yet it created an enormous problem for me...a conflict of whether to tell Iskandar or not. We were so young. Can you understand?" Unhesitatingly, she said, reaching her hand to her son, "François, my handsome boy, is Iskandar's son. I am blessed with François. But never have I informed Iskandar that he has a son by me. I chose, correctly I believe, not to interfere with his life and cause him difficulty or pain greater than he already felt. I prayed for guidance, hoping I wasn't wrong all those years. So, I did not respond to his many letters, preferring to allow him to be free in America."

Madeleine stood again to stretch her legs, looked at Milhelm, then turning, went to Sara and said, "I hope I have been correct in that decision so that his life would be better, without added complications. I did not want him to come to me out of guilt, but to be free. He sought freedom in America and I was not going to interfere. I believe in my heart that one day, some way, if it be God's will, we will find each other again." She set her jaw firmly as she stood straight and boldly said, "I believe we will." She then sat down and waited for a response. Any response. She felt more confident having told her story and, no matter what their response, she was strong again. As she waited, she knew she had said and done all she could. She had now, finally, been totally honest, come what may. And this strengthened her.

Madeleine said softly, "I hope you can forgive me for not wanting to tell you these things when we first arrived."

Sara, listening intently and uncomfortable with what she was hearing, began to shift her position on her cushion, and looked directly at Milhelm, hoping to see in his eyes his reaction, his emotional impact. This kind, loving man who saved Iskandar's life more than once, hesitated several long moments before he cleared his throat. Milhelm, a kind man, filled with sensitivity, could think of no reason to judge or condemn either his brother or his brother's lover. Yet, he knew he had to respond. Remaining expressionless, he eased Madeleine's heart by reaching across for her hand while holding her gaze. With his very large hand, he squeezed it gently, expressing much of the same sensitivity she had felt from Iskandar. She hoped that his message was that she and her son were *partie de la famille*.

He spoke in a low voice. "Madeleine, dear lady, you have lived in Douma with us...Iskandar's family...for nearly five years. We happily invited you both into our home, fed you, protected you, and welcomed you and your son."

Confused by his use of past tense, she began to worry again.

Milhelm continued, now deferring to François, "I have always had a strange bond, a close, warm feeling toward your son. He is about the same age as my brother when I last saw Iskandar." He turned toward the boy. "In so many ways, François, you remind me of him. And finally now I know why that is, and I'm relieved. I didn't know what to think. And yet, I couldn't have suspected this." Milhelm sat back in his chair for a long moment, drawing a deep breath, and then exhaling before continuing, "Thank you for telling us this story. It had to be as difficult for you to tell us as it was for us to hear you. We now must welcome you both into our family. But," he paused, holding up his index finger, "our customs and traditions cannot permit this sensitive situation to become known in the village. It is vital that what you have told Sara and me be kept in this room. Don't you agree, Sara?" he asked as he turned to Sara who was still in a silent state of mixed emotions of sadness, joy, and amazement.

Sara's love for family, for Katrina, Iskandar's mother, was deep and caring. Her thoughts raced back decades. She knew she could not say anything that would offend their memory. She leaned toward Madeleine and said in her soft voice, "My dear, when I first saw the gold cross I myself designed and had made by a cousin in Beirut more than thirty years ago, I thought the worst. I thought for a moment that the cross had been stolen from Iskandar, or even that someone may have beaten and robbed him. That is why now I feel a sense of relief." She sat back. "And, more so, why I am so glad you have shared your love for our dear Iskandar with us. I am grateful." She paused. "You are a kind, caring woman. You have endured much suffering in your silence. Of course, we welcome you. Yet, I believe that for you, for François, for Iskandar's memory in our village and for the entire Thomé family it would be better that you and François leave the village soon, before your secret is found out."

"Ohh," breathed Madeleine, not wanting to hear that thought. "Must we leave Douma?"

Milhelm, in his wisdom, and trying to absorb what he had just heard, broke the tension in the room by asserting control of the situation. He cleared his throat, slapped his thighs and stood up. "I will go to Beirut tomorrow and seek out family there to find accommodations for Madeleine and François. They will have to be told and we must help them as much as we can. The war is over now, and the city is safe."

"Then it is settled," Sara responded quickly, looking to Madeleine. They all stood together, with Sara reaching to embrace Madeleine and kiss her on both cheeks, and then embracing and kissing François likewise. François went to Milhelm who firmly embraced his brother's son before turning to Madeleine, followed suit and did the same. Both smiles and tears enveloped the small group of co-conspirators as they expressed their release of tension. They all sadly agreed that it was best for everyone that Madeleine and her son go to Beirut...and leave Douma.

Milhelm and Sara knew, of course, that Iskandar was now married, and from letters from Boston over the years prior to the war, that he was happy with Helene, a good, Syrian girl, and had two children. Yet they had come to love Madeleine and her son, so when they discussed all they had heard, they decided it was not their place to tell Madeleine of Iskandar's life in America, nor, God forbid, tell him of Madeleine's life after he left her in Marseille.

"That can bring no good, Sara. We must not interfere with the lives of these two people. We cannot, on our own, involve Iskandar's American family. We'll leave that to God's will."

"Yes, Milhelm, that's what I believe too. Yet, we must do all we can to help her. She needs love and support. And don't forget, François is Iskandar's son and your nephew."

"*Khali* Elias, we need your help to solve a dilemma in the family," Milhelm whispered softly to his uncle as they sat at a small table sipping the thick, pungent, hot Turkish coffee from the clear demitasse glasses outside the café on Hamra Street in Beirut.

"Tell me," he responded kindly with a quizzical look, completely devoted to his family member, "What is your problem, Milhelm? Of course I will do what I can," Elias, the elder, smiled warmly, casually asking, not having any idea what was coming next.

Milhelm leaned forward toward his uncle, whispering even lower so not to be heard by ears belonging to those who need not know. "When my brother, Iskandar, left us in 1920 bound for America, he visited your brother, Uncle Hanna, in Marseille where he stayed for six weeks awaiting his ship to America…"

Milhelm took more than an hour carefully explaining to Elias all the details, as he knew them from Madeleine. "She is an excellent, very stylish, smart woman who is an experienced couturier and would be perfect as a dressmaker and, maybe, companion to a wealthy Beirut family. Coming to Beirut from Douma now would be especially good for our family. Unfortunately, she cannot stay in Douma; the village is too small."

"Perhaps I can speak with my friend Anthony Kabani. He is now back in Beirut. He travels all over the world, and Mrs. Kabani is not as well as before the war. Perhaps she would welcome assistance. I will see what I can do. You say he is truly Iskandar's son? You are certain, are you not?" Gesticulating with his hands for emphasis, he added, "My merciful God."

"*Oui*, Elias, and *shookrun*," Milhelm said, shrugging his shoulders and holding up his open palms, silently asking "what can I say?" Mixing his French and Arabic as did many Beiruti, he patted his uncle's hand as it lay on the table. "When you see this boy, François, you will know. He is Iskandar. The similarity is remarkable. I will return to Beirut next week in hope that you are successful. Then, I pray, you can tell me to bring Madeleine and her son…your nephew François, to Beirut to meet Monsieur and Madame Kabani."

"Your story explains something to me too, Milhelm. Too often during the war, there were spies in Beirut looking for a Madame Moreau. We did not know she was the same woman. My memory is not so good, but now I believe I did meet her briefly when she arrived in Beirut, but I made no connection. Thank God she went to Douma with her son. Imagine," he murmured, "imagine if they had been found out by the Nazis. Iskandar's son, your nephew, could have been killed. Imagine!" Then with a questioning frown, Elias asked, "Milhelm, what ever happened to those Nazis who were searching for her? Did you see them?"

"Yes, Elias, I did," Milhelm replied succinctly, "Yes, I did."

That was all that was ever said.

Madeleine and François had spent nearly five wartime years in safety and relative obscurity in Iskandar's remote mountain village of Douma. They walked the paths he had walked, visited his school and very classrooms, sat at his desk, and played backgammon on the same mosaic towleh board still in the same home. They walked the hills up to the orchards, harvested the apples, olives and plums from the same trees Iskandar had tended as a boy. And now they anxiously waited for word from Beirut.

On the bright, cloudless summer day following Milhelm's visit with Uncle Elias in Beirut, whereupon he informed Madeleine and François that they would be moving to Beirut, hopefully to live with Mr. and Mrs. Anthony Kabani, the two decided to be alone for a few days with their own thoughts as their time in the village would soon be over.

"*Maman*, before we leave Douma I have to see the place where, as a boy, my father nearly lost his life in the snowstorm. We must go there."

So, they decided to climb the torturous trail up the two mountain ranges to the east.

Madeleine gestured, looking down into the lush Bekaa Valley, "Look at that magnificent valley down there, François. That's where your father swept wheat grains with his little hands. Can you imagine?"

After taking in the dramatic scene and Iskandar's childhood role in it, they walked down the steep, winding footpath to the floor of the Bekaa Valley. The next day they packed a lunch, and followed the same paths Iskandar had climbed back up with his heavy burden of wheat before he was caught in that unexpected snowstorm so long ago. They found the same large protruding stone overhang where Iskandar had been carried to warm his feet during that fateful day.

"I feel so close to my father, *Maman*," François spoke to his mother as they stopped and sat side by side under the stone shelter. "I'm very happy we came to Douma. Except for America, this must be the safest place in the world for us. And it has given me a chance to understand why my father had to go to America, why he was unable to stay with us in Marseille. I wish so much I could be with him." Lowering his head, with tears forming, he whispered to her, "I have come to love the people of Lebanon. They have such a desire to live! And be free."

"As do I." Madeleine responded to her son. "I have had Iskandar so deeply in my heart that I have been unable to love another man as completely as I love your father. Yet, Philippe was a good husband for me, and a generous loving father for you. We must always feel grateful for him. I was unable to let him know how totally I loved your father. There was little room in my heart for him or any other man. And now, my son, we have been fortunate that the truth has set us free." Embracing her son, she murmured, "I love you so much, François. You have become much like your father in many ways. You are exactly as he was when we were together in Marseille. Exactly. One day, I know that we will be with your father, but now, we must continue to live our lives, do our best and endure his absence. And so, we will move on and begin a new adventure in Beirut. Perhaps we will return to Douma in time. I know you like Katrina very much, and she likes you. You are cousins, and you should remain close friends. After all, she has the same name as your grandmother." Then standing, ready to go, she added, "Let's return to the village, make preparations to go to Beirut, and offer our thanks to God and to our family for the kindnesses we have received from them and from the village."

Before they left the shelter of the stone overhang, they embraced, feeling so close to Iskandar, admiring him, missing him, and more deeply understanding and loving him.

When you work you are a flute through whose heart
the whispering of the hours turns to music.
Kahlil Gibran

CHAPTER 9

Beirut, 1945

Madeleine sat with her hostess and spoke, "*Merci*, Madame Kabani. We are very happy to be welcomed in your home. I will make you the finest dresses in all Beirut, and will enjoy being your companion. My son, François, is a bright, well-mannered young man. I'm sure you will find him a source of joy as I have. He will help you also. Now that Lebanon is a free and unoccupied country, we should all enjoy an easier time."

Madame Marina Kabani responded with a slight wave of her hand, "Madame Moreau, I am pleased you will join us. Elias speaks very well of you and tells me your husband Monsieur Moreau was Director of the *Resistance* in France. That was a very important position, was it not?" she asked rhetorically.

She continued, looking directly into Madeleine's eyes, "We must all do the best we can under these trying conditions. Monsieur Kabani continues to work very hard, and as more areas become liberated, especially in Africa, his travels have increased. Sadly, I am not able to endure the pace and activities as I once did. There are always obligatory entertaining events at each city, and it has become too much a responsibility for me. I am glad you can help me assist my husband in these cases. This has been a very painful and challenging time for us here in Lebanon. It seems our place as a trading center however, does bring us prosperity, even though the war years were difficult for everyone." She sat quietly for a moment. "It has been the destiny of the Lebanese to be in the path of history's conquerors. We have been a place of refuge for so many over the ages. Alexander the Great led the Greeks as they conquered Sidon and Tyre in the south, then Egypt. Then came the Romans who took all the cedars they could and used the Bekaa to feed their armies. Our land provided refuge for the Jewish people during the invasion the Europeans call the Crusades. And now, my dear, Lebanon is even a refuge for you and your son, François." She drew a deep breath before adding, "We are a hospitable and proud people; proud of our heritage, proud that our fathers have rebuilt it each time, and grateful to be here for you. My husband, Anthony, is already rebuilding all over Lebanon, Palestine, Iraq, and even Kuwait. He has that amazing resilience and tenacity. But I can tell that you, my dear, have the same characteristics."

Changing thoughts, Madame Kabani continued as her eyes swept the large room, "Ours is a large and beautiful home, and the views from the terraces are beautiful. So are our furnishings, because my husband and I have brought beautiful art treasures from all over the world. We have entertained dignitaries here many times and, I pray now that this awful war is over, we will do so again."

Madeleine's eyes followed her hostess's eyes and marveled at her magnificent home.

"Meanwhile, Madeleine, you and I must do the best we can to provide a respite for Monsieur Kabani, a happy and beautiful retreat for him." she concluded.

Madeleine and François soon found themselves in Beirut in the home of one of the most respected families in the Middle East. Mr. Kabani had been in the trading business since 1926 when he bought his first truck from the American, Mr. Dodge, as a result of his visit to Detroit. He wanted to improve and expand his already successful transport business by means of mechanized travel. A man of vision, he was always looking for ways to bring his region to the same economic levels as the West. He established the first motorized transportation of goods between Beirut and Damascus, then from Damascus to Baghdad, replacing his and others' camel caravans. As his transportation business thrived, he naturally became a Chrysler dealer for the mercantile-starved Middle East, starting in Beirut, then Sidon, Damascus, and Jaffa before venturing to Baghdad, Amman and the Gulf States. In 1933, when oil exploration development and petrol sales began to dramatically change the region, Mr. Kabani was well positioned to import and market throughout the Near East the needed equipment, cars, trucks, spare parts, and other goods and commodities from America and Europe. Because of his business ethics and the reputation of keeping his word and his willingness to take on every profitable challenge, his companies became among the most trusted, reliable, and successful in the region, providing a gateway to the rapidly expanding and profitable markets of the "Near East" as it was called in the 1940s. While the decade of the 1930s was devastating in America and throughout Europe, the Near Eastern countries were just getting started. They were, in many ways, decades, and in some places, centuries behind the developed world. As the world demanded more and more oil and its progeny — lubricants, gasoline, and diesel fuel — the Near East economy grew exponentially, finally able to afford those commodities produced in the West.

When Germany began its military sweep across Europe in 1938, world demand for oil skyrocketed. America and Britain sought alliances with the Saudis, the Al Sabah emirate of Kuwait, and Iraq's king. European and American oil companies, which had created Aramco, were positioned to meet the insatiable demand for oil products to feed the Allies' wartime machine. Saudi Arabia, with its almost unlimited and easily accessible oil reserves, became the "golden goose," the treasured ally. King Saud Abdul Aziz, who united the Arabian Peninsula tribes, mostly by siring children with the daughters of the various tribes' leaders, created a family dynasty and controlled much of what became the world's known oil reserves. In time, King Saud became the most important client/friend of Anthony Kabani, channeling his country's needs through Kabani Enterprises. Saud, the world's richest man, personally enjoyed the *laissez-faire* culture of mostly Christian Lebanon. He spent many delightful evenings at the Kabani home enjoying their parties, accompanied by his entourage. Soon, as word spread, Sheikhs of the ruling families, the Al Sabahs in Kuwait, the Al Khalifa, of Bahrain, the Emirates, and the Al Thani family of Qatar sought to partake of Monsieur and Madame Kabani's soirées. The Kabanis became the hosts of royals who chose to travel from their native countries with their more constraining social mores and regulations to enjoy the world of the freedom-loving Lebanese in Beirut and their province-wide sense of *joie de vivre*. Kabani Enterprises became one of the principle business beneficiaries of royal largesse, while keeping in close touch with their far-flung network of associates and partners. Mr. Kabani and his family were welcomed everywhere.

Monsieur and Madame Kabani's four sons, all well-educated at Beirut's American University of Beirut (AUB), the Sorbonne in France, or Cairo University in Egypt, and ultimately at the London School of Economics, followed in their father's footsteps. They became his surrogates, representatives, and personal delegates to maintain the Kabani reputation for honesty, integrity, and capability. Their word was their bond. The region's power brokers, royalty, and functionaries welcomed their acumen, integrity and their involvement. It was a very profitable arrangement for everyone.

Anthony Kabani admonished his sons, "Do not become part of the political world; work with it, maintain ties with all factions, but stay out of the fray, and you will survive. We do not seek power. Be friends with those who have the political power, and those who one day may have the power. We are traders, careful business people. We are Phoenicians."

By 1945, the four Kabani sons were in their thirties and forties. During the war, one was in New York, another in Cairo, the third operating in Amman, Jordan, and the fourth in Baghdad. Annually, they visited their parents in Beirut, Anthony's home base, preferring to otherwise remain at their stations with their families. Madame Kabani accompanied her husband to visit their sons, enjoying the respect of her community and her husband's associates.

"My dear," she said, turning to Madeleine, smiling, "we now have homes or apartments in Amman, Baghdad, Athens, Alexandria, and Paris. Of course, we have not been able to visit Paris during the war as it is so difficult there, and it is not so easy for me to travel as before. But one day I wish to return there. It is such a beautiful city. I'm sure you agree. Despite what others may say, I am glad the French surrender meant Paris and its treasures would not be destroyed by that madman, Adolph Hitler. What a pity that would have been. Such beauty would have been lost to future generations. And for what? It would have been a tragedy. So, as for me, I will remain here in Beirut with my friends and visit Paris when I can. It is, after all, a beautiful city as well, but from this room, each day we can watch the magnificent sunsets as the golden glow glistens on the Mediterranean Sea. I always feel God is watching over us as I watch the sunsets."

Madeleine's life during the next two years in Beirut was especially exciting. She and Madame Kabani grew close, always conversing in polished French, and enjoying each day. As Madame Kabani needed new dresses and accessories for social engagements, entertaining and attending palace events following Lebanon's independence, Madeleine designed the most elegant attire for her, shopped in the finest boutiques, and became a most welcome customer. Many times, she would be invited by Madame Kabani to accompany her to events. Other times, Monsieur Kabani insisted she accompany both of them not only to assist Madame Kabani but also to be part of his party. As a result, Madeleine DuBois-Moreau soon became part of the Beirut social scene, enviably associated with the Kabani family and its reputation, and recognized in the upscale Hamra shopping district as such. Others in Beiruti society and in the finer boutiques welcomed her and treated her as though she was actually a member of the Kabani family. Her life was enriching, safe and comfortable. She came to crave the Lebanese way of life.

François also enjoyed similar benefits as a student at the American University of Beirut (AUB). He was popular with his colleagues, and, being quite a handsome, well-mannered young man with the added bonus of being "almost a Kabani." His presence was always welcomed.

By late 1946, Madeleine and François were becoming fixtures of the social scene of Beirut. All was more than wonderful for this forty-ish beautiful, charming associate of Madame Kabani from Marseille and her 26-year-old son, refugees in Beirut who had become a part of Lebanon. They loved Beirut and had come to live beyond their wildest dreams…far in excess of what they imagined that fateful day they arrived on the docks in 1940.

Madeleine always fit in easily. Since she was a little girl, her mother had taught her the importance of social graces. Daniella had taught her, and Madeleine had listened. "Watch the polished ladies of wealth, my clients and learn. Do as they do, behave accordingly. Always be a lady," her mother would admonish. "Stand very straight and tall with hands by your side, smile, be gracious, kind and generous, and by all means, my child, spread your smallest finger. And never point."

"François," Madeleine would in turn, later admonish her son, "I have been teaching you since you were a child those same lessons my mother taught me. It is remarkable that they have served us well so that we are accepted, even welcomed, into the finer homes of Beirut. The people of Beirut are kind and wonderful people, are they not?"

François replied with a smile, "Yes, *Maman*, but after all, I am Lebanese too. I believe we are both Lebanese in our hearts. We speak Arabic fluently and have learned the customs. We have become part of Lebanon, don't you think?"

"Yes, son, that is exactly what I think. We are French, but we are Lebanese also. Your father would be very happy knowing this...and I believe he will, in time."

In truth that which you call freedom is the strongest of these chains, though its links glitter in the sun and dazzle your eyes.

Kahlil Gibran

CHAPTER 10

Beirut, 1946

The French *Resistance* grew out of a disparate collection of French citizen groups, which began fighting the German occupation forces from the outset of the German invasion in 1940. France was in political turmoil even before 1940 and was politically weak. As a result, the *Resistance* effort, a paramilitary outside the government, consisted of every conceivable political and economic leanings of society. Publishers of underground newspapers, Catholics (including priests), rural farmers, communists, Jews, *émigrés*, and liberals formed small groups that provided first hand intelligence, formed escape routes for Allied soldiers and airmen trapped behind enemy lines and harassed German forces.

When the collaborating French Vichy government was formed, they fought it. They included armed guerilla groups that blew up bridges, sabotaged transportation lines and power grids. Even the communists got involved after one year. Taking their orders from Moscow, they had their own agenda. With the German-Soviet Agreement signed in 1939, they became an anti-war group, which led to its leaders being arrested. The Party position reflected the Soviet relationship with Germany, and for the first year of occupation, communists were considered enemies of France. Despite inter-party conflicts, many collaborated with the Germans while many opposed that position. But Germany broke its pact with Stalin and invaded the Soviet Union in 1941. That's when they began resisting the Germans.

By June 1944, the *Resistance* numbered 100,000 and became politically and morally vital to France during the German occupation and for several decades afterward.

Following the war, the government was provincial and almost hopelessly divided, reflecting the political unrest, with various groups fighting for control of the French government. Socialists, Communists, Conservatives and those seeking revenge against collaborators created a chaotic period when more than 35,000 members of the *Milice*, the Vichy Gestapo, thousands of Communists who sided with Germany prior to Germany's invasion of the Soviet Union, and anti-Gaullists were tried and executed for collaborating with the enemy. France was unable to unite. Only the continued presence of the *Resistance* and its moral, pro-France high ground was able to provide a meaningful example for others to follow. By October 1944, only four months after the June Normandy invasion, the *Resistance* boasted 400,000 members, up from 100,000 in June, constituting a viable constituency for the rest of the French people to follow.

"What better way to unite the French people," declared the French newspaper *Le Figaro*, "than to honor the leaders and members of the *Resistance*? Isn't it time these brave people who risked their lives for the French people be properly recognized?" Encouraged by the overwhelming support of public opinion, the government and non-government institutions joined together to locate and honor those brave souls who fought for freedom.

During the years 1945 and 1946, the French government undertook extraordinary and comprehensive post-war efforts to recapitulate what happened in France after the German invasion in 1940, which brought forth the effective and vitally important efforts of the *Resistance* and Monsieur Philippe Moreau's successful leadership. All of France became aware of his importance and what the *Resistance* did to insure the liberation of France, especially the successful Allied invasions of Normandy and Toulon/Marseille. The people of France were grateful to him, and the government endeavored to convey their gratitude to those survivors of the *Resistance* and widows and widowers who survived. After the French government was able to locate them, they sought to personally convey that appreciation. As a consequence, they sought out Madeleine Moreau, and with the close and friendly relations with Lebanon's government, and after extensively searching for her, they found her in Beirut.

In late 1946, Madeleine received an invitation from the French Ambassador in Beirut. Hoping to learn of the war's impact on her native home of Marseille and what happened to her mother, Philippe and Hanna, she had the Kabani driver take her to the embassy. Curious and apprehensive, about his invitation regarding "an important subject," she was concerned and quite nervous as to why she would receive such a request from the ambassador of her native country. The ambassador welcomed her with a characteristically French flourish and slight bow. "Please sit down, Madame Moreau. I have much to tell you," the French ambassador spoke softly and with great respect as he gestured to the burgundy leather couch handcrafted in the mountains of Lebanon, opposite his matching chair. "May I offer you juice, coffee or tea, Madame?"

"*Merci*," Madeleine replied as she properly took her seat on the couch, white kid gloved hands clasped in her lap, head held high. "I am honored that you have invited me to visit with you, Monsieur Ambassador."

The ambassador continued, smiling, "What I have to say to you, Madame Moreau, may shock you, will surprise you, and, I believe, will make you very proud."

She remained puzzled by his statement, tilting her head slightly in an alluring, yet wondering manner.

The Ambassador poured coffee for them both, then stepped behind his impressive mahogany desk and sat down in his leather chair. He pulled a large, flat envelope sealed with red wax from a drawer and placed it in front of him.

Folding his hands together and resting them on the envelope, he hesitated for maximum impact, then leaning toward her for emphasis, he began, "As you may know, your husband Philippe was unfortunately killed while performing most important work for the French people during the terrible German occupation of our beloved country.

"His work was incredibly vital to the successful liberation of France and he is at this moment being recognized with enormous gratitude by a private French foundation, yet not by the government. This is I hasten to explain, because we, the official body of France, cannot be officially involved. The French people and its government are most grateful to your husband, Madame. This particular foundation, with government approval, is dedicated to the welfare of families of the brave deceased members of the *Resistance* during the war.

"The recognition of your husband's extraordinary leadership is shared by all those in positions of influence and authority, including leaders of the Allied Forces and by General Dwight Eisenhower himself, Prime Minister Winston Churchill, President Charles de Gaulle, and even President Harry Truman. They know that without his leadership in organizing the *Resistance* into an effective coordinated force, the Allied invasion at Normandy would not have been successful and all of Europe could have been lost. Forces of the *Resistance*, organized under your husband's leadership, prevented the Germans from being able to deliver their vaunted panzer divisions to the northern front. The *Resistance* delayed all German efforts to stop the invasion! Your husband's leadership, organization and instructions were incredibly successful. Trains carrying those tanks were deliberately delayed with planned accidents by the train engineers, and tunnel explosions. It was fantastic and so vital. Actually, many believe we won the war because of your husband, Monsieur Philippe Moreau, my dear Madame." He paused, allowing his last comment to take effect.

"His work required that, after Normandy, he immediately go to Marseille to prepare the *Resistance* in southern France. His new headquarters were secretly based within the *Panier* district in that city. It was very dangerous there with 15,000 Germans garrisoned in the city. Under great pressure and personal danger, Monsieur Moreau created an effective program of sabotage by the Free French Army in preparation for, and in coordination with the United States and the Allied invasion, which freed the entire southern region in August of 1944. That invasion at Toulon and Marseille was also quite successful due to Monsieur Moreau's planning and leadership.

"Ironically, while he was in Marseille, he stayed in the home of your mother and

Hanna Chalhoub. Hanna was Philippe's principal contact there, providing offices, safe apartments, information, coordination, and assistance in every way to drive the Germans from the south of France. He and your mother were indispensable to efforts in preparation for the Allied bombardment of Toulon and Marseille, and the Allied invasion called Operation Anvil. After completing his plans prior to the invasion, Monsieur Moreau had to leave Marseille to meet with colleagues in Denmark. Sadly, it was during the siege of Marseille that your mother and Hanna were killed. John Giordano of Toulon, their friend and a respected Free French compatriot, was meeting with them at the time. He was fatally wounded as well. They were among the thousands who suffered so much during those days when the battleships and Allied bombers were trying to rid the area of German forces. German artillery and errant Allied bombs bombarded the *Canebière* while they were there dining, German shells hit the restaurant directly." He lowered his head in a show of respect. "I am told that, gratefully, they did not suffer."

As the ambassador paused, looking up from his papers, he focused on Madeleine's eyes. "I am profoundly saddened to have to tell you these events concerning your mother and your husband, my dear Madame Moreau. Philippe left Marseille in early August, leaving your mother and Hanna, his dear friends, to travel to Copenhagen to coordinate with the Danish *Resistance* leadership. It was there that he was found by the Nazis and assassinated. This was a tragic turn of events for all of us.

"Without his extraordinary leadership, it is believed by his grateful countrymen, as well as the English and the Americans, that France would still be occupied by the hated Germans and controlled by the terrible Vichy government."

As he finished reading his papers and commenting, the Ambassador looked at Madeleine with an empathetic expression and continued.

"Madame Moreau, it has been my privilege and my sad duty to tell you these details, as dreadful as they are. Tragically, millions of French people died during 'this nasty business,' as Winston Churchill described the war. But it is certain even more French and, indeed, American and British, would have suffered and died had it not been for your husband, Philippe Moreau."

Concluding, he spoke with authority as he rose from his chair and stood quite straight. "It is my great honor to inform you that a grateful nation wishes to extend to you its thanks by permitting and endorsing this private foundation's actions to honor your husband's name with monuments in Paris and Marseille. In addition, they wish to give you a token of our appreciation in the amount of one million French francs, to be used by you in any way you wish. I regret that there is only our gratitude and enormous thanks to give you for the incredibly brave and loyal activities carried out by Monsieur Hanna Chalhoub and your magnificent mother."

Unclasping his hands, the ambassador picked up the envelope, stepped around his desk toward his visitor. Perplexed, Madeleine, with a look of sadness, took his cue and rose from her chair. The ambassador came to her, stood stiffly, and with great respect, leaned toward her and, with French elegance, formally kissed her on both cheeks. He then bowed in respect, stepped back, extended his hand to her and gave her the envelope containing a letter signed by the president of the unnamed foundation containing the official cheque in the amount of one million francs, and an invitation to come to Paris and Marseille for the presentation and unveiling of the monuments.

Madeleine, caught completely off guard by this presentation, felt suddenly weak and gratefully sank down in her chair. She remained motionless for several moments while she read the official document shaking in her hands. She reached into her leather handbag, retrieved a lace handkerchief and lightly touched her moistened cheeks.

"Please forgive me, your Excellency. I am very sad, although very proud. I have lost a wonderful husband, my mother, and her dear friend and mine, Monsieur Hanna Chalhoub. I have lost so much, but I am also honored and proud." Then, with a nod of her head and the beginnings of a slight smile, said, "Of course I will go to Paris."

She again sat quietly thinking, and then asked. "You say none of them suffered? Is that true?"

"Yes, Madame, that is what I am told. While they agonized along with all of France during the war, they did not suffer at the end."

"One question, Monsieur," she whispered, leaning forward and raising her hand. "Was Marseille totally destroyed by the bombardments? I mean, were the holy places destroyed?"

The ambassador carefully flipped through his papers, scanned the appropriate pages, and looked back at Madeleine.

"It appears most of the churches were left intact. Though, of course, there was severe damage everywhere. However, since Marseille is the city of my youth, I am pleased to say the most prominent church, Marseille's pride, although it was temporarily the German headquarters, was left virtually untouched. Of this I have official confirmation. It remains as beautiful as it was before the war. The German commander wisely surrendered to the French commander only a few minutes before the church was to be bombarded by the Allies and destroyed. It was so imminent that it is almost a miracle it still stands. Do you know the cathedral Notre-Dame-de-la-Garde?"

Madeleine, watching the ambassador's face carefully, suddenly gasped, brought her hand to her opened mouth and cried aloud, "Oh, my God, thank you God." She wept quietly, both hands covering her face.

"Is that place important to you, Madame?"

Nodding, she replied between her silent sobs, her shoulders shaking slightly, "More than I could ever describe to you, Monsieur. So much more."

Collecting her thoughts and remembering her proper etiquette, she continued, "I am so sorry for my outburst, Monsieur Ambassador. I must be alone now, *s'il vous plait.* This has been a most difficult moment of remembrance and, yet, gratitude for me. I do hope you understand. Would you kindly have someone locate a taxi for me?"

"Of course, Madame."

Safely settled in the taxi, she leaned back against the backseat cushion, closed her eyes and sighed, "*Mon Dieu*! What shall I do now?" She felt emotionally drained and alone with her thoughts as she returned to *beit* residence Kabani tightly holding onto the envelope containing the pronouncement and the cheque.

Madeleine couldn't help but think of Marseille, her mother, Hanna, and her loving moments with Iskandar. She knew she needed to be alone with her memories for she knew that her life was now going to be so very different. For too long she had been torn by the conflict of being Madame Moreau and yet loving Iskandar. The war and its casualties had now created a new world for her. Philippe was gone; her mother was gone. And as a result of this news, she was drawn to Marseille by a new powerful tug. She knew she had to revisit the city of her youth, and she felt, quite naturally, the yearning to go back to their place atop *Les Calanques* where she left her childhood and became a woman with her first love. She knew she had to take whatever time it required seeking the truth within her, to clarify her feelings and determine her life's new course. Now, as a result of Philippe's heroism, she found herself actually made even wealthier, having received a large inheritance from Philippe's estate months earlier by virtue of her marriage to Philippe Moreau who was quite wealthy in his own right. She felt a sting of guilt for not being able to totally commit her heart to Philippe, subconsciously longing for the embrace of Iskandar, her first true love.

As she rode in the taxi to the Kabani residence for respite, she knew she must be with her hostess, and now her mentor, who was anxiously awaiting her return. But Madeline held back, not ready to share the entire message from the Ambassador.

"Oh, Madame, Kabani, I am overwrought with mixed emotions. My heart has belonged to Iskandar Chalhoub since we met in 1920, but now I find myself filled with a sense of guilt and unworthiness accepting these large rewards because I married Philippe Moreau. What am I to do?" she fretted. "I am truly mixed up. Should I give away that which I have received?"

"My child. Didn't you tell me you told Monsieur Moreau about your love for Iskandar?"

"From the beginning, Madame, from the very beginning. He always knew. Although, yes, I was true to Philippe and a good wife to him throughout our marriage. And it was a good and beautiful marriage, Madame Kabani. I know that, and I know Philippe felt it was."

Madame Kabani, receiving an emotional Madeleine she had not seen before, had not known what had happened at the embassy until Madeleine explained everything to her but she could easily tell that her friend was distraught. Sensing her sadness and confusion, Madame Kabani, in her nurturing manner, listened quietly and then spoke as she reached for Madeleine's hand as she sat beside her. "You should be alone for awhile, my child. You must look deep inside yourself and find your desires. You must clear your head. Be only with God. Let Him guide you." Then, patting her hand affectionately, she softly concluded with "Take your time, *y'slemlie Allah Ma'ak*. May God be with you."

Madeleine couldn't get rid of her nagging conflicting thoughts, the emotional conflict that tore at her heart so much. She decided to open her mind and focus on the needs of others as a way of getting away from her own personal concerns and agony. These moments of introspection brought both pain and solace to Madeleine as she tried to determine what to do with her life.

After several days of strolling alone in the gardens in thought and meditation, she had Madame Kabani's driver take her to downtown Beirut where she walked in solitude for several hours on the Corniche high above the sea. She sought out a café there where she could sit quietly among strangers, contemplating as she gazed at the sparkling sea. As she looked around her, she witnessed many who suffered so much more than she and François during the Allied bombardment to rid Lebanon of the Vichy presence in 1941 and 1942. She saw children with missing limbs, mothers and fathers limping from their wounds, and felt so much empathy for them. She became convinced she had to find a way to help them. As she watched, she felt an urge to be an anonymous observer, to think alone, not to converse with them. As she sat at the table by the railing, high above the placid sea, she sipped tea, leaned back, calmer now, and closed her eyes to the world around her.

Memories of her mother, her youth, and her life in Marseille as a young girl in simpler times flooded her consciousness. She was grateful Daniella was with Hanna at the end, and that the end came swiftly and without suffering. Then her thoughts turned to Iskandar. "The cliffs were our place," she whispered aloud, gazing at the sea, thinking of his touch, his smile, their love. She recalled Marseille and the serene beauty of the sea from the hill overlooking the magnificent cerulean waters, much the same as Beirut. Every detail of her moments with Iskandar seemed to fill her mind. She was again overwhelmed by feelings of sadness mixed with loss and guilt. *Should I have stayed in Marseille to be with Hanna and Maman? No*, she quickly decided.

When she opened her eyes, she watched as a mother in torn clothing walked toward her table with two small maimed children. Her remembrances quickly dissipated as she was struck by the sudden appearance of this woman who had lost an arm, probably in the bombardment that destroyed the lives of so many in Beirut. The woman's eyes made contact with Madeleine's as she held out her open palm asking for money.

"Madame, *s'il vous plaît?*"

Madeleine looked closely at the woman and her two sad-looking little girls in ragged clothes and unkempt hair tugging on their mother's skirt, their eyes beseeching Madeleine to help. The oldest girl was walking with crude crutches as one foot dragged; the other had a bandage over one eye. Madeleine instantly felt great sympathy for this woman and her children. "Of course," she nodded with a loving smile, handing the mother a more than generous amount of money.

The mother stared at the sum of money given her and almost wept, her eyes filling with tears of gratitude. Looking into Madeleine's eyes, she bowed in respect and whispered, "*Shookrun*, Madame, thank you so much."

The more Madeleine looked around her, watching the people at the café and along the broad Corniche, the more she realized that many people, so many children, more than she had imagined, were injured from the bombardments. They are innocents, she thought, as she began to realize how fortunate she was, and very grateful for her son's health and safety.

Her thoughts went to François. He is there, across the boulevard at the university. Safe, not wounded, like these poor souls. *Merci, mon Dieu.* Compelled to do more, she reached into her purse and beckoned to the woman. "Come back here, Madame. I have something more to give to you and your children. They are so beautiful...with such big brown eyes." She offered the woman another generous amount, holding the woman's hand and closing it around the money. Then, on impulse, she stood, reached out and embraced the woman. After a moment, she crouched down to hug the children. "They are darling."

She stood again and, placing her arm around the woman's shoulder, asked, "Do you come here each day?"

"*Oui*, Madame, *merci, merci beaucoup*," the woman replied with a sad but grateful smile. "It is so terrible. I am so proud and I hate doing this but I must beg to feed my children. We have no food, no home. We do the best we can. Thanks to God, many people are kind and generous."

As the woman turned to leave Madeleine's table, she spoke, "*Allah ma'ak*." Be with God.

"*Allah ma'ak*. I shall see you again," Madeleine promised.

After she finished her tea, Madeleine paid the garçon and walked out of the café perched high above the Mediterranean overlooking Pigeon Rocks. She suddenly had a wholly different, less self-oriented view of the world and of Lebanon. Into her life had come unpredictable events of monumental impact. First, her father's death in the World War I, then Iskandar completely fulfilling her need for passion and love; her son, François, Philippe, the war, then her escape to Douma...ah, lovely Douma, and now, enormous wealth and, incredibly, the enormous change in her financial capabilities and new found concomitant responsibilities, She experienced an epiphany-like awakening to the plight of others, a more realistic awareness of the suffering that surrounded her; the wounded, the poverty, the misery of the poor a revelation. A change of her spirit. She gazed out at the sea, thinking, for a long time. Then, she turned away from the sea. Her eyes swept the city landscape, including the ruins remaining since the siege. For the first time, she truly witnessed the heavily damaged apartment buildings, the pushcarts bearing goods, the young boys trying to sell anything, some begging. Most were in torn clothing, most without shoes. All looking hungry. She thought about Iskandar when he was very young. He too was very poor. She saw children everywhere. Some very young playing in the streets, others, unable to play, simply sat and watched.

Feeling a sudden sense of urgency, she walked to the curb and signaled the oncoming car. "Taxi!" As she climbed into the backseat, Madeleine instructed the driver to take her to the Kabani home.

Exhilarated, and with a swelling sense of enlightened determination, she entered the luxurious residence and sought out Madame Kabani.

"She's in her room," said the maid in her perfectly starched white blouse and black skirt.

Madeleine climbed the staircase energetically and knocked at the bedroom door.

"*Entrez!*" said the voice of Madame Kabani from behind the door.

Excitedly, Madeleine quickly turned the polished brass lever handle and entered the room. Breathlessly, she declared, "Oh, Madame, I must speak with you! After a most difficult week, I have now had a most incredible day." She was excited to share her experiences of her day. And then, with a positive smile, her voice at a higher pitch, of joy Madeleine told of her visit with the woman and her children. "I have seen for the first time what I must do with my life, how I can help others." Pausing for a breath, she continued. "I have decided to use the money from France and do something for these poor children of Lebanon. This is my country now, in my heart, and I cannot bear witnessing the suffering without doing something." Madeleine was passionate as she described her thoughts, her vision to make life better for the orphaned and under-privileged children of Lebanon.

"Oh, my dear, these few days must have been extraordinary emotional experiences for you. I am so sorry for you. And yet, I am happy you have found your way back from the despair you experienced after your meeting with the Ambassador. What an amazing turn of events for you to deal with so suddenly. War is so painful, for those who suffer so much, for those who must mourn. I am glad I am here for you, dear Madeleine. There is so much to comprehend, isn't there? As Homer wrote, Even those who must stand and wait, they also serve. You are right, my dear. What a wonderful decision! I'm sure Monsieur Kabani will be happy to assist you in your efforts. He will be home soon. Let's discuss your intentions with him this very evening. Perhaps he will have some suggestions. And I am sure our friends can be convinced to participate."

With François and Monsieur and Madame Kabani at the dinner table that evening, Madeleine enthusiastically repeated her day's events. She carefully and deliberately explained her vision, her plans to do all she could to provide medical help, rehabilitation, and housing for those whose lives were so terribly affected by the war. Her passion was obvious and contagious. "I am very excited about this, Monsieur Kabani. Will you help me?"

Stunned by this turn of events, he replied, "Of course, my dear. This is an excellent proposal. We can do this together. There is so much to do. So many Lebanese suffered during the war. I will speak with my friends. I am sure they will support your efforts as well."

"Monsieur," she asked with her head lowered modestly, "Another favor...I also need your counsel and guidance. Will you please help me protect my funds? You are so much wiser than I about these issues."

"If you ask, certainly I will be happy to watch over your new found funds. You have been given a great deal of money. I think it is a good time for you to invest. The world is rebuilding everywhere. I myself have recently invested heavily in the United States. There is much opportunity at this time in Europe as well. Your funds must, at first, be secure. And if we invest them well, you can accomplish your desires to help the poor of Lebanon and still not substantially reduce your largesse. *Insha Allah*, God be willing."

You give but little when you give of your possessions.
It is when you give of yourself that you truly give.
Kahlil Gibran

CHAPTER 11

Paris, 1947

Using their Lebanese passports, François accompanied his mother to Paris to participate in the French foundation's honor to Philippe. During their stay, he enrolled at the Université du Paris, the Sorbonne.

"Paris is so beautiful, François, truly one of the most beautiful cities in the world. It's good that the Germans didn't destroy it. At the time, surrendering the city without a fight didn't seem to be so brave. Many French were opposed and wanted to fight the Germans instead. But now, it is seen as a most wise decision. You'll enjoy your stay in this loveliest of cities here as you attend the Sorbonne.

"You will meet so many fascinating people from all over the world now that the war is concluded."

Within a few days, ceremonies were held in the city honoring the heroes of the war, especially Philippe Moreau, with appropriate monuments standing in the prominent parks.

Later that day, as she sat in her compartment on the train to Marseille, listening to the clickety-clack of the wheels on the tracks, she focused on her return to Marseille, the city of her youth, the city where she fell in love with Iskandar. She watched the forests and gently rolling hillsides transform to vineyards, broad expanses of open land, farms and lakes as central France passed by and the terrain of Aix-en-Provence in southern France passed by her window. She recalled François' parting remarks, "Remember, *Maman*, the love of so many who have come into your life" Madeleine, now a beautiful woman in her mid-forties, some twenty-eight years later, was still in love with and remained committed to Iskandar.

As the train began to slow, Madeleine, by herself for the first time in her life, felt a strange sense of *déjà vu*, but as a visitor, not as a citizen

"Taxi! Please take me to a hotel on the *Canebière*."

The driver, noting her chic clothing and expensive luggage, respectfully and silently delivered her from the rail station to the elegant Charles V Hotel, as she requested.

After she checked in and her luggage was placed in her suite, an anxious Madeleine DuBois-Moreau stepped out of the hotel, stood on the hotel's entry way, took a deep breath, and looked around She happily saw many familiar sights, but, sadly, many other familiar buildings were run-down, many still showing damage from the invasion. Perhaps the *Canebière* had indeed seen its better days too. She reminded herself that, after all, since she left, twenty-eight years of depression, turmoil, social street battles, political unrest, and even war, to say nothing of the Germans' cruel occupation. All in all, she decided, Marseille had survived, even though a bit worse from wear.

Speaking to the hotel doorman, she said, "Well, it looks like this part of Marseille got its share of damage, though I remember this area so well.

"Have you been away long, Madame?"

"*Oui*, Monsieur. I left Marseille just before the Germans invaded. It seems like centuries ago," she said sadly, almost looking down.

She knew the restaurant where her mother and Hanna had been hit by German artillery and avoided looking in that direction. She preferred not to think of their last moments. Rather, she simply stood at the curb for a few minutes. Even though her striking beauty attracted stares from the passersby and nods with tipped hats from the gentlemen, she was not distracted from her mission. She knew exactly what she wanted to do, where she wanted to go, what she wanted to see. She couldn't wait another day. It must be now. She stepped to the left to find her way to *Vieux Port* and then walked to the *Panier*. She had no time schedule. She was now, for the first time, independently wealthy, had no obligations to anyone or anything. Her son...all that remained of her family...was safely ensconced where he should be, in Paris.

And so, she would do as Madame Kabani had admonished with true love and elderly wisdom: "Take as much time as you need, my dear. You must savor this time in your life. You have earned it. You deserve to find your true inner emotions. You are never alone, as God is always with you. Have faith, my dear. Remember the beauty of your loved ones, the passion of your youth. If you do, you will find the truth. Listen to an older woman, Madeleine. Go and find the enrichment of your spirit. Nourish your soul and be not afraid. And when you do, let it be a magnificent moment. Then, when you are where you must be in your heart, return to us."

Madeleine knew Madame Kabani was correct. Her sagacity convinced her of what she must do no matter how long it took. Suddenly, walking on the cobblestone sidewalk along the port, she was aware of an older, well-dressed man who stepped directly in front of her as if he was a close friend. His face was filled with surprise as he thought he was gazing on Madeleine's mother, Daniella.

"*Bon soir*! Madame DuBois, is it really you? *Mon Dieu*! How can this be?" He looked very closely at Madeleine's face. "Oh, pardon, I am so sorry. You startled me because you look exactly like the woman my Uncle Hanna loved during *le guerre*." Sensing her hesitation, he quickly asked sincerely, "Are you her sister? Do you know of whom I speak?"

Madeleine looked at the swarthy Lebanese man staring at her quizzically, and then turned her head and saw that she was, in fact, standing at *Place de Liban*, the Lebanese label of *Place de Lenche*.

"Daniella Dubois is my mother," Madeleine nervously responded in a loud whisper, stunned at his statement but pleased to have her mother remembered in this way.

"Well, I knew your mother and Monsieur Hanna Chalhoub. They were most popular here in the *Panier*, especially during the war. Everyone believed your mother to be the most gracious and beautiful woman in the south of France." Then, hopefully, he asked, "May I join you, Madame?"

Feeling quite safe and secure in her familiar locale, she replied, "*Merci*, Monsieur, but I prefer to be alone at this time. And I must leave soon, for there is something I promised myself that I must do today, before the sun sets. But you have been most gracious." She barely noticed as he bowed in respect and stepped toward a remote table.

She looked at the tables and chairs scattered across the plaza and, feeling slightly dizzy, almost as though she was floating, realized that she had somehow found herself at the Café Liban, Hanna's restaurant, not in the summer of 1920, but rather, now, in the summer of 1948.

Her eyes searched the plaza. She gingerly sat down at a table near the entrance to the restaurant. Automatically searching her purse for her compact, she carefully powdered her nose, then hand signaled the *garçon*. "A glass of wine, Savignon blanc, *s'il vous plait*."

She thanked the waiter, and sipped delicately from the wineglass, lost in her own nostalgia while looking at the familiar buildings on three sides of the plaza. She couldn't help but remember every detail of that evening so long ago when she, just a 16-year-old with great feelings of anticipation, had come to this same place with her mother to meet Iskandar. It was as if she somehow had stepped back not only in time, but had also instantly morphed into the happiest moment of her life, which was when she had stumbled on the cobblestones, then tripped and stumbled into Iskandar's arms. She smiled as her thoughts went back to the moment when she was walking down the gentle slope of the cobble-stoned walkway and saw dear Hanna, his hair carefully combed as always, and his young, so handsome nephew that she was about to meet. How very foolish she had felt stumbling, yet happy at how it had prompted Iskandar to leap spontaneously from his chair to come to her assistance. Such a gentleman he was, she remembered lovingly, exhibiting his thoughtfulness and concern for her at that awkward moment. She had wanted to impress him, but her awkward spill, while embarrassing, had turned out to be a beautifully innocent, yet intimate, moment of their first meeting. She almost burst into laughter as she remembered her bizarre beginning with Iskandar! How wonderfully they fell in love!

She did not know what to expect from this visit to the place where she met Iskandar, but she was beginning to realize that the painful dilemma she feared would envelop her was not to happen. Rather, at least at this point, it was bringing a new perspective, a sense of reality, truth and acceptance. She felt the time she would spend alone in Marseille would allow her dreams of the future to build on the memories of her past and she would remain focused, young and hopeful. She also began eagerly to see the present, and look to the future with hope and confidence. She now knew what she must do to provide others with assistance. She would remember the past, but do her best to put it behind her and focus on her new life with its efforts to help others. It was a natural segue for her as she had always been a giver, but now she had a new direction.

She became aware that more and more people were walking by, then, glancing at her wristwatch, saw it was becoming late in the day. Spontaneously, her eyes looked to the east to gaze on the familiar Notre-Dame-de-la-Garde, the symbol of Marseille, the place she had taken Iskandar, the place on the hill where he had, in his joy with her, kissed her for the first time. Her body trembled as she heard the distant bells of the cathedral, recalling how they rang the moment he had kissed her that day, and again after they had loved on *Les Calanques*. It was magical. Two young people in love for the first time. She was sixteen, he eighteen. It was as though they felt at the time that God Himself was blessing their union. Now as she heard the first bells strike, her tears began to flow. "Six o'clock, exactly six o'clock. Oh," she softly asked out loud, "Iskandar, where are you today?"

She placed money on the table for the waiter, stood tall, and began to walk down the steps at the edge of the plaza. She waved to the Peugeot. "Taxi!" she hailed with her arm outstretched. She looked at her watch. She still had time.

The taxi pulled up to her place at the curb. "*Où allez-vous?*"

"Notre-Dame-de-la-Garde," she replied as she quickly climbed into the rear seat.

The taxi driver smiled as he looked at this lovely face in his rear view mirror. "Do you want to make the last service of the day, Madame?"

"Well, in a manner of speaking," she replied. "I would like to reach the church before the sun sets."

"*Oui*, Madame, we can be there very shortly."

In minutes, the taxi reached the slope leading to the cathedral. Madeleine signaled the driver. "Stop here, driver. I would like to walk the rest of the way."

Madeleine paid the driver and exited the Peugeot, collecting herself as she tentatively stepped up to the walk. Still not quite sure she was doing the right thing. She looked up the hill at the stone structure, the familiar bell tower, the glistening gold of the statue of Saint Mary at the pinnacle of the dome, and the surrounding pine trees that canopied the rugged stone of the hills. Her legs felt weak as she took her first steps up the steep ascending stone walkway. Almost instinctively, her right hand went to her head as she crossed herself.

The memories of this place were almost overpowering. She looked over her shoulder and gratefully saw that she was alone, isolated with her memories. The afternoon visitors had departed. Madeleine turned and crossed to the steps, counting them until she reached the quiet place where she and Iskandar had sat together that late afternoon. She looked at her watch. *Mon Dieu*, she thought, *I am almost there at exactly the same time.* Her eyes scanned the grassy knoll, the magnificent trees posing as sentinels.

Gingerly, now without hesitation, she stepped eagerly to the place overlooking the city and the sea where she had been with Iskandar, and sat on the bench at that very spot. After a long respite of gazing at the sea, she looked around the promontory with her chin propped in the palms of her hands, her knees supporting her elbows. She was a picture of a woman content in her deep personal thoughts. Assured that she was alone with her fondest, happiest remembrances for what seemed only minutes but was actually more than an hour. She whispered to herself, almost in a prayer, her eyes brimming with tears of love, "Oh, Iskandar. I want you, I need you, I love you. When am I going to be with you again? Come to me, Iskandar."

Madeleine partially blinked her eyes wearing a serenely wistful expression on her face, then closed them again. She knew now she had done the right thing in coming back here, the very spot they had shared so long ago. She was absolutely certain that she and her young lover would meet again; that God would make certain it would happen.

"One day, Iskandar, one day, you and I will return here together. This is our place, the home of our love. Soon, my love, *mon amour*. Soon."

As she turned her head, Madeleine watched the sun begin to set into the sea as it had so many times before when she visited this place with her son, remembering…watching.

Finally, satisfied, she stood up, smiled to herself as she straightened her dress, looked at her watch and moved toward the steps that would lead her down the hill. She was a happy woman once again, but also a woman who knew she was loved and now, a mature woman who had found a purpose beyond herself and her past.

Every afternoon during the following two weeks, Madeleine happily returned to the cathedral and to the promontory to be alone with her thoughts. She dined either on the *Canebière* or at the Lebanese cafés at the *Place de Liban*, savoring the memories, enjoying the food of the Levant.

She was convinced that she had found her place in the world, her best and most fulfilling course. God would help her, she deeply believed. She loved Psalm 46:10

which says: *Be still, and know that I am God.* With a renewed sense of purpose, she returned to her new home, Beirut, to devote herself to her honorable cause.

Back in Beirut, Madeleine set out to do whatever it took to fulfill her new purpose. Everyday, Madeleine eagerly ventured into the poorest parts of Beirut, locating rundown houses or damaged, small buildings where several families could live. She bought them at very good prices, paying the eager sellers cash on the spot. By repairing them with local workers, she provided jobs for many of the homeless who actually improved the very houses they eventually would live in. Her reputation for paying in cash brought many owners of buildings to her modest office, offering them for sale at significantly reduced prices, seeking cash, in strong American dollars.

"You are becoming known as a saint on the streets of Beirut, Madeleine," Madame Kabani exclaimed with pride, laughing with joy at dinner one evening. By 1950, Madeleine had built more than a dozen private, secular homes for the poor, two orphanages, several health clinics, and, enlisting out of work retired teachers, she created six small schools. She became known as a tireless leader in the welfare efforts to help the city's homeless children. She eagerly sought support from the various religious groups and their fund-raising efforts. She also became active in the restoration of heavily damaged apartment buildings, particularly in Bohemian West Beirut near AUB, to provide even more lodging for the poor. And as she progressed, visiting the orphanages each week, speaking to groups, even enlisting students at the university to volunteer for her cause, she attracted others who enthusiastically became part of her philanthropic campaign. "I am determined," she told every audience who would listen, "that we citizens of our city together must and will do all we can to help the poor, the homeless, the children." Within a few years, Madeleine's efforts were making a substantial and visible impact on the social and cultural life of the city, and her successes became known to the political and religious leaders of the city and throughout all of Lebanon.

Meanwhile, sound investing was paying great rewards for her too. Marcel Kabani watched over her investments, carefully soliciting advice from his network of financial institutions in Beirut, London, and New York. Indeed, her wealth was growing even as she invested so much in the foundation she had created with his help.

François, learning from his mother, became eager to participate in her causes. They decided that upon completion of his courses at the Sorbonne, he should spend a year at the London School of Economics, and afterwards return to Beirut.

As Madeleine involved herself in her charities, she became admired for her generosity and passionate dedication to the welfare of the underprivileged. She also carefully followed her son's progress at the Sorbonne. After giving considerable thought to what she should give François upon his graduation, she decided to have a Beiruti goldsmith make a ring identical to the ring given to her by her father in 1917. It would replace the one she had given to Iskandar.

"It must have the exact same design," she told the goldsmith. "Include a French cross with the initials F.D. on either side, for François DuBois."

And let there be no purpose in friendship
save the deepening of the spirit.
Kahlil Gibran

CHAPTER 12

Paris, Autumn 1948

"This is the most exciting city in the world," André mused to his friends, feeling very positive about their lives, and Paris itself. "You must explore it, celebrate it, partake of all that it offers," he smiled with a twinkle in his eye, "even its cultural facilities. Most of all, enjoy each day, *mon amis.*"

François was listening intently to his younger, passionate new friend and classmate, André Chacôn, a free-spirited student of French history, at the Café Mediterranean. They were sitting on black metal chairs with curved heart-shaped backs at a small round four-legged metal table on the sidewalk overlooking the River Seine in Paris watching the people, especially the pretty coed students, stroll by. This was François's favorite place to spend sunny, breezy afternoons after classes, often joining his collegiate friends, writers and artists, on what was known as the Left Bank, a meeting place of liberal-thinking students who, as a group felt they actually learned more from their conversations with each other than they learned in their classrooms. Their communal discussions, virtually an extension of their classes, were encouraged by the professors at the Sorbonne. The serenity of the river, just across the street, with its endless flow, reminded the students of the Université du Paris that life was not just a moment in the passage of time, but rather a process that should be explored to its fullest, and those thoughtful philosophical discussions were a vital part of the human experience. The professors encouraged their students to look far beyond the destruction of the horrendous battles and chaos of World War II where, except for the city of Paris, most of the major cities of Europe were almost totally destroyed. They were ravaged by the invading Germans who were determined to conquer all of Europe, or by bombardment by the Allies who were equally determined to destroy the German war machine and obtain an unconditional surrender.

Gratefully, Paris was spared the blanket bombardment of the Allies since the weak French government chose instead to surrender the city to Hitler so that its jewel, the locale of so much historical and cultural treasure, would not be destroyed. Even so, the German occupation was a terrible time of tension and abuse which impacted the French psyche for years.

"They were all crazy," André continued. "War is stupid. Young men must die so that older men can fulfill the dreams of their egos. It has always been and always will be, I suppose." He paused, leaned back, lifted his glass of chilled white wine, and sighed, "I prefer the ways of the poet."

"Ah, André, of course you do. You were spared, being a Parisian, the terrible onslaught of fighting. But, if you are being attacked, I believe you too will fight."

"François, you say these things, but, I think you too are a lover, not a fighter," he laughed.

François, now 28, and a few years older than André and his other classmates, and because of his stepfather's involvement in the *Resistance*, had a slightly different and more mature view of the war. He smiled, "Well, it is true that I never actually was part of the fighting. But I have seen the destruction of war, though mostly in Beirut and Marseille. And I can tell you, when someone is attacking your homeland, you will fight back, even to death. Yet, André, I think there is more at issue than ego. There is a sense of survival of one's freedom, family, and one's way of life and culture. It depends on one's point of view."

And so their daily conversations continued. Much discussion focused on the growing influence and threat of communism, not only in the Soviet sphere of Eastern Europe, but also because of the increasing instability that the communist threat presented in Italy, Austria, and in France itself. The war was over, but the political repercussions continued for years. Paris, like Marseille and many other major cities of Europe, was a beneficiary — guarded optimism, civility, cultural treasures, and fine hotels. The Sorbonne was its own oasis of freedom, intellectual discourse and learning. Students from all over Europe sought admission, not only because a degree from the university was a cherished symbol of an excellent education that, except for schools in England, was the finest a European student could hope for, but also for the personal relationships that would be beneficial in later years. One late afternoon, François was enjoying his second glass of wine with his friends, feeling a sense of euphoria, and a slight light-headedness. Cool breezes were blowing over them. The leaves of the sycamore trees that lined the avenue rustled lightly, a testament to new life. Small puffy clouds drifted above in the celestial blue skies. Their party of six was spending the late spring afternoon watching shoppers stopping among the small specialty booths in the open-air market for their favorite fresh vegetables and freshly killed chickens.

"The women have to shop everyday," commented one at the table. "They don't own refrigerators. Only the rich can afford luxuries like that. The cost is too dear for electricity, so they shop each day, only for the day."

"France will rise again," said another, with a shrug. "One day we will live like the Americans. They have so much there."

As André turned his head to look at the pedestrians, he directed François' attention to the tall, striking young woman walking toward them. Her beauty was not wasted on François. Not wanting to miss an opportunity, François boldly stood up and moved toward the sensual, dark-haired beauty. His confident, nonchalant swagger impressed the young woman.

"*Bonjour*, Mademoiselle," he smiled as he slightly bowed in respect, clearly seeking her favor. "Would you care to join us? I believe I have seen you on the campus. My name is François DuBois. We are discussing matters of great importance, solving the troubles of the world." He gestured with a wave of his arm toward his table of friends. "We invite you to join us for a glass of wine."

"*Merci*, Monsieur," she replied with a lovely smile. "Monsieur DuBois, you say?"

"*Oui*, please sit with us." He smiled as he pulled out a chair for her.

"And, I assume correctly, I hope, that you are indeed a student at the Université, are you not?"

"I am indeed. *Enchanté*, Mademoiselle."

"I can tell you are not French. Although you speak the language well, you have an Eastern accent. Where are you from, Mademoiselle?"

"No, I am not French, but I have lived in Europe, and one must speak French, *n'est-ce pas*? I am from Poland, although I have lived in France since 1937 when my family and I came to Paris. So I perfected speaking French although, as you say, I still have a slight accent."

"Well," smiled François, "you are a pleasant sight for a man, wherever you are from, and I am delighted to meet you. And now, let me introduce you to my friends. Then, with all his attention on her lips, he asked, "Tell me your name, please."

She didn't disappoint him as she spoke softly, "My name is Leah," she said with a slight, friendly smile, deliberately refraining from divulging her last name. She was still defensive and reticent, she knew, but felt justified as the war had caused her to be very careful with people she didn't know.

After all had exchanged courtesies, François delved further into his new lady friend's life while describing his own, his body language speaking volumes.

"Yes, I love Paris," she exclaimed with a friendly, easy smile as she surveyed the faces in the group. "Everyone has been so nice to me. The weather is lovely now, the leaves are turning into lovely colors, the rains have ended, the birds are in love, God is in his heaven, the war is over, and all is well in the world. At least here."

"Well, I think we are the fortunate ones," André interjected, keeping the conversation light, as most students he knew did, recognizing others had too many awful remembrances of the atrocities that had ended only a few years ago. The memories of loved ones who had been lost were now comfortably internalized, and most did not want to resurrect them, especially with strangers.

"We are all finding ourselves at new crossroads in our lives," François said, boldly moving to find out what he could about this lovely young woman who had now entered his life. "For example, I am part French and part Lebanese. I am studying economics. I hope to go to the London School of Economics for my advanced degree, and live in Beirut where there are excellent opportunities." Then pausing for effect, he added, "My mother is becoming involved in charitable causes there. I believe now that the war is over there will be an increase in international finance. Needs for capital investments and job-creating industries are enormous. Don't you agree?"

"Oh my," responded Leah, lowering her eyes from his face, "I have no opinion on that issue. My interests are more in the area of art history and world politics. You see, I hope to complete my studies and some day teach school. I speak five languages as well."

François, listening intently, reached to touch her hand that was resting on the table by her wineglass.

She watched as François touched her hand and, rejecting an initial response to withdraw hers, smiled demurely instead, willing to see where this conversation would go. François observantly noticed the almost quizzical expression on Leah's face turn friendly in a most brief moment, belying her internalized fear his forward touch triggered.

"Please do not fear me, Leah. We are all good-natured fellow students here."

"I am sorry, François. Forgive me. The war has made many of us reluctant to trust. I have had a difficult time trusting, for you see, I am Jewish, and Jews have had a most terrible time in Europe, especially the last ten years, even in France when Pétain's dreadful Vichy government took on the anti-Semitism of the Third Reich. So, I have a bit of difficulty relaxing with someone I don't know well...with almost all people, actually."

"I understand, Leah," he nodded, "but be assured that I am in Paris for only one reason, and that is to learn as much as I can while obtaining my degree."

"To be sure, Leah," interjected André, "there is a second, although subordinate occupation of my wealthy friend he has not yet admitted. He is a man who enjoys as much of his life in Paris as is possible. He is the perfect example of *joie de vivre*." Continuing, he laughed, "Oh, how he could play the innocent while hoping you will like him enough to have dinner with him later. Is that not so, *mon ami*?"

Leah looked from François to André, then back to François, as François replied quickly, feigning outrage at the pain of insult, yet smiling, "Oh, André, how could you? I am simply trying to be friendly. Certainly *carpe diem* is what I live by, but dinner hadn't even crossed my mind." Then, glancing at his wristwatch, continued, "But, as a matter of fact, it is getting late; it is nearly eight o'clock. Time has flown by. But isn't that always the way. So, it is either continue our discussion or go home to study, I suppose. On the other hand, my new friend," François said, now looking into Leah's demure eyes, "would you be interested in joining me for dinner?"

"Aha!" laughed André, both arms outstretched. "Thank you, *mon ami*, for proving me a psychic. I knew it! You are so predictable, François."

"But, André," he shrugged, still smiling, "how could I not invite our new friend to join us for dinner, eh, *mon ami?*"

"Us?" André exclaimed with a look of surprise on his face. "When did it become us? You rascal!"

"Just now," François laughed, "when you pressed the issue. What was I to do? She is, after all, a lovely, intelligent student who looks like she would enjoy more conversation with us while sharing the delicacies of a fine Parisian restaurant. Wouldn't you, Leah?"

She was amused at his audacity. "I can't help laughing at you two. And how could I resist your generous offer? You both are too silly for words."

"Well, André, you nearly got me into trouble, but it looks like we must be off for an early and perhaps intellectual dinner so that we all can retreat to our rooms for our studies which we all eagerly live for." François winked at André, "After all," he said with a thin smile of devilishness, "we are here for our collegial education, *n'est-ce pas?*" He silently wondered if Leah actually believed him as he unsuccessfully tried to portray himself as an innocent...clearly not an accurate description of one who appeared to be the oldest and most sophisticated of the group.

Leah remarked, "By all means, shall we have an early dinner so there will be time for our studies?" She smiled at André as if he were a co-conspirator.

"Yes," André quickly responded, "and maybe afterwards, we will escort our friend, François, to his flat to ensure he is home safely with his books." He paused and, with a wink, added, "Ahem."

They all laughed together at their joke on François.

"Enough," François laughed. "Let's just go have a bite to eat, shall we?" he said, recognizing it would be a better start with this new, tantalizing creature to go along with the joke, not press the issue, and come across as a good spirit. There will be another opportunity, of that I am sure, he thought to himself. Then he smiled, stood, and reached out his hand to Leah as she rose...and rose...and rose, until he noticed she was as tall as he.

"*Mon Dieu,*" François said to André too softly for her to hear, "she is magnificent."

That first evening went very well for everyone in the group, especially for Leah and François. The others enjoyed their own separate conversations throughout dinner. The two laughed together, drank more wine, relaxed, and forgot about their studies that night. François, in full pursuit, invited Leah for a walk along the Seine before walking her to her flat. Kissing her hand at the door, he invited her to join him the next afternoon at Café Mediterranean.

"Do you think another time you might like to dine on foods of the 'Med'?" he asked.

She smiled, "I don't know. I really haven't tasted those foods...perhaps."

"Well then, let's just find out," he responded with a confident smile.

"Tomorrow then," Leah whispered as she bent toward him, lightly kissing his cheek.

"Goodnight, *mon ami.* Thank you for a lovely evening and dinner," she said, closing the door as he turned to leave.

Once inside, she stepped into the kitchenette, which was actually part of her one-room studio apartment. "Here, kitty," she beckoned to her stray cat she had nursed back to good health, "I know it's late, but come here and get dinner." She poured milk into the bowl and watching, bent over, hands on her knees as her kitten lapped it up. "You know what my little kitty; I met a very nice man. He's very nice, funny, and handsome. Tonight was certainly special. But...we shall see what we shall see."

❧⸾⸙⸿

After their second evening together, François and Leah found they both wanted very much to be together often. To Leah, at 22, François was mature, considerate, sensitive, intelligent, and always with available money...more than the other students. She didn't question him on any personal issue. He was a pleasure to be with. He had not tried to paw her or pursue sex, at least not yet, which she found to be not only a surprise, but a pleasant and different experience, a welcomed behavior that drew her to him, leaving her wariness and reluctance behind. As a result, Leah was becoming friendlier and more open with François — and more vulnerable, allowing herself to let her true personality emerge. This was exactly what François was hoping would happen. He was sure she was still very cautious, so he responded accordingly. In time, he found her opening up more and more to the group, sometimes expressing her opinion on Europe's experiences, describing the fear the European Jewish community shared across the continent, and beginning to appreciate the friendly banter of the group, even as they laughed at their own jokes.

François was a charmer. He knew exactly how to behave properly with this lovely, sensitive Polish-Jewish refugee who had every good reason to be defensive, to be reluctant, sometimes petulant, sometimes shy.

"If I do not cause her fear or give her reasons to raise her protective defenses, then Andre," he confided to his friend, "her behavior will be more honest and her guarded natural insouciance would become apparent."

After a few weeks of newfound camaraderie, Leah began to laugh easier. François noticed a refreshing new bounce in her step. Life could be truly good, he had convinced her to her pleasant surprise."

"You know, Leah, I'm finding everything we do together is much more enjoyable this way. I'm glad you came into my life."

"François, I'm glad you said that, because I am very grateful for your friendship. I enjoy seeing you nearly every day, except when we're in our classes or studying at the library. You've added so much to my life here at the Sorbonne."

"We've spent so much time together. Andre wonders if we left school!" he exclaimed, laughing. "The best part, Leah, at least for me, and I sense the same for you is that neither of us has demanded too much, nor have we expectations beyond the realm of reality.

"Well, François, you made it clear from the outset that you planned to enroll at the London School of Economics after you graduate from the Sorbonne. I am so happy here, François. You have helped me rid myself of the demons of the war. It was so awful, but now I feel a sense of freedom that I have never felt before."

"It's the same for me, Leah. You somehow bring out the best in me. I can even tell that my priorities have changed somewhat. *Merci, mon amie, merci.*"

"I think I even study better now that we study at the library side by side."

"And more often these days, studying together in our apartments," she laughed and giggled. They spent many days together exploring the city, sharing its principal attractions, which added so much to their growing bond of affection. Both continued focusing on their studies, but there was no doubt their attraction to each grew stronger each day.

Although the idea of a long-term relationship was never discussed, perhaps because intermarriage of their very different religions and cultures might not be acceptable to either family, or simply because each had life goals that came first, they both felt an easy comfort in each other's presence. They too began to realize that they were slowly but surely falling in love. They never talked about it. They never feared it. It just seemed to be so natural, and so welcomed. It would be just a matter of time.

When love beckons you, follow him,
though his ways are hard and steep…
And when he speaks to you believe in him,
though his voice may shatter your dreams
as the north wind lays waste the garden.
Kahlil Gibran

CHAPTER 13

Paris: Late Autumn, 1948

"I am having a wonderful time tonight, Francois no matter how many times we have walked along the river together, it's always special."

I feel so close to you, Leah. I really am very fond of you, you know."

"I know, Francois. And I hope you know how I feel about our special friendship." As they held hands walking along the Seine one Saturday night following a special birthday dinner for Leah of pressed duck at the spectacular restaurant Tour d'Argent, one of Paris' finest restaurants, which overlooked the Seine and the lighted, magnificent Notre Dame cathedral, they simultaneously felt a romantic culmination of their weeks of friendship and affection.

It was a beautiful evening with a clear sky full of stars. The cool almost cold night air, with only a hint of a soft breeze off the river induced them to walk closer together. Leah's arm through Francois' reaching a favorite spot in their walk exactly opposite the cathedral, Leah stopped, and then responding to an overwhelming romantic feeling, turned to François, pulling his hand to turn him toward her. Her breasts grew unusually warm, almost hot, despite the cool evening air. She could no longer resist. Convinced completely she was in love with Francois, lust overcame her natural reluctance.

"I want you, Francois. Leah was ready to offer herself to him. "You see that young couple over there, François?" Leah whispered to him, lowering her eyelids, reflecting her growing sensations of sensuality.

"There, by the river, Leah?" he responded in feigned innocence.

"*Oui*, François. You see what they are doing?"

Smiling, he grasped both her hands and pulled her close to him. "They are in love, Leah."

"And so am I, François. I am certain of that." she whispered, resting her head on his shoulder. "Oh, please hold me."

"Of course!" François said, thrilled, feeling her body against his. His eyes closed as his emotions increased. "I want you Leah. You make me warm all over."

They embraced closely, eagerly wrapping their arms around each other, pressing their young bodies against each other. It was so natural after weeks of friendly companionship. Leah's firm, full breasts pressed against François's hard chest muscles, exciting both even more.

Leah, feeling François' swelling muscle, leaned against him even more, and murmured, "Ohhh, François, you feel so good. You excite me so. I can hardly breathe. This is so wonderful. I never thought I would feel this way." She could feel her palms grow moist and felt droplets form on her upper lip. "You know, don't you, that I have never been with a man before?" She lowered her chin in innocence. "I realize that may sound strange, but it's true. I just couldn't trust anyone to come close to me...until you."

Together they relaxed their tight embrace and pulled back slightly so that they were face to face, staring directly into each other's eyes, hoping to be assured their growing feelings and hopes were the same.

"Kiss me now, François," she offered.

"I love you Leah. I have loved you for a long time."

"Oh, Leah," he whispered as he moved his lips to touch hers. Her mouth opened slightly inviting him. He kissed her eagerly and deeply as he held Leah close to him, sensing her hips moving even closer against his, making him grow even harder.

After a moment, she pulled away slightly, whispering, "Oh, François, you feel so good. Perhaps...perhaps, my feelings are too good." She turned her head, wanting more, but not sure she should stay. "Perhaps I had better go home now, darling."

François sensed her hesitation, yet felt her desire for him. "Leah, I'm not sure how long I can stand this. For a long time, I have wanted you and now I am getting close to losing control. Let's go to my apartment. It's just over there. Either that, *mon amour*, or we must go over to that park over there...behind the hedges."

Convinced it was indeed their time, pulling his hand and leading him, she whispered, "Come, François, come with me. I cannot leave you. I must be with you tonight, my darling."

Together, they crossed the grassy area of the park, stepping without hesitation, through a narrow opening in the six-foot hedge and emerging through the green, thick bushes on the other side. They didn't know whether to laugh at the destruction of the path in the hedge they had created in their unstoppable haste or to sigh at their mutual nearness to sexual culmination. Without doing either, they fell to the grass, Leah hastily pulling up her skirt while François fumbled with his buttons.

Perched above Leah, on his hands and knees, François looked down into her moist eyes, filled with the sensual emotions of love "I am so very warm, Francois be gentle, my love."

She moaned softly with her eyelids lowering as she pulled him to her, "I want you now."

"Oh, Leah, you are so beautiful, so lovely. I have wanted you since the moment I first saw you that afternoon at the café. You are so magnificent. *Je t'aime, mon amour.*"

He gently moved on top of her as he tenderly fulfilled her wishes and his desires.

Afterward, they lay together, side by side, caressing each other, fondling, savoring the moment, smiling at each other, sharing.

She murmured, "I am so happy you are with me here tonight."

"You are more wonderful than I ever dreamed, Leah. I do love you so much."

She touched his lips with her fingers. "François, thank you for being so kind and patient with me. I am not experienced in these matters, and your loving was so beautiful.

"I have wanted you so much, Leah. I don't know how much longer I could have waited! But I'm glad we became close companions first."

After a few minutes of enjoying each other, with Leah stroking his chest and François fondling her breasts, Leah began inching closer to François, getting more excited. Her hand began to move down his chest to his hard stomach, then to his upper thighs. As she caressed him, he began to grow hard again.

"Leah, you are incredible," he whispered as she moved on top of him, then with a strong move, he thrust himself inside her feeling the height of ecstasy. "Go gently, but please don't stop. It is so incredible." She looked up into his eyes, ecstatic in their intimacy.

"My God, Leah, no one can surpass you. You have made me so happy."

The post-war years of Paris were an exhilarating relief from the awful dangers before, and with their new total freedom, these years would become a time of social change, of exploration by young people. With the massive rebuilding across Europe, fueled by America's Marshall Plan, money was flowing and political thought thriving, especially at freethinking institutions like the Sorbonne. There was a similar urging to be free and in love with life. Couples openly expressed their affections as France led the way worldwide in the sexual revolution and in fashion, while, in America, there remained a puritanical constrained behavior and strict social governance of the late 1940s and 1950s.

François and Leah enjoyed the following months free of constraint, happy to regularly share their time together in intimacy as they both pursued their studies, supporting each other.

But, in time, their life together experienced an unexpected and significant turn of events.

Leah broke the news to him the next summer, one afternoon as they walked along the Seine watching the clouds drift, the passersby, and the river with its inexorable flow.

She stopped to turn and face him. "I've been thinking a lot lately, my dear François, and there is something I must tell you now that the school term has ended." She hesitated for a moment. "I must leave Paris."

"What?" he gasped, stunned.

"Because I love you so much, this is the most difficult decision I have ever had to make. I must go to Palestine immediately to be with my own people, to help build a homeland."

François couldn't believe his ears. This news was such a shock to him. He clearly did not comprehend the deep-rooted emotions Leah felt. Yet, he cared for her so deeply. He believed they would never, ever become separated. He thought she felt the same way. Startled at what she said, he anxiously reached out to her.

"Leah, I love you too much to let you go. And I know you love me the same way!" Turning away, staring at the river, he now realized she had a much different agenda than he. Lowering his head, he turned back to hold her, saying softly, "I know I can't stop you, but I hope I can convince you to stay. You are breaking my heart, my Leah." He sighed sadly and looked to the heavens for help, then turned back to her. "Of course, you must do what is in your heart. I can only hope one day I will be able to understand. I certainly cannot understand you now."

She lowered her head against his chest, also feeling great sadness, and whispered, "You know you are the only man I have ever loved. And you will always be the only one. I hope...no, I know in my heart, my love, that in time we will be together again. Please, you must understand and forgive me, François."

"I believe we must find each other once again. I can never forget you, my love, my dear Leah. How can I ever have room in my heart for anyone but you? Perhaps you can change your mind? I don't want you to go, Leah!"." He tried without success to smile and somehow find a way to accept this tragic turn in his life.

They embraced tightly, holding each other for a long and emotional time as tears overflowed onto their saddened cheeks.

After what seemed like hours of agony, they both murmured to the other, "*Au revoir, mon chérie*" to each other as they stepped apart, arms extended, not wanting to let go.

François found that after Leah left and he was now alone, he really didn't find life at the Sorbonne as fulfilling, enjoyable, or enriching as before. He didn't laugh any more. He hardly ate for a long time. His friends noticed a lingering sadness. He thought of Leah every day, much of the time, but he forced himself to focus even harder on his studies, deciding reluctantly that he had to move on, accept fate's bombshell and come to his own self-actualization.

As he resumed writing weekly letters to his mother remembering her descriptions of his own father's determination to fulfill his destiny, he became convinced he could and should do the same. He came to believe that he too must find his own way to go "beyond the cedars." Francois also felt his lost love with Leah was too similar to his mother's with Iskandar better understood what she must have felt, and what strength she must have found to overcome her depression. "She showed me the way, he whispered to no one one day by the Seine, and if she could overcome this kind of depression, I guess I can too."

It was at François' graduation from the Sorbonne in the spring of 1949 that Madeleine attended and proudly placed the treasured likeness of her father's ring on her son's little finger.

"You make me so proud, François. I want you to have this ring which is identical to the one your grandfather gave to me before he went off to war. It is that ring I gave to your father as a symbol of my eternal love for him. And this ring, my son, is a symbol of my deep love for you. I believe if your father were here today, he would be so proud of you too, and express his love and pride as I do."

"Thank you, *Maman*." He smiled as his eyes moistened from her poignant gesture. "I will wear it proudly all my life. Wouldn't it be something if my father, even after all these years, still wears the ring you gave him?"

"*Oui*, François. Let us believe that he does treasure my ring as I do his cross."

François, yearning to broaden his knowledge, expand his horizons, and focus more on his career recalled his wonderful years in Paris during which he grew philosophically while living the good life in an intellectual atmosphere and experiencing the best years of his life. His continuing generous allowance from his mother provided him access to the finest restaurants and cultural events. He continued to live very well, partaking of the finer things in life. And yet, there was no one who could replace his beloved Leah. Also, as much as possible, he painfully put his rich memories of Leah behind him. Because he had to.

He enrolled at the London School of Economics, recognizing it was the finest school of its kind in Europe, one that would introduce him to American and British scholars and leaders in global economics. He could also sharpen his English.

While he concentrated on his graduate studies, he still found time to enjoy London and its sophistication, and time to expand his relationships with several lovely women, some students, and some simply attractive and wealthy. But nothing and no one could fill the void left by Leah's departure.

He received short notes from Leah from time to time. But they were too brief for him to know fully what she was doing and where she was now living. What she always wrote did remind him of her love, signing her letters with "I will always love you, François."

After he left Paris for London, her letters could not find him and he had no way of finding her. He was bound to simply wait for her to somehow contact him.

When you are sorrowful look again in your heart,
and you shall see in truth
you are weeping for that which has been your delight.
Kahil Gibran

CHAPTER 14

Kissimmee, 1944

"This war has been a terrible thing for everyone," Alexander commented to Helene and his father one Sunday afternoon as they listened to the news on the radio describing the latest battles. Like parents across America, their greatest fear was for their sons and daughters who were in harm's way. And while everyone across the country felt relatively safe from the destruction taking place in other countries, they worried constantly about the welfare of their children across the sea. Parents knew so little since all mail was censored for security reasons.

Michael, son of Alexander and Helene Thomas and grandson of Abraham Thomas was stationed in England, flying in the Eighth Air Corps. He was a pilot of a B-17 bomber who, with thousands of young airmen, daily bombed the factories, submarine bases, and rail yards in Germany. The assignment of the U.S. Eighth was daylight strategic bombing, which made them terribly vulnerable to German fighter attacks, flak, and artillery. Losses were consistently very high, often as much as fifty percent. And, like many of his compatriots, both American and English, he was, during these worst of times, just 19 years old. By the time he had ten missions behind him, he had experienced a frightening loss of friends and emergencies — dangerous experiences a man of 60 in normal times would not have encountered. And yet, he had not yet reached his 20th birthday when he had completed his twenty-fourth bombing mission.

Like every other American serviceman in Europe, he was not allowed to write home telling his parents where he was, what he was doing, where he was flying, and even what he did on weekend furloughs in London. Parents and families kept vigil with a lighted candle in the window next to a small flag, and lived each day in ignorance except for news reports on the radio and in the afternoon newspapers. As a result, letters from home were filled with newsy dialogue including reports of who recently got married, who had a social at their home, the weather, and the like. Some simply said, "We miss you...take care of yourself...we love you and hope we see you real soon." Other not so pleasant letters the soldier, air cadet, marine, or sailor would receive might be from his girlfriend or "three-day wife." When a letter came informing the combatant that his girlfriend back home had found someone new who was nearby, a "Dear John" letter, this terrible news in some cases drove the already depressed serviceman even deeper into depression or worse.

Because of the mail restrictions, most families were not aware of the condition of their sons and daughters except for the War Department sending representatives to tell families of the young man's status, either serious injury, lost in action, or death.

Helene and Alexander lived from day to day with concern for their son Michael. They were filled with anxiety, uncertainty...and no idea where Michael was...or if he was safe.

Helene did her best to keep herself busy at the church, helping in collection drives for the war effort, and keeping her home a place of respite for her husband and daughter. Her happiest times were in her kitchen when she prepared Alexander's favorite meals.

One afternoon in late 1944, she and Alexander would find their world changed forever.

Taking a moment to pause from chopping the lush parsley for the evening's *tabouleh* salad, Helene looked out the window overlooking the lake and fondly recalled watching Michael and Helena as young children racing to the shore and splashing into the dark waters of the lake. With a lingering smile, she returned to her dinner preparation.

Unknown to her, two uniformed U.S. Army Air Corps servicemen drove into her driveway in an Army green-colored Ford sedan. Stepping out of the car, they straightened their jackets and pulled on their caps. They carried leather satchels as they briskly walked to the front door of the Thomas home and knocked firmly on the door.

"Who is it?" called Helene cheerily from the kitchen.

"Mrs. Thomas? Mrs. Alexander Thomas?"

"Yes, yes, just a minute," she replied as she placed her knife on the counter, wiped her hands on her apron, and walked down the hallway to the front door.

"I'm coming!" she smiled with a welcoming expression for her visitors before she could make out the two figures standing at the door. Then, recognizing the uniforms, she thought, Oh...oh...why are they here?

As she neared the door, she could see the green-colored automobile with stenciled lettering "U.S. Army Air Corps" in white paint.

"Hello. I'm Helene Thomas. What can I do for you?" Nervously, she opened the screen door. "Won't you come in please?"

Removing their caps, they stepped into the foyer. The taller of the two spoke first. "Mrs. Thomas, I'm Air Force Captain John Reynolds and this is Captain Ray Jones. Is your son Captain Michael Thomas of the U.S. Army Air Corps?"

"Yes, he is. Why do you ask? What is it? Tell me...is he hurt?"

"Yes, ma'am," he replied as they followed Helene to the living room. "It's about Captain Thomas. We have been instructed to inform you personally that your son, Captain Michael Thomas, was killed in action over Germany."

"Oh, my God, not Michael!" she screamed. "Oh, my God...Michael..." Suddenly she felt very weak as she pressed one hand to her mouth, the other to her heart. Hyperventilating, she began to faint.

The two reached for her as she collapsed to the floor, sobbing, both hands over her face. The two airmen lifted her and took her to the nearby couch in the living room. Her shoulders shook as she struggled to sit up, thankfully with their help.

"Please, dear God, let it not be so..."

"Ma'am, we know this is a terrible thing for you to hear, and believe me, we wish we didn't have to be the ones to carry this message. We are so sorry, ma'am, so very sorry."

"How...how...did it happen? Do you know?"

"Yes, ma'am, we do know," replied the other serviceman. "We have a full report for you along with a citation of his bravery in action, and several medals he earned. From what the report says, he was quite a brave man, Mrs. Thomas. You can be very proud."

"Proud you say?" She lifted her head to look up at them and clearly replied, "I've been proud of my son all his life. He was such a good boy. Now I must find his father. Can you help me to the telephone? My God, this will kill Alexander. His whole life is for his son. Maybe I better tell him later, when he comes home..."

"Whatever you want Mrs. Thomas. We do have this citation for you, with much more detailed information. I can assure you that Captain Thomas surely earned the respect of his fellow airmen."

He pulled the citation from his case and began reading:

"Captain Michael Thomas's B-17 was one of two hundred and sixty flying over Germany that day. His was the lead bomber, the one whose navigator and bombardier guided the rest of the planes to the target. Observations of pilots of other planes nearby testify to his leadership and bravery. Despite attack by numerous German Messerschmitts and a sky filled with black clouds of flak, that is, thousands of pieces of steel exploding that could have virtually shredded his plane, Captain Thomas steadfastly, and at great risk to himself and his crew, flew directly to his primary target. Just after his plane flawlessly released its load of bombs, flak artillery hit his plane. The observing pilots believe it struck the plane's nose, ultimately fatally injuring Captain Thomas, the co-pilot and bombardier.

The plane went into a steep dive. Captain Thomas held the plane as steady as he could, allowing able members of his crew to parachute out. That bombing mission is believed to have resulted directly in saving thousands of GIs, hastening the war's end, and giving a solid boost of morale throughout the Eighth Air Force."

After reading the citation, the designated informant continued, "Mrs. Thomas, your son earned the Distinguished Flying Cross and A Purple Heart for bravery beyond all call of duty."

Helene sniffed and cleared her throat as she wiped her eyes as she tried to respond to the young men.

"I really don't know what to say...I just can't believe my wonderful only son is gone. But I do know thousands of boys have been killed, yet it is so very painful. I'm not sure I'll ever get over this news...I do thank you both for coming here today... still, I'm not sure how I'm going to tell his father. He loves Michael so much. A son is everything to a father. But..." she paused as she thought a moment.

After an hour, Helene felt she wanted to be alone with her memories of Michael. She stood to end the meeting she wished had never happened. Responding to her, the two messengers also arose respectfully and moved toward the front door.

"Well, Mrs. Thomas, if there is anything the Air Force can do for you, please feel free to call the number on the card. We're based nearby in Tampa. And here is the box with Captain Thomas' citations, battle ribbons, and honored medals for your safe keeping. His plane was shot down over Germany, and didn't return. We can only assume that the entire crew were gone and there are no remains. We are so very sorry".

Respectfully saluting her as she stood at the doorway, they stepped to their automobile, got in and slowly drove away with a goodbye wave as they departed.

Helene, taking a deep breath, decided to wait until Alexander arrived home after his workday. She felt she needed time and went to bed with her sadness.

After dinner, while Helene was not animated as usual, and Alexander, feeling something had happened, watched her. Rather than press her, he waited in silence. When she had finished eating only a portion of her dinner, she rose and looked at her husband while reaching out to him with her hands. "Alexander, come with me, I have something to tell you." They walked side by side out to the porch overlooking the lake.

After a few moments they began talking in hushed voices. Helena, still clearing the dinner table, was carrying several dishes to the kitchen when she heard first the raised tone of her father's voice. "What? Oh no, Helene, not Michael...not my son...oh God!" Helena's voice followed, "Oh, Alexander, I so wish I didn't have to tell you. This has been the most horrible day of my life. I love you, Alexander, and now we must accept this. It's happening all over America. Hold me, my love, hold me. I need your strength."

"Oh, Helene...my God...Michael... my son...my only son. I'm lost...I don't know what to say. We have always feared that this day might come. Now there is no hope…only the truth…oh God…" he stammered as he stepped to his favorite rocking chair, sat and silently gazed out at the lake as the setting sun behind him slowly allowed darkness to overcome the Thomas' home.

Helena, having overheard part of the conversation, rushed outside to embrace her sobbing mother. "Oh, Mom, not Michael!" she cried. "What are we going to do without him?" she begged rhetorically. "What are we going to do without my big brother?" Helena, now crying too, then went to embrace her father as he sat staring, dumbfounded, with years flowing down his cheeks. They remained together for several hours, long after the sun had set, in sadness and despair, lost in memories.

The next day, Alexander awoke, skipped breakfast, and, wanting to be alone with his lost dreams for his son, wandered to the backyard, walking through his beloved fruit trees, under the oaks, and out to the boat dock. He spent the entire day alone feeling lost, abandoned, cheated. He could hardly keep his breath… tears flowed down his cheeks as his throat choked up throughout the day, causing him to breathe with difficulty.

Helene spent the day in her house, her refuge, only venturing out to the porch in the afternoon to sit and watch her husband in his mourning, emotionally reaching out to him, being visible as he would glance back from time to time…

Alexander and Helene, in their own ways, close to each other and dedicated to their children, spent the next several days aimlessly existing in their pain, sorrow, and emptiness. They felt a gaping void in their hearts that only a parent who has lost a child could understand. Helena silently took over the household chores, allowing her mother to be free to do nothing but reminisce and wonder what might have been.

Alexander, feeling pain as never before, recalled the hurt when his mother died…and the terrible emptiness in his stomach and the pain in his heart when he had to leave Madeleine behind. But this was even worse, as though nothing before had prepared him for this day…nothing. "Dear God," he prayed, "what did I do to deserve this? Why? Oh, why did Michael have to suffer and then leave us? He was so young…so good. He was my heart, my eyes, my life. All I have endured, all I have done was for Michael and Helena…not for me. Please don't let anything happen to Helena, nor to Helene. Let us have peace. Help us…guide us." Then, gazing at the clouds overhead with his arms stretched out to the side, he exclaimed aloud, "Michael, where are you, my son? Where are you?"

Day after day he sat on the dock, his glazed eyes staring into space, alone with his memories, thinking, lamenting, and mourning his greatest loss. Alexander ached inside. Only when Wilbur came by after several days to check on his friend did he feel able to go to Helene and Helena, exhausted, drained, cried out.

"I have no more tears, Helene," he said as he embraced his wife. "I'm lost, but Michael has been with me all these days. Now I want us to be together, Helene." Looking around, he asked, "Where is Helena?"

"She was visited by her girlfriends who learned the news about Michael. I believe that after the Air Force messengers left me that day, they informed the mayor too. Then word spread quickly. I thought it would be better if she spent some time with her friends. You remember when the McLaughlin boy was killed in the Normandy invasion? Well, the town found out the same way. Alexander," she said softly, "Sit with me. We need to talk." Looking at him, she reached for his hand. "We must honor Michael. We must remember our son, and we must live on. We have to somehow be strong for our daughter. Helena needs to see us strong, don't you agree? Yes, my husband, we are sick with pain. Our loss is great and we will never get over...this." She stopped to breathe, stammering now, "... get over...I don't think I can even say the word..."

"Get over losing our only son, Helene?" Alexander interrupted. "I don't believe a father can ever get over the loss of his only son...not me, anyhow. But you're right, Helena. As always, you are right. Yes, we must honor Michael and we will. And, I believe that he would want us to continue living our lives, as difficult, as almost impossible as it will be. Yes, Helene, together we will honor Michael's courage and bravery. But it will be hard, Helene, it will be hard. He was my life." Then he added as he lowered his head, "No, Helene, I don't think I'll ever get over losing my only son."

After weeks of near sleepless nights, Alexander awoke one morning and went for a walk toward the lake, simply to think and be alone. He thought for a long time on all that had happened and what his life would be like without his son. Finally, his sadness gave way to acceptance. And he began to look at life in a different way.

"Meaningless!" he exclaimed aloud. "My life would be meaningless without Helene and Helena. Yet I haven't spent enough time with them, working all the time. That is wrong...and I must change my ways."

Until now he had worked diligently, more than anyone, more than anyone should expect, seeking financial security to be able to provide all he could for his family. But now, Michael's death had shown him how fragile life could be. He made a resolution that his future would become very different by focusing on the emotional needs of his family and the needs of others less fortunate.

Alexander, experiencing a veritable spiritual epiphany, began to develop interest in local charities. He knew from his impoverished youth the misery and pain of lack of food and medical attention. He became more aware of those who had so little as he inquired into the needs of others in his post-war community as he learned of veterans going through painful rehabilitation.

He became acutely aware of the enormous need of so many wounded. Each day he visited hospitals in Tampa or Orlando. He witnessed many unable to take care of themselves. These wounded veterans required profound assistance and were really only teenagers or in their early twenties. "They're so young," he would tell Helene. He was overwhelmed by the sacrifices these young people had endured for him, his family and the nation to preserve their freedom.

He even began to visit the children's health center in Tampa, then the one in Orlando. Each time he saw poor, hungry children, he remembered his own youth, recalling his difficult days with an empty stomach, watching his friends in the village begging for food. As he and Helene visited with these poor children, his throat would choke. His eyes would well up with tears; he felt their pain in his heart. Almost immediately, he would kneel beside them, embracing each child one at a time. He knew deep down how they felt. And he knew he had to find ways to help.

During World War II, Alexander and other successful businessmen had formed the Florida Cattlemen's Association, a strong financial and political force in Florida. Their influence at the capitol in Tallahassee was becoming as powerful as any group in the state. Now, Alexander, keenly aware of the health care needs of others, especially injured young people, met with his friends and proposed that they form a foundation to take the lead in providing health care and rehabilitation throughout the Central Florida region.

They started small, first focusing on the veterans' needs at the Tampa VA rehabilitation clinic, then creating new health centers in Sanford, Bartow, and Kissimmee as they sought more support from political leaders in Tallahassee and Washington. Alexander met with his cousins, the Chalhoubs, in Palm Beach, and friends in Miami to use their influence to obtain state involvement and financing that would improve the lives of poor families, handicapped children, and impaired veterans. He was turning his talents and focus in a new direction, helping those outside his family for the first time, becoming very involved in their health care needs. He tapped into his personal resources to finance the Boys and Girls Club in Kissimmee. He generously supported similar efforts for rehabilitation clinics in Tampa and Orlando.

He enjoyed having Helene and Helena accompany him on his visits to the hospitals, and clinics and welcomed their support of his endeavors. "We have the means to do God's work."

That is how, in the early 1950s, he met a fellow Lebanese immigrant in Miami, Anthony Abraham, who would become one of his dearest friends.

Your children's souls dwell in the house of tomorrow,
which you cannot visit, even in your dreams.
Kahlil Gibran

CHAPTER 15

In 1948, three years after World War II changed the world and her family forever, Helena Thomas enrolled in Vassar College, the same year François began his two years at the Sorbonne. Despite her father's "traditional" thinking and his wish that she stay nearby, Helena finally won him over. Alexander relented as he came to realize that his daughter was determined, independent and stubborn a mirror image of himself.

"What can I do?" he shrugged as he rhetorically asked his wife, Helene.

"Dad, I'm not ready to get married, and I want to see more of the world. Times are changing and I want to be part of it. I know that it may be hard for you to understand, but since the war, lives of women will never be the same. Many of us are not in a hurry to get married, have children, and ignore what we feel inside. Sure, I want children someday, but only if I find the right man, and after I have tried my own wings for awhile. During the war, Dad, women flew airplanes; they worked in factories; they were in the Pacific and in Europe. I think I am feeling what you felt when you left Lebanon for America to find your destiny. I'm so much like you, Dad, and just because I'm a girl doesn't mean I can't try, does it?"

Alexander, listening intently to his daughter, now a woman, and looking into her pleading eyes, couldn't decide if he was sad from lamenting the passage of his "little girl" into a young woman, or feeling pride and reluctant understanding. Somehow, his daughter profoundly reminded him of her mother when he first met Helene. She too was a "free spirit." And for an instant, she reminded him of his lost love, 16-year-old Madeleine when they met and he became so enchanted by her lust for life, her youthful exuberance and optimistic sense of adventure. After some thoughtful moments, he smiled and reached to Helena with both arms, with the love a father has for his daughter. As she stepped toward him to be received into his beckoning arms, they embraced and both felt loved…and trusted. Smiling,

Alexander held her close and tightly drew her to him. "I love you, my little girl, my dear Helena. You bring me joy. I hope you can understand too what I am feeling. It seems the lives of men are going to change because the lives of women are changing so much." He shrugged, "Perhaps that is the way our lives will be. *C'est la vie.*"

It wasn't easy for Helene and Alexander to say goodbye as she boarded the train at the Kissimmee station, bearing all sorts of luggage, hugs, kisses, farewells, and best wishes from all her high school friends that September day.

"*Allah ma'ak, y'slemlie,*" Alexander and Helene whispered into her ears as they hugged her and kissed both her cheeks. Write often."

While embracing, Helena whispered to her father, "Dad, you are going to be proud of me, I promise, but I think I want to be like you. I don't think I'm cut out to be a housewife. Times are different. It'll be fine, you'll see." Then she squeezed her father and kissed both his cheeks.

"I'm always proud of you, Helena!" he exclaimed.

"I love you, Mom and Dad," Helena yelled from the rail car steps. "I love you too," she yelled as she waved to her buddies and friends from school. "See you at Christmas, y'all."

As Alexander watched his beautiful daughter leave, he felt the same emotional pangs of emptiness and loss in his stomach that he felt watching Madeleine standing on the Marseille dock, so long ago, and he found himself rubbing her ring as he waved to Helena. "We will miss her terribly," he said to Helene as he wrapped his arm around his wife. They both felt their bodies slump with sadness, yet with pride and a sense that their "baby" was becoming a woman, stretching out her wings and leaving the nest.

"The house will seem very empty now with her gone," sighed Helene sadly as she closed her eyes, tears running down her cheeks.

Helena, meanwhile, put her bags away, settled in her seat, leaned back, closed her eyes, and with a silent smile of pride and feeling a sense of wonder, whispered, "Here we go! I wonder what it's going to be like at Vassar."

Helena's initial year at Vassar College was an adventure she would never forget. Everything and everyone were so different. Her classmates were mostly from the Northeastern states, although many came from major cities of Ohio, Michigan, and Illinois. She reckoned she was the only freshman from Florida. All were from upper income families, as this was, indeed, one of the finest, and most expensive, women's colleges in the country.

After World War II, women were becoming more independent, but yet not universally so. Lots of Helena's college friends clearly were sent there by their parents to become "perfect mates" for up-and-coming young men from wealthy families attending Harvard, Dartmouth, Brown, Yale, and the other nearby top Ivy League schools.

So, attending Vassar was a special introduction for Helena into an entirely different social world. The people were different. Their speeches, their interests, their social ways were all different. Almost all were from multi-generational wealthy, "old money," families. Some were down to earth, and others were, frankly, spoiled brats or "princesses."

She found the mountains of upstate New York exciting, especially during her first autumn with the colors everywhere. "I love the maples, especially when the sun is bright on them," she exclaimed. It was certainly different from the flat, open pastures and citrus groves of Central Florida. To some girls, she seemed like a backward "hick," but in time her confidence and Southern charm won over most of her classmates once they got past their initial elitist prejudices, though there were a few who let Helena know that she was "different," meaning less, and expected her to prove herself to them.

She was keen on getting good grades, especially in economics, accounting, and French: her favorite subjects. She also found time in the winter to learn to snow ski, especially after seeing her first snowfall that November of her freshman year.

In the spring, she learned to play lacrosse, wearing knee socks and skirts to play organized sports for the first time in her life. Already athletic, once she figured out the rules of this new physical game, she played well. But she wasn't that interested in team sports, especially when she was faced with the tricks a few of the girls played on her. Some seemed unable to accept a "cowboy" in their midst, her nickname to a few.

Some rode horses to be sure, but jumpers or dressage on English saddles, always formally attired, and quite strange to her. Helena kept slipping off the saddle. "Where's the horn, anyway?" she asked more than once.

Helena was really dedicated to her studies in her junior year. After two good years of excelling in Accounting, Micro- and Macroeconomics, and corporate finance, she was called in by her adviser.

"Thank you, Miss Thomas, for coming." Her career adviser, Frances Biddle, standing in welcome, nodded with a practiced firm business-like handshake and slight smile. "Do sit down, my dear." She was dressed in a tailored dark suit and crisp white linen blouse.

"Good morning, Miss Biddle. Have I done something wrong?" She perched on the edge of a chair and pulled her long, flowing dark brown, almost black, hair behind her ears and shoulders. She knew her hair was part of her identity at this campus occupied by mostly blonde or light-brown haired women.

"Oh no, my dear. On the contrary," Miss Biddle responded quickly as she sat down in her leather chair behind an antique, grand, oversized desk, selected precisely for its imposing size and shape in an effort to intimidate anyone who ventured into Miss Biddle's "lair of wisdom," as it was known among the dormitories. Helena registered Miss Biddle's formal, dark, pin-striped, mannish suit.

"It is my responsibility as your career advisor to be ever mindful of your progress here at the college. You know, although I am from Philadelphia, I attended Vassar, not Bryn Mawr, and though it may seem decades ago, it really wasn't that far in the past," she smiled as she spoke. "I graduated in Administration Studies with a minor in Sociology. Of course, that was before the war and, since then, there have been enormous changes in curricula as well as an explosion in career opportunities for women. It's about time I'd say."

Pausing, Miss Biddle carefully watched Helena's eyes for her silent response and seeing none, continued, "I think, strange as it may seem, the women of the world, certainly in America, must look to the events of World War II as the watershed of opportunities for women. It unleashed women as a group, proving to the men that we can indeed perform and even excel in many of the careers heretofore not available. I mean, it's obvious to anyone with half a brain, and that definition, I suppose, sadly, would clearly include most men," she laughed out loud at her joke, "that if women could successfully weld war planes together, fly them across the country as did the WASPs at only eighteen to twenty years of age, then women can, should, and must be accepted in the halls of corporate America."

Helena smiled at the sexist comments but made no reply.

"And that, Miss Thomas, brings me to your career discussion."

Helena stifled a smile as she observed Miss Biddle, heiress to a centuries' old Philadelphia blue blood family, go through her programmed presentation. The students referred to her as "Biddle." Her close friends in Philadelphia nicknamed her "Frankie." Every young girl in Philadelphia society had cute nicknames it seemed to Helena. Like "Marts" for Martha, "Middie" for Mildred, or "Boots" for Barbara.

Watching Miss Biddle, nearly a campus legend for her presumptive snobbery, pedantic speech, and yet, "right-on-the-money" information, advice and counsel, was something Helena had actually looked forward to. Each of the girls who had already gone through this junior year series of private meetings at the dorm laughed about the performance, the bashing of the "men's world," and championing the rise of women in business and the preservation of Anglo-Saxon cultural excellence.

After flipping through several stacks of files on her desk, glancing up and down with a frown, first at Helena's face, then back down to her papers, Miss Biddle found the file she was looking for. She lifted her head, exposing a prim tortoise headband keeping her hair pulled away from her face in the conservative pageboy style, and assumed an expression of superiority. Miss Biddle thrived on control and intimidation in keeping with Machiavelli's *The Prince* which sat prominently displayed on the dark mahogany end table by the couch.

Helena shifted in her chair, hoping the preliminaries would soon give way to substance. Furrows appeared on her forehead reflecting her growing impatience and concern. *Where is this going?* she asked herself as she looked around the tastefully decorated room with several exquisitely framed Currier and Ives prints hanging on the walls.

"As I was about to say," began Miss Biddle, smiling slightly at Helena to get her attention, "it is time we at Vassar present the best we have to offer to the best in our corporate community, Miss Thomas. Your excellent grades, your research projects, and comments from your professors indicate, in my opinion, that you could have an excellent future in banking. Perhaps even in international banking which is opening up nicely since the war. You are studying French and you speak fluent Arabic. I believe you have outstanding opportunities you must be aware of and should prepare for. It won't be easy, my dear. And you might get disappointed by America's corporate reception. But I think it's worth your while to seek such a career.

"The Rockefeller family is quite enlightened, and so that might make an international career possible for a woman at Chase Bank in New York. It is a fine institution as are J.P. Morgan, and New York City Bank. But I'd prefer you consider becoming part of Chase. You may even want to consider obtaining a Masters Degree in Economics or Finance.

"In sum," Miss Biddle concluded after twenty minutes of discussion, indicating she had reached her decision and singular advice, "if you agree, I will do what I can to help you become the first Vassar graduate to be placed in Chase Bank's International Department. My dear Helena, you are in exactly the right place at the right time. With your dedication, you should succeed very well, and, in doing so, pave the way for young women who will follow you. You will meet some of the finest and smartest people in the world. And with your Middle Eastern heritage, who knows where this could lead?"

Helena was stunned by this presentation, believing she would simply complete her years at Vassar, graduate, enjoy a few weekends in New York or skiing in the Adirondacks, then return to Kissimmee and get a job at one of the banks in Tampa, Osceola or in Polk County. Now, however, this conversation presented a whole new world she would never have dreamed existed. And she liked the feeling of adventure it brought her. She was encouraged, and began to change her opinion of this austere woman.

"Miss Biddle, what if I was interested in locating in New York and possibly joining Chase Bank. What is your advice to me? And do you really think a woman, especially a cattle rancher's daughter from Central Florida could obtain a job offer from Chase Bank that isn't just a glorified secretary's job, or someone's assistant with no real career possibility?"

"It's true my dear that you would probably find returning to Central Florida more comfortable, not nearly as stressful, and monumentally simpler and easier, but without much of a future. And I believe that while New York City can be a frightening challenge to most anyone, to a person as adventurous and intelligent as you, it could be that you would find the experience extraordinarily rewarding, difficult as it might be. It's not as civilized as my hometown of Philadelphia to be sure, but it is the banking center of the world. You would be in a new environment that surpasses almost anywhere else in the world. The men may find in you a competition they will try to undermine, and maybe even try to do you in. So, if you decide not to consider this option, my dear, I certainly understand. At the same time, I have already spoken to Carole Whitaker, your classmate, about the same possibilities. You know 'Car' don't you? She's from the Whitaker family of Haverford outside of Philadelphia. She is considering the same option I'm presenting to you."

"Oh sure, Mrs. Biddle. 'Car' and I are close friends. She's one of the nicer girls I've met from Philadelphia. Some of the others are such snobs, you know. But not 'Car'."

"Snobs? From Philadelphia?" snorted Miss Biddle in mock insult, thrown aback by this charge as she brought her hand to her breast, clearly chagrined at the label by this "cowboy" from Florida. "What do you know about snobs, Miss Thomas? I can tell you a few things, and Philadelphia is, contrary to popular opinion, hardly a place that condones snobbery, my young impetuous friend. Justifiable pride to be sure, but not snobbery. Please rethink your opinion, my dear."

"If you say so, Miss Biddle, if you say so." Helena smiled as she contritely lowered her head, looking up from the tops of her eyes, knowing she had made a *faux pas*.

"So, do I understand you would be open to pursuing this course of action?"

"Miss Biddle, I really appreciate what you have told me. I believe that yes, I would like to pursue what you've described. But I think I should speak to my parents. Maybe tonight." Shaking Miss Biddle's hand in a formal good-bye, she rose and left her office with a constrained excitement she had never felt before.

"Today is the greatest!" she whispered to herself as she nearly ran out of the Administration Building.

Though they are your children,
you may give them your love but not their thoughts,
for their souls dwell in the house of tomorrow,
which you cannot visit, not even in your dreams.
Kahlil Gibran

CHAPTER 16

Kissimmee, 1949

One Sunday afternoon in late summer, Abraham visited his son at Alexander's lakefront home. Sitting side by side in rocking chairs on the porch, looking out over the expansive grassy lawn with scattered fruit trees and beyond to the breeze-blown, choppy waters of enormous Lake Tohopekaliga, they spoke with a strange foreboding sense of nostalgia.

"You have done very well, my son," he murmured with a sweep of his arm, "and I am proud of you. You have made a good life. Your wife Helene is wonderful and happy. That is a good sign. If a wife is happy, it is because her husband takes care of her needs...all of her needs. She adores you, and like you, has been devoted to your children. And now you are involved with many others' needs. I have watched you now these past, my goodness, nearly thirty years, and I am grateful to have you as my son."

Abraham paused, his forehead slightly furrowed between his eyebrows, eyes squinted, still gazing across the lake wistfully, searching his mind for the right words. Alexander couldn't help but wonder where his father was going with this because he had never begun a conversation quite the same.

"I have decided, Iskandar, to return to Lebanon." He hesitated briefly, looking into Alexander's eyes for a visceral response. "I am in my late seventies, Milhelm is now a grandfather, and I miss Douma. I want to see my other son again. And I want to hold his children while I can. It is time, *Baba*. You are secure; you have fulfilled your destiny...your mother's wishes. Shortly, I will make arrangements."

Pondering his true issue, he tried to play down the potential danger in his next question of his son. "But, there is something I wish to discuss with you, *Baba*," (Abraham used his Arabic pronoun in referring to his son as he always did in personal discussions) "something I have wanted to discuss with you since the day I saw you arrive in New York from Marseille. I felt it best to wait for you to tell me, but you never have. So, now, I must ask you. Of course," he shrugged, "you don't have to tell me if you do not wish to."

"*Biyee*, what is it?" Alexander felt there was a deep concern in his father's carefully chosen words but had no idea where this conversation was leading. "You tell me you are leaving America now after so many years. My God, how wonderful it has been for me to work beside you all this time." Alexander laughed, "There have been terrible days and wonderful days, and there were days I was so angry with you; sometimes you are so stubborn. Sometimes. But there were so many good days; so many wonderful experiences. We have had a joyful life together."

"I am stubborn, Iskandar?" Abraham waved his arms in the air as he shifted in his chair, his voice increasing in pitch several notes. "You think it is I who am stubborn? How can you believe that? It is you who has been the stubborn one!"

Abraham laughed and slapped his son's thigh. They laughed together, enjoying a not so frequent happening. But, as both knew, they were secure with each other and they had done their best under very trying conditions: carving out a life as immigrants in a strange but free country, in the South Florida sub-tropical frontier with its swamps, droughts, floods, freezes and hurricanes. They came from not even being able to speak the language, too embarrassed to try lest it be too obvious that they were different from others. Now after nearly four decades since Abraham arrived, they were a significant and prosperous part of the regional community, well respected, and considered equals among their peers, influential in the politics of the agricultural community and at the state capitol in Tallahassee. They had done extraordinarily well.

"Even now, Iskandar, it is said that if a man seeks to become governor of Florida, he must first visit the Stewart brothers in Bartow, the Parkins in St. Cloud, and Alexander Thomas in Kissimmee. That is something, because this could not have happened in Lebanon. We were not of the right families, but here in America anything is possible. How I wish Milhelm had come with you." He paused to reflect. "It is too late now, so I must go to Douma and help the family, perhaps build them a home large enough for the entire family. It is still a very poor village."

"And, as for those houses I built for the poor workers here in Kissimmee during the years before the war, I will give them to our tenants. You don't need them. There are thirty-four now, and they have been good tenants. Before I leave, their homes will belong to them. Even after I leave, you must continue to send goods to our village."

"And your question, *Baba*. What is your question to me?" Alexander asked with a quizzical look.

Abraham shifted again in his rocking chair, faced his son and cleared his throat before he spoke.

"Your ring," he pointed to his son's hand. "What is the meaning of the gold ring you have worn on your finger since you first arrived in America? You and I are not people of jewelry. You have not even worn a watch on your wrist, yet you have never removed that ring. Why is that?"

He was caught off guard. "It is nothing," he shrugged and turned his eyes away, not wanting to discuss the ring's meaning. He simply didn't want there to be any conversation about Madeleine because his sense of honor would cause him to feel betrayal to Helene and his family. It really was still on his finger out of habit more than anything else.

"It is something, Iskandar." Abraham raised his eyebrow. "It is important to you. You may not want to tell me, but it is not nothing, my son," he emphasized, as he focused on Alexander's eyes.

"Not now, *Baba*." Alexander smiled at the father he had always adored, always respected, and stood up. He slowly stepped down from the porch to the grass at the last step, knowing he must be honest with his father. He could not shrug this question away. His father deserved better.

"Walk with me, *Baba*," he said as he turned to look back at his father.

The two men, both with a slight thinning of hair, and nearly the same size now, a bit overweight, their belts slightly lower on their stomachs, strolled together on the broad green grass expanse toward the lake. Alexander led the way to the fruit trees and reached to his favorite tree where he picked a mature, burgundy-colored pomegranate so native to the Lebanese mountains.

"Ah, *remáhni*," smiled Abraham.

"You see this fruit, Father? Like the fig trees and this pomegranate in my yard I have planted, I preserve my heritage so I will never forget the important times of my early life. I often walk here alone, tasting, when I can, the wonderful fruit of home. They remind me of mama and the village. It makes me happy."

Abraham could see his son's eyes moisten as they always did when Alexander was feeling something dear deep inside.

He handed the *remáhni* to his father who rolled the round, firm ball of fruit in his hands, feeling the hard, brittle skin, remembering the pomegranates that grew on the terraces of Douma before the locusts and the famine.

"Yes, Iskandar, I understand, holding this beautiful *remáhni* in my hands. It does bring me warmth and good memories."

"And this," Alexander said to his father as he reached into his pocket, "this is a stone from the mountain I brought with me so long ago. It was the last thing that I touched from the path above the village before I began my walk to Beirut. I have carried this stone with me since my last day in the village. It is always with me to remind me of where we come from. I will never forget my roots, *Baba*."

"But what does a mountain stone and a pomegranate have to do with your ring?"

"It is very much the same." Alexander, smiling slightly, whispered as he lowered his head in careful thought while fondling the ring with the fingers of his left hand, "This ring reminds me of my wonderful visit in Marseille. It was given to me by a dear friend, a friend of Hanna's as well.

Abraham touched his son's arm and said, "A good friend gave you that ring and you've worn it everyday most of your life? That is a good friend, son, a very good friend. I am happy for you."

He put his arm around his son's shoulder. "Was she very beautiful?" Abraham asked with a loving sort of mischievousness, delving.

Alexander nodded yes silently and smiled. *My father is so wise.*

Abraham could see from the look on Alexander's face that he had said all he was going to say about the ring. Noticing Alexander's slightly embarrassed responsive smile while listening to him, he also knew that the "friend" whose ring his son wore had to be very beautiful and very important. He didn't press the issue, realizing that Alexander had withdrawn, concentrating on his memories of Marseille. He could see his son growing pensive as his son's fingers gently fondled the ring. He felt Alexander's inner conflict, shrugged his shoulders and began walking ahead alone.

Alexander lifted his head and spoke to his father in a low and melancholy voice, "That was many years ago, *Baba*." He tried to explain but was unable to remove the memories.

"Another time, Iskandar. Tell me another time, if you wish." He turned and reached for his son, wrapped his arms around his shoulders, received the same from his son, and felt a special warmth of a father-son embrace as they stood beside the beautiful lake, soft breezes on their faces, drifting clouds, and the sound of silence broken only by the lapping of the waves on the shore. It was an important moment of love, of mutual respect and bonding.

As he held his father, Alexander whispered to him, saying, "Yes, *Baba*, I remember her with great love. If you hadn't been waiting for me here, I would have stayed in France to remain with her. She was that important to me. But I have not permitted those memories to be part of my life with Helene. Helene is a magnificent, wonderful woman and fine mother of my children. She and my children have been the most important people in my life. As you are. ."

He did not speak of the cross his mother gave to him, now with Madeleine, as a symbol of his commitment to her, his first true love.

Except for their tragic loss of Michael, life had indeed become very good for Alexander and his family.

As they talked together, remembering, Abraham spoke. "My son, as I taught you when you were a boy in Douma, you have been a good teacher to your children about life. May Michael rest in peace," he whispered as he made the sign of the cross. "I have watched you with them…here in this very place…instructing them how to respect the land, to grow living things, to graft fruit trees…when and how to prune them, to respect the earth, to remember your heritage. Michael became a fine young man because of your closeness to him, Iskandar. We are a people who treasure the bonds of family and hold God close within the family. It is only because we have been so close that we have survived."

They were indeed very close as a family, and all who knew them recognized that as a strength. Yet, still dealing with the loss of Michael, they had overcome many challenges and difficulties, and had faced conditions that had brought down many of their neighbors, especially during the Great Depression when no one had any money. Everything was hard, sparse and trying. But they had survived the worst of times and, when conditions improved, together they enjoyed the best of times. They thrived through devotion to family, hard work, dedication, determination, faith, and to be sure, a stubbornness that would not let them quit under any circumstances. Quitting or giving up simply was not part of their beings, their heritage. They counted on each other throughout those years. Faith and enduring, resilience and tenacity were their strengths.

All of these characteristics were to be tested as 1949 came to a close. Helena, becoming more independent and more grown up each year, was in her junior year at Vassar. Wilbur was very much involved in running the businesses. Alexander found himself more and more involved in his continually expanding business enterprises of cattle, banking, citrus production, and juicing plants. Even so, he was very much focused on his growing philanthropic endeavors in health care.

His charities had become very important to him. He found himself increasingly networking with "the boys in Tallahassee" seeking state grants and support for establishing new hospitals and rehab clinics. Other times he represented the Florida Cattlemen's Association, and helped form the Florida Citrus Federation of growers, producers and transporters. Although Central Florida was still very rural, sparsely populated with small towns and few cities, it was becoming very important as a producing region.

Alexander was a very busy man in the prime of his life, dedicated to his daughter and wife.

Smiling, Helene proudly announced at the country club the night they happily celebrated their 25th wedding anniversary, "Alexander's life is his family, his businesses, and his charities. Our home is my domain. He is my husband, and I am his wife. We are and will always be partners. I pray we will be together forever." She laughed, "For at least another twenty-five years!"

The gathering of friends stood and applauded their beloved neighbors after her brief statement.

They belonged here, she knew, and the love of her friends and family showed on her happy, radiant face, especially when Alexander stood, walked over to her with a proud smile and embraced her.

But it was not to be.

Some of you say, Joy is greater than sorrow,
and others say, Nay, sorrow is greater.
Kahlil Gibran

CHAPTER 17

May: Vassar, 1951

Having just completed her final exams at the end of her junior year, Helena felt really good about her grades and her college career. Gazing out the window, she thought about entering her senior year in the fall and how amazing it all was. She smiled at her roommate and said, "Next year should be a blast, Lucy!"

The phone rang loudly in the hall interrupting Helena's thoughts.

"Hello?" answered a sorority sister walking by, "Pi Phi house." Then she shouted, automatically, "Helena, it's for you. It sounds like it could be your Dad!"

Helena ran down the hall, grabbed the telephone and eagerly said, "Hello?"

"Helena, this is your father."

Your father? She knew instantly something was wrong. He never spoke like that unless he was very serious, very concerned. His voice was unusually nervous and sounded urgent.

She asked quickly, "What is it, Dad?"

"You must come home immediately. Your mother needs you by her side. She is very ill. It's serious. I need you here. And I need you now."

"Oh, my God," she stammered, "What? What is it?" Her heart was racing, not understanding how her mother could become so ill so quickly, with no warning.

"We are not sure, but we believe it is cancer. Come tomorrow, Helena. Call us as soon as you make your travel arrangements."

"Oh, my God, mama has cancer?" Helena uttered again as she put her hand to her head in disbelief at this frightening picture in her mind of her seriously ill mother as she hung up the phone. Tears welled up in her eyes and overflowed down her cheeks. Lucy and her other sorority sisters joined her in her room as she fell on the bed sobbing. She knew cancer was a certain death sentence.

Early the next morning they helped her get to the station where she caught a train for New York City. Her heart was filled with dread the entire seemingly endless trip home on the train, from New York to Philadelphia to Atlanta, Jacksonville, and finally Kissimmee, where she was met at the station with warm embraces from her father. While happy and grateful to see her, he could not disguise the ache he felt in his heart. This impending, frightening unknown thing called cancer had crippled his beloved Helene. By now, she was so weak that she was in bed almost all of the time.

Quickly they climbed into the car and drove to the house where Helene had had her nurse help her dress and brush her hair so that she would look her best for her daughter's arrival.

"Take me to the porch facing the lake," she had requested of her nurse. "I want to be there when Helena arrives. Not in the bedroom."

And that was where she sat in her rocking chair looking out over the lake, relishing her view she loved so much, her favorite place that gave her peace and serenity, when Helena leaped from the car and ran up the steps to the front door.

"Mama? Where are you, Mama?" she cried out, running through the house.

"Out here, Helena," she called out weakly. "I'm on the porch. Come to me, my darling. Give me a hug. Oh, Helena, I'm so glad you are here."

She rushed to her mother. "Mama, what is it? You were so vibrant and happy at Christmas. What could have happened?" Helena's eyes began smarting, so she turned her face away so her mother would not see her sadness and fear. She could easily see her mother had already lost a lot of weight. Her cheeks were hollow, her eyes deeper.

"It's pancreatic cancer, darling. It happened so fast. We didn't have any warning. At first, I just felt sick, like the flu or something. I thought maybe I was just tired after the busy holidays. The doctor didn't think it was serious either, so I took his advice and went to bed, took some pain killers, and simply waited to get better. Then, a few weeks ago, the pain began. It has gotten worse, darling, and no one knows for sure what to do. The doctor is hopeful, but so little is known about this disease. But now, at least, I am happy because I have my family with me. Even my parents, my sister Julia and Sam are here too. Everyone seems so worried. Your father has been wonderful, God bless him. Your father hasn't left the house since this all began. He refuses to leave me alone. He has grown so much more sensitive since we lost Michael in the war. I'm afraid for him, Helena."

Each day, Helena tended to her mother as she watched her grow weaker and weaker. On Sundays, she drove her into town to church and to see her friends. Alexander and Helena brought friends from the hospital auxiliary, the church, and Helene's social club as often as they could. Each day Helena and Helene sat side by side on the porch talking "girl talk," looking out over the lake as long as Helene could tolerate sitting, a blanket over her shoulders.

Actually, Helena began to find these hours, extending into days and weeks, a mixed blessing. While her mother's health deteriorated at an accelerating rate, she treasured their hours together.

"I love these quiet times with you, Helena. I'm sorry you had to rush home from school." She constantly held, patted or simply touched her daughter's hand as she spoke to her, not wanting to let go.

"Don't even think about that, Mama. I am so glad we have this time together. It's bringing us even closer." She turned her head as her tears began again, not wanting her mother to see.

She listened intently as her mother recalled in whispers her youth in Boston, growing up with her sisters, describing what it was like during the "Roaring Twenties," Prohibition, then coming to this frontier town of Kissimmee, becoming part of "cattle country," and what it was like being married to Alexander.

"He's a good man, Helena. Your father had nothing. Your grandfather started here as a railroad notions peddler, as they called them back in those days. And, with all their hard work, long hours, dedication and determination, they provided you and me with a home...a beautiful home...food on the table, and, most important, he gave me you and your brother Michael. I will be forever grateful to him for my so many blessings."

She stopped for a moment and gazed out over the familiar waters of Lake Tohopekaliga, then turned to her daughter. "Helena, there is something I think you should one day speak to your father about after I'm gone. He has always shared everything with me. We always spoke of his boyhood days, his life before we married. He has always been faithful to me. But there is one thing he has never talked to me about. When we first married, I asked him to tell me about the ring on his small finger. He has never removed it. It's the one with the French cross in the middle with the letter "D" on the other side of the cross. All I know is a dear friend gave it to him in Marseille where he stopped over on his way to America. He was 18-years-old. He told me that it was a reminder of where he came from so that he would never forget his humble beginnings. He had so little when he arrived. That ring was his most valuable possession. He was penniless. He had only that and the clothes on his back, a small valise, and that silly stone he carries in his pocket. I believe it reminds him that he was so poor as a boy that he could not stay in France, but had to continue to America. Your father never wanted to forget that no matter how successful he became, he came to America to be free, to find his destiny and fulfill the wishes of his mother before she died. That's all. He has told me over and over how much he loves us and that he believes his mother knows in heaven that, indeed, he did fulfill his destiny with me, with you, and with Michael. It nearly killed him when Michael died." She paused, then added with a slight smile, "And now with his success here in America..."

"He always said he only wanted freedom and opportunity."

"So, Helena, that is all I know of his mysterious gold ring. Perhaps there is more. Perhaps not. Perhaps it reminds him of a young love. I don't know, and I never pursued the issue. It didn't matter. What came before me has not hurt me, and I accepted it. One day, you might ask your father to share the story of the ring with you after I'm gone. But I want him to know that if it belonged to his love before me, he should not feel any guilt. He should know I never thought anything of it. Tell him that, Helena…for me. Do you understand?" She yawned, "I'm tired now, Helena. Please take me to my bedroom. I feel sleepy."

It was only three months after Helena had received the call at college to immediately come home when her mother went to sleep for the last time.

That afternoon, after visiting on the porch overlooking the lake, Helena helped her frail mother into the wheelchair and pushed her inside to her bed in the master bedroom on the first floor. After helping her onto the bed as Helene winced with pain, though never complaining, Helena lovingly reached for the light blanket and pulled it over her mother's shoulders.

"Glass of milk, Mother?" she asked.

"Actually, Helena," she replied with a wan smile, "I think I'd like a glass of your father's orange juice."

"I'll squeeze some right now, Mom," Helena laughed as she stood and stepped toward the kitchen.

She grabbed the best Temple oranges from the refrigerator and squeezed them for her mother, then added the sweetest juice from the Honeybells. Calling out to her father sitting in the den to come join them, Helena poured three glasses of juice, put them on a tray, added a small vase of flowers, and carried it to the bedroom.

They toasted together as a family. Helena carefully lifted the glass to her mother's lips for a sip, and then placed it on the nightstand. Fluffing the pillows, she gently helped her mother lie back down. Helene softly rested her head on them and gratefully closed her eyes, smiling peacefully.

They all held hands as Alexander kissed his wife on the lips, whispering, "Helene, I love you so much. Always know that."

"Iskandar," she replied in a weak voice, "I am a lucky woman to have had your love and shared so much with you. Don't be sad, my husband." Then, after a breath, "Helena will need you now more than ever. And, Iskandar," she smiled as she used his native name deliberately, "please be good to yourself. Life is too precious. Don't be alone too much."

Helena, standing near her parents as they tenderly expressed their love to each other, felt tears welling in her eyes. She stepped to the bed, pressed her cheek to her mother's, kissed her on her lips and told her how much she loved her.

Alexander and Helena continued to sit on the edge of the bed holding Helene's hands, sensing that the end was near. Helena was stroking her mother's hair when she felt her head turn.

Helene's eyes closed and she quietly, peacefully exhaled for the last time. Then she was gone from their lives.

Alexander, experiencing a *déjà vu*, recalled the last moments he had shared with his own mother when he endured the same tapestry of sadness, deep love, and the almost unbearable sense of losing one's mother. Just like what Helena was going through now. He recalled the sharp pangs of loss, the sense of despair of a mother, and now a devoted wife leaving him forever. And he began to cry.

"Don't do that, Daddy. If you cry now, I'll never get through this," Helena whispered, putting her arms over her father's shoulders as she felt her own tears begin to flow. "I don't think I'll ever forget her last minutes. I'm so glad we were here with her. I think that made it easier for her," she said as they hugged.

Alexander thought to himself, Helena is calling me "Daddy" again instead of "Dad" which she has used since she turned sixteen. She's my little girl again. He reached for her again.

After they hugged, Helena looked into her father's eyes and whispered, "I love you, Daddy."

And let today embrace the past with
Remembrance and the future with longing.
Kahlil Gibran

CHAPTER 18

Helene's death was a major blow to Alexander and Helena, and, to the entire community. Like most families of the Mediterranean, the wife-mother is the glue of dedication and love that holds families together. She had carried the emotional burden of the family, smoothed over all frustrations, disappointments and conflicts within each member's life. "Momma" then "Mom" could and did solve everything. Every childhood sibling argument, scratch, bruise, or wound physically or emotionally got better and its pain mysteriously disappeared when she gently touched or kissed the "wa-wa." She was an angel, doctor, psychologist, arbitrator, healer, sounding board, and storehouse of love and loyalty. She raised the children, she defended them when necessary. She taught them all she knew, arranged all birthday parties and social events and maintained relationships. She had helped Alexander with his English writing and speech, and then sat beside Michael and Helena as they did their schoolwork.

And while the Thomas family was close and appreciative, they never knew what hit them when Helene passed from the scene. There became an absence that left her home so empty, a vacuum that seemed to virtually remove the air from the house. For Alexander, who had relied upon Helene for so long, there was an enormous loss of his companion, his partner in all things. She nurtured him and was always beside him, even in the darkest hours. She prepared the food for his table, supported and understood him, and constantly reassured him of his importance in her life, in the life of the community, and in the lives of their children. She had a unique way of making sure he knew he was appreciated. She knew that "if Daddy, *Biyee*, is happy, everyone is happy." When as a child, helping set the table, Helena might ask, "Where is the head of the table, Momma?" Helene would reply with a smile, "Wherever your daddy sits is the head of the table." Alexander never felt the slightest competition from his wife, his helpmate. She was never a burden. He ran the businesses, working long hours at the store sometimes six and seven days a week, whether at the store, on the ranch or in the groves. Helene was mistress of their home. What she said in the home was the rule, as her husband never expressed disagreement in front of the children.

In their early years together, he had tried but never really could fully appreciate her loneliness in her new home away from her family because he was too busy, too focused on survival in his long days at work to be very involved with her emotional needs. He was on a mission then, anxious to make a good living to provide them basic needs like a home, food, a better future for them and the children. He was so frugal, resisting buying anything, never forgetting his humble beginnings when money was almost non-existent and nothing could be wasted. His clothes were always the same: dark wool slacks, white long-sleeved dress shirts that he wore open-necked with his sleeves rolled up two folds. He was content to wear his clothes until they wore out, and would have but for Helene taking care of that problem too. He always wore the same pair of laced, black, smooth-toed shoes, which he shined daily himself. He had one pair of boots for when he was on his horse or working in the pastures.

Now, only days after her funeral, he was suddenly aware of how lonely he was missing Helene. The house was empty. Its heart and soul was gone.

What now? This house is too big now, he said to himself as he walked from room to room, subconsciously looking for his wife.

Helena had returned to Vassar College to complete her senior year. Alexander's father, Abraham, had returned to his beloved mountains in North Lebanon more than a year before Helene had grown ill. Michael was gone. And Alexander was alone…again.

And now, in 1952, at the age of fifty, Alexander was by himself in his beautiful but silent five-bedroom Victorian house situated on the shore of Lake Tohopekaliga overlooking the expansive rolling lawns to the lake shore, the boat dock, his garden, and his favorite giant oak trees. He still loved admiring and picking the fruit from his pomegranate and fig trees, and grapes from his small vineyard, all reminders of his youth in Douma. For years, Helene and the children harvested the young wada-areesh, the grape leaves, in the spring, while the new leaves were soft and pliant, so they would always have the leaves available for rolled grape leaves served with lemon juice or *laban* yogurt just as Alexander had eaten in his homeland as a boy. He loved that Helene always cooked his favorite meals for him: *kibbee, tabouleh, yabrah, imjadara ma' roz*, and *khobaz*. He appreciated her tasty *baba ghanoush*, the tangy eggplant and sesame oil patè, and her ever present hummus.

And now, she was gone. Their home, her palace, was without its mistress. He was alone and quiet much of the time. He recalled Helene's infectious smile, her laughter, her humming as she prepared meals in her kitchen. It was so comfortable with her all those years. During the warm, breezy summer afternoons when business was slow and he didn't have to work until dark, they had walked together under the huge moss-draped oak trees they had preserved. He remembered fondly when they bought the land for their new home soon after their wedding. Helene had come with him to this hot, unfamiliar new frontier of Central Florida, away from everyone she loved and everything she enjoyed. But now, as he walked alone among the oak trees, almost every day that first year after the funeral, pondering his new life, seeking solace from his grieving, he found that he better understood her feeling of emptiness and loss as he himself now felt this gut-wrenching loneliness.

"Helene..." he cried out as he looked back from the trees to the Victorian railings of the porch, fully expecting her to be standing there where she always stood at the top of the steps by the post of the porch at the white railing. She would watch him with a loving smile, cherishing his presence, the father of her two beautiful children. She had always let him know that their companionship and marriage had completely fulfilled her. He felt rewarded by her.

But this day, like every day since her illness, he looked but didn't see Helene standing there. "I miss you, Helene," he spoke aloud as tears welled up. Then, he would turn and continue his stroll, alone with his thoughts, feeling the grass crunch under his feet, the familiar breeze on his face, watching the thunderclouds form in the summer sky. This became his daily ritual every afternoon since Helene's passing.

Even after taking the advice of his friend Abigail, and hiring a housekeeper and cook, Alexander still felt alone. So much was irreplaceable. He kept himself busy each day going into his office after sitting alone, eating the breakfast his housekeeper had prepared for him. He would read the morning paper on the leather couch, sipping coffee, with not quite the same familiar taste as Helene would prepare for him, then sitting at his desk answering correspondence, making his daily telephone calls to friends and business colleagues. Then, he would eat a light lunch consisting of soup and a sandwich, which soon became a very boring and uninteresting ritual. It wasn't like being with Helene when they often shared a mezza of olives, cheese, hummus, grilled lamb and salad, all eaten with *khobaz*, pita bread. As with Helene in those days, after his daily lunch he would drive to the ranch, saddle his horse, and ride, now alone most of the time, among his cattle, viewing his land, and thinking.

Many days, he found his solace on Sheikh as he would saddle up in the mornings, meet Wilbur, his closest friend, and ride through the herds in the pastures. They had been riding together, almost as brothers, for nearly thirty years, Wilbur in his sweat-stained, well-worn Stetson, and Alexander in his. They knew each other's mannerisms and priorities. Sometimes Wilbur would answer Alexander's questions before being asked. They were very close. Both understood the goals of the Thomas ranch, a major part of the growing, prosperous Thomas Enterprises, a conglomerate respected throughout Central Florida, one of the largest beef production areas in the United States. The brand ATA was respected by everyone in the business from the feed providers to the railroads, from the trucking lines to the buyers, and from the major meat wholesalers across the country. Although people now rarely saw the master of the ranching family, they knew and respected his name.

Gratefully, Alexander was still an integral part of the leadership of The Florida Cattlemen's Association, wielding quiet but powerful influence in the office of the Governor, the halls of the State of Florida Senate and the House of Representatives in Tallahassee. He was a significant part of the financial strength of the important Central Florida counties, and was often consulted for his opinion on many issues confronting the enterprise and quality of life in Florida.

It was during the early 1950s when the U.S. Senate Reform Committee was investigating gambling in Florida, that Alexander and his Polk, Osceola, and Orange County colleagues were asked, "How far do you want this investigation to go? It could embarrass some powerful Florida leaders, especially in Miami and Jacksonville."

Remembering his son Michael's sacrifice, Alexander took the lead and became spokesman for the group, reflecting the conservative nature of Central Florida and recalling the returning veterans he tried to help. He responded forcefully, "My son, and the sons and daughters of many Floridians, rich and poor, white and black, fought in World War II to preserve freedom for all of us at great cost. Young lives were lost, limbs ripped from their bodies; they suffered much pain and destruction. Dammit! I don't want to see all those sacrifices wasted so that the poor souls in our state can lose everything they have at the gambling tables and casinos. No sir, we'd just as soon gambling in Florida be stopped, at least as much as it can be. So, go as far as you need to to get the head of that monster. Don't worry about who you find. Let the chips fall where they may."

The Kefauver Commission did just that, and many said they could not have gone so far had the determined but politically savvy Senator Estes Kefauver from Tennessee not gotten the green flag from the powerful cattlemen of Kissimmee, Bartow, Tampa, and Sanford.

With all of Alexander's charities and activities, he still maintained his original shop on Broadway even though he had sold his father's store when Abraham returned to Lebanon in 1949. He significantly expanded beef production to help meet the growing, almost insatiable demand for more and more beef products during the years following World War II. He often remembered swearing years ago, "I promise I'll always have plenty of food for my family."

The nation and Europe were faced with enormous pent-up demands for almost anything that could be produced. By the late-1950s, Americans were awash in money, demand, and a newfound ability to produce almost anything the world needed at breakneck speed, an enormous departure from the moribund isolationism of the 1930s. Indeed, the "Sleeping Giant," as described by the Japanese Admiral after the attack at Pearl Harbor, had indeed awakened. Parents, mostly those who grew up with very little during the 1930s and 1940s, became determined to have and to provide for their children all that they didn't have while growing up. As more and more families acquired more and more pets as never before, all sorts of beef products were called on to provide food for this new phenomenon.

As a result, Thomas Enterprises was thriving beyond Alexander's wildest dreams. Earnings skyrocketed, each year far exceeding those the year before. Americans were traveling more on vacation, and many began leaving the cold winters of the North for the South. Visionaries declared there would be a major population shift from the northern "Rust Belt" states to the "Sun Belt" states, and Florida, with its disproportionate enormous coastline, pristine beaches, more than adequate supply of water and other resources, and temperate year-round winters, was sure to benefit. Land values began to escalate during the 1950s. Pastureland for which Alexander had paid only $2 or even $16 per acre was now worth over $100 per acre. His 30,000 acres were now of enormous value, more than three million dollars.

Even with all this happening around him, Alexander, a widower, found the days, weeks and months after Helene died to be empty and depressing. He missed Helene so much that staying alone in the house without her familiar voice was almost unbearable.

Some days he would sit on a porch chair and think about his youth in the mountains playing with his brother and his cousins, climbing the olive trees and the larger ancient cedars. Nostalgia had become his pastime, it seemed.

Other times he would recall his early years in Kissimmee, the embarrassment he shared with his father at not speaking English well, of being "different" for the first time in his life, being with his first American friend, Abigail, learning from her, and admiring her all those first days in America. He vividly remembered learning English from this young, exciting woman who might have been the mother of his children, but for her mother's prejudice and his father's insistence. He remembered Abigail's father, Big John, and the store he opened at eighteen. *Eighteen? Could I really have opened a store when I was just eighteen years old? My God, I was in a big hurry!*

And then he would recall sitting under the oak tree behind his store during the long, slow summer days, with his back leaning against the trunk, whittling a piece of wood with his penknife he always carried with him, or practicing with his sling.

He smiled as he remembered the day he first met Helene in Boston. How cute she was at fifteen. And how lovely a woman she became by the time he went back to marry her. And how loving and loyal she had been as his wife, a dedicated mother of his children, and a caring daughter-in-law of his father. *All those years, even during the difficult times, she was by my side...all those years she never complained. How lucky I have been, he thought. How very lucky. And now, Helene, you are gone.*

"All I have are the memories," he confided in Wilbur on more than one occasion. "Michael is gone, and now Helene."

Once, he paused as he gazed across the pasture and said, "Wilbur, with all that we have built, I am still so empty. I'm not the sort to be alone."

One Sunday afternoon, with no work that had to be done, he took a walk across the lawn down by the lake. His thoughts deepened as he reached down, pulled up a long leaf of grass and stuck it in his mouth. His thoughts turned to the three women he had loved. *I had to watch my mother die too young. I had to leave my first true love, Madeleine, in Marseille. Now I must face life without Helene. Even my father has gone away. And my only son is gone.*

It was while riding across the pastures that he began to catch himself subconsciously fondling the worn gold ring on his small finger he had received from Madeleine.

He often found another haunting thought in his mind: Helena will someday be married, raise her own children, and find her own destiny. That is how it should be, for it is written, "where you go, your children cannot follow...and though they came through you, they are not from you. You cannot be with your children forever." He found himself reflecting on that as he reread the thought-provoking book *The Prophet*, written by Kahlil Gibran, his countryman. This book of philosophy became his companion and made him proud. He had nearly memorized the book, he loved it so. It also provoked him into finding acceptance, healing, and a sense of the realities of life.

And so, on that particular day, reflecting on all these thoughts, he decided, *I must find what God wants me to do with my life now that it has changed so very much once again. I will pray on this. There is so much to do outside of myself. Many things. I can do more for the handicapped, for the poor children. I can prepare for the changes that are sure to come to Florida very soon.*

His life was a continuing metamorphosis from focus on survival, work and success to a more spiritual, giving response toward his human side and a growing passion for helping others.

It is when you give of yourself you truly give.
Kahlil Gibran

CHAPTER 19

Alexander's Epiphany

Alexander rarely attended social events during the first year following Helene's death even though others invited him to dinners, parties, soirees, and to political rallies in Orlando, Tampa, Miami and Tallahassee. Events he reluctantly agreed to attend were only those to which he would not have taken Helene. He just couldn't bear visiting people who would ask him so many questions and express their sympathy.

While he guarded his privacy and stayed in the Kissimmee area most of the time, he began to make time to visit his good friend Anthony Abraham and the Elias family in Miami, his cousin Elias Chalhoub in West Palm Beach, and the Barakat family in Jacksonville. Sometimes, when he didn't attend his own Episcopal church in Kissimmee, he would drive over to Orlando to visit his sister and attend her small Antioch Orthodox church.

Meanwhile, the recognition of Thomas Enterprises as one of the more successful businesses in Central Florida allowed Alexander to delegate more and more as he was becoming a sought-after contributor to local health organizations providing health-care therapy, aid to the poor, and especially to underprivileged children's causes. His wisdom was sought even by boards of civic and business organizations of which he was not a member.

In Miami, Anthony Abraham, a treasured friend of Alexander, was building his automobile dealerships into a very successful operation. Alexander made it a point to buy all his vehicles from Anthony.

Anthony convinced Alexander to invest jointly in beachfront properties and vacant lands near the growing Miami International Airport. During the 1950s, they even ventured into investing in South Palm Beach County by purchasing farming tracts there. Sometimes they bought quarter sections of one hundred-sixty acres at a time for the going rate of $50-$70 per acre. During the 1950s and 1960s they occasionally bought property in Delray Beach and Boca Raton for $10,000 per oceanfront lot.

During Alexander's visits, they would spend a lot of their time together at Anthony's house just talking about life and sharing memories as they played their favorite table game, *towleh* backgammon.

"You can't beat oceanfront land, Iskandar," Anthony would say, addressing his good friend in his native language as they visited in his Miami home, "especially if you can live with the bugs! Water is like gold, you'll see."

"I don't know. They're asking a lot of money, Anthony. In Kissimmee, lakefront lots go for $500." Alexander's mind wasn't focusing on business as much as before, and Anthony could sense he had lost a lot of enthusiasm for work and was much more inclined to speak of life since he lost Michael and Helene.

Anthony, more familiar with land prices along the southeastern coast, and with a different perspective because he was from the North, would only smile and reply, "Iskandar, trust me. It will be like gold in time. You'll be pleased with these purchases in a few years. We have to be patient, my friend, and we can afford to be since taxes are so low."

Anthony and Alexander had much in common, the foundation of their long friendship. They both had come from poor beginnings and were almost the same age, Alexander being two years older. They arrived at almost the same time from Lebanon; Anthony in 1922 and Alexander in 1920. They both were young during the "Roaring Twenties" and fought the good fight during the rock-poor '30s. And both were anxious to succeed, were somewhat impetuous, but learned their lessons well from the land and stock market crashes.

Anthony began his career in Chicago in the industrial north, and had experienced the terrible stock market crash more than did Alexander. But both were convinced from that experience that they would be better off owning land, not participating in the stock market or trusting banks. They looked to their basic businesses and land ownership for their success.

"I like land, Anthony. I can touch it, walk on it, look at it, and to me, land is the best you can leave your children."

They both had a common vision of Florida's future and were convinced long-term investing in Florida real estate was a wise decision.

"I did well in Chicago, Iskandar, but I got tired of the snow, the cold, and the difficulties of living in the north. That's why I moved to Miami. And I think lots and lots of people will continue to do the same. They will need new houses and places to shop. Yes, Florida's future looks good to me."

They spoke often of how wonderful it was to be in America, and how grateful they were that their fathers came to America. Both felt very fortunate to have prospered beyond their wildest dreams.

"We have received so many blessings, Iskandar. Just look at us. We have food to eat, clothes that fill the closets, financial security. We must find a proper way to give some of it back to America."

"I agree, Anthony," Alexander nodded in assent as he raised his small glass filled with *arak*, now milky-white from the melting ice, "and that is why I've gotten so involved in the health clinics for veterans in Tampa and Orlando. And as for you, I know how you have been helping the children of Lebanon by helping a new group finance new hospitals there, and even here in Miami."

Anthony smiled. "But we can do more, Iskandar. I've been looking for something that all of us from Lebanon could do together, even as we would still continue to help our own individual communities."

"We could pool our resources and bring in the Barakat family from Jacksonville, too," responded Alexander enthusiastically.

"And the Haddads and Mansours in Orlando and the Maloofs in Tampa," added Anthony. "Okay, let's have some fun. How about a game of *towleh*? We've had two glasses of *arak*, so we should both be bold in a game."

"Right you are, Anthony," he laughed in response, "and we both should be easy to beat too."

One day, the following month when Alexander was back in Kissimmee, the phone rang while he was at his desk reviewing the monthly figures from his various enterprises.

"Hello, Alexander Thomas speaking."

"Mr. Thomas, this is the operator calling. I have a person-to-person call for you from Bishop Anthony Bashir."

Alexander's mind raced, remembering his favorite cousin and childhood neighbor in Douma. They were playmates as boys. Anthony was now a bishop, he remembered, Metropolitan of North and South America, the largest church of Syrians and Lebanese in America. Then he heard the deep, familiar voice over the phone.

"Hello, Iskandar. How are you today?"

"Anthony, it's good to hear from you. Your voice is so clear. Are you in Florida?"

"No, I'm in Los Angeles on an important mission and I need your help. Something wonderful is happening and you need to be part of it."

"You know, Anthony, the only time I remember ever saying 'no' to you was when we were boys in Douma and you warned me not to climb to the top of that tall cedar. You were right. That was the day I fell and broke my arm!"

Anthony laughed, "Yes, I remember." He chuckled again, "You were so sure of yourself. But you have always been sure of yourself. I remember you once told me, 'I want to be sure of myself ninety-five percent of the time and correct at least fifty percent of the time.' I never forgot that, Iskandar."

"Thank you, *y'eini*. What can I do for you?"

"There is something you should know, and that's why I'm calling. Danny

Thomas has begun a crusade. He is fulfilling a pledge he made to St. Jude years ago to build a shrine, and that shrine, he has finally determined, will be a hospital for sick children. It is to be called St. Jude Children's Research Hospital. Fundraising has begun by his friends in Los Angeles, New York City, and Detroit. Christians, Jews, and Muslims are joining together to make this dream of Danny's come true. It is a labor of love, of faith."

"Now," he continued with his sales pitch, "all Lebanese in America are being called on to join this crusade. This hospital can be the single best way for all of us to thank America for the freedom, opportunity and prosperity that we and our families have received in this great country. Danny has formed a fundraising organization named ALSAC, which stands for American Lebanese Syrian Associated Charities, and Aiding Leukemia Stricken American Children."

"That sounds pretty impressive," Alexander interjected as the bishop took a breath.

"It is! This hospital will be located in Memphis."

"Memphis, Tennessee?" Alexander asked, surprised.

"Yes, Iskandar, Memphis. There are very good reasons that I'll explain later. I believe so much in this cause that I'm urging all Antiochan Orthodox churches in America to join in this crusade to find a cure for leukemia that kills more than 90% of the children with this cancer."

"Cancer! I hate that word," Alexander thought as he remembered Helene's pain.

"Iskandar, it's one of God's challenges to us. He's calling on us as human beings to find a solution. You must help us, cousin. Danny has taken on this mission and I can tell you, he has dedicated his life to it. He has already brought the Lebanese together with his success in Hollywood, and makes us proud of our heritage by making us laugh with his weekly television program."

Alexander smiled remembering the last episode of "Make Room for Daddy." Listening patiently, he waited for his passionate cousin to pause so he could respond. He also remembered that terrible illness robbing him of his beloved Helene.

"Now you've caught my attention. I've watched Danny's show every week for a long time. It's obvious he's proud to be Lebanese. And I really laugh at his 'Uncle Tanoos.' I think we all can identify with him since we all have our own version of 'Uncle Tanoos.'"

The Bishop picked up on his cousin's interest and, being an experienced at fund-raiser, knew exactly what to say next.

"Danny is having fund-raisers in most major cities, including Miami. Mike Tamer is committed to this cause, Iskandar. He is a one-man campaign, and running this massive effort. He's from Indianapolis, the president of the Midwest Federation. Can you believe it? He took a year off from his business to devote himself to raising funds for St. Jude! Mike is the driving force with Danny."

Enthusiastically, he continued, "Danny is looking to his people, and I'm asking you, to help be responsible for funding the operating costs of St. Jude." He paused just a second to catch his breath. "Most of the money needed to build the hospital has already been raised, Thank God. But we need more. You've been without Helene for some time and hardly anyone in our community has seen you lately. Now it's time for you to get involved in this wonderful cause. Be a leader. I am aware of your generosity in Florida. Anthony Abraham down in Miami keeps me informed. It is good you donate so generously, Iskandar, and now I am asking you to give even more. Your cousin Elias Chalhoub is already on the Board of Governors. I want you to join him."

Alexander could always count on his cousin to find a painless way to get in his pocket. He smiled, knowing the Bishop was wearing a slight smile as he went to his favorite closing.

"I am counting on you to match Anthony, Iskandar."

How many times he had heard the Bishop utter those very words when he stopped by to visit on those occasions while he was in Florida. The scenario was always the same. After a fine dinner served by Helene, they and the children would sit around the table for hours listening to Bishop Bashir, one of the most revered Lebanese in the world. He was beloved by all, no matter what church they belonged to. His sincerity, humility, and dedication to God's works were renowned. His quick sense of humor was always part of his persona that endeared so many to him. "Even the Pope is my good friend, Iskandar," he would say with a proud smile.

Anthony paused and Alexander heard him whispering, "Here, Danny," as he handed the telephone to Danny Thomas, "speak with your brother."

Listening to Danny himself and feeling his enthusiasm, Alexander was quickly convinced that his decision now was not if, but how much. After Danny made his pitch, Alexander knew he was committed.

"I'm with you, Danny, and I have friends I will speak with."

Danny then moved on and asked, "Can you come to Miami and meet with Mike Tamer and me? There will be a fine dinner. It's being sponsored by Anthony Abraham. Do you know him?"

"Know him? I sure do," Alexander replied, thinking how much more he was going to have to donate to keep Anthony at bay! At the same time, he felt a little upset with Anthony for not calling him first.

"How long has Anthony been involved? When did he agree to sponsor a fund-raiser?"

Alexander was just like the others in his community. Now he was in friendly competition with his friend, exactly what the Bishop and Danny were hoping for.

Danny knew his brethren. "Nobody wants to be first and nobody wants to be last." He laughed, understanding what Alexander was thinking. "I just now spoke with Anthony and asked him. Bishop Bashir and I have been on the phone for hours setting up dinners around the country. Why do you ask?"

"Well, Anthony and I are very close and he'll brag to me about underwriting the Miami dinner without me. And now it's too late. So why don't I organize another dinner in Tampa? Then you could make both cities on the same trip! As a matter of fact, I'll even match Anthony's contribution!" Alexander laughed.

"Okay, Iskandar, I'll call Anthony and tell him. But be prepared, you know Anthony, if he finds out what you are doing, he might even increase his contribution."

"Well, let me know if he does. I wouldn't be surprised," Alexander chuckled, thinking. "God, I love being part of this family. Let me know your schedule, Danny."

"I'll have my office contact you later today, Iskandar. The Bishop sends his warmest regards. *Shookrun. Allah ma'ak.*"

With a smile, Danny placed the phone on the cradle and shook hands with Bishop Bashir as he jammed one of his legendary cigars in his mouth.

Alexander felt uplifted from this conversation as he hung up the phone and swiveled his chair around to look out the window of his office at the lake he loved so much. Pulled out of his doldrums, he now knew he would be among people of his homeland on an important mission…together. He felt included now, not alone.

He leaned back, chuckled to himself and murmured, "I wonder how much that phone call is going to cost."

All these things shall love do unto you that
you may know the secrets of your heart,
and in that knowledge become a fragment of Life's heart.
Kahlil Gibran

CHAPTER 20

Alexander's Path Takes a Turn

Nearly two years after Helene's death, Alexander knew he would have to stop living in the past and find a way to begin a new life. He felt a deep sense of emptiness without a woman's love. Alexander never liked being alone, although in truth one couldn't tell by watching him. He always seemed so focused on his work.

Sitting still in his saddle each day looking over the herd, often crossing one leg across the horse's withers, leaning back in the saddle and feeling the breezes on his face, a Stetson hat protecting his eyes from the bright sun, Alexander, not as content as he looked, would proudly survey part of the thousands of acres of his holdings and meditate on his life, thinking of where God would take him now that he had no companion.

He found himself thinking more and more of Madeleine, unable to escape the gnawing feeling in his stomach, the increasingly aching affection he still felt for her that he had been able to put aside in respect for Helene for so long. There remained a sense of uncertainty, a chapter in his life that never truly closed. He began to realize that his thoughts of Madeleine were becoming a larger part of his consciousness after relegating those memories of his first love and the weeks they shared in Marseille to his subconscious years ago, where they had remained undisturbed for nearly thirty years.

Even though he could keep very busy most days, his afternoons and evenings were very lonely. More and more he found himself thinking of his lonely life, of Madeleine, recalling the loveliness of her face, her smile, her touch, her laughter… the ring…Notre-Dame-de-la-Garde…*Les Calanques.*

He was very much aware that he had to respect Helene's memory, yet he was inching day by day toward a new confrontation with his destiny.

By Christmas of 1958, Helena flew in from New York where she had gone to work for Chase Bank after obtaining her Master's degree. She did indeed find the culture at Chase to be friendly toward the few women who worked in the International Corporate Finance Department. Her year of graduate school at Radcliffe, the only quality graduate school where women could obtain such a degree, helped her career possibilities enormously. Coupled with her fluency in four languages, Helena's skills were growing in great demand. She was often asked her views on the opportunities to do business in Europe and in the Arab countries of the Middle East. Since her father had often explained to her the culture of Beirut, the international banking of that key city and profit center, she was well versed, and becoming an important resource of insight. It also helped her career that she had spent the months following Radcliffe working in Paris and Geneva in an exchange program with Credit Suisse. When she could, she would travel to other cities and spend "familiarization periods," as the bank called them, in their offices in Beirut, Athens, Amman, Baghdad, and Dubai. She had become one of the few true internationalists in the bank, called on to make sure those who would travel to those countries representing the bank were well versed in the local cultural protocols. In a word, she had become an important asset to the international post-war vision of the bank's global interests, to say nothing of her polished and graceful beauty that often belied her sharp mind and perspicacity. She was determined to succeed in her career, and, like her father, was resilient, and tenacious. She conscientiously watched and learned from everyone around her, chose her mentors carefully, was sensitive to interoffice politics…not participating…which only added to her mystique…and aligned herself with her mentor and the bank's leaders.

"Daddy," she told her father during one of their bi-weekly telephone conversations, "I really love travel to the Near East. I always get chills when I'm asked to visit our offices in Beirut, thinking of you as a young man there."

"Did you ever get to Douma?"

"Gee, Daddy, it's always so rushed…in and out. Most of our meetings are at the golf club near the airport south of Beirut. I even met Mr. Anthony Kabani who owns the club. He's so nice."

The bank involved Helena in much of their Near East growth so that by the end of her first year at the New York offices, Helena was considered a "rising star." But of course, the possibility of joining the upper ranks of any major bank in America was still exclusively for men, and she knew it.

She knew, therefore, she might not stay with Chase under those circumstances more than five years. After that? Who knew? Maybe the tugging in her heart to return to Florida would be too much to overcome. Yet, she was determined to learn all she could, advance within the bank, make friends and business contacts of those she would bump into again, making sure she left favorable impressions everywhere. What Helena, this striking, tall, olive complexioned beauty, found was that men wanted to be around her. Her ebullience, founded on solid self-esteem and confidence soared when she stepped into a meeting, smiling and upbeat. She was not at all intimidated, and became more and more comfortable as her involvement grew. Her loyalty, love of life, and ready smile made her all the more attractive. Her laugh was infectious and disarming.

She was very smart in banking and had learned and believed in the bank's purpose: "We lend money to help good companies, we want it back, and we charge interest for using it. What's so complicated about that?"

She had indeed made her father proud as she had promised, and when she came home for Christmas, she announced her holiday plans.

"I can only stay a week, Dad. I promised to go on a bank conference trip to Garmisch, near Munich, for New Year's. We'll all go skiing too. I hope you don't mind, *Biyee?*"

"You're skiing in West Germany? Why not Switzerland?" asked Alexander.

"Actually," smiled Helena, "we have found that the West German companies have come back strong during the ten years since the end of the war, and several leaders of European industries will be there. France too has grown, but their political situation, like Italy's, is still a problem; too many Communists and banks hate Communists. Now, with the success of the Marshall Plan, the European countries have really rebounded. So, after our holiday in Garmisch, a team of us is going to be calling on companies in Munich, Frankfurt, Stuttgart, and Marseille, France. I think I'll be in Marseille for more than a week."

"Marseille? Why Marseille?" Alexander quickly asked in a pronounced tone of voice that surprised his daughter. The sound of the city's name stirred Alexander as he subconsciously twisted the ring.

"Our research indicates there is a terrific potential in Western Europe, particularly in France, West Germany, Spain, and even Switzerland. But Credit Suisse has a virtual monopoly in Switzerland for now. Spain and even Portugal have some strange laws that are so different from English Common Law that we are familiar with. So, we think we can do just fine by focusing on England, France, and West Germany, and staying out of Spain and Portugal for the time being."

She continued enthusiastically, "Marseille has always been a vital port of call and departure for shipping and trading companies. It has quite a history too."

This last remark got Alexander's attention. "Yes, it certainly has quite a history, Helena," he replied, with a slight smile, remembering, as he thought of his own history there while he rubbed the ring with his left hand.

"I may spend a lot of time in Marseille as well as Paris, Dad."

"Hmmm," said Alexander. "So, you will be in Marseille after New Year's. Do you know that I lived in Marseille for nearly six weeks, Helena?"

He looked at his hands and saw his finger fondling the ring. When he looked back at his daughter, he saw she too was watching him rub the ring. Helena felt a twinge of nostalgia as she recalled her dying mother's wish that she someday ask her father about his ring. Alexander saw her eyes move from the ring to his eyes, tacitly asking him to say something. He put his hand away.

"Of course, I was just a boy then, in 1920, after the first war."

During these times alone or when Alexander visited his sister and her family in Orlando, his emotions would do battle in their ambivalence. Leila had her husband, her home and her family, including three grandchildren, and he was happy for her. But his visits reminded him too of what was missing in his life. Without Helene in his life, he really had no sense of belonging to someone. Helena's life was full and moving on. Yet, he felt lonelier than he could recall. His desire to change that caused him to think more and more of Madeleine, and their love and intimacy in Marseille. He realized that those characteristics he loved in Helene were so similarly lovable in Madeleine. Both loved life, both were nurturing, and he had loved both. While his love for Helene had culminated in marriage, his deep affection for Madeleine had never truly been resolved. There was a growing sense of urgency in him that he had to bring that relationship to a resolution or he would never be at peace with himself. It was time to do something!

During his drive home from Orlando, his thoughts turned completely to Madeleine. He resolutely parked the car in the gravel driveway near the door, and with a newfound attitude of determination walked briskly from the house to the lake's shore. There, under a darkening thunder-cloud filled sky heavy with moisture roiling above him, he stepped onto the wood planked dock and walked to its end two hundred feet out into the lake. With a firm jaw, he placed his hands on his hips and stared out into the distance, just as he did on the ranch or in the groves when he had faced a major decision he had been pondering for some time. While looking across the lake, then up at the power of the clouds, he felt a sudden sense of energy that seemed to pull him from his two years of malaise.

He knew he needed to make a decision. This could not go on. It was getting too painful. Indecision was something that was always difficult for him to live with. Creases in his brow brought by serious thought gave way to a thin smile that began to form at the corner of his lips as he looked across the large lake whose surface was broken by choppy, steady wind-driven waves lapping at the dock's pillars. He looked up at the dark gray thunderclouds, building and churning as they threatened to bring a powerful, seasonal storm. A single osprey sailed with the wind across the lake. The quickening wind, brought by the cooling rain clouds, suddenly increased in strength and seemed to be sending him a signal. Facing into the wind, he brushed his thick gray-speckled, dark brown hair to the side as he felt it respond to the wind. His deep brown eyes opened larger as though he was looking east across a vast ocean. He thought deeply for a long time and became transformed, his teeth clenched as his hands formed two fists down by his side. He felt energized and empowered by finally coming to a decision. The first lightning flashes struck offshore brightening the lake's surface…then a sharp thunderclap… and another bright flash.

Alexander shouted into the wind as if to reinforce his solution. "I don't want to be alone anymore…Why should I? It is time…I will find her. I will go to Marseille and find Madeleine, no matter how long it takes. I will find her!" He shook his fist at the sky. "It is time. I will go now!

"There…it is done…I have decided!" He stood tall and rigid and stretched his arms to the sky, beseeching its powers.

He was convinced that he would find her no matter what it took or how long. He now knew it! At this moment of decision, of his commitment, he absolutely believed God's universe would conspire to assist him in his quest. Another major flash of lightning seemed to make his point. Then seconds later, another even louder thunderclap.

That evening he excitedly called his daughter in New York to tell her he was going away for awhile and was anxious to get started.

"Helena, when I finally decide, I cannot delay taking action any longer. That's who I am."

At first, Helena assumed that he was probably returning to Lebanon to revisit his childhood village of Douma. But then, remembering her mother's words, she paused on the phone and swallowed thickly before asking what she knew was a very personal intrusion. She simply couldn't stop herself.

"*Biyee*, does this new upbeat sound in your voice and your decision to travel have anything at all to do with the ring you always wear on your finger? Are you going to Marseille?"

Alexander's forehead furrowed quizzically as he listened to Helena's question, surprised at her query. He then realized he would have to be absolutely honest with his daughter and try to explain that this trip would in no way reflect any lessening of his devotion to his family. He knew it would not be easy, but he had to be totally forthright with her to spare her any pain or confusion.

"Yes, Helena," he said with a mixture of compassion and forthrightness, "I am going to Marseille. I need to begin my new life. I must try to locate a dear friend from long ago. I'm sure you will understand, *y'slemly*. Tomorrow, after I see Wilbur and deal with business, I'll fly from Tampa to New York. Please arrange a room for me in the city. We'll have dinner the next evening and discuss my trip. I'll explain everything to you and we can discuss whatever you wish."

"Thank you, Daddy. I would like that."

Helena felt relieved and a bit apprehensive, sure his explanation would be difficult for both of them. She felt a strange sensation while listening to her father initially like a co-conspirator with him, then experiencing a brief sense of betrayal to her mother.

But she remembered her mother's admonition when they spoke those last days, "Life is for the living, my darling. You have a full life ahead of you. Live it.

And don't let your father be lonely. I know he loves me, but he must move on. He is still young. And if you ever hear the story about the ring as I asked of you, remember, I know he has always loved me, and anything that happened before our life together was not important to me or to our marriage. Never forget what I tell you now."

Helena, comforted, looked forward to her father's visit all the more.

Your reason and your passion are the rudder and sails of your
seafaring soul…let your soul exalt your reason to the height of
passion, that it may sing…
Kahlil Gibran

CHAPTER 21

New York, 1959

Two days later, they met at the Waldorf-Astoria Hotel. Helena squeezed her father's hand across the table and lovingly smiled at him as they sat in the hotel's elegantly decorated dining room. Their booth was in a quiet corner. Fitting, she thought, for they needed time without distractions.

"This is nice, Daddy. I'm glad you came here so we could have this time together."

Deciding that the Waldorf was an appropriate choice for her father's visit, she had made a reservation for him there. She knew that he would never have selected the city's most expensive hotel, staying true to his frugal nature and lack of self-indulgence. But, she felt that he had worked very hard all his life, had reached a respectable level of wealth and prominence, and deserved the very best. So, at the last minute, she had booked him a suite.

Now here they were, father and daughter, to discuss this new adventure of his, totally out of keeping from all she knew of her father's rural life in Kissimmee. She was quite surprised at her father's behavior and certainly had mixed emotions about his sudden decision to go to Marseille, France.

Helena felt a slight disappointment, or perhaps a semblance of pain. She had a fear that possibly her parents' relationship had not been all it had seemed to be, that maybe a secret life, somehow, had been kept from the light of day, so to speak. *Did my father truly love my mother, she asked herself, or was it just a surface relationship? No,* she thought, *it was real. But who or what is it my father is seeking to find? How much does that person mean to him?* During their dinner, Alexander deliberately delayed presenting the real reason for their meeting and tried to start the evening with light conversation in a fatherly way by asking about his daughter's career and other aspects of her personal life.

Helena, curious, yet keeping her professional demeanor in order to control her inner turmoil and eagerness to hear her father's words, enjoyed telling her father about her life in New York. Finally, anxiously waiting to hear about his intentions, she brought up the true subject of his visit.

"Please, *Biyee*, tell me what is on your mind, what you are feeling. Daddy, I want to know. Look at me and tell me what this is all about, what it means. Please," she repeated, looking deep into his eyes.

Alexander felt his daughter's hand squeeze his as he looked with love and concern into her eyes. As he did, he could see her eyes moisten, belying her vulnerability. It was a poignant moment for both of them. He could not hurt his daughter...his only child. He had to be honest in a way that she could understand without condemning him. Alexander knew he had to present to his daughter his entire story to assuage her concerns as best he could, not completely sure she would understand, recognizing her closeness to her mother, especially in the final weeks of Helene's illness. For an instant he mentally connected her pain to his when his own mother died while her husband, his own father, was away. Uneasily, he began…"Helena, my lovely daughter, you embody all the dreams of your father and your mother. I love you, and I loved your mother. I revere her memory and am grateful to God for our many years together, for the gifts of you and your brother, and our sharing of our lives together for so many years. But, it is hard for me now, and has been since your mother passed away." He paused to gather his thoughts though his eyes never left hers, then continued speaking almost in a whisper, carefully and gently, "I cannot live alone. I have too much love to give. I am aching inside, *Biyee*. I believe your mother would feel the same way. After having a happy marriage for so long, it is too difficult. The emptiness, the loneliness. It makes me sad all the time."

He reminded himself to be very sensitive to Helena's concerns. Although she was now a mature, educated and bright woman, she was still her mother's only daughter and that bond they had always shared would very naturally cause her to be protective of her mother's memory even though she respected and loved her father.

Softly, deliberately, he told her, "Helena, after my mother died, may she rest in peace, *Allia hummah*," he wiped his eyes and continued, "when I was very young, at her urging, I decided I had to leave the mountains of Lebanon. I left all that I knew and everyone who was dear to me, except my father and sister who were already in America. I had to leave my brother, my home, my cousins, my beloved village, my mountains, and my ancient cedars of our homeland. I was an innocent 18-year-old boy."

As he recalled his youth, Helena knew he was terribly saddened. She watched with emotion as his eyes moistened while he spoke of his memories.

"You know some of my history, but I am now going to tell you about a part of my life no one else knows. I am going to entrust with you a part of my life I have never shared with anyone. You must trust me, and you must accept with love what I tell you because it is the truth. Your mother, *Allia hummah*, may God rest her soul," he whispered, hoping Helena understood. "Your mother did not ask about my past and it was never an issue between us. I gave my whole life to her and to my children. I don't believe I have to tell you that I have been totally committed to my family. You know I have been, Helena."

Helena nodded, her eyes heavy, as she listened, not yet sure where he was going, nor was she totally comfortable with this conversation. Nervously shifting slightly in her chair, she reached to her purse for a tissue and dabbed her eyes. She knew they were getting close to something that could cause her to lose control.

A bit wistfully, he looked across the table at his beautiful daughter, seeing her for the first time in a stylish business suit. He sat back, sipped from his glass of water, placed the corner of a napkin with his free hand to his lips, and took a moment to think while gathering his thoughts, their eyes locked into each other's. He spoke in a low soft voice as he leaned toward his daughter, both arms folded on the table, carefully choosing his words. Helena's eyebrows pursed, causing a crease between them as she wondered how his words were going to impact her feelings.

"I bunked in steerage on an old World War I converted Turkish steamer ship from Beirut to Marseille to board another ship to New York. I hoped to get to New York quickly and meet my father, but I had to stay over in Marseille six weeks before I could leave for New York."

"Was the trip difficult, *Biyee?*" interrupted Helena, prodding him, trying to ease her father's concern for her sensitivities.

"I can tell you it was awful…the worst experience I have ever had. I got sick almost all the time just like everyone else and spent most of my days bending over the railings. I was fresh from the mountains and had never been on a boat. I have never sailed on another ship like that again, and likely never will. My friend Butrus and I leaped, literally leaped, onto the pier when we reached Marseille, we were so grateful." He smiled, breaking the tension he felt in his muscles. As the words he spoke struck him, he laughed. "We were very happy to be on land, in France, and off that old boat!"

For the next hour, Alexander softly described the six weeks of his stay in Marseille, leaving out no detail. She could tell from his voice he was recalling truly happy times in his life. His face brightened and his demeanor seemed uplifted and cheery. And she was pleased. He told her of Uncle Hanna and Daniella. He described his adventures and his growing feelings toward Madeleine, his first love, this 16-year-old vivacious beauty. He told of the days in the parks, *Les Calanques*, the day on the cliff, and the moment she gave him the ring and he gave her his treasured cross.

Helena asked to hold the ring. Alexander slowly twisted the ring from his finger as he watched Helena's face. Then slowly, he handed it over to his daughter. It was the first time he had ever let anyone touch Madeleine's gold ring.

"So that's how you got this," she exclaimed with a look of wonder on her face.

"She was the most beautiful, most charming creature I ever saw, Helena. She swept me off my feet. She was 16, two years younger than me. Can you understand? For a long time I couldn't think of anything or anyone but her. Yet ever since your mother and I married I have always focused on the present each day. Although I have never removed this ring, I have always been devoted to your mother and you children. However, I must confess to you that after these two years since your mother's death the memory of Madeleine has re-entered my thoughts during my loneliness."

He took in a deep breath, then let it out slowly, trying to ease his tensions. "This is an unresolved part of my life. It lingers with me and haunts me. There is a void, an emotional emptiness. Can you understand what I'm telling you? I must somehow find a resolution. I owe it to myself. Actually, Helena, as I think about this situation, I believe I owe its resolution to you as well as to myself."

Then relaxing back into his chair, he lowered his eyelids as his hands twisted his cloth napkin. Wanting to connect with his daughter, he reached for Helena's hand. "As you know, I am a passionate man. I do not love for a moment or a day. When I love, it is totally and forever. I will always love your mother. Yet, I must admit to you that I still feel love toward Madeleine."

He stared into her eyes looking for a sign, hoping she understood.

"Helena, I was surrounded by love when I was young. I lost that love when I lost my mother, when I was only 12 years old. I loved and still love my brother, Milhelm. And only two years ago I lost my wife, your mother, my life's companion. Before that, I lost my only son, your brother Michael. Now, however, I cannot continue without doing everything in my power to resolve the feelings I have for Madeleine. She is the only one left for me, Helena."

Then he hastened to add, "This in no way takes from my love for you, nor for your mother's memory. It is separate. It is vital. It is my destiny that I must follow that path until I find her. I promised long ago to return for Madeleine, but we lost touch before I met your mother. Now, I will search for her until I find her, or find out what happened to her. You'll simply have to understand, and know that I need your support." He was now almost pleading with her.

Helena listened intently and, surprising even herself, began to recognize how proud she was of her father. She had inherited her father's intense warmth and passion. She could do nothing but listen with a sense of love, compassion, of even a feeling of vicarious excitement for her father. She leaned back, having let go of her father's hand, and lowered her eyelids while the beginning of a small smile crept onto her face as she accepted her father's plight. She searched for the words to let her father know she understood, surprising even herself, and that she did not find what he felt and told her to be offensive to her or her mother's memory. She, in her young, yet independent and worldly way, understood that he had to do what he had to do. Her very thoughts caused her to smile and nod her head to him. She did not feel threatened, but felt instead empathy, a compassionate, stronger emotional bonding with her father. She also knew it would be impossible to change her father's mind. That, she knew, would be unfair, casting a sense of guilt on him, causing him great conflict. It would be an exercise in futility…an exercise she was not about to initiate. In a way, she identified with his dilemma, his devotion to his heart's yearnings. It reminded her of what she had read in Kahlil Gibran's *The Prophet*. It was that book her father had given each of his children on their sixteenth Christmas, explaining that *The Prophet* was written by a close friend of Uncle Salim in Boston, now deceased, and that Gibran was from Bsharre, a village north of and very close to Douma, his own village. "Read the chapters on friendship and love, especially the chapter on children, and you, our gift from God, will better understand what life is truly about," he had said when he gave her her own copy.

The Prophet was very popular at Vassar she remembered. Much of it was used in her philosophy classes as well as by the girls in the dormitories and sororities as they talked in groups at night, discovering and exploring their philosophy of life, relationships, friendships, and, of course, love.

"When Love beckons to you, follow him," Helena spoke aloud, remembering Gibran's words as she looked at her father.

"Oh, Daddy," she exclaimed, reaching for his hands, "I love you so much. Please, go find her. Find Madeleine, follow your heart, Daddy. It would be selfish to ask you not to. And Momma was not a selfish person. I know she would understand. She always told me her life was totally devoted to your happiness, Daddy." Helena felt her eyes well up. Wiping her cheeks she continued, "I know you were always devoted to her. She would want you to be happy and as fulfilled as possible."

"Thank you, Helena. Your mother was the most wonderful, most giving woman a man could ever hope to find. She was selfless. She nurtured. She gave. She understood. I know that I tried to be the same way with her. That is why I do not feel a sense of betrayal or guilt. Believe me, since your mother died, I have prayed a lot for guidance, for acceptance, for strength, and for understanding. Now I am at peace with God and the memory of your mother. But it was most important that you listened to me tell you what was in my heart. I can't tell you how much I appreciate your understanding and your encouragement to resolve these haunting emotions I must deal with." He smiled and held out his hands to her. "*Allah ma'ak.*"

She squeezed his hands as she whispered to him, looking into his deep brown fluid-filled eyes, "*Allah ma'ak*, Daddy."

And since you are a breath in God's sphere
and a leaf in God's forest,
you too should rest in reason and move in passion.
Kahlil Gibran

CHAPTER 22

New York, 1959

Sitting in his seat by the window on the flight from New York's Idlewild Airport the next afternoon, Alexander felt relaxed, optimistic yet anxious, like a great burden had been taken from him following his painful but positive visit with Helena. He had been torn by the compelling need to be honest with his daughter, though very much aware that there was a risk she might possibly resent his desire or, his need to search for his first love. He sought a message of forgiveness from Helene through Helena's response, indicative of a daughter's bond with her mother. He had asked himself that question a hundred times before reaching New York. Thank God she understood.

He was grateful that his only daughter was as empathetic toward him as she was protective of her mother's memory. And it made all the difference to Alexander as he turned his thoughts from their conversation to the searching journey he must now make. Helena's office had arranged his itinerary from New York to Marseille. He would fly from New York to London, then to Paris. From Paris, he would ride the train to Marseille where he would begin his quest to find Madeleine and recapture the memories of his youth.

Throughout his transatlantic flight, he realized that while he was, as was his nature since boyhood, optimistic that he would indeed find Madeleine. As he gazed out the window of the airplane, he also felt the growing sense of reality that it had been nearly forty years.

"Forty years!" he whispered to himself. "Who am I kidding?" It was the question he had not yet allowed himself to think about. Instead, as was his nature, he kept all negative thoughts pushed back, not allowing them to deter him from his goals. "Be sure 95% of the time," he said to the window.

His cupped his right hand under his chin as he rested his elbow on the seat's armrest. Helena had convinced him to travel first class, contrary to his frugal habit of not frivolously spending money on himself.

"You deserve it, Daddy," she had smiled at the hotel. "Let me take care of your travel arrangements. We have a travel department at the bank that will make all the preparations, including drivers in every city. You should travel like the bank's executives. They often make very successful and important business contacts in first class too." She had arranged window seats for him on each flight, giving him the option of visiting with his neighbor or not, enabling him to courteously avoid conversation if he chose. He was, after all, on a mission, not a pleasure trip.

Reluctantly, he had accepted her advice. Now comfortable in his over-sized seat, he was glad he did.

Helena had arranged for a connecting flight to Paris after Alexander had insisted that he did not want to take the time to be transported into London for a few days layover. "I want to get to France as soon as possible," he had told her. "London can wait until later. Get me to Paris," he had insisted. He had to wait three hours anyway because he still had to go through customs and London's Passport Control before being permitted to leave the main terminal to be transported to the separate Air France terminal for his continuing flight. By the time he had verified his luggage transfer in the early morning light, passed through the second passport control booth, stepped down to the concrete pad where the connecting plane rested, and climbed the steps to the door of the Air France propeller-driven DC-6, he was aware he was nearly exhausted. It wasn't until he finally boarded the plane, walked the few steps down the narrow aisle, found his seat and settled in, that he could relax. His body was tired and drowsiness quickly overcame him. He fell asleep thinking of Madeleine as the wheels left the runway and the flight was en route to Paris, France.

The man standing in the terminal was holding a sign reading:
"M. A. Thomas."
"I am Monsieur Thomas," Alexander said, recalling his French.
"Monsieur Alexander Thomas?" inquired the man.
"Yes, that is me."
"Come with me, Monsieur. The car is waiting for you at the curb. I am to take you to The Maurice Hotel. I will go now and collect your luggage. Please wait here for me."

He marveled at his daughter's attention to detail.

The driver flagged a porter, handed him the luggage coupons and instructed him to bring the suitcases to the black Peugeot at the curb. With a nod, the porter followed his instructions. Within minutes, the driver had placed Alexander's four suitcases in the trunk of the taxi, settled in, and began the forty-five minute drive into the city.

The sedan pulled up to the curb at the Maurice Hotel in the middle of the city. Immediately, the formally attired doorman opened the rear passenger door allowing Alexander to step out. Alexander barely noticed the tall, stunningly lovely brunette woman stepping into the taxicab in front of his after she left the hotel with two suitcases.

"Welcome to the Maurice Hotel, Monsieur. Your name, *s'il vous plait?*"

"Alexander Thomas. I'll be staying one night, perhaps two, sir."

Early the next morning, as the sun's brightness entered the room through a crack in the drapes, Alexander awoke in his room with a start. He looked at his watch to check the time. As accustomed as he was in Florida to always get started at 7 a.m., waking in response to a wake-up call in Paris now at that hour was just two in the morning in Kissimmee. Still, he was anxious to begin his first full day in France. He remembered he had made an appointment at the U.S. Embassy to make the staff aware of his mission in France, to gain advice in accomplishing his task and insight as to how best to proceed. He picked up the ornate French-styled phone from its cradle and waited for the operator's voice, then ordered breakfast. He enjoyed his Continental foods, especially the croissants with local cheeses and jellies, boiled eggs, coffee, and juice. "Hmm," he thought with a smile, "this juice is really good!" He couldn't help but smile at himself as he compared it to his own orange juice. As he sat at the table on the terrace balcony of his luxurious suite, he couldn't help but peer over the ornate wrought iron railing and look around the city, marveling at its broad expanse of dense buildings anchored by the famous Eiffel Tower, Paris' tallest structure. *It's not as tall as I imagined.*

When he stepped back inside the suite with his cup of coffee, he surveyed its elegant interior. He was in one of the most desirable hotels in the world, he reminded himself as he selected a period Louis XIV chair, sat down, slid back, and felt the smooth, taut fabric and, for a moment, while admiring the exquisite furnishings, couldn't help but remember the bare furnishings in Uncle Hanna's apartment in Marseille that he had shared with Butrus so long ago. He smiled at the incredible contrast.

Remembering his father's admonitions, he told himself aloud, "Never forget your beginnings. Remember your roots, *Biyee,* and you will stay humbled and happy. Enjoy the fruits of your labors, yes, but never forget."

After his morning shower, he shaved and dressed, remembering to check outside the door for his shoes. The porter had told him to leave his shoes at his door so they would be shined for him before morning. Alexander had, for his entire life in America, shined his own shoes. In Douma, and even in Kissimmee, shining shoes was a luxury few, if any, could afford. Certainly, as a boy, his well-worn shoes and sandals were more for protection than for dress. But in Europe, he followed their custom even though, out of habit, he had made sure he had brought his own shoe polish and brush.

After his meetings at the Embassy where he was instructed to call on the Consul General in Marseille, he ate lunch, and undertook a preliminary meeting, as he was advised, at the government Hall of Records in Paris where he received a perfunctory lesson in records search, but no information of value. After a fruitless, frustrating morning, he returned to the hotel.

Anxiously hoping to find some answers in Marseille, he caught a taxi to the central rail station to board his train to the south of France. He would arrive in that port city before nightfall, where he knew he would spend his first of many evenings at a certain café on *Place de Liban*. He could hardly contain his emotions as he boarded the train, checked his luggage, and took his window seat. His thoughts immediately turned to Madeleine. "I'm coming for you, Madeleine. I'm coming back to Marseille, finally, my love," he whispered to himself as he looked out the window, his heart filled with anticipation. As he watched the countryside pass by, his mind began playing with his imagination. *How can you expect that she will be in Marseille after all this time? Are you acting like a foolish old man? You are, after all, fifty-six years old acting like an infatuated teenager. Do you really expect she will look the same? Do I? Will she care anymore? Does she have a husband? Does she have children? Is she even alive? What am I doing? Am I really being fair to Helena?* A frown formed on his face for a moment as he thought about the wisdom of returning home. *After all*, he reminded himself, *she had never written to him in response to his many letters.*

But he knew he was doing what he had to do to fulfill his heart's desire and find resolution, or he would never get on with his life. He had fallen deeply, completely in love with Madeleine. She was his passion, his soul mate. She would always be so. His mind couldn't stop focusing on the total bonding they both had felt toward each other and the belief that God had blessed their union. He remembered…how they had become essential to each other…the electric sensations he had felt just seeing her each of those days in Marseille…the powerful and exciting emotions that were beyond anything he had ever felt before or since…the spontaneous outbursts of joy, of love, of mutual attraction, of their laughter…almost giddiness… as they explored each day together, enjoying every moment. She had become a vital part of his life so quickly. "Your soul is entwined with mine," he murmured aloud to no one, staring out the window watching the vineyards of southern France whiz by, almost as a blur, reminding him it would not be long now.

You are and will always be my life's love, dear Madeleine. Wherever you are, I will find you. I swear it.

"Marseille…Marseille, *s'il vous plait*. It is time," the conductor announced as he approached Alexander's row of seats, interrupting his thoughts.

Alexander felt the train slow down as the conductor stopped at his seat, bracing his feet as the train slowed, responding to the steel brakes being forcefully applied to the wheels.

"We are here. And thank you Monsieur Thomas for telling me your beautiful love story. It is wonderful that after all these years you did not forget, that you are seeking to complete your destiny. You are a determined romantic, are you not? Perhaps your heart is, in truth, French," the conductor chuckled.

"*Merci*," Alexander smiled to the conductor. "I'm grateful that you were not too busy to listen to a man who has lived a full life, who was too poor when young to remain with the first love of his life, but had to wait thirty-eight years…thirty-eight long years to determine it was time, time to find his lost love, time to follow his heart." His voice grew firm, "We have but one life to live, only one, and none of it should be wasted. Indeed, I did not waste those thirty-eight years. I had a wonderful marriage. I worked very hard and did well. I was loyal to my dear wife and we raised two lovely children. But after she was taken from me, I found the only way I could be fulfilled was to leave everything and find my lost love, Madeleine." He loved saying her name aloud. "And now, here I am, returning to where we first met, to trace our steps, to recover the love of my heart, my very soul I left behind so very long ago. I am here once again. And I thank you, sir." He shook the friendly conductor's outstretched hand.

"*Bonne chance, mon ami.*"

Moments later, Alexander departed the train with a small wave to his new friend. Outside the terminal, he signaled for a taxicab, instructing the driver, "Drive me to the *Panier* by the Joliette pier, *s'il vous plait*. I am late, very late for a reunion," he smiled with new energy.

"You wish to go to the docks, Monsieur? Would you not prefer your hotel or a restaurant on the *Canebière*?"

"Later, driver, later, but first, if it is still there, please take me to the *Place de Lenche*, or as it was called, the *Place de Liban*."

Alexander first wanted to go to the familiar *Panier* to revisit the spot where they first met. Then, he would have the driver deliver him to the Charles V Hotel on the *Canebière*, not far from Madeleine's mother's shop he had visited so many times long ago when he was young.

And let your soul direct your passion with reason,
that your passion may live through its own daily resurrection,
and like the phoenix, rise above its own ashes.
Kahlil Gibran

CHAPTER 23

Alexander carefully watched the mostly five-story stucco buildings pass by as he settled in the backseat of the taxi, remembering, but also noticing how much things had changed, which increased his apprehension. There were new buildings everywhere, especially along the *Vieux Port* and the *Panier* waterfront.

"Everything seems different here by the port, driver," he remarked aloud. "I can't believe those rows and rows of new buildings along the *Quai du Port*."

"*Oui*, Monsieur, ." the taxi driver sought to explain,

With a scowl he reminisced and responded to Alexander's question, "This part of the *Panier* was destroyed by Hitler and the Vichy government because they are so close to the rail yards and the port. They knew the *Panier* was a breeding area for anti-Nazi sentiment. Then it was heavily bombarded during the 1944 invasion to rid the city of the Germans near the end of the war. After the war, the rubble was removed and the government rebuilt these more modern apartment and office buildings. They are handsome, don't you think?"

"And so new looking. Alexanderr retorted, "The *Panier* has always been known for its older buildings, a place for poor immigrants, is it not?" Then noticing a cluster of flowering bushes, he exclaimed, "Ah," Alexander commented, "I remember this park although the flowering trees, benches and shrubs seem different and new."

"Well," his driver replied over his shoulder, "Much of that park was replanted after the bombardment. There were many new *jardins* built in tribute to the French who lost their lives during the war. That particular park, dedicated to those of the *Resistance* who lost their lives, is lovely, don't you agree?"

Acknowledging the beauty of the new garden, Alexander's emotions on his quest began alternating between angst, nostalgia and excitement. His eyes scanned the old commercial port, now filled with small sailboats, mostly pleasure crafts, and fishing boats.

"Do the fishermen still sell their catch each day along the docks on the *Panier* side of the quay?" he asked the driver as he pointed in that direction.

"No, Monsieur, actually the fish market has relocated to the north end of the *Vieux Port*, closer to the *Canebière* where it is more convenient. It's not as large as before, but still, the fishermen daily offer he best fresh fish, escargots, while other merchants now offer goods like wine, handmade candles and soaps, flowers and perfumes. Still, he fresh seafood is the main draw for shoppers even today."

"Well, it's still beautiful, but so different." Now, driver, please take me to *Place de Lenche* for a few minutes. I wish to see if a certain cafe remains today."

Alexander felt a little dizzy as he sensed being a mental observer of Madeleine and himself when he was eighteen years old, a sort of "out of body" experience.

A few minutes later the driver waved his left arm. "There is the Café Liban. Perhaps that is the restaurant you wish to visit," he said, pointing out the window. "Do you recognize what you are looking for?"

Then, he asked, "Monsieur, would you like to stop here now or go directly to your hotel?"

Alexander sat up in the seat, looking up at the plaza with its familiar tall sycamore trees and their paper-thin, multi-colored trunks' skin and large green leaves shading the tables and chairs beneath.

"I've seen what I want to see, driver," Alexander responded, settling back into his seat behind the driver. "Yes, please take me to the hotel."

Thinking he might earn a good fee if he attached himself to this American tourist, the driver said to Alexander over his shoulder, "Monsieur, *pardon moi*, would you like me to be your driver during your stay in Marseille? I have lived here all of my life. I was born here in 1910, before the first Great War. Perhaps I will be familiar with all that you need to find, or to ask about. And I have many friends in the Lebanese community as well."

Lost in his thoughts for a moment, Alexander replied, "I am looking for an old friend since before the second war. Do you think you can help me?"

"Well, *je ne sais pas*, it will be difficult but I'll try. I know many people, and the police are my friends. We shall see. Try me. Oh, Monsieur, my name is Jacques du Chavelle."

Alexander nodded, "Let me think about this. My name is Alexander Thomas. I'll check into the hotel, rest, and take a shower. I'd like you to return in two hours to pick me up. I particularly wish to be taken to the Notre-Dame-de-la-Garde before the sun sets."

"*Merci*, Monsieur Thomas. I will return in two hours."

"Thank you, Jacques. Six o'clock then."

Minutes later, Alexander exited the taxicab as the doorman opened his door to welcome him.

"Welcome to the Charles V Hotel, Monsieur. May I deliver your luggage?"

"*Merci*," Alexander smiled as he nodded before he stepped to the heavy glass double entry doors. He was pleased with the elegance of the lobby, with its period furnishings. His feet felt the change from the polished marble floor to the plush carpet as he stepped to the registry desk.

"Passport, Monsieur? Kindly fill out this card. And how long will you be staying with us? Ah, Monsieur Thomas, welcome, sir," he exclaimed with a pleasant smile, "we have been expecting you. Everything is in order. The bank confirmed your arrival just this morning. I will have your luggage taken to your suite immediately. Welcome to the Charles V Hotel."

Alexander couldn't keep a small smile form on his lips as he noted the incredible contrast when compared to his arrival at Uncle Hanna's office so many years ago.

As he stepped into his luxurious suite, Alexander, turning his head to view the entire space, smiled broadly, and said aloud as he opened his arms and surveyed the room, "Well, Butrus, Marseille is certainly different than it was for us in 1920, thanks to Helena's cosmopolitan tastes and my good fortune." Then he whispered to himself, "Now, if I can find Madeleine, everything will be perfect."

After unpacking and showering, Alexander lay down to rest, placing his head on the finely textured white cotton down pillows with their crocheted fringes and fell fast asleep.

Promptly at six o'clock, the taxicab pulled up to the curb. Alexander was waiting, standing at the curb before the hotel's entry.

"Very good, Jacques. Let's go to the cathedral now. I would like to visit awhile and look at the sea at this special time of day."

After a brief but poignant visit to the cathedral, he had the driver take him to the Corniche, passing by the Jardin du Pharo, and farther east to *Les Calanques*.

"Stop here, Jacques," he instructed, tapping the driver's shoulder.

"Here?"

"*Oui*. I want to look at the cliffs here and the small cove below," he gestured. "These are important places for me."

For the next fifteen minutes, while his driver stood beside the Peugeot and waited patiently as he kept an eye on his passenger, Alexander retraced the familiar places he had walked hand in hand with Madeleine, looking and thinking.

Over there is where we were. He smiled, remembering, as he looked toward the grassy spot where he and Madeleine had shared their love and whispered, *Here you are, my beautiful Madeleine. And here I am.* He sat down on a stone ledge and, facing the sea, gazed at the same panorama they had shared so long ago. The sun was nearing the horizon. He looked to his right and focused on the sea, smiling as his thoughts focused on Madeleine, their closeness, their sharing, her face. He could never, ever forget.

After the sun started to set and before darkness began to envelop the sea, Alexander looked around one last time, then walked hesitatingly to the waiting taxi. Suddenly, he stopped for just a moment, looked back over his shoulder and whispered, "I will be back. I will return to this place with you, my beloved Madeleine. I promise."

"To the restaurant, Monsieur Thomas?"

"*Oui*, Jacques. *Place de Lenche* and the café."

Alexander watched the vaguely familiar streets pass by the taxi's windows. He focused on the older buildings, small parks, new hotels and office buildings, eager to spot a particularly significant sight.

"Here we are," spoke the driver, over his shoulder. "Here is the *Place de Lenche*, or *Place de Liban* as the Lebanese call it. Go up those steps and you'll see the Café Liban, on your left."

"Hmm..." replied Alexander, "it's amazing. The park and the apartments really look so much the same. The café's sign is newer, but the restaurant is still there! The front of the buildings have improved, some of the shutters look the same, some look freshly painted, but the tables are placed almost exactly as before, and I see the backgammon games on the tables. Isn't that something? It is said that 'the more things change, the more they remain the same.' It is true, *n'est-ce pas?*"

"Yes, it is true," replied the attentive driver. "Would you like me to return to take you to back to your hotel, Monsieur?"

"No, *merci*. I'll find my way back. I'll enjoy the walk."

The minute Alexander stepped from the taxi onto the stone street and walked up the stone steps to the restaurant's front door, carefully stepping between the tables and chairs so not to disturb the customers, or bump into the hustling waiters in their familiar outfits, he felt a powerful poignancy sweep his consciousness, much like what he felt at the cathedral and on the Corniche. Everything was familiar to him, causing delicious memories to flood his consciousness.

"My God," he said aloud, "the memories are so strong. I had no idea I would feel this way." His eyes seemed to glaze over as his mind went back, and yet they saw so many things that made him seem miles away.

The waiter, noticing how distant his customer appeared, interrupted Alexander's thoughts, asking, "May I help you, Monsieur." Like the other waiters, he was dressed in black pants and white shirt, a small white towel apron tucked in his waist. He had a thick moustache, typical of Middle Eastern men. As customary, all the waiters serving the clientele of Café Liban were men. And just as customary, the person at the cash registry by the front door was the co-owner, a serious-looking, dreary woman, perhaps in her sixties, dressed in a dark burgundy dress with a black hand-crocheted shawl draped over her shoulders, her long graying hair twisted into a bun in the back. Her expression and facial lines belied her destiny. She had worked hard most of her life, much of it tending the cash register in the restaurant she and her husband owned. At the instant Alexander stepped in, the lady smiled with a friendly welcome that relaxed him. By the look on her face and her demeanor, Alexander quickly formed a more favorable impression of her, hoping she would know something of Hanna, Daniella, and Madeleine.

"*Ahlen wa sahlen*," she greeted him, immediately recognizing Alexander as being of Lebanese or Syrian heritage. "*Ibn* Arab? Are you the son of an Arab?"

"*Oui*, I am Lebanese."

"Ahhh…welcome. Please come in and make yourself comfortable, Monsieur. But you are American, aren't you?"

"Yes, but I was born in Lebanon," he proudly responded. "Let me guess. Are you, with your husband, the owner of Café Liban?"

"We bought it from the estate of the owner at that time, Hanna Chalhoub."

"Oh, my God," replied Alexander, "Hanna was my uncle. Can you help me? I am seeking to find a dear friend who was close to my uncle, *Khali* Hanna, many years ago. Did you know him and his friend Daniella DuBois?"

Her face lit up, her eyes widened as she smiled. "Yes, of course, we knew Hanna and Daniella very well. We were terribly sad, and angry, when they were lost during the invasion."

"*Mon Dieu*! How did it happen?" he exclaimed, shocked, never having heard anything about the war's impact on his uncle or Daniella. From 1939, neither he nor any relatives in Boston received any word, mail or otherwise, from Marseille or Douma. Most didn't write letters as news was never good, and government restrictions made writing to America almost impossible. Alexander was totally ignorant of any events in France or Lebanon for more than fifteen years, difficult as it may seem. He too had his life struggles in America during the Great Depression, and while he often thought of his brother Milhelm or Uncle Hanna, there really was little reason compelling enough for him to actually correspond.

His mind raced as did his questions, making the woman smile. "Please tell me as much as you can. When was it? Was Daniella's daughter, Madeleine, with them at the time? Would you sit with me and tell me all you know? Uncle Hanna and Daniella were very good to me when I was here years ago." He didn't want to go into detail regarding Madeleine just yet, but grew hopeful at this possible opportunity to pursue his inquiry.

Looking around the restaurant, he noticed the growing number of diners entering the café as the evening began in earnest. Empathizing with the owner, he quickly added, "Madame, I realize your evening is just beginning and you are busy, but if I could have just a few minutes with you, I would very much appreciate your kindness. I have just flown in from America on an important personal search, and I need your help." Now energized, and six hours ahead of Florida's time, he was not tired although he had had a full day.

"Perhaps I will have more time to spend with you tomorrow, but come sit a moment now with me," she replied tentatively, looking him over, satisfied this man would not be a problem. "I'm always happy to visit. Here, we will talk at this table."

Alexander could tell by the table's location and lack of settings that this table was her choice as she could see the entrance and the kitchen door from the same chair.

In unison, they sat down on the wooden chairs at the table, and, after a moment, were served glasses of wine.

"My name is Wedad. Now, tell me your name, where you have come from, and who you are." She folded her hands, placed them on the table and looked straight into his eyes.

He returned her direct gaze and started, "I am from America. My name is Alexander Thomas. My Arabic name, before Ellis Island," he smiled, "is Iskandar... Iskandar Chalhoub Thomé." For a brief moment, he recalled Madeleine whispering, "Iskandar." His eyes began to moisten as he began telling the proprietor of his past. He instantly felt a rapport with this woman, perhaps, with a willingness to be naively candid and hopeful the possibility existed that she and her husband could help him. He became very relaxed and forthcoming, gesturing over the table as he described his stay in Marseille.

"I first came to Marseille from Beirut in 1920 when I was on my way to America," he began. "I stayed here, in this very building, for six weeks as a guest of my Uncle Hanna. How did you know him?"

"Well, Iskandar, this is a large but in many ways a small community of Lebanese immigrants here in Marseille. We know almost all of our brothers and sisters here, especially those of the *Panier*, and for decades, most of us have attended the same churches, St. Mary's Antiochan Orthodox and the Catholic Church on the hill. Although, I must say, since the Middle East war, many new people have settled here, mostly from the south of Lebanon and from Palestine. But until 1947, most of us were very close, almost like one extended family, as they say. Now, it is much larger and more diverse." She lifted her glass as a demonstration of friendship, then sipped from her glass. "Excuse me," she smiled as she turned and beckoned to the man moving towards her, "here comes my husband, George. He knew Hanna very well."

George, slightly shorter than Alexander, had a handlebar mustache, dark olive complexion, a balding head, and wore a cream-colored, long-sleeved silk shirt and black trousers.

"George, meet Iskandar," she said as George extended a thick, calloused hand to Alexander. "He is seeking information about an old friend of yours, Hanna Chalhoub."

"*Mahrharbahr*," George smiled, returning Alexander's. "Of course. How can I help you, Iskandar?" he asked as he pulled out one of the four wooden chairs at the table and joined his wife and her visitor. "Hanna was a very popular man in Marseille, especially the *Panier*. And after it was found out what he had secretly done to assist the *Resistance* during the dangerous Nazi occupation, the city of Marseille almost built a shrine to him. The entire local Lebanese community wanted to honor him. Yes, he was a good man and a good friend, Iskandar. Now, what can I do to help you? Tell me. I can take a break right now. You have come at a good moment. One hour later and I would have had to ask you to come back tomorrow."

Alexander sat back, sipped from his glass, and ordered a mezza platter of hummus, *baba ghanoush, kibbee, zeytoon, tabouleh, jibneh*, and pita. "This will hold me for the evening," he smiled. "I love this food so much." Then after a bite or two, he paused and, looking directly into the owner's eyes, said, "George, I'll get right to the point. I am on a mission. I have come a long way to find someone and must start here. This is where my story begins. I hope you can help me find Madeleine DuBois, daughter of Daniella DuBois, close companion of Hanna Chalhoub." Alexander paused to take a long breath, trying to determine how much he needed to share with this man. He decided not to go into the details of his relationship with Madeleine, at least not at the moment.

"Iskandar, I will help you all that I can, but I must tell you, Hanna and Daniella were killed during the American invasion of Marseille in September of 1944. They were together and, *Allia hummah*, may they rest in peace, they died practically in each other's arms. They were on the *Canebière* in a restaurant dining when an errant Allied bomb hit that restaurant directly. There were many innocents killed those days from so many poorly aimed cannon shells and bombs. I do not know what happened beyond their being killed at that time. I do know that Daniella's daughter, I believe her name was Madeleine, was not with them. By then, she was a grown woman and married." He caught himself and added, "I believe she had a child. Yes, she had a son."

"Married? A son? Ohh…" Alexander, stunned by the words, frowned, disappointed, then asked with a bit of sadness in his voice, "Did she still live in Marseille at that time?"

"Well, no," he responded, "she left Marseille just before the war actually began. No one knew where she went. Her husband was a leader in the *Resistance*, and a marked man. The Nazis were after him all the time. He and she simply disappeared one day.

"She disappeared?" asked Alexander, opening his arms in wonder. "Does anyone know where she went?"

"*La'a*," replied George, "no one heard from her again, even her mother. And Hanna didn't speak of that either. Her husband was gone much of the time, meeting with groups all over France, never sleeping in the same place two nights in a row. Perhaps he sent her to a safe place. Maybe Switzerland or America?" George's forehead furrowed as he looked to his wife, then questioned himself and Iskandar. "I do not know, my friend," he shrugged, holding both palms up. "I do not know anything more, I am sorry to say."

"Yes," Marie nodded, "her husband was deeply involved in the Underground, and Hanna was close to him. He provided "safe" houses here in the Lebanese sector of the *Panier* throughout the occupation. Monsieur Moreau traveled a great deal. Daniella's daughter stayed here before the invasion. We never saw her or heard of her during or after the war. Never."

George agreed. "*Oui*, that is so. I do not believe she was in Marseille during the occupation. Of course, we assumed she was safe, did we not? But perhaps she died during the invasion, or later, during the war?"

"*Oui*, you are correct. Madeleine left Marseille before the Germans came, but I do not know where she went. No one, to my knowledge, knows where she went, or how, or why, really. Maybe she went to Sardinia. Or maybe she was killed."

Alexander joined the conversation, looking to Marie, "So, you say she was married to a man named Moreau, and lived in Marseille until the Germans arrived. Is that as you understand it? And then she left and never returned, *n'est-ce pas?*"

"Well, Iskandar, that is my understanding. We were close to Hanna, but not to Daniella's daughter. I am not sure if anyone I know has more knowledge than this. It has been nearly twenty years. Let's see, no, it has been even longer. Most people here now arrived after the war. Perhaps the authorities will have more information, but, of course, many records were destroyed during the occupation."Alexander watched George's face as he lowered his eyes, adding softly, "I am very sorry, Monsieur." George looked toward the door and stood as he saw a couple enter the café.

"*Merci*, George, for all of your help. I very much appreciate your time. I can see you are busy, and that this is going to take more investigation, but I have time. Now I must go, but not before I congratulate you on your fine foods and your superb *arak*. And most of all, I am very grateful you have kept the Café Liban intact and similar to what I recall. It holds many wonderful memories for me." He bowed his head to George and Marie as he stood to leave. "*Shookrun.*"

"*Afwan*, you are welcome."

As he walked to the door, he stopped and turned back to his new friends, "Thank you again. I will return to visit with you."

"*Insha Allah*, Iskandar." Maria added, "When exactly did you last visit with Hanna and Daniella here at the café?"

He thought for just a moment, "It was during the summer of 1920, a long time ago", he remarked wistfully.

"1920?" she exclaimed. "Indeed, yes. So much has happened since then, don't you agree?"

"Beyond your wildest dreams, Madame," Alexander replied quickly with a dubious smile, and repeated, "Beyond your wildest dreams."

"And tell us, Iskandar, where are you staying in Marseille?"

"I am at the Charles V Hotel," he said, standing in the doorway entrance to the café.

"And for how long?" Maria asked.

"For as long as it takes, Madame. For as long as it takes," he answered, the second time in a whisper to himself as he stepped through the doorway into the cool, balmy night.

You would measure time, the measureless and immeasurable.

Kahlil Gibran

CHAPTER 24

Marseille: The Search Continues

The following day, at the end of his meeting with the U.S. Consul General, Alexander, having listened intently to every word and deciding there really wasn't much the Americans could do to help, determined that he would need to follow the only sound suggestion he heard: "Try the local police department. Perhaps they can help you."

And so he did. But the Marseille police station was of little or no help, being preoccupied with current local crimes, including predominantly, the importation of illegal drugs. They had no time to assign personnel to missing persons, especially those missing during the war.

"Monsieur Thomas," the officer gesticulated with his arms, "you must understand three things. First, the person for whom you are looking may be dead. Second, there are no records of any sort to which we have access…so many were destroyed by the Nazis during the occupation and the Allied invasion. Third, we have no information of anyone by that name. I'm sorry, but we're not able to help you."

Alexander felt frustrated that there seemed to be no one who knew of Madeleine's whereabouts or when she was last seen or heard from. Yes, Hanna was well known, but even he, after such a long absence, was becoming only a vague memory to many, and nonexistent to most, especially the postwar generation. Most of his closest friends were also killed during the war, and most of those who weren't left Marseille very soon after the war as life became almost unbearably difficult in the cities. Food was so very scarce, transportation systems and streets were wrecked, buildings shattered, water often unavailable, and electricity sporadic at best. Many escaped to the countryside where they could farm to feed themselves. It was only after the U.S. aid, as part of the Marshall Plan, the enormously generous gift to Europe from the U.S. under President Truman, and spearheaded by America's outstanding Secretary of State George C. Marshall, that cities in France, as well as the other European countries began to rebuild themselves into livable communities. And that took several years. By 1950, the demographics of Marseille had changed dramatically, impacting the culture of the citizenry. As a result, the Lebanese community changed almost completely. Many had left for other places, to their extended families in Lebanon, Syria, Canada, and the Americas. So, Alexander faced a near vacuum of people who might have even known Hanna or Daniella, but certainly not Madeleine.

Day after frustrating day, extending into endless weeks, Alexander called on everyone he could think of who might be helpful, no matter how remote the possibility. Every day he was at the *Place de Liban* and the *Canebière* asking shopkeepers, clientele, gendarmes, and taxi drivers, who seemed to know about everything and everybody except the whereabouts of Madeleine DuBois. Some older residents on the *Canebière* knew of "Daniella DuBois and her adorable daughter," but they had less than precise memories, or knew of nothing after the German invasion.

Each day was a frustrating experience for Alexander. He was not accustomed to this kind of fruitless endeavor. He always felt like he could make things happen. But here, every day was empty for him.

At least four times each week, Alexander visited the Café Liban where he would lunch or visit in the late afternoons, make acquaintances, renew his backgammon, sip *arak*, dine on a simple mezza, and ask questions of those diners who looked old enough to possibly know something. He spent many hours at the café sipping the pungent thick Turkish coffee from a demitasse cup, one of the many lingering traditions of the Ottomans that most Lebanese continued to cling to. He, Maria and, most often, George would talk of many things. Sometimes the subject would become Lebanon. He became a familiar habitué, sometimes drawing sympathetic glances from those who noticed him so often.

"What do you think of the U.S. Marines in Beirut? Do you agree your President Eisenhower did the right thing, Iskandar?"

"I think so, George. It seemed to me the political difficulties in Beirut with the infighting of the powerful political families will need U.S. involvement for a long time. I'm glad Lebanon stays close to France and the West and doesn't align with the Soviet Union. This whole 'Cold War' thing has me concerned. I don't like politics that much anyway, and maybe it's because I am Orthodox, since we have no aspirations concerning the presidency in Lebanon. As you know, only the Maronites can ascend to the presidency...it's in the Constitution. They send their children to school in France ensuring that close bond, counting on the power of France to keep them in place. So yes, George, I supported Ike in that decision. I hope they can keep Beirut and Lebanon at peace."

"*Insha Allah*," replied George with a smile. "More coffee, Iskandar?"

And so it went...the weeks now extending into months...as he sought information in cities outside of Marseille, including Paris, Aix-en-Provence, Le Havre, Lyon, and Toulon...most of France. Still, nothing. Alexander's time in Marseille was somewhat exasperating, yet, pleasant enough, being around his countrymen. He became frustrated, unsure what to do next, where else to look or with whom to inquire. He wondered to himself many days, What am I doing? Maybe I should go home. "No," he would whisper in response to his own words, "no, I cannot. Not now. Something is sure to turn up. Yes, it's frustrating. Everything is beyond my control. All I can do is continue my search…and wait."

His inherent tenacity that would not let him quit his mission was sorely being tested, and he knew that.

"Day after day…nothing!" he muttered, shaking his head.

It was in Alexander's twelfth month of residence in Marseille when someone who had heard of his search came to his hotel one late afternoon. He didn't realize how long he had been here and was about to fly home to reassess his actions when one evening he received the phone call.

Rarely did his hotel phone ring, so Alexander anxiously reached for it. "*Allo?*"

"Monsieur Thomas, there is a visitor here in the lobby asking for you," said the concierge. "He says he has information you may find interesting. Would you prefer to meet with him your suite or in the lobby?"

"Neither," replied Alexander rather eagerly. "Ask him to meet me in the lounge. I'll be right down."

"As you wish," replied the concierge efficiently, wanting to help his hotel's continuing guest.

Alexander, encouraged, yet not quite ready to be too optimistic, reached for his tweed jacket, brushed his hair back, grabbed his wallet and keys, and stepped to the door, hoping for some news beyond what he had been hearing for so long: "I'm sorry, Mr. Thomas, but we cannot help you in your search as much as we would like to."

Alexander strode quickly to the elevator. As he stepped out of the elevator onto the marble lobby floor, he expected to see someone approach him. He looked to the concierge at his small desk. The concierge made eye contact, smiled slightly and nodded his head toward the lobby lounge.

Alexander received the signal and stepped across the lobby to the lounge where a man stood waiting.

"Monsieur Thomas, the American?" the man asked. "I think I can help you."

Alexander, after an endless time of seemingly dead-end information, looked at the man suspiciously, surveying him closely with concern. He was a few inches shorter than Alexander, about the same age, and was dressed in a modest French dark blue suit that a mid-level bureaucrat would wear. Lebanese in appearance, he was olive-skinned, with silver hair at his temples and wispy strands of hair atop his balding head. He seemed a bit shy and had a worried expression on his face.

"I am someone who worked for many years as assistant to Monsieur Hanna Chalhoub. I have heard of your investigation. Can we sit and talk?"

"Of course," Alexander answered as he led this man, who appeared to be sincerely eager to help him, to a booth in the corner of the bar.

"Let's sit here," spoke Alexander, gesturing toward the booth. "What is your name, Monsieur?"

"I am Amjad Hamra. My family is from Tyre on the southern coast of Lebanon, but I, myself, have been here in Marseille since the end of the first war in 1919. My only job was working for Hanna Chalhoub, your uncle. I was his assistant, bookkeeper, and collected his rents for more than twenty-four years until his unfortunate death in the late summer of 1944. We were very close, Monsieur, very close. He trusted me with his business many times when he traveled, and I trusted him in his fairness and appreciation for my efforts. He was a very generous man, Monsieur Thomas. I respected him very much."

Alexander, watching, listening to every word, nodded as the man spoke, keenly interested in what he might know.

"We were close for many years even though he was a Christian and I am Sunni Muslim. We trusted each other completely. But now he is gone and I miss him. I miss my friend so much. He had no family, you know. No wife, no children. Only his work, his buildings, and Daniella. He intended to leave everything to Daniella. Did you know that?"

Alexander couldn't believe his ears. Mr. Hamra seemed to know so much and sounded so sincere, so honest. He was surprised at the revelations of this stranger.

"Why do you come to me at this time?" asked Alexander. "And, if I may ask, what do you wish from me? Or do you have new information for me?"

"Oh, Monsieur Thomas, I do not ask anything of you. Monsieur Chalhoub told me of you many times, wishing you were his son. He told me except for life's twists and turns, you might indeed have been his son. And," Amjad continued, "since I thought of Monsieur Chalhoub as my uncle, you would be my family too. When I first heard of your questions in the Lebanese section of the *Panier*, I wasn't certain what you were doing or who you were. But, after so many months following your path, I decided I should try to help you. After all, Hanna left most of his buildings to me. Did you know that? He had written in his will that all he owned would be given to Daniella DuBois. But, if she was not alive, it would be given to me. Of course, I did not know that, to be sure. And now I am a wealthy man because of him. Perhaps, sir," he paused, looking at Alexander, studying his face, "perhaps I can help you. That is my desire, so in some ways I can help further Monsieur Chalhoub's hopes and dreams for his 'almost son'."

He paused again. "I do not want to mislead you, sir," the man continued, looking directly into Alexander's eyes, "I do not know where your friend Madeleine DuBois is today. But I do know some things that may lead you to that information.

Would you like me to continue, sir?"

"Yes, of course," Alexander interjected without hesitation, filled with renewed hope, "please continue. I am here in Marseille on a mission of my heart, and if you can help me, I am most interested in what you have to say."

"Mademoiselle DuBois was a lovely young woman, Monsieur Thomas, whose heart was broken when you left her. Yet, she did the best she could. She was just a young girl, you see. Several years later she met Monsieur Philippe Moreau, who was a close friend of Monsieur Chalhoub's. He was much older than Madeleine DuBois and quite wealthy. Life was difficult in those days and she found it necessary to marry this well-respected man who could take care of her."

Alexander, listening intently, suddenly began to feel great regret and sadness. He felt a sickening sense of having abandoned Madeleine and leaving her to the fates. He had to hold back his emotions as Amjad Hamra shared his detailed information. He did not know anything of Madeleine's life after he sailed on to America. He had no way of knowing…eighteen years old, very poor, totally dependent on his father, no responses to his many letters to her. Yet, he felt somehow responsible for Madeleine's fate. Alexander's stomach tightened. He began to ache from his past actions.

"Monsieur Hamra," whispered Alexander, "this is so difficult. I am appreciative of all you are telling me. I have loved this woman since I arrived in Marseille in 1920, some forty years ago, and now, you tell me she had to marry because times were too difficult for her. And now, I feel that I abandoned her and must do something." Alexander wiped his face with his handkerchief in silence.

His heart heavy, he continued, "I promised her I would return for her. But, I didn't until now. I let her down. Perhaps, perhaps," he repeated, "she is even now married. And perhaps she has several children. I have no way of knowing. But, my heart tells me she waits for me as I long for her to return into my life." Taking a deep breath, Alexander continued more humbled, "Amjad, I am reminded of the words of our countryman, Kahlil Gibran, as he wrote in his book, *The Prophet*, when Almitra spoke of Love. Those words are so true to me. They haunt me every day. Do you remember? I think they are burned in my mind. I remember these words:

> *When Love beckons to you, follow him,*
> *Though His ways are hard and steep.*
> *Though the sword hidden among his pinions may wound you.*
> *And when he speaks to you, believe in him.*

"And so, my dear man," Alexander said as he waved the waiter to the table to refresh their glasses of wine, "I ask you to tell me all you know that I may find Madeleine, my first love."

Amjad smiled. "Well, Monsieur Thomas, I will do all that I can, and with pleasure. There is a man who lived in Marseille for many years, Jean Pierre Armand, who now lives in Paris. Perhaps he can help you. He was a close friend of Monsieur Chalhoub's and was in the *Resistance* throughout the war. You are aware, are you not, that Monsieur Chalhoub was extraordinarily helpful to the French underground, the citizens' army against the Germans?"

Alexander shook his head, and with his hand beckoned the man to continue without delay. "Please continue, Monsieur Hamra."

"Yes, sir, happily, but I wish to keep my facts straight, as I am not the young man that I was, so bear with me."

"Of course, please continue at your pleasure. I have time, as much as you need," Alexander replied with a grateful smile.

"Jean Pierre Armand was very much involved, as I said, in the *Resistance* during the war as a high-level agent based in Marseille, and, on occasion, in other cities nearby, like Toulon. He worked very closely with Philippe Moreau, who was at that time Director General of the *Resistance*, a very important man, and Madeleine's husband. Monsieur Moreau was a brave man, very intelligent, and somehow successfully brought the various *Resistance* groups together. At the beginning, there were three major groups across France. Very dedicated to France to be sure, but they would not or could not coordinate their efforts. Politics, sir... always politics." He paused as he shook his head. "Even so, the Germans came. But Philippe will long be remembered as a French hero. And, I believe that Jean Pierre Armand, a dedicated man to the *Resistance* who was very close to him, may have the information you need. I recommend you find him. There remains a small separate office in the French Defense Department in Paris for those who fought in this way. They may have the information for you. It's almost a secret agency, Monsieur Thomas, with its documents not for common knowledge, so you must be cautious. They jealously guard their information for, as they say, 'security reasons.' I am sure you understand. It would be like trying to obtain information from your CIA or FBI, *n'est-ce pas?*"

"I understand, Monsieur Hamra. And I thank you for this information. I will leave for Paris in the morning. *Merci, merci beaucoup.*"

They both stood and acknowledged each other with a slight bow before Hamra departed the hotel.

Alexander had followed too many false leads during the past six months resulting in nothing but more frustration, so he cautiously restrained himself, not yet willing to believe he had begun to find an avenue to some answers. In fact, he had not. Still, Amjad Hamra seemed knowledgeable and sincere.

"George," he asked his friend at the Café Liban later that evening, "tell me what you know of Amjad Hamra."

"Of course, *mon ami*," he nodded as his eyebrows raised up, "Amjad was Hanna Chalhoub's protégé for many years, and one of the luckiest men I have known. Do you know that Hanna gave him these very buildings after his death in 1945? He is now my landlord and a good man. Why do you ask? Are you interested in Marseille real estate?"

"No." He laughed at the thought. "I think I have all the real estate I need at this time. I met Amjad and he told me of a man who might have helpful information in my search. Have you ever heard of Jean Pierre Armand?"

"Yes, of course, but many years ago. He was here in Marseille during the Occupation. I believe he was involved somehow in the French Underground. But, I must tell you, I was not involved in those things at that time. Only a few Lebanese in Marseille dared to become involved in the *Resistance*. It was too easy for the Germans to kill us and suffer no retribution. If they killed the French, the French fighters could and would retaliate, you see. As for us, we were too vulnerable." He paused before continuing, "But I do know he was a close associate of Hanna's. I should have told you before, Mr. Thomas. I simply didn't think of him. Forgive me, please."

"Please do not feel badly, George, this is a complicated search." he smiled. "I leave for Paris in the morning. Perhaps I will return with the information I am seeking. It depends on how cooperative Monsieur Armand is and what information he has at his disposal. Until then, *mon ami*, *au revoir*, and thank you for your encouragement."

For even as Love crowns you so shall he crucify you.
Even as he is for your growth so is he for your pruning.
Kahlil Gibran

CHAPTER 25

Throughout the train ride to Paris the next morning, as he watched the vineyards, pastures, farms, and rivers of southern France pass by, Alexander's thoughts were about Madeleine's life after they parted. He was consumed with questions. Only a few shared weeks in their youth were reality. But in his mind they had grown into a lifetime of enormously important emotional fantasy. Thus realities of the mind, giving him a sort of roller coaster of agony then ecstasy, sadness, then joy, emptiness, happiness, frustration and anger at himself. He thought about the questions he would ask of Jean Pierre Armand, and what he would say someday to Madeleine.

"Driver, take me to the National Defense Department office building," Alexander instructed the taxicab driver at the central Paris railway station.

In deep thought, he hardly noticed the Paris skyline and all the people on the sidewalks as his taxi drove slowly, inching its way through the crowded streets. Finally, the cab stopped at a large downtown government building. "We are here, Monsieur," the driver announced over his shoulder.

"*Merci*," Alexander said as he handed him a generous fifty francs.

"*Merci*," replied the driver, seeing his tip.

Filled with optimism, Alexander strode briskly to the entrance of the building and went directly to the security officer sitting solemnly at his desk in the outer office to get directions to the French *Resistance* Division.

"Oh my," the officer replied to Alexander's query, "I am so sorry to tell you, Monsieur. That division has been eliminated as of the first of this year," the guard announced sternly, shocking Alexander from his optimistic mood.

"Eliminated? What do you mean eliminated?" Alexander raised his voice to the guard. "Goddamnit! How could they just eliminate an entire department? How can this be? Is there anyone left I can speak with? I am seeking a meeting with Jean Pierre Armand. Do you know of him?"

The guard raised his eyebrows at Alexander's outburst and, maintaining his composure, responded, shrugging at the impatient American, "Of course I know of Monsieur Armand! He came here every day. He was a kind old man, very friendly with many stories about the war, you know. I myself don't know much of the war. I was a small boy, you see, but it was most difficult, I remember, Monsieur. But Monsieur Armand told me many exciting stories of the *Resistance*. He was one of its high level officials, a wanted man, you know. It is so sad," the guard's voice trailed off.

"What is so sad?" asked Alexander, now almost pleading, exasperated.

"Well, perhaps you don't know, Monsieur. You are from America, after all, aren't you?"

Alexander sensed a bit of cynicism in the guard's voice and questioned gently, "What happened? What is so sad?"

"Well, when the offices were eliminated, closed down, Monsieur Armand, who was Director General of the division, was devastated. He became very depressed from the date he was informed of the closure. Of course, he was not a young man, and it seems," the guard continued, speaking a bit more delicately, "that his sole purpose in life was taken from him. His wife and children were killed by the Nazis during the war, and all he had left was his work, looking after veterans of the *Resistance*. When that was taken from him, we believe he died because he had no further purpose. No one needed him. He died of a lonely heart."

"He died? Good God!" exclaimed Alexander, now a bit embarrassed, increasing the pitch of his voice. "Jean Pierre Armand is dead?"

Alexander thought for a moment, then asked the security guard, "When did Monsieur Armand die?"

The guard looked at his calendar, "Hmm, let me see. Yes, it was three months ago. Yes, three months ago next week, Monsieur." He looked up from his desk, and wearing his most official expression of importance, said impatiently, "Will there be anything else?"

Dejected, he stomped his foot on the marble floor. "No, I don't believe so, Monsieur," he answered the guard. Then, turning to the exit, he stopped. "Forgive me, but he was my last hope. Are there any other veterans of the war who also served in the *Resistance* who you can refer me to?"

The guard, sensing Alexander's desperation, answered, "Perhaps, if you explained the purpose of your inquiry. I can direct you to someone who can help you." He lowered his voice, "For example, if you are seeking a person who was in the *Resistance*...?"

"Well, yes...I am. If you could direct me to someone, anyone who may have such information, particularly with regard to Marseille, I would be most grateful, sir."

"In that case, may I suggest that you see André Duval? He is familiar with the Veterans Administration Department and may be able to help you."

"*Merci, merci,*" responded Alexander with renewed hope.

"Go to the second level, Room 206."

After waiting for Monsieur Duval for more than an hour to no avail, and growing in frustration, Alexander decided to leave and return the following day. He had left most of his belongings in Marseille, so he carried only an overnight valise as he walked to his hotel, expecting to remain in Paris for just one or two nights as he had hoped.

The next morning, Alexander returned to the same rudimentary offices at the Defense Department building, and waited again, this time successfully, for André Duval.

"Please tell me how I can help you, Monsieur Thomas," the well-dressed official said coolly to Alexander as he ushered him into his small, austere, but functional office that lacked any décor whatsoever.

Alexander found a chair opposite him, separated by a small wooden desk, and casually looked around before addressing this obviously low-level, low-pay government bureaucrat, whose sole incentive was to stay safely in his position until his pension arrived, some ten years into the future.

"Well, Monsieur, I am on a mission to find someone, and I have reason to believe if I can locate Philippe Moreau, then I will be able to locate the person I am seeking."

The official responded, "Did you say Philippe Moreau? The same Moreau who was so instrumental in the *Resistance* during the war?"

"*Oui,* Monsieur, the same man," replied Alexander with a nod. "Do you know how I can find him?"

"Well, Monsieur Thomas, if you are seeking the same Philippe Moreau who was Director of the *Resistance* during World War II, I am afraid I have bad news for you. Unfortunately, he was killed in 1944. Moreau was high on the list for assassination by the Nazis, and was shot dead."

"Oh, that is very sad. I am sorry to hear this news…sorrier than I could ever explain." Alexander shook his head, subconsciously realizing that could mean Madeleine could perhaps, now be a widow. "Did Moreau have a family? Would they be in Paris?"

"Sir, please…understand, sir…it has been more than fifteen years since his death, and while we do our best to maintain contact with French veterans and their heirs, that is only true if the heirs are receiving any pension benefits from the government. Let me see if we can locate the necessary files and determine the current status of Monsieur Moreau's survivors."

"Thank you. I appreciate anything you can do."

"Certainly, but it will take some time. I will have to delegate the file search to a member of our staff, and, unfortunately, we are always understaffed. You understand, don't you? Also, I must tell you, there will also be a slight fee for our services."

"*Mais oui*, I expected that. I will certainly pay whatever you charge."

"Very good. Will you be staying in Paris?"

"Yes," Alexander replied, "I am staying at the Maurice."

"Ah, the Maurice. That is one of the finest, most expensive hotels in all of Europe. Excellent choice. I am sure you will be quite comfortable while you are here." The official smiled warmly, and sensing a good personal opportunity to obtain several fees from this wealthy American, Duval smiled again and continued, "Perhaps you should enjoy your stay in Paris while we find out what we can. The costs will be appropriate to our efforts. I will contact you at your hotel. It could take a few days though."

"A few days?" Alexander asked incredulously.

"Yes, sir. We will do the best we can."

"Well," Alexander replied, "I will count on you. Perhaps it will help if I paid you double the fee in advance in case you must ask several people to assist you." Alexander thought it would make his case a priority and speed up the effort if he opened the gratuity door for Duval without offending him, recognizing that this official, like most, felt underpaid and unappreciated while struggling to make ends meet…so, why not offer more funding?

"Ah, thank you, Monsieur. I believe that suggestion could enable me to hasten the process of mobilizing my staff assistance. Let us say, day after tomorrow. Can you return to my office at eleven in the morning? I will know at that time if there will be any additional costs."

"Until day after tomorrow. Then." Alexander stood, and with a cynical smile shook hands with the official before leaving. "It's nice to meet you. Thank you, Monsieur Duval." He was being overly pleasant, knowing this man could choose whether to find the information, or simply declare it lost!

He stepped from the office, closing the door behind him.

At exactly 11 a.m. two days later, Alexander knocked on the door of Room 206.

"*Entrez, s'il vous plait*," the familiar voice called out.

Alexander turned the knob, opened the door and entered.

"Ah, Monsieur Thomas, I have some news for you. Please sit down."

"*Merci*, Monsieur Duval. Please don't hesitate. Tell me of your findings."

"Fortunately, after a great deal of searching, we have located the file section for Philippe Moreau. It was difficult even though he was a hero in the war. However, our news is both good and not so good, Monsieur." He shook his lowered head.

Alexander's optimism and upbeat emotions took another nosedive. "What is the news, Monsieur Duval?"

"Well, Monsieur Thomas, as I told you, our work and our files are relevant to those Free French Army veterans and their families who are still alive and receiving government pensions."

Alexander looked quizzically at him. "I don't understand."

"It seems that although Monsieur Moreau was part of the French Underground, or *Resistance* as they were also known, he was not officially part of the French government's armed forces. Members of the army were, of course. But those members of the *Resistance* never became eligible for pensions. Alas, they were never officially qualified. As a result, there are no records of any pension payments whatsoever to Moreau's heirs. I am afraid that as far as the Veterans' Administration Office is concerned, we are without any information whatsoever that could help you." He shook his head sadly, "I am very sorry, Monsieur Thomas."

"Damn!" Alexander's face fell as he slammed his open hand on the desk, accurately reflecting his disappointment and prompting the official to speak again.

"Perhaps there is another way, Monsieur. I have a suggestion for you. I urge you to enlist the assistance of a very good private investigative agency. They are freer to search records and make inquiries than are we government employees…privacy laws and all that. You understand, I'm sure. So many resources and contacts have been utilized by these independent agencies since the war. It's possible that one of them could be helpful to you. I have cards here from two such firms. I suggest you consider this approach because I believe you would be wise to obtain quality private assistance in your search rather than seek answers exclusively on your own. There are so many possibilities for discouragement if you are not aware of the necessary sources, and, of course, you are not familiar with the French rules and regulations for obtaining government information. We must get many approvals to search files. And, while this is 1962, we are still finding ourselves with incomplete files and information. All our work is still done by hand with so much time required to process all the files. It is a laborious, time-consuming task, Monsieur. You need specialized help. I am sure you agree?"

"You are right, Monsieur Duval. I would appreciate the cards of your contacts."

After two quick phone calls from Duval's desk, Alexander had appointments to meet with representatives of "the best in Paris," as Duval described the two firms with which he had previously arranged for a fee when the prospective client made his initial deposit payment.

"So," he mused, looking at the business cards, "I will meet these gentlemen at the Maurice Hotel today at 4 p.m. Thank you, Monsieur Duval. We will see where this path leads. I will make my choice by this time in two days. And if they are successful, I will return and reward you handsomely."

"Until then, Monsieur Thomas, good luck. I am certain that whichever agency you select, you will be pleased. Both are considered very trustworthy and effective."

Alexander took the official's advice and, after interviewing representatives of both firms, selected the one he felt most comfortable with, paid a generous retainer fee, and scheduled a meeting two weeks hence. He felt relief at his decision and felt more confident with others assisting him in his search.

Two anxious weeks later, Alexander and the detective from the agency met for lunch at a quiet sidewalk café near the hotel.

"Good afternoon, Monsieur Thomas. It's nice to see you today." The man stood at Alexander's able. He was tall, good-looking, wore a trim dark suit and was impressive in his manner.

Alexander looked up and, with a welcoming smile, said, "Sit down, please, Monsieur Trudeau. Do you have information for me?"

After sitting down at the table, the detective deliberately opened his leather briefcase and pulled out a thin file, hoping to impress his new client. "Monsieur Thomas, we have been researching every government agency that could conceivably have information, yet we continue to find nothing. It is very frustrating. But we will continue looking. I will contact you as soon as we locate anything that will lead us to resolving this situation. Do not despair, Monsieur Thomas. If Madame Moreau is in France, we will find her. I asked you to meet me here today because I do have something to show you. We found this in a private archive, a museum of sorts, in a small village on the outskirts of Paris that was devoted to information on the *Resistance*, the French Underground as we called it, and its activities and individuals. A daughter of one of the *Resistance* members lives there and is the self-appointed 'Keeper of the Legacy'."

Alexander looked at him quizzically and said, "Yours is the first bit of news I've had in more than two years that is not negative. Tell me what you have."

Jean Luis Trudeau looked directly at Alexander and, handing his client a copy of a newspaper clipping, said, "We found this newspaper article that we believe has merit. It is the first indication that Madame Moreau actually exists or even existed. At least this indicates she was alive in Paris in 1948. But that, of course, was fourteen years ago. Where she is today is unknown to us at this time." He added, "It also states in the article that her son accompanied her."

Alexander clenched his hands to this unexpected news. "She had a son?" Alexander wondered aloud, "I think that this is a profound bit of news, Monsieur. That means she wasn't killed during the war, doesn't it? And it means she was in Paris after the war!"

Alexander studied the article that included two small, somewhat blurry photographs. One was of Moreau. The caption and story told of a private foundation committed to honoring the members of the *Resistance*, and the dedication of a memorial to Philippe Moreau. It began, "In gratitude of the heroic leadership of Philippe Moreau…"

Alexander's eyes moved almost instantly to the second small photograph. The caption identified the two individuals in the picture as: "Monsieur Rene Chounard, Director of the Chounard Family Foundation, presents a certificate to Madame Madeleine Moreau at the site of the new memorial…"

Alexander's hands began to tremble as he looked at the photograph. He was clearly shaken, seeing for the first time any evidence that Madeleine was still alive, at least after the war. His eyes were dancing at the sight of Madeleine's face. Without any hesitation, he burst out loud, "My God, it's her! I cannot believe it, but it must be her. The photograph is so small. Oh, my God, Monsieur Trudeau, you cannot imagine what I am feeling. If this is truly her, we must now find her!"

"Yes, that is our goal, and if she is still alive, we will do everything we can to locate her."

Alexander, excited at the news, yet afraid to become too optimistic, tried to restrain his emotions once again. "*Merci*, Monsieur Trudeau. Thank you for this news. As you locate any new information, I can be reached through my hotel concierge." Relieved, he stood and reached out his hand to conclude the meeting. "Until then, *au revoir.*"

Alexander returned to his hotel room and decided to call Helena with the good, albeit incomplete, news. He checked his wristwatch as he sat at the small desk in his room.

"Let's see, there's a six-hour difference between Paris and New York this time of year. So, it's just after nine in the morning in New York."

"*Allo*, how can I help you, Monsieur Thomas?" the hotel's operator responded.

"Person-to-person, please," he instructed, "to Mademoiselle Helena Thomas at the following number in New York City, America."

Moments later the phone rang. Alexander anxiously reached for the Florentine-looking telephone and brought it to his ear. "Fancy phone," he mumbled.

"Monsieur Thomas, I have Mademoiselle Helena Thomas on the telephone for you."

"*Merci*, operator. Hello…Hello…Helena?"

"Yes, Daddy, I'm here. It's so good to hear from you. You must have some news, I haven't heard from you since you left Marseille for Paris. What's happening, Daddy?"

Alexander spoke eagerly to his daughter. "The investigation firm I hired has finally come up with something."

"What is it, Daddy? Tell me," she responded to his excitement without a second's hesitation.

Alexander described his meeting with Jean Louis Trudeau, the clipping, the photographs. "Based on this clipping, we believe that Madeleine was in Paris at least in 1948. We cannot be sure she is still here or even that she is still in Europe, much less France, so we still have much to do. But it's the first evidence we have found..."

"That's wonderful, Daddy," she interrupted, "I'm happy for you. I must tell you though that Uncle Anthony in Miami has been trying to reach you. He says it is important. He wants you to join him and other members of the Board of Governors of St. Jude in Memphis. Can you call him or should I tell him you are out of the country?"

"No," Alexander replied, "I'll speak with him. I'm feeling good right now. I must admit, *Biyee*, I've been very frustrated and discouraged for far too long. Call Anthony back and tell him I'll try to reach him as soon as I can."

"Okay, Daddy, I'll do that. Good luck."

"Bye, Helena. I'll be back in touch."

Alexander waited for his daughter to replace the telephone in its cradle before replacing his. "God, I love that girl," he whispered to himself, grateful for her understanding, as he sat back in his chair.

"Iskandar," the familiar voice said, "I'm glad you called. We've been worried about you — the family, all your friends at ALSAC and St. Jude. We've missed you. You've been gone so long. Are you alright, *khai-yi*?"

"Yes, Anthony," Alexander spoke into the telephone, "I am better today. At last I have some news."

"Good," responded Anthony, "I hope the weather is cooler in Paris than it is here in South Florida."

Alexander asked, a bit nervously, "What's on your mind, Anthony. What is so urgent?"

"Iskandar, you need to come back, and very soon. We have been working on the new St. Jude Children's Research Hospital for several years now. The time has come for all of us to witness the fruit of our labors. Danny Thomas wants us all to be in Memphis for the official grand opening of St. Jude's Hospital. Bishop Bashir made me promise I'd get you there, *khai-yi*, and now you need to come. We broke ground in 1958 about this time, if you recall. That was the same year President Eisenhower sent the Marines to Beirut ... God, what a mess that was. You know, Iskandar, the opening will be our proudest moment. And, for Danny and his family, it is the fulfillment of his promise so long ago to St. Jude. Imagine, Iskandar, it was only five years ago that you and I got involved in this dream of Danny's when Mike Tamer, George Simon, Bishop Bashir, Danny, and Fred Gattas convinced us to join in, at a time when all they had were drawings and a dream."

"Yes, Anthony, I remember. You can tell Danny and the boys that I'll be there."

Anthony replied, "Good, Iskandar." Anthony told Alexander the dates, schedule and function highlights. "I'll have a telegram sent to you. The events are in two weeks. I'll count on you to be with us."

Alexander replied, "That's fine, Anthony, I'll be there."

The next two weeks passed slowly with no new information as Alexander planned his trip to Memphis. Almost daily, he called Jean Louis Trudeau inquiring, "Any news today?"

The response each time was always the same disappointing, "I am very sorry, Monsieur Thomas, but we do not have any new developments. There have been so many futile efforts...so many dead-ends...but we believe that eventually we'll find something."

En route to the airport before departing, Alexander stopped by the offices of Trudeau Investigations, Ltd., and left a packet of information explaining how he could be reached while away. In addition, as his parting comment, Alexander said to Jean Louis as they shook hands, "Contact me as soon as you have any news. And if you cannot reach me, call my daughter, Helena. Her information is here in this envelope."

Trudeau responded with a reassuring smile, "We will be in contact immediately when we have something to report, Monsieur Thomas."

Trudeau had grown personally involved in the romantic search of this American. He believed this man deserved results, and felt as if he were drawn into this effort beyond a simple business transaction. He was determined to see this through to resolution no matter where it led. Alexander had proven he would bear whatever the cost.

They embraced and the investigator kissed Alexander on both cheeks in the French tradition. "*Bon voyage.*"

You give little when you give of your possessions.
It is when you give of yourself that you truly give.
Kahlil Gibran

CHAPTER 26

Memphis, TN, Spring 1962
St. Jude Children's Research Hospital Grand Opening

Alexander arrived in Memphis the day before the grand opening of St. Jude Children's Research Hospital and, as always, checked into the Peabody Hotel, the "home away from home" for all members of the Board of Governors when in town to attend board meetings, committee meetings, or other gatherings of the hospital or of ALSAC. This was the funding arm of volunteers, most of whom were of Lebanese heritage, with some of the Jewish faith, and some of the Muslim faith.

It was late in the afternoon when he arrived.

The clerk at the front desk asked, "Shall we have the bill sent directly to your offices as always, Mr. Thomas?"

Alexander nodded, finished filling out the registration form, looked up and, with a smile, acknowledging the soft lilting Southern accent, replied, "Thank you, yes, as always." He noticed the clock on the wall behind the clerk as it approached six o'clock.

"Pardon me, Mr. Thomas, but I would like to say to you and all other members of St. Jude's Board of Governors how much all of us here at the Peabody admire you for giving of your valuable time and paying all your own expenses. We find it remarkable that St. Jude pays for all expenses of the children, their parents' visits, food, room, and medical expenses. It's unheard of anywhere. That's very unusual, you know. For all of us here at the Peabody and, I think for all citizens of Memphis, we thank you for being here. St. Jude is a wonderful contribution to Memphis and to Tennessee."

Alexander smiled proudly and replied, "Thank you, young man. It's our way of thanking America, and helping Danny Thomas. It's for the children. Give Danny all the credit." With a feeling of warm pride in his heritage, in his friends, and in his fellow board members, Alexander stepped into the elegant lobby full of families with children. He then watched with amusement the march of the mallard ducks as they left the fountain waters where they had been swimming all day to step down the wooden steps to the red carpet and waddle to "their" elevator that would take them to the rooftop to complete the trademark march which concluded each day at six o'clock sharp. The ducks would not reappear until the next morning when they would step from "their" elevator onto the red carpet and march back to the fountain. Giggles of joy from the children and parents, crowding closer to get better views, accompanied the procession as onlookers thrilled to this daily ritual.

Alexander watched, enjoying the parade, relaxing, and feeling good upon his return to Memphis, the Peabody, and to his dear friends at St. Jude.

It was good to return to America after months and months of fruitless searching, agonizing over what appeared to be a futile, exhausting search for an impossible dream. He had been away from his family, his businesses, and his friends for too long. And, as a result, he felt a sense of being strangely disconnected from his previous life.

While his friends on the Board of Governors of ALSAC and St. Jude let him know by their words and behavior that he was respected and missed, he knew he had been separated for what seemed an eternity. The worst part to him was that as a result of having put his whole heart into his search for Madeleine his emotions were indeed frayed. He needed a break with friends. His colleagues in America had reached out to him, but it was clear his agenda had taken him on a different path from them for too many months. He knew he had to dedicate himself to his search. It was very important for him. And while he understood there was no guarantee of success, his tenacious optimism made him really believe there was a strong possibility he would locate Madeleine even though he had waited more than forty years. Forty years!

Because he had waited so long, and so much of his life had transpired, he blamed himself for his lack of success. Yet, he also reminded himself he could not have conducted his search for Madeleine sooner. After all, he insisted in his mental debate, he simply could not have returned to Marseille to find Madeleine from the date he married Helene. And never did he receive even one letter from her. So, he began to understand that questioning himself was an exercise in futility.

He didn't know whether to keep going or go back to his life, to move on. He was considering these thoughts in silence in his room at the Peabody Hotel when the phone rang.

Anthony Bashir's voice was on the line, "Iskandar, join us in the ALSAC hospitality room. All your friends are there. Danny is 'holding court' and wants all of us to join him in Suite 777. Your cousin Elias and your buddies Joe Ayoub and Fred Gattas haven't seen you yet. You're family, Iskandar. I'll come get you in fifteen minutes. Be ready."

Shaken from his thoughts, Alexander smiled, thinking they weren't going to let him be alone too much.

"You are my brother, my friend. We are worried about you. No one knows what's bothering you, and we're not going to ask. But, we want you with us. See you in a few minutes, Iskandar."

"I'll be ready. Thanks, Anthony."

Alexander listened for the "click" signaling Anthony had placed the telephone on the cradle slowly, not sure if he was actually ready for a mixer. He softly hung up the phone.

As he was finishing dressing after a quick shower, he heard a knock at his door.

"Be right there, Anthony."

Alexander opened the door and found Anthony, Fred and Joe waiting for him. All jovial, they grabbed Alexander and ushered him down the hall to Suite 777. At the door, Marlo and Terre, Danny's daughters, were waiting. "Come on in," they said in their young voices. "Daddy's waiting for all of you."

The suite was filled with members of the board, wives, and friends. The mood was quite jovial. Almost everyone was standing, most with a drink in one hand, the other free hand gesticulating as one on one conversations loudly filled the air.

Danny stood up from the sofa where he had been sitting with his son, Tony, and several other board members. Raising both hands for attention, he spoke aloud the second he saw his daughters signal that everyone was in the suite. "*Ahlen wa sahlen*, come in and gather around me. I have some very interesting news for all of you."

The bartender asked of those just arriving, "What'd you like to drink fellas?"

"Scotch on the rocks," they answered with grins.

"You've got it."

After a few minutes of congenial exchanges, Danny asked for quiet and their attention. "Gentlemen, we did it," he announced with his familiar wide grin. "As you know, I made a promise to St. Jude Thaddeus when I was at the lowest point in my life, and together, we made the dream come true. I'm grateful you're here to share this exciting news!"

He continued, "Mike Tamer carried most of the load these past years. He's my hero. And so are you men, your families, your wives, your children. We have also fulfilled a promise to our heritage." Pausing to look at the many familiar faces around him, he continued, fumbling his ever-present large cigar in his fingers, "And, as you know I've said, as I believe, if a man isn't proud of his heritage, he has no heritage. We, together, share a wonderful heritage as Lebanese, Syrians, and as Americans. Now, together, we have unified in thanking America as never before. And I am so very proud to be among you. You honor me."

They all applauded their leader as some yelled out, "No, Danny. You honor us!"

After a moment, smiling and very happy, he looked around the room and continued, "And now, I have some exciting news for us all. The President of Lebanon has invited us to come to Beirut and be his guests for a gala celebration.

He and our countrymen are aware of what we here at St. Jude have done, and he thinks it appropriate that we come to the palace in Baabda to receive a grateful thanks from Lebanon for continuing the tradition of our Phoenician ancestors in traveling the world, being successful in our trade, doing so in peace, honoring our heritage, and exemplifying all that is good in our history." Then he stopped for emphasis, looking around at the faces watching him, anticipating. "Of course," Danny said smiling to his friends, "you are those about whom he is speaking. I'm just a saloon entertainer who did good."

That self-deprecating remark brought forth loud laughter, and comments like one who yelled out, "That's true, Danny...Sure, Danny, you're just a saloon entertainer, movie star, friend of Doris Day, dreamer of honorable dreams, uniter of our people, most famous, most beloved Lebanese-American in the land...Yes, Danny, just a saloon entertainer!" They all laughed at the joke.

Danny, feeling proud of what he and his countrymen had done, spoke loudly above the crowd, "The most beautiful part of all of this is that it is for the children! We must always remember what ALSAC stands for and never forget it: Aiding Leukemia Stricken American Children. Never forget!"

"Now," he continued firmly, "we must not stop here. We must do all we can to support our doctors, nurses, and researchers. We must give them all they need to rid the world of this terrible disease."

"I'm proud," he said in all seriousness, his voice lowering, reflecting his mood change. "I am proud to be a beggar for the children. And that's what I want all our people to be: Beggars for the Children. Even though we dedicate our beautiful hospital tomorrow, with nearly ten thousand people expected there...can you believe it?...ten thousand people will come to watch the doors of St. Jude open for the first time," he was on a roll now, "...even though we dedicate the hospital, we truly have only just begun. We must find the cure. We must treat every child at no cost to their families. We must provide the very best care. Never forget this. Our job has only just started. And we will succeed."

"*Insha Allah*!" echoed several in the crowd in unison.

Danny took a deep breath and, with tears of gratitude moistening his eyes, he spoke again, "*Shookrun*, my friends, my brothers." Then with a bow from the waist, "I thank you for all you are doing. Thank you."

After a moment of respectful silence, some of the proud, extraordinarily successful men of the Board of Governors from throughout America shifted noticeably on their feet. They all felt a sense of goodness, of enrichment and human fulfillment in pursuing such an honorable goal. These feelings would remain with them for years and bring energy to their lives.

Danny spoke again, "Mike Tamer will fill you in on the invitation to go to Beirut. The President wants it to be in mid-June, a time of rebirth, a time when those of us from the mountains will be able to travel to the villages of our birth without being blocked by deep snow. Those from the Bekaa or the south can go anytime," he grinned again.

Mike thanked Danny and began describing the proposed gala in Beirut and travel arrangements.

"The President asked us to select those Americans of Lebanese heritage who have exemplified the finest characteristics of success, philanthropy, ethics, and character that Lebanon can honor. Actually, we created a committee to do this. It was comprised of the most respected individuals we could find in America. Bishop Anthony Bashir was the chairman. There were a dozen on the committee. No one in this room, excluding the Bishop, was on the committee, not even myself or Danny. The ambassador from Lebanon selected many of the committee members. He also asked President Eisenhower to select members. Members came from each of the various religions Orthodox, Melkite, Maronite, Judaism, and Islam. He stopped for a few moments to let all of this sink in, then concluded by saying, "Of the fifty members of the Board of Governors of St. Jude and ALSAC, thirty were selected. Another twenty outside the Board were also selected. They were chosen not only because of their support of St. Jude, but also in recognition of their many years of active, dedicated philanthropy, humanitarianism, career success, reputation of honor, ethics, and always their remembering and honoring their heritage: Lebanon. Those selected will be formally contacted. We ask that you be prepared to go to Beirut and stay in Lebanon for seven days during June." He flipped through his papers making sure he hadn't forgotten anything, then continued, "Please coordinate your travel plans with my office; all airline and hotel reservations can be arranged with us to make it easier for you. And," he laughed, "as usual, you'll be sent a bill. You know, St. Jude pays only for direct hospital costs, research, and patient care."

Everybody joined in the laughter. Albert Harris called out, "Mike, after seeing those sick children today, none of us minds that at all. It's the least we can do."

"Alright then," Mike finished, "after this week here in Memphis, the next time we'll all meet again will be in London where we'll get on the Middle East Airlines flight to Beirut. May God bless you all."

At breakfast, on that dedication weekend in Memphis, Alexander visited with several of his friends on the Board and, sitting next to Danny, he found himself listening to Danny's lovely and supportive wife, Rose Marie, talk about their children's hopes and dreams, and Danny's vision into what he wanted St. Jude Hospital to become. And yet, as he listened, he found himself thinking offaraway places…Marseille, Paris, and now, Beirut and his village of Douma.

"Imagine, Danny, in a couple of months we'll be in Beirut. I haven't been back. God, I wonder if I'll recognize anything."

Danny turned in his seat and, lighting his ubiquitous, enormous cigar, replied,

"It's going to be wonderful, Iskandar. Y'know, I wanted to take the family several times, but something always came up. Four years ago it was the politics in Beirut, and Ike had to send in the Marines. Then, it seemed there was a movie or series commitment, just when things were calm in Beirut. But I'm really looking forward to getting up to Bsharre. I love that place. It's beautiful, Iskandar."

"Yes it is, Danny," Alexander replied with a smile, "it is so beautiful with the cedar forest and that six thousand year old cedar by itself. And Gibran's birthplace. It's magnificent. But right now, Danny, in February, the snow is so deep, I don't think you could get there."

Alexander laughed, "That's true, Danny. Lebanon is a most incredible, tiny country. They even grow bananas all along the southern coast. Bananas! Can you imagine? And the largest apples you ever saw. Remember, its mountains hold more water than any place in the Middle East, and in the Bekaa Valley, there are ponds and streams where you can hunt birds, ducks, and fish to your heart's content."

"I'm really glad we are going together," said Danny with a smile of pride. "We've all done some good things here in America, Iskandar, but I have to tell you, St. Jude Hospital is really the pinnacle of my life, my dear friend. And it brought so many of us together. That's one of the things I'm most proud of, along with my children." Danny reached to the ceramic bowl-like ashtray and flicked his growing cigar ash. "I mean, look over there, there's George Simon and his family from Detroit, the Shakers from Chicago, the Thomas family from Wilkes-Barre, Elias Chalhoub from your neck of the woods, and on and on. Young Dick Shadyac is new here, and I can already tell that he will be extremely dedicated to us and be a significant presence. He's a good one.

"And soon," Danny continued, "soon, the sons of all these guys will pick up where their fathers left off. I tell you, Iskandar, I am damned proud of what we've done here. We are going to save a lot of children. And while we're doing it, we're thanking America for our opportunities and our blessings. And now we'll be going to Beirut together. Man, I feel good."

Alexander smiled, put his arm on Danny's shoulder and said with complete sincerity, "Danny, like most of these guys, I've done well in America. I've had two beautiful children. My daughter, Helena, is going to be thirty-two this year. As you know, I lost my son in the second war. And then Helene died too. But I have to tell you, being a part of ALSAC and St. Jude has been really important to me. You and the hospital pulled me from a sad time. I'm grateful I could be part of this hospital and part of your dream. Thank you, Danny."

He paused, then continued, "Still, I'm involved with something personal. I have to go back to France soon. I'll meet you and the others in London. If that's not possible, I'll fly to Beirut from either Paris or Marseille. I've got some important business to conclude there, one way or another."

"Till Beirut then, Iskandar," Danny replied, patting Alexander's shoulder. "Good luck."

As Alexander got up to leave Danny to his family and others who wanted to visit with him, Danny also rose, and, with pride showing in his eyes, embraced Alexander. While hugging, these two friends kissed each other on their cheeks, pulled apart, smiled and, almost in unison spoke, saying, "*Allah ma'ak*. Beirut in June."

And let your best be for your friend.
If he must know the ebb of your tide,
Let him know your flood also.
Kahlil Gibran

CHAPTER 27

Tampa, 1962

Early the next morning, Alexander placed a call to Paris. "And what news do you have for me, Monsieur Duval? Anything new?"

"I am so sorry to tell you, Monsieur Thomas, but..."

"Nothing?" he interrupted.

"No, sir. We cannot find Madeleine Moreau anywhere. We know she's not in France. We have covered all of Europe. Still, nothing. She seems to have completely disappeared. We've been in close communication with Interpol, and with our associates in Switzerland, Britain, Sardinia, and Spain. But nothing has come of our efforts. We do know she was briefly in Paris in 1948 when Philippe Moreau was honored, but that is all, except that she stayed in the Maurice Hotel for a few days that year. Apparently, from their records, she has not stayed there since. I am sorry, but one never knows what will come up in these matters. Don't be too discouraged. Perhaps in time...

We'll keep the file open, but cannot at this time encourage you."

"Time? Where the hell could she be? She must be somewhere! Find her, dammit!" he angrily demanded in frustration as he banged the desk with his hand.

He leaned back in his chair behind his desk and pondered. Then he realized that the memories would not go away and the aching need to find Madeleine would grow even stronger. He was lonely and needed the presence of his first love if at all possible. During the following days, Alexander busied his life in Kissimmee, trying to set aside his emotional battle. Occasionally, he visited his sister in Orlando. He visited the clinics he supported; and he met with his friends, the Stewarts in Bartow.

Still, as much as Alexander got more involved locally, evenings at home were the loneliest times for him.

Over the next several weeks at home, Alexander began more and more to re-involve himself in his enterprises, not accepting the fact that he might never find Madeleine, but thinking that at this time, it was better for his daughter and himself that he not become too deeply engrossed in a disappointing and stressful effort that might not result in a successful conclusion. Weekly calls to Paris were all he could do anyway. He realized that being in France didn't really improve results. It was an unfamiliar sense of impotence, of not contributing to his mission …having no influence to resolve his problem. He hated having to rely totally on others in this situation. His inability to make things happen was driving him crazy. It was at these times he would remember Psalm 46:11, "Be still and know that I am the Lord." He had to face the fact that there may not be anything more he could do and that, as agonizing as it was, he would simply have to let God take over and resolve it for him.

As his business life got more active, he began to feel somewhat better, being reminded of the many blessings in his life. He telephoned his beautiful daughter each week, and met with Wilbur, who managed the ranch so well in his absence. Sometimes he would drive to Tampa to visit his special friend Abigail, one of the few people he could always confide in, who knew from him his desperate search for Madeleine. Now widowed, she resided in her bay front home, He needed to see her now.

"Well, dear friend, how are you feeling today?" Abigail asked the moment she saw him at her door. "Any news? Come in and let me give you a hug."

"Hi, Abigail, it's good to see you."

"As I see you these days with such sensitivity and warmth, I'm so grateful we've stayed close all these years. Isn't life strange, Alexander? My mother kept us apart, although I have to bear the responsibility because I was not courageous enough to defy her when I cared for you so much. She would say, 'He's not for you, Abigail…a nice man, but of a different world. You can be friends, but that's all.' I'm sorry, but I was too young, weak and naïve, I guess."

"That's history, Abigail," Alexander replied in a soft voice as they embraced, "that's behind us. Let's speak of today…of the future."

"Alexander, I want to tell you something I've been thinking about for some time. Sit down." Looking at him, she said, "My husband, Bill, was a good man, but he couldn't stop his drinking. In truth, I am convinced he was always jealous of you. You came here as an immigrant with no money. He had every privilege: social prominence, family, wealth, good looks, but he never felt adequate. He never felt he had earned anything. I think he was in great pain. It was awful watching him even long before he took his own life that day…and very bad afterward for me too, but now he is finally at peace. And I am finally at peace. And, dear friend, I hope soon you will be at peace. But you aren't now, you know." Her eyes focused on his as she drew her breath. "I'm going to tell you something." She pointed her finger at him and spoke firmly. "You must either fully devote yourself to your search for Madeleine, or you must find a way spiritually to completely put her and your past with her behind you. If you don't do this," she admonished, watching his face with all seriousness, now sitting beside him on the couch in the living room, putting his hand in both her hands, "then, your emptiness and your sadness will rule your life. You will lose your passion for life. And that, Alexander, would not be fair to Helena, not to yourself, nor to your friends. This has lingered too long. It's time, Alexander, for you to decide."

She paused, thought for a moment and continued, looking into his sensitive eyes, "You were there when Bill died. You embraced me, and spoke strongly to me. You advised me to take charge of my life and move on. And you were right. And now, that is what I'm doing for you." Then, sitting straight up, and changing the tone of her voice from one of sympathy to firmness, said, "Alexander, make your plans now. Go back to Marseille. Find her or not, but end this search one way or another. It's been long enough. If you find her, bring her to me. She and I have much to talk about. If you don't find her soon, then as you told me, it will be time for you to get over it and get on with your life. You need to know. And so do I. You know how much I love our deep friendship. Now go, and may God be with you."

Alexander listened to what he knew had to be said to him. He had to come to a decision. "Thank you, Abigail. I guess I needed to hear those words from you. I think you are right." He slapped his thighs and stood up. "It's time to bring this search to an end one way or another. I'll always be grateful for your support and your love. I have to be in Beirut in June and I've decided to go to Douma to visit what family I still have there. I haven't been back since I left so many years ago. I'll simply leave it in the hands of God and the detectives in France."

As he stood at the couch, she reached out her hand so he could assist her as she arose. "I've been thinking," he said, "I'll leave next week, spend a few days in France, see if there is any news, and then meet with my friends in Beirut. I'll be sure to see you before I leave."

Nodding her head, she smiled and said, "I'll come get you and take you to the airport."

He stepped to her so that they could embrace as very dear, very special friends.

In early June, as they had planned, Abigail picked up Alexander and took him to the Tampa airport for his flight to New York that would connect with his flight to Paris.

Alexander's flight that day took him to Idlewild International Airport in New

York. After an early dinner with Helena in the city the night before, he got a cab to the airport and boarded Air France flight 202 bound for Paris. Alexander spent the six hours on the plane thinking about his life, about his children, about Abigail, about his charity efforts, but mostly he thought about Madeleine.

As he perfunctorily responded to the inquiries and deliveries of food from the attractive stewardess, he also realized how quiet it was in the new jet's cabin. Then he noticed the middle-aged woman sitting next to him put down her magazine as she sighed.

"Life is so unpredictable," he said softly to her. "Here I am, nearly sixty years old, searching for my first love, when she was sixteen and I was eighteen. We spent an incredibly beautiful six weeks together in Marseille forty-two years ago. How do you explain such a phenomenon?" he asked her rhetorically. "How do you deal with such a thing?"

Then, not able to stop himself, he told this listener his story of Madeleine and how she has remained in his heart for so long, so endearingly.

She nodded from time to time and replied, "Sir, there is no way you can rationally explain such matters of the heart. It is like faith; either you have it or you don't, you either feel it or you don't, and, in all candor, you either deal with it or you don't. If you want my opinion, since you told me about your story and you asked me, I'd say to you, you have to see it through. You have to exhaust yourself seeking a conclusion or you'll never be at peace. Find her. Either she's still hoping for you to find her, which, as a woman, I believe is true, or she has a full life, a husband, a family, and has no room for you. In either case, you must find out. You have to continue your search or put it behind you."

She paused, looked to the attendant, waving her hand to get her attention, and asked for refills of her glass of wine and his iced tumbler of Scotch. When that was done, she turned, looked into Alexander's eyes, reached for his hand, and said, "I can only speak as a person who just met you tonight, heard your story, and sensed your emotions, but I do believe you will find this lucky woman." With a smile, she added, "I wish I had a handsome, sensitive man like you looking for me."

She leaned toward Alexander to look out the window. "I think we have crossed the coast of France. The weather seems fine." Sitting back, she turned and whispered to him, "Yes, I do believe you will find your Madeleine."

After landing at the bustling Orly airport, Alexander was once again driven to the Maurice Hotel.

He showered, had a leisurely breakfast, and arranged to meet with Monsieur Duval at the hotel.

Duval sat beside him in the lounge. "*Allo*, Monsieur Thomas, and welcome again to Paris. I really am sorry to say to you, sir, that, still, we have no new information to offer you. Nothing. Madame Moreau is nowhere to be found. There is no record of her marriage, death, pension, hotel reservations…nothing. She must be outside of Europe. We simply don't know."

"You say you searched everywhere?" responded Alexander with a sigh of exasperation. "I expected this would be your report. It is so frustrating to me. If you find anything, anything at all, please contact me through the Charles V Hotel in Marseille, or contact my daughter in New York. You have both numbers. After a few days in Marseille I'll be flying directly to Beirut and staying at the Phoenicia Hotel."

"Yes, Monsieur Thomas. I can honestly tell you that we have done our best and have come to the conclusion that we are not able and will not be able to locate Madame Moreau. In all likelihood, I am sorry to tell you, we believe she has passed away. We are no longer convinced that she is still alive.…Good luck to you, sir. Good luck," he repeated because he truly wanted this man to succeed in his search.

"You may be correct, Monsieur Duval…you may indeed be correct. If she is still alive, I will find her. But I must be successful soon or I must assume that is no longer possible. And that decision I must make soon, I am very sad to say."

Alexander spent three days in Marseille before leaving for Beirut, often visiting his friends at Café du Liban, the *Canebière*, paying homage at Notre-Dame-de-la-Garde, and sometimes preferring to sit alone quietly on the promontory he shared so long ago with Madeleine, anticipating that it may indeed be the last time he would visit the site. He had great difficulty finally accepting the possibility that Madeleine would not be found, that she may indeed have passed away, and that he had waited too long. He was sad and felt a sense of deep futility after two years of his frustrating, exhaustive search. He was coming to the point of accepting that he would never find her.

Finally, on June 11, 1962, Alexander boarded the Mideast Airlines flight to Beirut.

When love beckons to you, follow him,
Though his ways are hard and steep.
Kahlil Gibran

CHAPTER 28

Beirut, April 1962

François leaned back in his luxuriant chair as he pulled away slightly from his large mahogany desk. Each morning he arrived at his office at 8 a.m. to examine and analyze financial reports before the telephone began ringing with its incessant demands. After a couple hours of concentration, he liked to turn his chair toward the large windows of his corner office on the thirtieth floor of the Credit Suisse building in West Beirut overlooking the usually sparkling Mediterranean Sea and enjoy his coveted view.

He loved his work as an investment banker with Credit Suisse, one of Europe's most highly respected banks. His years at the London School of Economics had served him well. In only a few years, his education, his personal style, his relationship with the Kabani family, and his fluency in three languages enabled him to become a friend and financial advisor to Arabic speaking rulers of Kuwait, the Gulf States of Bahrain, Qatar, the Emirates, and Saudi Arabia. Many were now fluent in French as was he, but few could speak English as he did. His talents were highly regarded, especially as his clients from Europe and America visited Beirut. He was often called on to host visitors, taking them to the finest restaurants and to the elegant Casino du Liban which rivaled the best in the world, including Paris' Crazy Horse Saloon, and the casinos of Monte Carlo and Las Vegas. He was also popular among his mother's growing circle of commercial and philanthropic leaders.

Life was very good for François who was frequently asked to speak on global economics to students at the American University of Beirut, the finest university in the Near East.

Yet there was something missing.

François' heart belonged to the most beautiful, sensual woman he had ever met...his lover in Paris...Leah. All he ever knew was what she had written him when she abruptly left Paris to go to Palestine in 1948...so long ago. He never received further information of her whereabouts or activities...just her words that she would always love him.

He had never forgotten her, even as he had progressed in his work.

During his late morning respites, François loved to clear his mind as he gazed in the distance, sometimes watching ships sailing the sea to and from the ports of Beirut and Jounieh.

"Looks like a storm brewing," he said to no one in particular as he noticed the scattered rain drops begin striking against the large glass panes…pinging … a staccato sound that he enjoyed.

It was spring of 1962, and while there was turmoil among the powerful political families, it was much calmer in the city after President Eisenhower sent the Marines into Lebanon. Beiruti businessmen and bankers, who always seemed to stay above the fray, remained as apolitical as possible, the wisest course for economic survival, a posture the Lebanese traders had perfected over centuries of invasions and internecine battles.

And to the south, who knew whether the Palestinians and Israelis would ever find a way of occupying the same land. So far, since 1947, the Israelis were in control.

Such were the thoughts of François Moreau, Vice-President of Investment Banking in the Near East offices of Credit Suisse during those difficult years that Lebanese had to survive. But this particular morning would be different for him.

As he enjoyed quiet concentration during his brief reverie, the telephone beckoned with its familiar "buzz-buzz." As he reached for the telephone, he went through his typical decision: French or Arabic?

"*Allo*," he answered in French. "François speaking."

"François?" the soft feminine voice responded breathlessly in French. He instantly recognized the lilting familiar voice from his past that had resided in the recesses of the most private places in his memory cells.

Unnerved, his throat suddenly tightened and his hand began to shake. "Leah! Is it you?"

"*Oui, mon chéri.* I am in Beirut, at the airport."

"At the airport? But why? Are you coming or going?"

"I just flew in from Paris, François. Our Paris. Do you remember?"

He couldn't help but smile, almost breaking into a happy, nervous laugh, at the sound of her voice…all it took for his emotions to become charged with sensuality and joy.

"Do I remember? Oh, Leah, yes. Of course! I have never forgotten you."

"Nor I you, my love…nor I you."

"But, Leah, you left with just a note. And now it's been…what…nearly fourteen years? *Mon Dieu!* Can I see you? Will you stay in Beirut? For dinner at least?"

"*Non, mon chéri*, I must be here only to go south to Israel. You remember, don't you, that I had to leave Paris to help my people. I knew then as I know now if I saw you instead of leaving you the note, I might never leave you…ever…I still love you so much, François. Are you married now?"

"Married? To another? How can you ask such a thing? You still fill my heart, Leah. And while I have lived and continue to live a wonderful life, I have something missing in my soul. You are that something, Leah."

"Perhaps, François, when times are better and I have done all I can do, then perhaps, I pray, I can be with you. It is so difficult."

"What is it you are doing, Leah?"

"Don't you remember, François? I told you in Paris, and I cannot speak of my mission at this time. But, please know that you are always in my thoughts and that I will always love you. And soon, I hope we can be together. This insanity has to end, God knows. As for now, I must go on and yet keep you in my heart."

His emotions bounced from excitement to disappointment to joy to anger. "This is terrible, Leah! How can we love each other so deeply and not be together? What kind of destiny is ours?"

"One day, François, I promise we will be together…forever." She nodded and waved to the airline agent who signaled it was time to board the plane. Her voice lowered. "For now I must say *au revoir*, my love…until later."

"*Au revoir*, my love. Be safe."

He stared at the telephone in his hand as he heard the taunting, disconnect tone. Frustrated, yet grateful to hear her voice once again, his mind raced back to Paris and his days at the Sorbonne, especially his evenings with Leah in romantic Paris.

"She is magnificent," he whispered aloud to the room, to no one. "And like it or not, I still love her so much. Just the sound of her lilting voice, her laughter, makes me excited. My lover, my friend!" Then he laughed, "My elusive ghost!" But he knew that he had no choice but to accept his destiny, so resignedly he thought, "One day, *Insha Allah*."

He set the telephone back on its cradle and turned to the darkening clouds in the west, over the sea, to better understand that Leah and the sea were alike…in the case of both, he seemed to have no influence to change the path of either.

"*Mon Dieu*. I think I now have a better appreciation for my father and mother's life, he thought wistfully. Am I destined to repeat their love affair?"

Your joy is your sorrow unmasked.
Kahlil Gibran

CHAPTER 29

Alexander's Return to Douma, June 1962

Alexander, in a window seat as usual, watched the blue waters of the Mediterranean slip beneath the plane's wings as he anxiously awaited his return to Lebanon.

"Forty-two years…it's been forty-two years," he said softly to the lovely Lebanese attendant moments after she announced to him, "We'll be descending shortly, Monsieur. Our arrival in Beirut is on time. Welcome home."

"Forty-two years," he whispered again to himself as he continued looking out the window at the cloud-flecked sky as it met the high, rugged snow-capped mountains beyond the city. He had deliberately sat on the left side of the plane so he could look to the north of Beirut as they began their southern descent west of the meandering shoreline of Lebanon. He watched the mosaic pattern of the majestic mountain ranges, while feeling a surge of strong, poignant emotions in his body. His skin tingled at the thought of returning to his homeland.

Home. I'm coming back home. He almost started shaking at the thought. Instantly, memories of his childhood in Douma flashed through his mind. He was feeling his deep love for Lebanon.

"Miss," he spoke to the attendant as he pointed out the window, "those are the mountains where I was born. Look! You can still see the snow on the high mountains. Even in June the snows will be there."

"It's so magnificent, Monsieur. I can see why some call Lebanon the 'Switzerland of the Middle East.' No wonder the Lebanese always come back. My friends and I snow-ski in the mountains of Lebanon, and within less than an hour we are water-skiing in the sea. Amazing!"

"That is true…" he smiled proudly, with a twinkle in his eye.

His gaze on the shoreline of Beirut jutting out into the sea cast an excitement in his heart. Looking to his left, to the north, he could see the coastal town of Tripoli, then Byblos, then Jounieh with its large port, and beyond was Beirut. Up the mountains to the east of Tripoli he focused his eyes on the terrain hoping to recognize where his tiny village of Douma was located. Its unique shape would be recognizable, but it was a bit too hazy to clearly see it. He could see the patches of cedar forests, snow on the taller mountains, and the greening valleys of olive groves as they responded to the warming of spring.

As the Mideast Airline's Flight 109 descended, it banked gently to the west, then back to the east to begin its approach to the Beirut airport just a few miles south of the city.

As the stewardess returned to her jump seat toward the front of the plane, Alexander braced himself for the landing. Shortly, the tires squealed as they safely struck the tarmac runway.

His emotions were high. *Home. This is almost too much*, he smiled to himself.

"*Yallah*," shouted the airline representative impatiently waving to the disembarking passengers as they left the plane, "please follow me to the terminal gate marked shaish. There you will find the immigration and custom officers."

Alexander climbed down the steps of the airplane ahead of most of the passengers who were eagerly seeking the gate. When his foot touched the tarmac, he carefully looked all around him. "Beirut," he whispered in amazement. He had never even pictured what it would be like if he ever returned, so the sensations were simultaneously exciting, unfamiliar, and unexpected. He breathed in the familiar smells of the nearby sea blending with the odors of the airport.

"I left by ship…an old, slow ship…and I return by jet airplane," he laughed and said aloud. "Amazing!"

After he concluded passing through customs, Alexander emerged to the large, noisy baggage area where several planeloads of passengers were waiting for their baggage to arrive. All bags were being hand placed on a stationary, sloped bank, crowded by anxious travelers hoping to find their suitcases, boxes and bags filled with everything from clothing to gifts for relatives.

The ubiquitous porters moved through the crowd with their hand wagons. "Do you need help?" they asked everyone.

Alexander watched, not feeling a sense of urgency, but preferring to "people watch" as he noticed everything. In the jostling crowd there were people from all regions of the Middle East and several countries of Africa. There were black-draped Muslim women from the more Islamic and fundamentalist nations, including Yemen, Sudan and Oman wearing their different styles of *abeyehs*; Saudi or Kuwaiti sheikhs in their fabulous woolen cloaks, and *keiffeyehs*; Egyptians, Jordanians, Syrians, and Iraqis in western dress emulating the attire of Europe. Europe's influence is still very strong, thought Alexander as he observed the crowd. The faces were a mixture of all shades ranging from the white-faced Syrian and Europeans to the tanned Lebanese to the brown Egyptians and visitors from the Gulf States. Fascinating, Alexander thought, and so different, the whole world is here, it seems. People from everywhere, coming to the *laissez-faire* Lebanese society. The balance of Christians and Muslims seems to work here, at least for now. Of course, the difficulties of the late 1950s, and need for U.S. forces to quell the street battles in 1958 were the manifestation of the seemingly endless internecine political jousting. Even so, Alexander was confident that the resilience and tenacity of the Lebanese culture were so strong that they would come back very well indeed.

We always come back, he remembered.

"Taxi!" he shouted at the curb. As a cab pulled alongside, he ordered, "Take me to the Phoenicia Hotel."

The taxi pulled up to the curb at the hotel, where Alexander paid the driver in Lebanese pounds he had acquired at the bank exchange branch in the airport.

"*Shookrun*," responded the driver, smiling, as he opened the rear door while accepting his fare plus a generous tip.

"Thank you, driver," Turning, he went into the hotel where he was met by a uniformed doorman.

"Your bags, sir?" he asked in French.

"In the car please, and yes, I'm checking in for a few days," Alexander responded as he handed the doorman a gratuity.

He entered the ornately decorated lobby featuring a mixture of European-design furniture, area oriental rugs spread on polished Lebanese marbled floors, and Middle Eastern wall hangings. Crystal and gold light fixtures sparkled above. Alexander admired the fabulous décor of the renowned Phoenicia Hotel, one of the finest in the world.

Alexander's eyes fixed on a woman in an affeyeh who was kneeling on a small oriental rug in a remote corner of the lobby, kneading dough on a flour-dusted tray. As he walked toward her, along with several others, she threw the flattened dough into the air until it widened to a round sheet eighteen inches across, like a large pizza pie with a very thin crust. When she had achieved just the right thinness and size of the dough, the woman looked up at the crowd and smiled proudly. With the dough in both hands, she gingerly spread the pie-crust shaped dough across the bottom of an inverted stainless steel bowl that was already becoming hot from a small charcoal fire on a bed of stones in front of her. The woman looked up at the crowd and smiled again. Quickly the very thin dough began to bubble from the yeast as the thinner parts and edges began turning brown. In just a few minutes, the thin dough was baked into bread.

"Her presence is a way of reminding ourselves and our visitors of our heritage and culture," spoke the hotel concierge to no one in particular, but loud enough for Alexander and several observers to hear.

"*Attinee khobaz*," spoke a man standing next to Alexander.

"Ten pounds, sir," responded the woman modestly, then, gingerly lifting the bread from the convex bowl, she exchanged it for the fee, handing the man the full sheet. He folded it in half, tore it, and offered the other half to Alexander.

"Would you like part of this *khobaz*?" asked the man as he turned his head toward him wearing a proud smile.

"*Shookrun*," nodded Alexander, accepting the generous portion the man had torn from his bread as though he was tearing a newspaper.

"Ahhh, it tastes so good," smiled Alexander.

"It always does, especially when it is just baked. It's the best bread in the world," he said smiling, waving his arm around his head.

He savored the warm soft bread, inhaling the fragrance of his youth.

"Iskandar," shouted Anthony Abraham from a few feet away. Alexander recognized his familiar voice, calling him by his Arabic name. "I'm glad you are here. We were concerned about you since you were the only one of our group that didn't meet us at Heathrow. You're just in time. The gala and awards ceremony are day after tomorrow."

"*Mahrharbahr*, Anthony," smiled Alexander, putting his arm over his friend's shoulder. Alexander was about three inches taller than his friend, yet they were otherwise equal in so many ways, respecting each other as brothers.

Everyone, including Anthony and his wife, were planning to visit their family villages the next day.

"Marie and I are going to Zahle tomorrow to visit her family. Are you going to Douma, Iskandar? It's an open day with nothing scheduled, although we are all warned to be back in the hotel by noon Saturday for the big event that night."

"Well, Anthony, I think I'm going to take a taxi up to the village. I haven't seen my brother in so many years. It's time. But since my father died in 1956, and my brother has never written...I'll never understand that...I really want to go there." Then, he thought a minute before continuing, "Quite frankly, Anthony; I'm not sure what I'll find. When I left, conditions were so terrible. My memories are not happy ones. When my mother died, part of me died. But I love the mountains and the cedars. I'll go see who's still there."

"Of course, you must. After all, it's been more than forty years, and how many times do we come back to Lebanon anyway?"

"You're right, Anthony. It seems you always are. I think I'm sad that I'm alone here. Helena's not with me, and I have been totally unsuccessful in France. It's so strange. Madeleine is nowhere to be found anywhere in Europe. I don't know how much longer I'll continue looking for her. But right now I'm not feeling so good."

"Maybe you should have brought Helena, Iskandar. She would have loved to see Beirut with you, I'm sure."

"Helena couldn't leave her work. I would have loved to show her where we came from. Maybe another time soon. Still, it's exciting to be here, Anthony, and I'm looking forward to the drive north. I might go up to Bsharre with Danny. It's beautiful up there in the mountains. That's where both our families are from, you know."

"Kahlil Gibran too," responded Anthony quickly. "That's right, Gibran lived up there."

Then, changing the subject, "Have you ever seen the Jeita Grotto just north of Beirut? The stalactites and stalagmites are fabulous…among the most incredible in the world."

"Good idea, Iskandar. We'll go see it. A bunch of us are going to the casino tonight. Why don't you join us? It'll do you good. Come on, we'll have some fun. They say it's as good as Las Vegas, and a lot like in Paris! We're meeting right here in the lobby at 8 o'clock. In fact, why don't you join Marie and me earlier for dinner in the hotel restaurant?"

"Maybe I'll do that, Anthony. Thanks. But first I'm going to my room, take a shower, and telephone Helena."

Later, they enjoyed a delicious dinner of local fish, *hashweh*, *kibbee*, and eggplant *soufflé*. Later, part of the larger group assembled in the lobby to go to the Casino du Liban up in the hills above Jounieh in two vans. The drive at night was spectacular looking down at the city lights.

"Not all of us are here tonight. The others are getting an early start in the morning," announced Danny to the group in the van. "As for the rest of us, we're going to have a good time, so let's go. Everyone be ready to have some fun! Look at that view! What a city!" he exclaimed, pointing.

They gathered on the casino balcony on the western hillside overlooking the shoreline and the sea. It was a startling vantage point. They could look down on Beirut with the flickering lights from the homes, apartments, tall office buildings, and shops…a city of over one million people during the best of the halcyon days of the early 1960s when indeed it was the "Paris of the Middle East." The view was magnificent.

"Beautiful isn't it, Iskandar?"

"I'm glad I came, Anthony. I do feel a lot better. And looking down on Beirut tonight is a sight I've never seen. It's incredible!"

"It's great to be here for all of us, Iskandar. They treat us like visiting royalty; everyone is warm and welcoming, friendly to a fault. I love our culture. It's too bad more Americans don't visit here to see for themselves."

"It's a real eye-opener for me. I've been so involved in my businesses. But now, I am reminded of my heritage, where I came from. It's really something isn't it, Anthony?"

Marie turned from gazing down on the city, and, looking at her friend, said to him in a soft voice, "Maybe you should consider bringing Helena back here next year, Iskandar. It would do her good to see where her father and his father came from."

"Good idea, Marie," responded Alexander.

"Maybe your life will find a new direction now that you have returned to your village," spoke Anthony pensively as they stood side by side at the railing of the balcony, looking down on the city a thousand feet below. "Maybe something good will come out of our visit, my friend. We all were peasants, went to America, became peddlers, and, thanks to God, we succeeded. And we helped others. So, Iskandar, rest easy and feel good about yourself, and your life. You are still young. Put yourself and your life in the hands of God, my friend. You may be surprised at what He has in store for you. Maybe you'll even find a beautiful Lebanese woman here in Beirut," he chuckled, only half kidding.

Alexander patted him on the back. "You're right, Anthony. Thank you."

"Hello, fellas," spoke Fred Gattas as he sauntered up to them "Are y'all enjoyin' yourselves here?" Fred's Memphis accent made them smile. His speech matched his southern drawl.

"Fred," Alexander replied, "I've lived in Central Florida for forty years and I don't think I've ever heard as thick a southern accent as yours or Albert Harris'."

Anthony joined with Alexander as they both laughed.

"Waal," Fred responded, accentuating his West Tennessee drawl even more, joining in the humor, "ah know y'all make fun of ma accent, but I'll tell ya, if I didn't talk like this in Memphis, my business would surely go away. They'd think I was a Yankee or sumpthin' else."

"No, sir," George Maloof stepped in and spoke, "Fred, nobody would ever call you a Yankee, at least not in Cleveland. Your drawl is so thick, I can hardly understand you sometimes. Even when you speak in Arabic, you have a drawl. It's really funny to listen to you talk 'Suthin'," he added, mimicking his friend.

"You boys having a good time?" It was Danny Thomas with his ever-present cigar. "I'm having a terrific time here myself. We're going to drive up to Bsharre in the morning and we might be going to Damascus on Sunday after church. Anyone want to join us?"

Everyone was feeling a sense of renewal, of camaraderie. After they all enjoyed a couple of hours in the casino, they assembled at the front glass doors where they would meet the limos that would take them back to the hotel. The evening was a pleasure for everyone that night. Yet, all of them anxiously wanted to make a pilgrimage to their home villages the next day. Some even planned to make a second visit to their relatives' homes after the awards ceremony two days hence.

"Okay then, we'll see you at the Saturday night events," Danny announced in the hotel lobby as he and his family turned to leave.

"Heck," Fred said to the few remaining in the group, "none of us did what we did at St. Jude's for an award. Don't get me wrong, fellas, ah'm right proud to be here and ah'm surely honored to be among such a crowd of you successful guys. It's excitin' just to be part of this."

"Don't give us that 'I'm jus' an ol' suthern farmboy tryin' tuh make a livin' and y'all are so rich compared to me' stuff, Fred," laughed Emile Hajar, from Boston. "We all know you're the wealthiest guy in Memphis. You've got a beautiful family, and without you there might not have even been a St. Jude Hospital. So, brother, just let us stand in your shadow and we'll be grateful."

Fred laughed at the friendly teasing and they all enjoyed their exhilaration, buoyed by the visceral sensations of actually returning to their homeland, most, if not all, for the first time.

The deeper that sorrow carves into your being,
the more joy you can contain.
Kahlil Gibran

CHAPTER 30

On to Douma

The next morning, Alexander gazed out the window at the sea as his taxi drove north along the coast to the center of the port city of Tripoli. The taxi then turned sharply right at the key intersection downtown. He felt his weight shift in the back seat.

Kassem, his driver, turned his head, looking at his passenger sitting next to him. "We will be going up the mountain now. We should be in your village soon, *Insha Allah*," spoke the driver to Alexander in his native Arabic, Alexander fully comprehending.

"*Shookrun*," he replied, looking at his watch. "We should be in Douma by eleven o'clock then. Stay with me; depending on what we find, we may drive north from there."

"*Na'am*," the driver replied, nodding his head. "Do you like my car, sir? It's a five-year-old Mercedes. I take very good care of it. My brother's son is an excellent mechanic. He takes care of the motor and brakes for me. I shine it each day. Of course, if I didn't the dust from these mountain roads would be as thick as bread!"

During the forty-minute drive up the winding mountain road, Alexander noticed most of the pavement was only wide enough for one car, with occasional spots where a car could pull over to allow another car or truck to pass by heading in the opposite direction. It was a well-worn passage that in some places in centuries past was just wide enough for single file soldiers to march across the mountains down to the sea, adequate for the invading Greeks before Christ. It was first widened by the Romans to provide room for their war wagons, then later by the Islamic movement followed by the Crusaders. Over the centuries, this very road served as a trade route and connected the region to the port. It was only in the mid-twentieth century after World War II that the government was able to widen and pave part of the trail with asphalt, still barely wide enough for two cars to pass.

All the way up the curving, winding mountain road, the car careened along the edge of the precipice, too close for Alexander's taste. He guessed that the driver, in his mid-forties, was trying to impress his customer with the capabilities of his prestigious car. They were now high in the mountains overlooking the lush olive groves two thousand feet below.

"Take it easy, Kassem," Alexander finally shouted over the din of the noise of the wheels on the road. "We've got plenty of time. I know this road from my youth. But when I traveled here, it was a dirt path. I did it on a donkey or wagon. I've come too long a way to end it on this road, no matter how pretty this car would look down that ravine!"

"Yessir," replied the driver, "whatever you wish."

"Kassem," Alexander spoke after the car slowed down and the sounds softened, "How long have you lived in Beirut? Tell me of your family."

"My family came from Jerusalem in the late 1890's. At that time, Palestine was the commercial center of the eastern Mediterranean, Jaffa was a major port, and Beirut was a small port town. Things began to change so much early in the 1900s when many Europeans began migrating into Palestine, a place for people of all religions. It was prosperous and peaceful. That is when we came to Lebanon. Opportunities seemed to be better here for us, so my family came to Beirut. My wife Ramza's family lives in the South. They have stayed there because we are Sunni Muslim, and the Shimal, the North, is mostly Christian. Of course, the Druze live in the Shouf Mountains east of Beirut. You know, Mr. Thomas, it was the same in Palestine from centuries ago. We had Christian villages like Bethlehem, the birthplace of Jesus, Ramallah and Nazareth. Others consisted of Jewish villages or Sunni or Shia Muslim. We each stayed with our own kind, even though we all got along with each other and traded among the villages. However, we all prefer...no, I must be honest...required our children to marry within our own religions. But we got along very well. That is, until the war."

Having listened to Kassem recall his story for twenty non-stop minutes, Alexander, unable to resist as he realized more and more he was getting very close to Douma, responded by briefly telling his own story, including some aspects about Madeleine. While some things were simply no one else's business, he felt almost comfortable sharing his emotional burden to this driver whom in all likelihood he would never see again.

"I left my village as a very young man...just a boy actually, in 1920. My older brother chose to stay in the mountains, but I felt a better future awaited me in America. My mother urged me to follow my father there to find my future. And since I trusted her wisdom completely, I did just that. I have not returned to my village for more than forty years, Kassem. I don't even know who is still alive here. So, this is a very significant trip for me. While I believe I have accomplished all I could in America, I am very happy to return to Lebanon, yet I have no idea what awaits me in Douma."

"My friend," Kassem replied, "there are many destinies in our lives, I believe. Only *Allah* knows what will come."

Just at that moment, near the top of the mountain, Alexander spotted a familiar large stone on the valley side of the road just ahead. He almost shuddered at the familiar sight. It was still elongated, flat and about three feet tall and five feet long. "Stop the car, Kassem," he called. "Stop the car right here. I want to get out for a few minutes right now."

Alexander waited for the Mercedes to completely come to a stop before opening his door. "I'll need a few minutes, Kassem." He walked across the road to the stone with Kassem following closely, gazing down the valley, seeing the village of his birth far below with the houses strewn along the steep terraces. He chuckled as he fondly slapped the stone as if it was his close friend. Not much had changed in the village.

"See how the village looks like a scorpion from here, Kassem? He said, admiring his village, pointing below. "And see how almost all the rooftops are red? They are that way because legend says that it is to remind everyone of the blood that has been spilled here over the ages by our young men in protecting these mountains from the invaders. Sixteen times, Kassem. Can you believe it?"

Alexander, gesturing in various directions, told his new friend of the ancient cedars, how so many had disappeared at the hands of everyone from the Phoenicians on, ultimately defacing the mountain ranges of northern Lebanon.

"See those olive trees there on the valley floor by the river? Some of those trees are more than a thousand years old."

"Yes, Mr. Thomas, I know. My family had many ancient olive trees in Palestine."

"Up there," Alexander said, pointing up the mountain to his right, "are the orchards, or what's left of them.

"Legends say my family has lived here since before Christ. And yet, I went away like many others to seek a better life.

"And now," Alexander continued speaking with his head looking down, "I am returning to the place of my birth. My father is gone now; my mother died many years ago, and I'm not sure what I'm going to find. I'm searching for my brother and cousins."

"Mr. Thomas, I believe your heart is filled with emotions and that you might be a little afraid of what awaits you down there, but I also think that you must accept whatever you find. Sir," he beckoned softly, looking at his watch, and gestured to the car, "I think it is time to drive on to the village."

Before Alexander moved, he looked at the ground, digging his hand into his pocket and endearingly feeling the stone he had carried from this very spot so long ago when he last looked back at his beloved village. As he held the stone memento in his fingers, he looked again to the rooftops below. He recalled the very sensations he had felt that morning so long ago when he left Douma to seek his destiny in America. His eyes began to moisten from nostalgia as he remembered his mother and his childhood. He thought of his brother and how he had watched over him. He remembered his mother's gentle hands. His heart began to swell as he felt himself breathe deeply, looking, wondering what awaited him.

Then, he stood tall, squared his shoulders, wiped the light perspiration from his forehead, and turned to Kassem.

"Let's go. It is time for me to walk in Douma once again. But it is difficult for me. Do you understand?"

"Of course," Kassem replied, "it is always difficult to go back home, and for you...after all these years..." his voice trailed off.

The black four-door Mercedes slowly entered the main street of the village at the south and reached the center of the town's *souk*.

"See the stone sarcophagus there with the cedar tree at each end in the middle of the *souk*, Kassem?"

"*Na'am*," he responded.

"There..." continued Alexander, "you can read the plaque...it has the date of 350 B.C., acknowledging the arrival of the six Chalhoub brothers and their families to this place. Legend tells of my ancestors who came so long ago from the Golan in Syria to settle here. The plaque speaks of that date as the founding date of this village. Remarkable, isn't it? At the time, this was a heavily forested mountain range thick with wildlife: bear, deer, even lions, some say, and birds of all kinds."

Kassem slowly continued driving down the village road.

"We are here, Mr. Thomas," Kassem intervened. "Point to your house."

"Over there, Kassem. You see the small square stone building? That is where I was born. It looks so much smaller now. My God," Alexander exclaimed with a drooping mouth, viewing the modest...no...almost barren structure about eight feet in height. "You see this, Kassem? That is where five of us lived. My God, this is too much," Alexander whispered again, feeling a strong sense of humility, of warmth, of reconnecting to his soul. "I am stunned with memories, Kassem. I can't really describe my feelings. There are so many...my youth, joy, pain, agony, love...they are all there." He reached deep into his pocket and withdrew his stone companion, fondling it in his hand. *We are here, my friend, we are home again.*

They stepped from the car, and looking at the house, Kassem asked, "Yes, Mr. Thomas, but what of the very large house next to your birthplace? What is that?"

"That must be the new home my father built when he returned to the village after the Second War. He told me that he would build a new, larger home for Milhelm and his family. That must be it. He would never sell the land. No one in my family has ever, for centuries, it seems, sold our land. Soon after he finished the house he wrote to me about it, but I haven't heard from anyone else in years. Only after the war when they needed help. Then the letters stopped."

Alexander stepped from the taxicab, asked Kassem to return in two hours, and turned to walk the ten steps up to the newer main house, stopping at the top to look at the old stone house…hovel?…to his left.

"Milhelm?" he yelled at the door as if he had left only the day before. "Milhelm?" he repeated his call.

"*Na'am?*" came the response from a woman's voice inside. He heard footsteps and then the heavy front door opened. "*Ahlen wa sahlen.* Welcome!" A pretty, young woman spoke with a smile, customarily stretching out her arm as a gesture of welcome, beckoning Alexander to enter her home. He reckoned she was in her early thirties.

"*Mahrharbahr,*" spoke Alexander, smiling. "Is this still *Beit* Chalhoub, the Chalhoub family home?"

"Yes, yes it is. *Shooishme?* What is your name?" she asked, looking directly at the visitor.

"I am Iskandar Thomé Chalhoub," Alexander replied, and then asked, "Shooishich?"

"I am Katrina." With a friendly, innocent smile, she responded in English, sensing her visitor was American.

Alexander couldn't believe his eyes. The vivacious fair-haired, light-complexioned, young woman looked so much like his mother the last time he saw her so long ago. He was totally caught off guard by his mother's name. "Katrina, you say?" he gasped.

She smiled broadly as the rays of the sun stroked her auburn hair when she stepped outside the door to speak to this man who was unfamiliar to her and surely to almost anyone in the village. Of that she was certain. But his face would certainly fit in the village, she thought. He could easily be part of this family.

Alexander was struck by the familiar aromas emanating from the kitchen in the rear of the house. There was an unmistakable smell of the blending of sautéed onions with a hint of garlic, and fresh bread baking in the oven. His thoughts raced to his youth, remembering the very same aromas he would smell as he came home from school to find his mother at the fire in their three-room home.

His sensations were almost overpowering: peace, a touch of sadness, compassion, and comfortable familiarity. Eager now to enter the house, his heart was filled with a deep sense of "coming home."

Katrina couldn't take her eyes off her visitor's face. "You could be my Uncle Iskandar, son of Ibrahim. You look so much like my father."

"Yes, that is exactly who I am," he replied with a broad smile.

"But Iskandar Thomé *Ibn* Ibrahim Chalhoub is in America. I have never met him, but I believe he is there. Why do you now come here, sir?"

"I am here because this is my home. I am with a group returning to celebrate St. Jude Hospital in America, and to visit my family." He smiled, hoping to reassure the attractive young woman who reminded him of his own daughter. "I have come to see my brother." He added softly and endearingly, "You look very much like someone I knew many years ago."

Alexander hoped there were elders inside because she was not yet convinced. His eyes looked beyond her into the sparsely furnished home with its smooth, white plaster ceiling and walls, and large Oriental rug on the streaked, polished Lebanese marble floor. The austere walls had framed family photographs placed strategically over the couch and in the adjoining open dining room.

"I am Katrina, youngest daughter of Milhelm Thomé Chalhoub," she said proudly, but in a friendly tone.

"Katrina?" Alexander asked. "Did you say Milhelm is your father?"

"Of course. I have two brothers and a sister. Mother and I take care of *Biyee*. He is not well, you know."

"No, I do not know. I must see him immediately. What is wrong?" Without waiting for an answer, he stepped to the side of Katrina and strode into the living room, looking for the only apparent place that could lead to a bedroom. "Is he upstairs?"

"*La*," Katrina shook her head. "His bedroom is there," she replied, pointing with her hand. "But who are you, sir? I heard you say your name, but I don't believe it."

Losing his patience a bit, he sharply replied, "I am your uncle. Now take me to your father…please."

Surprised by the stranger's authoritative response, Katrina quickly led Alexander to her father's bedroom.

As he stepped through the doorway, his eyes went straight to the bed on which his older, beloved brother lay, then focused on the face on the pillow.

Alexander felt a sense of shock in his body as he saw his big brother.

"Milhelm," he said hurriedly as he stepped quickly into the room to the bedside. "Milhelm," he whispered. "What is the matter, *khai-yi*? What has happened?" He saw that his brother, always a very large man, was thin and weakened, without much energy. He looked so forlorn in his plain white *abeyah*, his body-length, cotton robe. Alexander, eyes moistening from his emotional impact, sensed that this was what he must now wear all the time.

Alexander turned to Katrina and whispered. "What happened, Katrina? Tell me, what is wrong with my brother."

Now convinced Alexander indeed was her father's brother, she opened up to him. "My father suffered a severe stroke two years ago and hasn't been able to speak much since. It has been very difficult for him. He was so strong, so important in the village. But now…" her voice trailed off as she looked sadly into Alexander's eyes. She continued, "He will know you, I am certain, even though I didn't recognize you, uncle. Go to him. Embrace him. Let him know you are here."

Alexander softly stepped to the bedside of his brother. "Milhelm," he whispered in his ear, "Milhelm, it is Iskandar, your little brother. Oh, my Lord," he said as he bent over and kissed his brother's cheek. As he did, he noticed a teardrop on his brother's cheek, and then saw his brother's eyes were filling with tears. A slight, but growing smile of familiarity formed on Milhelm's dry lips. His right arm and hand were clearly limp across his chest. Alexander had seen the signs of stroke in Florida's VA hospitals.

Alexander pulled up a chair to the bed and reached over to hold his brother's strong left hand, thankful now that he didn't further delay seeing him.

"His hand is still large, much larger than mine, and it is warm," Alexander said to Katrina as he turned his head to look at her through his own tear-filled eyes. "And he just squeezed my hand. His grip is still very strong," he sighed in relief. Then, looking up at the ceiling, he thought, *Oh, God, I pray I am not too late to be with my brother. Thank you, God.*

"His left side is still very strong. But his right side is weak and paralyzed. He cannot speak well," Katrina told him.

"Does he have adequate medical care?"

"Some. But he could use more. He has been depressed much of the time, but perhaps with your visit, he will feel better about trying harder. Aside from his paralysis and inability to speak, he is in good health. But he is sad most of the time."

Alexander gestured as he asked Katrina to leave him alone with his brother for a few minutes. Welcoming a respite, she exited, looking over her shoulder at the two men touching each other in joyful reunion.

"Oh, Milhelm, I'm so sorry I took so long to come home." As he began speaking to his brother of his life, his children, and his love, both Alexander's and Milhelm's eyes filled with tears, grateful for this surprise visit, remembering their youth together.

"Forty years, Milhelm. Forty years. It's been so long…too long, *khai-yi*. I love you, and we must do whatever is necessary to help you get well."

Two hours later, when Kassem returned to the house at the appointed time, Alexander asked him to leave him and return later in the day.

"I wish to stay today with my brother as much as I can. It has been too long. We have so very much to share."

Throughout the remainder of the day, Alexander stayed with his brother, taking a break at times to let him rest or sleep. He accepted Katrina's offer to walk to the *souk* with her.

As Katrina took her uncle's hand, they went down the stone steps to the now paved street.

"Let me show you our church, uncle. It is old, but it is beautiful. You know how much a part of our family life it is, don't you?" Then, she added, "We can pray for your successful return and for *Biyee*."

"Oh, yes, Katrina," Alexander replied proudly. "The church has always been very important to this family. It was for me when your father and I were very young."

After entering the solidly built stone edifice with the steeply sloped, red-tiled roof, and enormous hand-carved cedar front doors, they sat in the family pew to pray together for Milhelm's recovery. As Alexander leaned back, he instantly felt his body press against the familiar hand-hewn wooden seat and backrest. The sensations reminded him of the many Sundays he sat next to his mother, with his older brother on her other side. Sweet memories of his childhood and of the devotion and love of his mother enveloped him. He subconsciously gripped his niece's hand tightly.

After silent prayers, he turned to his niece and whispered, "Faith, Katrina… faith can move mountains, your grandmother would always say. So, we will look to God for His healing power. You know, Katrina," he continued, looking around the wood and stone interior of the ancient church, "this church looked enormous to me as a boy, but it doesn't seem so large now. Ahhh…the same icons are here."

"It's a small church, and ours is a small village, but I'm sure it seemed different to you as a boy." Then, simply looking at his saddened face in wonder for a moment, she added, "I'm so grateful to be here with you, Uncle Iskandar."

Then she smiled, trying to change his melancholy mood. "Let's go to the *souk*. Perhaps you will see some familiar faces."

As they walked the village's main street to the center, Alexander noted that the short lanes sloping up or down off the street were still mostly gravel and unpaved. The steepness up the slopes was still severe, demanding superior leg strength. He recalled how, as boys, he and his brother always felt strong.

"It hasn't really changed all that much has it, uncle?"

"No, Katrina, it hasn't. It seems very much like I remember. Even after forty years. A few homes are new and larger, of course."

As they got closer to the *souk*, they exchanged greetings with more and more pedestrians strolling in the opposite direction, some of whom appeared familiar, most not.

"By the way, Katrina, how is Aunt Sara?"

"Aunt Sara? Oh, uncle, she passed away three years ago."

"Oh, I'm sorry." He felt that now familiar poignant sense of guilt. Too late again, he agonized.

"She and my father spoke often of you. They missed you so much over the years. I think when Aunt Sara died, she took with her many family stories…even secrets," she smiled. "She knew everything, didn't she? Everyone always deferred to her. She could have been the sheikh of the village if she were a man."

"She was the matriarch of the family, for sure. And very strong," Alexander added with a smile.

Then she turned to him and asked, "Are there any people you would especially like to visit while you are here?"

"Actually, Katrina, I'm really here to see your father and our family, and to just walk the streets of the village. I think I'll sit here in the *souk* for a few minutes until we go back to the house."

After he looked around for a while, watching the villagers stroll in the market area, Alexander noticed he was feeling an almost overpowering swell of nostalgia with a mixture of joy and sadness, yet, embracing the warmth of being "home."

"Look up there, Katrina," he said to his niece sitting behind him. "That small grove of cedars is where your father and I played together back in the early years when we were boys. We would go up the mountain to the apple grove, then climb the cedars so we could look at the sea. And down there, in the valley, we would join in the olive harvest. Ah me," he sighed, "those were the simple days. We were very poor then. But everyone in the village was poor."

"We too are without much, Uncle. And I have to say, compared to cousins in Beirut, we are very poor here in the mountains. But we survive, and we are happy. We have a saying here...'We wish you enough.' Don't you see? Enough... enough food, enough sunshine to brighten your life...enough rain to provide for your needs...but not necessarily do we wish for more...'things,'" she smiled. "I like that view, and that is why I am very happy here watching over my father. My brothers and sisters are in Beirut. But I like it here in the mountains. We feel very rich here, although we have little money. The summers are cool, dry, and we have many visitors. Of course, the winters can be very cold, as you know. But it is true, my heart is here," she added after a sigh, looking across the *souk*.

"Well, Katrina, I too feel your sense of pride, of contentment here. Now, let's go back to the house and see your father."

Alexander stood, stretched his arms, and gave his niece a warm embrace. "I am very proud of you, Katrina, for your dedication to your father. And your mother? By the way, where is she?"

"Oh, *Imei* is in Tripoli for the day, visiting her sister. She will be disappointed that she didn't see you. But you will return soon, won't you? I know she will look forward to your next visit as will my father."

"I will be back, Katrina. Perhaps tomorrow, depending on what happens at our event in Beirut, but surely by Monday. So tell your mother I wish to see her. Let's assume Monday. Alright?"

"Yes, Uncle. Monday for sure. Now, let's walk back to the house."

As they turned, Alexander's eyes moved across the small village *souk*, up toward the mountains, then down to the terraced vineyards...the fruit trees in the distance lining the slopes...the olive groves below...remembering. Everything reminded him of his childhood days. Some made him smile. Others made him sad.

He shrugged his shoulders and responded to Katrina's call, "Come, Uncle. We must go." She was full of life, exuberant, and totally concerned for her father's welfare.

He stepped toward her, following until he caught up with her, and then together they began to briskly walk back to "*Beit Milhelm*," Milhelm's family home.

Alexander stumbled abruptly on an uneven step and decided to sit on the bench under the family grape arboretum next to the house. He patted the seat and beckoned for Katrina to sit beside him.

"He saved my life more than once, Katrina," he exclaimed fervently, "and now it is my turn to help him. Oh, Katrina, I am so sad for him...I waited too long to come." Alexander was angry with himself. "How I looked forward to sharing this time with your father. I love him so much. He watched over me all those years of my youth. He was so alive, so strong. Katrina. Your father was my hero. He literally saved my life when I was caught in a snowstorm up there," he said in a soft voice while pointing to the ridge of the mountains above them. "And now, he cannot speak to me with his voice. Damn!"

"But he is speaking to you with his eyes. You have made him very happy with your visit. Yes, he would have so much enjoyed sitting here, visiting with you. Before his stroke, he spoke about you all of my life, Uncle Iskandar. He still tries sometimes but it is too difficult for him. He told all his children how carefree and daring you were and how proud he is of you," Katrina said consolingly. "Always he has spoken of you with pride. He sometimes regretted not going with you to America. But I believe he has been very happy here in the mountains. It has been hard, to be sure. We have had to do without much, but we also have our family, our friends, the family church, and our heritage. We are people of the mountains. You understand, don't you?"

He nodded with an understanding smile.

"We all looked to you during those very hard days after the war. There was a food shortage and we had few clothes. The shipments you sent us helped us through those harsh, cold winters. We survived as a family and stayed together. I don't know if my father wrote to you then." She shrugged her shoulders. "Perhaps it isn't part of our culture. Anyway, then he got sick and very depressed and couldn't write." She smiled. "My father is a wonderful man...a kind man. He never succeeded in business, but what a good man."

Alexander thought how very different this was from his own prosperous way of life. Listening to Katrina's soft voice of compassion, he realized her presence had brought him to renew his appreciation of his family here in the village of his birth. "I have so much to be grateful for, Katrina," he said as he gripped her hand, looking into her eyes. "For so many years I was mostly absorbed in my work. I lost my son, Michael, during the war. Then, when Helene, my wife, went to sleep, I became very lonely. I am sorry now that I didn't come back then. But I never received any answers to my letters, so, I thought everyone was fine and doing well. But now, I can see what happened."

Katrina spoke to him, bonding with her uncle, "Perhaps I can tell you now, knowing you will understand. My father was a proud man as you are and could not write to you to tell you he needed help. He could never have done that. He didn't want to bother you all those years. And then," she took a deep breath, pausing, "when he suffered his stroke, he wasn't able to speak or write. He suffered in silence. He didn't want us to tell you. I don't know why. We didn't know what to do. And we don't know what secrets he has inside. But I am sure he is very happy you have come now. And now he may regret our not writing to let you know. Men are too proud, I think," she shrugged. "Maybe your visit will help him get better."

Alexander frowned slightly, "I should have come years ago. I think I have waited too long for too many things. I have missed very important appointments with two people I love very much. And now I must live with the knowledge of what might have been here, Katrina, and in Marseille."

"Marseille?" she asked.

"Yes," he replied, "but it's a long story. It began when I was very young, on my way to America. Perhaps one day I will tell you about it. But not now. We must only look to helping your father. And now, I need to use your telephone."

"It's in the living room, Uncle. We just got our telephone only two years ago. It's been very hard to obtain one ever since the war."

"So long?"

She shrugged again, accepting.

They stood and embraced.

"Let's go into the house now."

Alexander sat for a moment thinking, calling on his nearly fifteen-year involvement and financial support at the VA hospital's therapy programs in Tampa where he had worked after his son died. He had also been supporting a prominent rehabilitation clinic in Orlando. He knew more could be done for Milhelm, and although he was not sure how much his brother would improve physically, he knew having regular therapy sessions would certainly improve his attitude, and, he knew that as his spirits improved, so too would his physical condition.

"I will have a new sturdy wheelchair sent to you, Katrina," Alexander told his niece. "Whatever is available, I will have it sent to my brother as soon as I get home. Then you can take him to the *souk*. He'll like that." Alexander didn't need reminding of his brother's needs. Nor did he need any request to act. He became totally preoccupied with his brother's welfare. "We'll do what needs to be done, Katrina. I'll need your help though."

His initial call was to St. George Hospital in Beirut. He spoke in Arabic to the Medical Director. Alexander was determined to succeed in bringing help to his brother.

"I want the best physical and speech therapists you can find. Full time. Let them alternate every other day at the hospital and then here with my brother. I will be responsible for their full salary and travel costs. If you will agree, then I will pay you in advance for six months at a time." On a roll now, he added, "In addition, I'm sure you have certain needs at the hospital that we can discuss. Oh," he remembered, "and a new wheelchair. We need a wheelchair now." After reviewing the various options the hospital could offer to a paying family, a welcomed situation to be sure, they both agreed the hospital would begin treatments immediately. Relieved at what the director told him, he responded, "*Shookrun*," confidently as he completed the call, feeling helpful and assured.

"Katrina," he said as he placed the telephone in the cradle, turning to her, "I have arranged for St. George Hospital to provide whatever your father may need in medications, therapy, and for his comfort. I know you will continue to watch over him and be my liaison. We will communicate regularly and I will arrange for you to be properly paid. I want to do anything and everything I can do for my only brother. For him and for our mother and father. Do you understand?" He wrote on a notepad as he spoke. "Here is Dr. Nabeel Zein's name and phone number. He is the man I just talked to. Stay in touch with him."

"Of course," Katrina replied, "but Uncle Iskandar, I cannot accept any payment from you. I will ask that you give it to St. Mary's, our family church, instead."

"Certainly, how 'American' of me." He smiled, understanding. "Yet I want to provide for your needs whatever they become. You are my brother's daughter, which makes you my daughter as well."

"And now, Uncle, let's walk to where your mother sleeps. She's up there on the hill by the church next to your father, my grandfather, my *jiddou*."

They walked side by side up the winding path, and as they came closer to the graves, Alexander again felt his chest heave with emotion, catching his breath, remembering his mother's gentle, enduring love, and his father's love and strength. The moment they arrived at their graves, he fell to his knees.

"Thank you, Lord," he spoke softly, "thank you for bringing me safely to my home, to the place of my birth, and to my brother. And thank you for reminding me of so many blessings you have bestowed on me." He felt it. He knew where his heart was. His transformation was becoming complete. He covered his grieving face with his hands as his tears overflowed.

As he spoke, Alexander felt himself experience a sense of willingness to accept whatever might come into his life. He was wonderfully impressed by Katrina's unselfish devotion, but not surprised at her exuberant acceptance of her life, of having so much less in a material sense than he had experienced. So refreshing, and so lovely.

"Thank you too, Katrina, for teaching me simply by being who you are. But I shouldn't be surprised. Your father was, at the same time, incredibly strong physically, and yet generous and giving, with the sensitive soul of a poet, like Gibran."

Later, as Kassem held the Mercedes car door open for him, Katrina whispered, "*Allah ma'ak*, Uncle Iskandar, go with God, and know we all love you. Please come back soon. And next time bring Helena." They kissed each other's cheeks. She eagerly hugged her uncle, wrapping both her arms around him.

Alexander pulled his face back a few inches and said, looking at her face, "You have the face of your grandmother, Katrina. So lovely, so beautiful. You and Helena both carry her in you. *Allah ma'ak*, Katrina," Alexander whispered once again as he lingered, looking into her eyes before climbing into the waiting taxicab.

Now speaking from inside, before he closed the door, he said, "I must go to Beirut now, but I will return Monday before I leave for America. And I will come to see you and my family very soon after. You have restored my faith. *Shookrun*, dear Katrina, *shookrun*. You are my family, and you have entered my life at a very important time."

He sat back into the front seat of the taxi, heaved a sigh, and looked back to see his niece dabbing the corners of her eyes with her lace hankie as he too felt an overflow of tears and wiped them from his cheeks. She is such a joy.

The taxi surged up the mountain road as Kassem confidently pressed the accelerator pedal, calling on all 360 horsepower under the cab's shiny hood he had buffed during the afternoon.

After a few minutes as the powerful car climbed the steep incline to the ridge, Alexander, tapping Kassem on his shoulder, alerted Kassem, wanting him to stop ahead. "Kassem, there is the stone on the right! Stop the car. I want to look from there one more time for a few minutes."

Alexander emerged from the front seat of the cab and stepped to the familiar stone once again. More at ease with himself, and having filled his thoughts with Katrina and Milhelm, recalling so much of his childhood, and feeling better about the fact that he had not been successful in his two-year search for Madeleine, he became absorbed in the view of his village, the mountains, the valleys, the olive trees, and his beloved cedars in their clusters on the mountain slopes.

Finally he spoke. "Well, Kassem, I have come full circle now, more than a full lifetime, more than forty years later, and I have fulfilled my destiny. I have achieved my mother's wishes and gone beyond the cedars…she was so wise. Even more, Kassem, I have returned to my roots. Now where will my life lead me? I must think about that."

"My friend," Kassem replied as he stood beside Alexander and put his arm around the shoulders of his new friend, "you have indeed fulfilled your mother's dying wishes. You know that she and your father sleep together in peace, and you know they wish only for your peace of mind. So, do that for yourself. Find your heart, follow it. Do as Gibran admonishes, and realize that we do not know what *Allah* has in store for us. Muslims believe, as He speaks in the Quran: 'Only God, and there is only one God, knows what awaits us even in the next minute.' So dear friend, now that you have returned to your homeland after so many years, you have found your youth, your brother, and your family, and perhaps you have found yourself, the most important thing. You must live, truly live, knowing God has something very good in store for you." Kassem smiled and returned to his place behind the wheel. "We must be on our way to Beirut where you must begin the rest of your life."

As Katrina watched the black Mercedes leave the village and ascend the winding road up the mountain, her eyes focused on the sharp bend in the road higher up where she knew the car would stop.

That's the spot everyone enjoys a brief, but important moment to look down on the village rooftops. Then, as she saw the Mercedes pull to a stop, she smiled. She knew he couldn't see her from such a distance, but she waved her arm anyway, connecting to her father's beloved brother one last time. But he did see her and once again nostalgically remembered Madeleine standing on the pier in Marseille.

As Katrina turned and walked up the stone steps to the door before entering her home, she hesitated, looked again up the mountain road and thought for a moment. Uncle Iskandar said he thought he was too late for two important people in his life, and he mentioned Marseille. I wonder if he meant the woman who came here during the war when I was a little girl. She was from Marseille. Yes, Madame Moreau was very beautiful. And she had a handsome son who looked just like Uncle Iskandar.

Katrina leaned against the door, thinking…and smiled, closing her eyes.

Didn't she move to Beirut? My father would know. I wonder if that woman is the same person Uncle Iskandar spoke of? I wonder if he knows she's in Beirut even today?

All these things shall love do unto you that
you may know secrets of your heart and
in that knowledge become a fragment of Life's heart.
Kahlil Gibran

CHAPTER 31

Alexander, deep in his memories as a young boy, sat quietly thinking as Kassem drove. He couldn't take his eyes off the surrounding mountains as the taxi wound its way down the narrow, winding road to take him back to Tripoli, then the hotel in Beirut where he would dress to attend the President's gala that evening.

Alexander recalled, "It snows so much up there, another 3000 feet above the village, that we had to put a door in the roof so we could enter the building when the snow was deeper than the building was tall." He laughed, remembering. "It was so hard then. My life was terribly difficult here as a boy...we had nothing. I mean nothing, Kassem. My mother was a saint. We were everything to her. I loved her so much. And my brother, Milhelm. What a man. But how he suffers now."

Kassem, concentrating intently as he carefully steered the Mercedes at a slower rate of speed this time, replied, "Yes, I am sure it was hard, Mr. Thomas, but wouldn't you agree that your difficult experiences as a child better prepared you for the years to come?"

"Oh yes," Alexander replied with a smile, "I'm certain you are correct. For sure, it has been very hard most of my life. Life During my youth life's experiences somehow taught me it was not supposed to be easy, and it certainly wasn't easy; that it would be difficult, and," he chuckled, "There were times when I thought it was too difficult to continue."

"But you never gave up, did you?" Kassem smiled.

"Give up? Never!" Alexander responded firmly, shaking his head. "Giving up was never part of our way of life. We were always taught to believe we were given certain capabilities from God and that it would be an insult to squander those talents. Besides, when you are born in the mountains as rugged and as harsh as these, my friend, you cannot give up or you will suffer too much. When you are shown this as a child, as you get older, you don't question the tests of your skill and determination. Your youth is your foundation. Here, your future is a rocky one. It is not so easy just being born in Lebanon anyway. We Lebanese use our abilities, our skills, and our tenacity just to survive. We have no riches, no valuable resources, such as oil or enormous farmlands. So, we have learned to call on our minds, our values, our culture, our determination, our faith, our heritage…even in America."

Alexander felt himself becoming more and more aware of his blessings, and more accepting of his life as he experienced this time in the mountains having seen his village once more, being with his beloved brother and Katrina. In many ways, he was drawing on the psychic reserves that had waited for him for so many years. He was still experiencing an epiphany of spirit that bode well for him. And he was becoming braced in strength for what may come.

"Kassem, you were correct when you spoke to me at the stone on the curve in the road overlooking the village. Only God knows what the future holds for us. When I was having trouble in my business and things were going bad, like when the freeze killed our entire harvest and almost wiped us out, I said I will do this or that and my father used to tell me: 'If you want to make God laugh, tell him your plans.'"

Kassem laughed at the joke, turned his head to look at his passenger beside him. "Your father was a wise man, sir, and you must know that your abundance comes only from Him. Therefore, be still…and wait for Him." Then, changing the subject, he asked, "I think tonight you and your friends will be with the president at the gala. Isn't that so?"

"Yes, we are all here from America. Danny Thomas is our leader. We are here mostly because of him. He is a great, kind and wonderful man.

"This is a wonderful honor, Kassem. Most of us were just simple peasants who left our homeland when we were poor and very young. Now, we are Americans. But we always remember our Lebanese heritage with pride. As Danny often tells his friends, 'He who does not honor his heritage has no heritage.' And he is correct."

"So," Alexander continued, "we come here now to restore our love of our homeland and our heritage. In America we have been proud of our culture, our beliefs and our history." He chuckled proudly as he continued, "We came from the Phoenicians, and, now we return to be with our families and are being honored by our homeland. Some have labeled us "the New Phoenicians." Maybe that is so, and therefore one could think our work is complete, but it isn't. I personally still have one more very important task to complete. After I return to Douma to stay with my brother, I must return to France to conclude one way or another my search for someone very important to me. I pray she is still alive."

Kassem, still listening, pulled the taxi to the curb as they reached the port city of Jounieh, just north of Beirut. "I want to show you something," he said to Alexander. "I will show you a place with the most beautiful sight of Beirut and the sea. There you must be quiet for a moment, pray to God and ask for his blessing."

After a short drive up the winding mountain road, tightly lined by small homes, trees, and bushes, Kassem turned the car onto a paved overlook.

"We are here at my mosque. Speak with God here as you view this most incredible sight."

Alexander stepped from the taxi, washed his hands in the fountain, removed his shoes, walked into the mosque and knelt on the carpet to pray.

After thoughtful solitude and prayer, Alexander emerged from the mosque feeling much better and silently climbed back into the taxi.

He was quiet in thought for the rest of the drive into the city.

"Thank you, Kassem, for stopping at your mosque," Alexander said to his driver as he exited the cab at the front entrance to the Phoenicia Hotel.

"Shall I come pick you up early Monday for your visit to your brother?"

"Yes, I'll see you here at nine o'clock."

"*Insha Allah*," Kassem replied as he skillfully pulled the Mercedes away from the curb into the noisy, busy street.

"Iskandar!"

He heard his name as he entered the lobby. It was Bishop Anthony Bashir.

"Hello, Anthony," he replied as he wrapped his arms around his cousin's shoulders.

"Did you have a good visit in Douma? It's still beautiful, isn't it?" Anthony asked. "We all had a wonderful time. But I ate too much *kibbee* and hummus. I'm full!" he laughed as he patted his stomach.

The lobby was active with others in small groups, chatting and gesturing, all of whom who had spent the past two days at the villages of their parents, where they were born.

"We went to Ehden and Bsharre way north. It was very cold there, I must say!" Danny was speaking to the cluster of men in the lobby. "Isn't this great?"

"Yes, Zahle was so much bigger than I remember," added George Simon, with a proud smile.

"And the Bekaa is very busy…they are planting vegetables and wheat. The vineyards, and citrus trees are filling with new growth. I couldn't get over the rivers and ponds," said another.

"Well, it's quite a homecoming for all of us I must say. This is amazing. Looks like the Marines cooled this place down in '58," said Emile Hajjar.

"Just in time, I'd say," interjected Joe Ayoub. "They've had a bunch of trouble here. There always seems to be political turmoil in this part of the world."

"And it might get worse in the '60s some have said, especially in the South," spoke a new face with a familiar voice. "I'm glad I live in California. The Bekaa was wonderful, but California's San Joaquin Valley is where I live now, and for that

I am grateful."

"Butrus, is that you?" Alexander turned his head as he heard the voice that jarred his memory. "My God, Butrus," he exclaimed, using Peter's Arabic name. "How the hell are you? I didn't know you were here. I didn't even know they allowed Californians here," he added, laughing at his own joke.

"Yeah," Anthony added, "Floridians are always surprised when Californians are invited too."

"You know, guys, that's exactly how we feel in California about Easterners, especially those from that backward state of Florida. You should come out west if you want to see how the more advanced Americans live."

They all laughed at the friendly rivalry, relishing in their common bond.

Recalling their trip to New York, Peter pulled Alexander aside. When they were sufficiently separated from the group, he embraced Alexander, kissed both his cheeks and started speaking excitedly, "Iskandar, it's been so long...forty-two years! I don't know why we never get together. My home is your home, you know."

"I know, Butrus, but the first years were so hard. I worked with my father six, sometimes seven days a week, just trying to get ahead. Times were very hard... then later the Depression...when times got a bit better after the war, I had too much to do, it seems. I don't know where the time went, *khai-yi*, but it's been too long that's for sure."

"Well, when we get back, we'll have to do something about that, *khai-yi*. Besides, I understand your wife died. There are lots of nice ladies in California if you ever find enough time to come visit. I live near Stockton, and there are some wonderful Greek families there." He paused, "Wait a minute, Iskandar, what ever happened with that beauty you fell in love with in Marseille? What was her name? Let's see..."

"Madeleine, Madeleine DuBois." Alexander reacted quickly since she seemed to be on his mind most of the time.

"Yes! Madeleine. She was a lovely young girl. Boy, Iskandar, I remember how totally in love you were, and how you suffered on the ship to New York. My God, you were miserable. But then, if I remember correctly, both of us were seasick and throwing up most of the voyage. I haven't been on a boat since." He laughed heartily.

"Me either," Alexander replied. "I don't even go on the boat fishing in the lake at my home anymore. I did agree to take out my son and daughter when they were young; they loved it. Not me. Boy, I hated that ship."

"Well," Peter asked, "what ever happened to Madeleine? You said a hundred times on the ship you were going to go back and get her. Did you?"

Alexander wasn't prepared for this exchange with Peter, the only person in the world who would know about Madeleine. He took a deep breath, and answered his friend from 1920, "No, *khai-yi*, I never went back. I wrote her many times...many times," he reiterated, "but she never responded to my letters. Now, I'm convinced I waited too long. My French investigator thinks she passed away."

"Yes," Peter interjected, "I remember you wrote her on the ship almost every day. You were a lovesick puppy, Iskandar. I never saw a man so in love. No letters? How can that be?" He was surprised.

"I was eighteen, Butrus, and she was sixteen."

"Hey, is that the ring she gave you that night, Iskandar?" he asked as his voice pitch went higher while he stared at Alexander's finger.

"My God, Butrus, you remember that too?"

"Of course I do. Hell, you rubbed that ring all the time. Do you still wear that ring every day, even now?"

"Yes. Yes I do. I have never forgotten Madeleine. I was a good husband and a good father to my two children, but I must confess, I have never stopped loving her. It's not something you make yourself do…it's just something that happened to me, and I've never gotten past it. But I didn't let it impact on my marriage. Since Madeleine didn't respond to my letters, I was able to devote myself to Helene…she was such a wonderful wife to me, and mother to our son and daughter. I couldn't betray Helene. But after her death, Madeleine re-entered my mind, and I have been searching all over Europe for her for nearly two years."

"Two years?" Peter repeated startled. "My God, Iskandar, it's been more than forty years! That's a long time to stay in love with someone you haven't even seen for so long!"

"Maybe I'm being incredibly foolish. I don't know.

But I do know she has been in my heart all that time, and I cannot stop wanting her with me now. I didn't ask for this, Butrus, but it's something I can't explain… even to myself."

He continued, putting his hand on his friend's shoulder, and looking directly into his eyes, affirmed, "I tell you, if she is still alive, I will find her. I will never forget her."

"And if she is married? And has a bunch of children? And grandchildren? And if she's not even alive?" Peter asked quizzically.

"Well, I haven't thought about that possibility because I can't. She was only sixteen, for heaven's sake. Married? Not possible."

They both laughed, easing the tension of their conversation.

"If she's married, then I'll shake her hand, shake his hand, and wish them a happy life."

"Liar. You couldn't do that. I sure as hell couldn't do that. You're fooling yourself. After the love of your life shows up again after forty-two years, you think you could do that? I don't think so. I think," Peter continued with a mischievous smile, "if you find her…"

"When I find her…" Alexander corrected him.

"Okay, when you find her. But I think you won't even be able to speak. Forty-two years? You'd better have me with you, my friend."

"Sure," Alexander laughed. "Sure, I'll find her and bring her to California."

They both laughed, nervously to be sure, but they laughed, remembering their closeness as youths.

"Gentlemen," Danny said as he walked up between them, putting one arm around each, "we all need to begin to get ready now. The bus that will take us to Baabda, the Presidential Palace above Beirut, will be here at seven o'clock. Why don't you two join the rest of the guys in my suite for a quick drink, some conversation, and some local tidbits like hummus, *fistok*, and *jibneh*? Say in an hour?"

"Thanks, Danny. See you there."

Later, as they left the bus at the president's palace overlooking the city, the sun was just setting into the Mediterranean.

"Beautiful sunset, isn't it?" more than one asked a friend standing nearby looking at the sea.

"Yes. My God, that too reminds me of Madeleine, Butrus. The most wonderful evening of my life was that day I loved Madeleine on a grassy spot on the cliffs overlooking the Mediterranean Sea in Marseille. I always felt if I were to die after that, I had lived the most wonderful full life."

"Everything reminds you of Madeleine, Iskandar," Peter laughed. "Maybe some things more than others, I suppose, but you haven't stopped saying her name since I met you."

"I suppose you are right. Maybe I need to find a way to just hand it over to God."

"You think?" Peter laughed. "Now you're making some sense. Look for her, sure, but don't let it take over your life, Iskandar." Then stepping to the entry, he beckoned. "Let's go inside and have a wonderful time with the president."

The visiting delegation walked as a group from the buses to the broad, polished Lebanese marble staircase, climbed the dozen steps to the landing at the double doors, and one by one entered the anteroom at the foot of an arched stairway that led to the reception area. They gathered together and were led up four more marble stairs. They almost gasped as they entered the enormous ballroom with ceilings almost forty feet high, ornate décor, multiple huge sparkling French Renaissance chandeliers, and, at the far end, an elevated stage. To either side were many tables with cream-colored damask cloths set for eight each. A large number of people were already in the room enjoying beverages and hors d'oeuvres served by the abundant number of strolling white-gloved, formally attired servers, men and women, dressed in black trousers or skirts and white shirts.

Two of them approached the group asking graciously, "Champagne? Wine?

Orange juice? Tea?"

The servers, sensitive to the various religious constraints of the mixed populace, offered the variety of beverages customary in the more westernized Arabic countries of the Middle East, among them, Lebanon, Jordan, Iraq, and Syria. Juices were offered for those of Islamic faith.

Danny spoke to the group that had not yet dispersed. "I understand there are individuals here who live in Lebanon, mostly in Beirut, who also are receiving awards for their philanthropy from the president this evening. I think it best we not cluster together, but rather, mingle around the room with the local guests. Let's get to know them and introduce St. Jude to this crowd."

At his cue, Alexander and Peter began a slow stroll across the gleaming marble floor, admiring the grand ballroom.

"Extraordinary, Iskandar, isn't it?" Butrus asked, still deferring to Iskandar as he had on the ship when Alexander was eighteen and he was fifteen. Peter waved his arm in a sweeping motion, indicating the spacious room, accoutrements and décor that were deserving of their attention. They stopped briefly to listen to the soft background music played by the orchestra on the stage at the far end of the ballroom.

"The music is really nice too, don't you think?"

"Yes," Alexander replied. "You know, Butrus," he continued after taking a sip from his champagne glass, "when we lived in Lebanon, we were so poor, so apart from the political world here, I doubt we could ever have dreamed of entering this building even as employees. Now, we are here being honored by the president. Extraordinary! This whole experience is extraordinary." He lowered his head and whispered softly, "I'm sorry now that I didn't talk my daughter into coming with me."

"Yes," Peter acknowledged, nodding, "But we didn't expect this. I know I certainly didn't. I thought we'd have dinner and receive a decorative box containing a certificate maybe. Not this. Look at this room...the marble floors, the impressive Corinthian columns, the glistening chandeliers. It's magnificent. I must say, the president sure knows how to throw a party! We all came from the most humble, poorest origins, Iskandar, and in America, our people today stay away from politics, even in our smallest towns. So this really was never part of our consciousness. Maybe it will take another generation."

"Let's walk across the room," Alexander suggested. "We have a few minutes."

They strode together across the great room toward a cluster of men and women standing in a small group with the smiling, hospitable president. The women were in expensive, elegant evening gowns, most direct from Paris, hair coiffed to perfection...and the jewelry...so opulent, so exquisite, and so tasteful. These were the *crème de la crème* of Beiruti society for sure, Alexander thought.

His eyes suddenly focused on a tall, dark-haired elegant woman in the distance who stood very straight, arms gracefully at her side. She looked like an international fashion model. Contrasting with her tanned skin, her ivory sequined gown shimmered in the glow of the myriad of lights emanating from the crystal chandeliers. She was strikingly beautiful. The close-fitting strapless dress accentuated her slender figure. Many of the other women standing nearby were also dark-haired, some fair-haired, with olive or fair complexions, but not as tall or slender as this particular woman. Her elegance was pronounced by her subtle smile and her regal stature. As he looked from a distance of a hundred feet across the large room, his eyes focused on her face, her almond-shaped eyes with sensually lowered eyelids, her thin, arched eyebrows, the straight aquiline nose… Alexander's eyes were frozen to the woman's face. He was captivated. He couldn't move his eyes. She was the most beautiful creature he had ever seen. She seemed strangely familiar.

"My God, Butrus, look at that woman. She is lovely, so exceptional. I feel like I've seen her before."

"She's pretty, yes, Iskandar."

"Does she remind you of anyone? Who could she be?"

"I don't know, but I'll try to find out," he answered as he stepped away.

Alexander knew he couldn't stand in the middle of the room by himself. He would be too obvious. He looked around the room to obfuscate his stare; he didn't want to appear rude. He stepped to the side, toward a small cluster of men to blend in with them.

His eyes quickly returned to the woman. He couldn't help himself. After a few moments, he took two tentative steps toward her. She was still conversing with the young man. He watched as she placed her hand on his arm and laughed. Their faces were near each other's. Both were smiling at each other affectionately.

Alexander's emotions began a roller-coaster ride. He was drawn to her, wanting to be near her, to speak with he, to hear her voice..

An aide standing beside and slightly behind the president leaned toward him and discreetly whispered near her ear. "Sir, the American delegation has arrived. You asked me to inform you."

The president smiled silently, and nodded. Then, gesturing to another aide who quickly came to him and asked, "Sir?"

"Joseph, tell my wife the Americans are here. We will allow them thirty minutes to socialize before I need her beside me for my welcome. Kindly inform her now."

"Yes, sir." The aide bowed, turned sharply on his heel and strode across the room to the president's wife who was at the moment standing, visiting with her longtime friends, Mr. and Mrs. Kabani.

Tilting her ear to the aide, she listened to the message, smiled graciously, turned to her husband and nodded in acknowledgement. Then, returning her attention to the Kabanis, she alerted them. "My husband expects to speak in half an hour after the Americans have had time to visit. I will go to him shortly."

Alexander again tentatively took a few more steps toward the president's group as if he might join them. At least he hoped that's what the others in the room would perceive.

A waiter, noticing his empty glass, stepped up to him. "Champagne, sir?"

Alexander nodded and exchanged his empty flute for a freshly filled glass from the proffered silver tray which he in turn nervously gulped down. "*Shookrun*," he said as he handed back the glass.

Then he discreetly asked the waiter, "Who is the handsome woman speaking with the President?"

"She is a prominent, well-respected lady here in Lebanon. She supports children's hospitals, clinics, schools and young artists. She is quite well known and much admired. Her name is Madame Moreau."

"Moreau? Moreau did you say?"

His mind began to race.

He felt his pulse quicken. His lips felt dry as his memories flashed by in his mind…that first night in Marseille.

His eyes magnetically returned to the beautiful woman. He saw her turn to the president, listen to him, smile and nod, then turn to the young man next to her.

Alexander, now emboldened, decided he had to find Peter who was across the room. To do so, he had to step even closer to the woman. Not wanting to be seen by her, he avoided her eyes, stayed behind the guests gathered in groups between them, and swiftly walked away in search of Peter.

The room was growing more crowded with several hundred attendees in formal attire who stood or strolled while conversing, laughing, sharing stories, some louder than others, some gesticulating, waving an arm, most smiling, all adding to the cacophony so loud that one could barely hear the soft classical music in the background. For Alexander, the air was getting thicker, making it hard for him to breathe.

"Butrus," he said as he finally found his friend.

Before Alexander could speak, Peter turned to him and smiled, whispering, "Iskandar, I found out who she is. Her name is Madame Moreau. She is French, not Lebanese. But she has lived in Lebanon since before the war, more than twenty years now. But she's only lived in Beirut since after the war. No one knows where she was in the country before that. I was just asking this man who she was and he offered all this information. She seems to travel in the finest circles of Beiruti society, and is here tonight because she too is being honored by the president for her outstanding support of under-privileged, handicapped Lebanese children. Can you imagine? She is quite the philanthropist and has raised millions of dollars to build children's health clinics, hospitals and schools. She is beloved here, they say."

Alexander nodded his head excitedly. "I have to meet her, Butrus. I must find out who she is. She could be Madeleine."

"Go, Iskandar, and good luck," he said as Alexander turned toward the area across the room where the woman stood. The great ballroom, with its high ceilings and ornate décor, was now almost filled with people. The older couples were already seated at partially occupied tables, and mostly Lebanese nationals and government officials were standing in groups, laughing and speaking in Arabic or French, sipping from long-stemmed crystal flutes. The volume of voices was substantial. It was growing louder, reflecting the exuberance of the gathering of honorees and their families and friends. But as he watched the woman near the president, he realized he was not hearing the din of voices as before. Suddenly, the room was becoming silent to him as he focused only on her, noticing the exquisite way she tilted her head, smiled, and gestured with her hand. Her movements seemed somehow wonderfully familiar to him.

He also knew that very soon an announcement would be made urging all the guests to take their places and then it would become very difficult if not impossible for him to get near her. He realized he would have to do something soon. He had only a moment to make his move. If the woman indeed was Madeleine, he had to know immediately. His hands began to moisten, reflecting his increasing pulse rate and anticipation. He felt his heart pounding in his chest.

Then, mustering his courage, he finally began to walk toward her, determined, yet very nervous. He anxiously stopped once again and stood very still while gazing at her. His pulse grew faster as his breath became shallower. He pulled his handkerchief from his breast coat pocket and wiped his damp brow.

He looked around and realized he was nearly by himself in the middle of the room. People involved in their own conversations were walking quickly past him across the room to their assigned tables. His nervousness was certainly noticeable to himself if not to others.

After an agonizing moment he took a few more steps and watched her turn as she lifted her head, laughing with the president. Her somehow familiar laughter stopped him again as his gaze froze on her. He was becoming more convinced now it must be Madeleine. But is that her? His feet felt stuck to the floor, unable to move further.

Madame Moreau's hair was swept up in a French twist, held with an elegant silver comb, revealing her entire beautiful profile. Her neck was long and slender as he remembered. Her shoulders and arms were graceful as she gestured with her hands while speaking. It was so long ago.

My God! It is Madeleine, he finally realized as he dared to step even closer, emotions exploding within him. He watched as she delicately brought her champagne glass to her full red lips and gracefully sipped the clear amber bubbly liquid.

His eyes couldn't leave her. At that moment, she laughed aloud and smiled at the president, apparently her close friend, as she lightly touched his arm.

There was no sign that she was with anyone else except the handsome younger man standing next to her. Then he saw that she affectionately placed her arm through his, Alexander became even more perplexed and felt a sinking sensation as he wondered if indeed the man was her escort.

He stood still as though his knees were locked in place, his eyes never leaving her. All the years since he met her in Marseille seemed to flip through his mind… all those years of unanswered letters…his two years of an empty, frustrating, fruitless search.

Time seemed to stand still. It was as though his legs couldn't move. The world stopped for him as he gazed on her and the younger man.

Not knowing quite what else to do, he took just three steps, tentatively walking slowly toward her, and was startled to realize he was now only twenty feet from her. Embarrassed, he stopped abruptly.

Suddenly, he felt she sensed his approach. She tilted her head slightly in his general direction, but not directly at him.

Then it happened.

Her eyes turned directly to Alexander's. She still had the same smile on her lips she had a moment before as she paused to study the tall, dark, handsome man in the expensive silk tuxedo coming toward her.

Then her expression changed. Her smile widened slowly. One hand went to her mouth for a brief moment. The loud sounds of voices in the room morphed into absolute silence for both of them.

Drawing a deep breath, she stiffened with sudden recognition. Her expression changed as she asked herself, *Is it him? Is it actually Iskandar?* Her heart pounded in her breast. Her knees grew weak. Her body trembled.

It was a magical moment when their eyes met and remained fixed on each other's as they stood motionless in a room filled with the sounds of music and conversations, but totally silent to them.

Waiting for her signal before continuing toward her, Alexander glanced at the younger man, then back to her. She nodded slightly to Alexander, beckoning him to come to her. He stepped cautiously to her. Their faces became very close.

Her eyes nervously left his and went to his left hand.

Madeleine brushed a tear from her cheek as her eyes filled. Her smile widened, still looking at Iskandar's face. Just a step away from her now, he finally arrived close enough to speak.

"It is you, isn't it, Iskandar? It is you," she cried in a whisper, then lifted her arms wide, inviting him to her.

Alexander quickly responded as he too opened his arms wide to embrace her. She gazed deeply into his eyes, her own now brimming with tears of joy.

They embraced gently at first, then brought the other even closer. Tenderly, they held each other in love. They were together at last. Their moment filled with their singular sense of ecstasy. They wrapped their arms tightly around each other.

"Oh, Iskandar. *Je t'aime*," she whispered passionately in his ear. He could feel the warmth of her breath as she brushed her lips on his ear. "I knew you would find me. I have yearned for you for so long."

He whispered, "Madeleine, you make me deliriously happy. Happier than I have ever been in my life. I love you so much."

Finally, as they reluctantly and gently released their embrace, but keeping their faces near, he asked, gesturing to her companion, "And, Madeleine, who is this handsome young man?"

Smiling softly, she looked directly into his eyes and whispered, "Iskandar, meet your son, François."

SUNRISE OVER BEIRUT

PART THREE

OF A

TRILOGY

The Art of War is of vital importance to the state.
It is a matter of Life and death,
a road either to safety or to ruin.
Appear where you are unexpected.
Attack your enemy where he is unprepared.

Sun Tzu

CHAPTER 1

Beirut, June 5, 1967
The Attack

"What the hell? What the hell is that?"

François DuBois, startled by an ominous sight low in the western skies, rose from his chair behind his large, polished mahogany desk, and warily looked out his floor-to-ceiling office window on the thirtieth story. He stepped around his desk to get closer to the window and squinted to focus on a distant row of distinct dots above the eastern Mediterranean Sea.

As he did each day, this Monday morning he arrived in his office at exactly 7:30 a.m. He enjoyed his early mornings, the quiet time to clear his mind before the busy day began. It gave him time to review his day's agenda and organize his thoughts. And he loved watching the sun's impact on the city and the sea, marveling at the color changes of the skies and the sea at sunrise. But this morning in Beirut was different.

François couldn't take his eyes off the western sky, still squinting while staring at the dots moving low in the sky that kept getting larger. Frowning, he looked at his wrist watch. It was now ten minutes before nine o'clock.

"Hanna!" he shouted over his shoulder, impatiently, "Come in here. Quickly! Now!"

Hanna, his devoted and trusted, bespectacled assistant, rushed in, alarmed by the sharp sound of his employer's voice that was filled with unfamiliar urgency.

"Hanna! Look!" He anxiously motioned west toward the horizon.

As they both stood side by side near the glass windows, cupping their hands above their eyes, François pointed to the distance. "What do you see, Hanna? There," he pointed again.

"Dots," Hanna replied excitedly, "yes, I see small dots, in a line."

"Those dots are growing larger and larger. Look carefully, Hanna," François urged.

"Yes, sir, they are." Hanna, frightened and concerned now, spoke softly and with a deeply furrowed brow. "What are they, Monsieur DuBois? What do you think they are, sir?"

"I'm not sure, Hanna, but I want you to get President Helou on the telephone," François ordered quickly, then blurted out, "Yes! Now I can see that they are jet fighters flying directly toward Beirut. And they are flying dangerously low." He began to hear the faint drone of jet engines. The jet fighters were becoming well-defined as they droned closer and closer toward them at supersonic speeds.

François took a closer look, unsure exactly what he was watching, nervously waiting for Hanna's voice, which felt like many minutes, but was really just a few short moments.

"I have the President's secretary on the telephone, sir."

"They're coming closer, Hanna! Get me the President, not his secretary!" he yelled impatiently. "Hurry!"

Seconds later he saw Hanna's head signal to him. François quickly reached for the phone.

"Mr. President, are you still east of Beirut in Baabda today?

"Yes, François, I'm still here in Baabda. What's happening?"

"I am in my downtown office, and at this moment I am watching what appears to be a squadron of jet fighters coming directly toward Beirut, flying very low, beneath my offices. I'd say maybe less than two hundred feet above the sea at most."

"Two hundred feet, you say, François?" President Charles Helou asked incredulously.

"Yes, sir, very low. They are below my feet!"

"That means they are intending to be unseen, even by radar and our defense system."

The noise of the fighters' engines was growing louder, increasing the sense of urgency and danger by the second, disturbing François all the more.

"Yes, sir, it appears that way to me also. That is why I called you first."

"Just a moment, François. Hold on while I call the Defense Minister."

"I'll hold, of course, Mr. President, but as you know, if they are Israeli jets, they will be over Beirut in less than a couple of minutes, and in less than twelve minutes they will cross the Bekaa Valley and be on the outskirts of Damascus."

"If they were sent to attack Beirut, they should be firing rockets and their guns any second now. Hold on. I will be right back to you, but you must immediately take cover, François, and get out of your office!"

"Monsieur Dubois," Hanna turned and cried out, frightened for his family, "Are we going to die?"

www.ingramcontent.com/pod-product-compliance
Lightning Source LLC
Chambersburg PA
CBHW050354030726
47503CB00006B/1849